A Temporary Memory

CROCUS VALLEY, BOOK 2

MARIE JOHNSTON

LE PUBLISHING

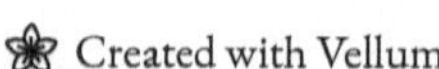 Created with Vellum

Nannying two adorable kids was a way to support myself until I got on my feet again. I wasn't supposed to fall for their stern single dad.

After a sudden, bad breakup, I land in a small town in the middle of nowhere, cut off from all my accounts and resources. I have a stalled dancing career, a mom in long-term care, and no money.

Then I meet Alcott "Cody" Knight. The type of guy I've learned to steer clear of—driven, rigid, and devastating in a suit. Only he also has two adorable kids, and he needs a nanny for the summer.

For two months, he'll pay more than I need to help my mom and myself. For two months, I'll take care of his kids, give them dance lessons, and see what a normal life could be like. For two months, I have to try not to fall for a guy who's hotter in jeans and cowboy boots than in a suit and treats me like I matter.

But my stay was only ever for a few months, to get back on my feet so I can get my life back. I might be used to leaving, but I can't stop wishing Cody and I could be more than a temporary memory.

For my brother. I'll miss you forever.

For new release updates, chapter sneak peeks, and exclusive quarterly short stories, sign up for Marie's newsletter at mariejohnstonwriter.com.

One

TOVA

"Excuse me, what?" I pushed my long hair over my shoulder so I could hear my rich-as-hell, good-looking dreamboat of a boyfriend, Frederick, better. I had to make sure I heard correctly. I had to ensure that my life was indeed derailing again—because of some douche of a man. My heart rate kicked up a notch and adrenaline dripped into my veins, all of it a slow preparation. The flight-or-fight response.

I usually fled.

I pulled the lapels of my blush-colored silk robe shut to hide the skip of my pulse fluttering at the base of my neck. My mom's words, back when she could string together coherent sounds, echoed through my head. *Never let them know you plan on leaving.*

"You heard me," Frederick said in his cultured, *I'm too rich for your bullshit* tone. He'd never used it on me, but it was most certainly aimed my way now. I hated that I wasn't surprised. If I gave myself time to look back on our two-year relationship, I'd see the buildup of his superior attitude toward me. I'd see it all so crystal clear. "That won't be a problem, will it?"

I had heard him. That was the issue, and absolutely, it was a problem. Yet, my mama didn't raise no fool. Nor did my grandma. And if both of them had, my grandma's life-long friend and partner, Thelma, would've taught me right. "I said I would choreograph and put on a show for clients tonight, but you know I don't do nudity." Mostly. "And I— I don't . . . I don't . . ." *Deep breath, Tova.* "I'm not a sex worker."

Behind me, Frederick quirked his full lips into an arrogant tilt and fluffed the crest of his blond hair with his fingers as he squinted into the crystal-framed mirror of my vanity. "No money's changing hands, Tova, my dear."

I used to think his *Tova, my dear* was precious, but it was quickly becoming a stain on my eardrums. The endearment turned out to be as much bait as the house Frederick had moved me into.

I was sitting on a pink, satin-upholstered stool in the bedroom I shared with him. The space was done with the most elegant touch, and he'd told me this vanity and the gold-crusted stool were his grandmother's. The house, this furniture, were all nicer than anything I'd had growing up. He'd relished indulging me. I hadn't seen the luxury for the trap it was.

I studied myself while Frederick casually acted as if nothing was amiss. Two pink dots glowed on my cheeks. My blush was usually a curse, unless I was performing. Then the dainty flush looked like part of my burlesque act, the sensual performance I'd worked hard to perfect and refresh while keeping slimy men's hands off me.

Booking gigs had gotten easier with Frederick's name backing mine, with him functioning almost like my manager. He'd coaxed me into giving up a day job I had adored to pursue my second job, burlesque, which I also loved. The ceiling for income with burlesque wasn't high, but not as limited as teaching kids how to dance. I could be my own boss while not needing a building with rent or a mortgage, insurance, or bookkeepers, and Frederick had connections.

I was a free agent. Or so I had thought.

I swallowed. "I didn't think you were a man who liked to share."

What red flags had I missed?

What would Thelma have pointed out as obvious in her growly smoker's voice?

The nicer the shell, the fancier the cage.

Men don't want to take care of you. They want to control you.

The more charming they are, the more they're hiding.

Frederick had charm and charisma. And he'd seemed so intent on helping me. I hadn't missed the warnings—I'd ignored them. He'd been my ticket to a stable future, but I'd been getting groomed to be his pet. While I was a sucker for a guy in a suit, he'd been hammering away at a cage.

Lines in the corners of his eyes winged out. He was older than me. Forty-five. His name had hooked me as much as his dapper appearance. Thelma would've hit me across the head with that red flag. Frederick Augustus Baldwin of the Augustus Opera House in Los Angeles. Frederick Augustus Baldwin *the Third*. Grandson of Augustus Baldwin, a famous opera tenor who married a big-screen darling in the fifties and had my boyfriend's pretentious parents, who hated me slightly less than they despised each other.

"It's an honor to share your *talents*." He stayed behind me, between me and the door. His impeccable black suit blocked out the reflection of the ornate bedroom in the mirror. I could see the door, taunting me.

What if I got up and walked out? Frederick was bigger than me. Would he get violent?

Did I want to find out?

I thought of Mom, and adrenaline flooded my veins. I couldn't risk discovering what Frederick would do to get me to stay.

"Two of the clients who will be in attendance tonight put tens of millions into my account—*each*, Tova, my dear. The least I can do is give them dinner and a show—and a private dance afterward." He put his hands on my shoulders and squeezed. "Don't you agree?" His grip tightened.

"Ow, Frederick. That hurts." I should know that calling out men's poor behavior never went well. I adopted a saucy pout to let him know I was still a harmless girl who thrived on his attention.

Ugh. The clarity was startling. I'd followed Mom's path closer than I cared to. The urge to be looked after, to have a little help in life, had been too strong.

He leaned down, his grip not loosening, and met my gaze in the mirror. His face was next to mine, and in his blue eyes was a hint of darkness I hadn't seen before. "A man shouldn't need to repeat himself, pet." Gah—the nickname! Another red flag waving in the wind. "You will do this for me, and you will let them know you enjoy it."

Like Thelma used to say—shit sticks.

I nervously licked my lips. My mind raced. I hadn't been at code-red levels of self-preservation since my mom's last boyfriend, when she dropped me at my grandmother's in Yorba Linda and ran. That guy eventually finished destroying Mom's life. Grandma passed away three years ago, not long before I met and succumbed to Frederick and his charm.

He'd plucked me when I'd been ripe for the taking.

Now I was in a golden cage, being told to flap my wings. Only this time, he wanted me to flap other things as well.

"Don't tell me the girl who shows her tits to random men night after night is suddenly a prude." He rose, freeing me with a suddenness that turned into more of a light shove. His snide laughter was dull against the tapestries hung above the bed and on the walls. "I thought you were a worldly woman. A lady with culture." In the mirror, I watched as he shoved his hands in his pockets and presented his profile, a pose that was so damn suave, but now I saw it was part of the mask he wore. "I'd hate to think I was wasting my time and money on a girl from the streets. I'd hate to think I offered you all this"—he held his arms out, making the cut of his suit even more impressive—"for nothing."

I steadied myself, flattening my hands on the cool oak surface of the vanity. My heart hammered against my ribs. Flashes of my childhood rose and disappeared in my head.

Mom packing me up in the middle of the night, telling me that if I didn't make a sound, I'd get to pick out a jumbo sucker. The way she'd trade duties with owners of dance studios. Usually, that meant sweeping and cleaning toilets. When I got older, I realized that, in one instance, cleaning toilets was a euphemism for sucking dick.

As an adult, I'd been through slumlords, lecherous directors, and narcissistic boyfriends. I thought Frederick was my ticket out. But he was all of them rolled into one, and if I didn't tread carefully, the little square door on my pristine cage would be glued shut and bumped against the wall.

"Of course not. You've been very generous." And controlling, if I was honest with myself, which I finally was. Frederick had influenced how I dressed, the way I performed, where I danced, and my finances. The last part stung and pumped a steady stream of panic into my blood.

I forced a smile that looked more like a maniacal stare. "It's, you know, going to take me a little bit to get used to the idea. I've been a one-man woman for a while." Like my entire life. I didn't dog on threesomes, polyams, or group sex, but none of them were for me, and that was okay too.

Apparently not to Frederick. He wanted me to strip naked tonight—something I never did—and . . . clean toilets.

My stomach twisted. I met Frederick after a show two years ago. Thelma told me I'd never find true love in the pockets of a millionaire, but I hadn't listened.

He crossed the room to me and patted my shoulders. "That's my good girl." Hearing his words curdled the protein shake I'd had as part of my pre-show routine. "They get a special show. And then a very special dinner."

He bent to press a kiss into my hair. I let my eyelids slide shut. Men like him weren't fooled easily. I opened my eyes to find him watching me.

"It won't change things between us, right?" I added a little extra whine to my voice. To him, I was the inferior partner in this relationship. I needed him to keep thinking that. "You won't think differently of me?"

He smiled, his blue eyes shining with a predatory gleam. "How could I, Tova, my dear?" He knelt down, lifted my curtain of hair, and tongued my earlobe.

A shiver wracked my body. I was nothing, if not a performer. I called on my skills and let out a breathless giggle that hid my nerves.

"I'll reward you dearly," he murmured, and my stomach heaved. "Something special, just for us."

A gang bang at your next board meeting, shit stick?

My lower lip stuck out in an expert simper. "Promise?"

Another wet, sloppy kiss along my neck. Ugh. I finally let the low-key disgust that I had experienced grow when he did this. I no longer found anything sexy about this man. My dwindling passion for him dropped harder than my credit score.

"You know I never go back on my promises," he purred.

He never made any.

The realization hit. No wonder he'd gotten one over on me. He was smoother than any crook I'd come across. Maybe I had been inferior, but that would end soon.

"You have a couple hours to prepare before the car arrives. Don't embarrass me." He straightened, yanked his suit coat down, and walked out of the room. He'd spoken, and his will would be done.

He was gone, but the room remained stifling. Had it always been this way? Had I only wanted to see the potential? I'd wanted to think this was my future, that after struggling for my entire life, I could have something that was mine. A home. And while I knew Frederick's house and cars and staff were his, I was confident that eventually I'd get there.

For a girl who'd lived her life so carefully, I'd tumbled right into a well-dressed trap with more money and resources than I could dream of. Yet none of them were mine, and Frederick controlled what should be in my name. In small increments, I'd molded myself in accordance with his advice. I hadn't noticed Frederick wanted a tool to make more money, and he thought me spreading my legs would earn him a nice bonus. Flattering as that was, Tova Grace Evanson was her own woman, and she was not making her mother's mistakes.

One day. One day, I would be able to live exactly how I wanted.

I got up and went to the door. The handle wouldn't move.

Locked in.

Disbelief spread through me. Why was I surprised? Yet I tried the door again, my brain refusing to acknowledge I'd never noticed the door could be locked from the outside. Had he changed the doorknob around, or had it always been like this? I'd been distracted by the elegance and hadn't bothered to look. Why would I?

I wasn't busting my ankle jumping out of a two-story window. Frederick would probably say something like, *You do your best work on your back anyway, pet.*

My circumstances would only get worse.

All I could think about as I tried to wrap my head around the situation that was becoming my reality was, *Good thing I'm prepared.*

After a clarifying breath, I returned to the vanity and picked up the bottle of my favorite rose-scented moisturizer. I squeezed a dollop onto my palm. Leisurely, I rubbed the cream into my shoulders and arms while my mind whirred.

Frederick and I had been dating for a month before he learned I was the ripe old age of thirty-one at the time. What number warning sign would that have been? His eye had twitched hard, but he'd claimed he had allergies. *The pollen, Tova, my dear.* Then he seemed intrigued by my life's story.

Because he thought my past, my mom, would make me easier to control.

Another squeeze, and I lathered my legs. I had the *special* performance in three hours. I could get my pre-show routine down to forty-five minutes, but I preferred to spend hours lost in my head, thinking of new moves, fresh skits, and upcoming venues to pitch myself to. Tonight, my mind was otherwise occupied.

The private event Frederick planned was supposed to

have been a treat. A private performance with only me, putting on my two special acts as Fannie Grace—a nod to my 1920s look and dance routines, plus two new acts I'd been working on that were more modern—at Frederick's suggestion. More seductive. Smaller pasties. Narrower G-string.

Ugh. I envisioned sticking those pasties on his nuts. No, getting them to stick to my breasts was hard enough. I could tie my titty tassels around his balls and knot them.

Thelma would high-five me.

Once I was done with the skincare routine, I checked my phone like I would do a social media update, spying on my nonexistent friends. The last two years had been so Frederick-focused I could high-kick myself, but it wasn't as if my life had been brimming with connections before that.

Except for the kids I used to teach.

I let out a gusty sigh. I missed the kids.

I grabbed my phone and tapped into the app for my savings and investment accounts that Frederick had set up for me. I was logged out. Shit. I put in my information. Incorrect password.

No. Chewing on my lower lip, I attempted to sign in.

Still an incorrect password. Imagine that. The asshole had shut me out of my accounts and cut off my access to my money. *Don't worry, Tova, my dear, my assistant will take care of everything,* he'd assured me. Had she gone into the system and changed my password, or had Frederick delighted in doing it himself?

I was flat-ass broke once again.

Well. That was that. Time for my perpetual plan B.

I went to the large walk-in closet. A small section by the door had been cleared for my stuff in the room that was as big as the kitchen in the home Mom had packed me out of and fled that last time. Should I have read into the minimal effort Frederick had made? Was he planning to shuffle me to one of the guest rooms while he found another dancer to fuck before sharing her with his clients?

Had he done this before? He seemed to have the play-book down.

I left my strappy, sapphire-blue underwear in place and stepped into the black velour tracksuit I usually wore to a venue. My hard-bodied black suitcase and a garment bag were packed with my costumes, my steamer, and duplicates of all my makeup and hair supplies. I'd worked too hard to be prepared.

I flipped over my suitcase and opened the lid. Inside was a sapphire-colored two-piece dress—my act included a strip-tease after all, the more articles to take off, the higher the tease—with fringe and sequins. My feather fans were tucked inside.

Digging underneath the supplies, I located the old phone I'd come to LA with. Thelma had made me keep it charged, and she insisted on a steady supply of minutes. Since both she and this phone had saved my bacon a few times, I'd dutifully done as she said.

Once the screen blinked on, I sent her an address and the time with the message, **I'd love to visit you soooon.** No specifics, in case Frederick found the phone. He'd only see a message to Thelma, who didn't live in California.

I wasn't a secret agent, I was just a girl used to limited resources. I hid the phone and went about packing a pair of shorts and a T-shirt from the old dance school I taught at. Nothing out of the ordinary. I had to play this right. Instinc-tively, I knew if I didn't, I'd be trapped for good.

A message blinked. **Got it, doll face.**

I blew out a breath, shut down the phone, and tucked it back into place. Like a robot, I went through the rest of my pre-show routine. Frederick used to tease me about my preparations. *You're not making international deals, pet.*

I was proud of how far I'd come as a dancer. No, I didn't get chosen as a Laker Girl. I wasn't on the big screen, but I didn't want to be. I needed to perform enough to earn a living and support my mom. Earning an income that didn't involve flashing my pussy to men as often as humanly possible was difficult. As tonight proved.

The door jiggled twice before it opened, and Frederick appeared, his eyes narrowed. "Time to go."

I acted as if I didn't know the door had been locked. "Of course." I held my chin up as I wheeled the suitcase behind me and followed him out the door and through the spacious hallways of his Beverly Hills mansion. Outside in the circular drive, a gleaming black car waited.

I had thought it was special he insisted we ride together tonight. Normally, he let me do my "burlesque thing" while he did "important businessman things" and mildly complained about the hours. I'd tease him that if he hadn't been one of my spectators, we'd have never met.

Not once had I questioned what a guy like Frederick had been doing at a hole-in-the-wall speakeasy. He was the type to get his steak served by Wolfgang Puck, not Bill from Albuquerque.

Thelma and her scandalous disdain for *Pretty Woman* had almost gotten me. I should have listened to her bitching about how h*e never would've looked at her twice if she'd been bagging his groceries instead of his dick.*

I got into the back of the Mercedes. Frederick slid in next to me and buried himself in his phone. Yet another thing he paid for and controlled. I posted the same pics of old performances I normally do to build excitement and gain an audience. Nothing out of the ordinary.

Don't ever call me on that thing, Thelma used to say.

Your prince might be a perv. I don't like pervs. Jimmy from the cul-de-sac was one, you know.

Jimmy from the cul-de-sac was a fifty-year-old from my grandma and Thelma's old neighborhood in Yorba Linda doing five to ten for the massive amount of child porn law enforcement had found on his "friend's" computer he was "just borrowing."

"Park in the back," Frederick said. His eyes glinted when he looked at me. "I don't want them to see the prize until you hit the stage."

My belly roiled, but I nodded. "You never get a second chance to make a first impression."

"Something like that." He spun on the heel of his expensive loafer and left.

I kept my breathing steady as Frederick unloaded me and my suitcase and escorted me all the way to the dressing room. The theater was eerily quiet. Where were the sound and light techs? The stagehands who arranged props? Usually, I was in a set with other performers, sometimes other burlesque acts, or musicians, or even comedians. Tonight, I was the only name on the marquee, and . . . this wasn't how it was supposed to go.

The dressing room was empty. Guys paid by Frederick and men who paid Frederick a ton of money waited for me to *perform.*

My hand gripped the handle of my suitcase so hard I wouldn't be surprised if I created divots. *Even breaths.* I hung up the garment bag and opened it like I had every intention of putting on my fringe dress, sequined bra, and kitten-heeled black velvet shoes.

Voices and laughter rang from the bar beyond the long hallway that led to the stage. On the other side of the dressing room was another hallway that led to the kitchen, the restrooms, and the emergency exit. An obnoxious alarm was supposed to blare if the door was opened, but the owner hadn't paid for the repair yet.

I checked the time. So close. I sat at the prep table I usually used with lights surrounding three sides of the mirror and started twisting and curling my dark hair until I looked like a 1920s flapper. When the last pin was in place, I situated on top the sequined headband with pale blue feathers that I would gift to spectators in the crowd.

Frederick popped in. "Everything good?"

No, dickwad, you know it's not. "Yeah," I said, my voice full of confidence. "I just have to get dressed."

His lewd gaze raked down my body. "Twenty minutes."

"Perfect." I checked the time. It was eight ten. On the dot.

When he disappeared, I counted to five before I dug out the burner phone. A new message was waiting.

Your chariot awaits. See you in a few hours.

A shot of relief dulled the sharp anxiety in my belly. I had started over plenty of times. This was no different. Maybe, for once, it wouldn't end the same way it always had: alone and betrayed, with only an old woman living in the middle of nowhere to bail me out.

My new beginning couldn't last long. I was down, but I couldn't be out. My mom depended on me.

I rose, took my Firecracker Red lipstick and scrawled out FUCK YOU SHIT STICK on the mirror, followed by the juvenile outline of a cock and balls. Then I lifted my suitcase and checked the hallway. Clear. Frederick thought I had no money and nowhere to go. He was wrong. I walked right out of the emergency exit with no working alarm to the car Thelma had waiting for me.

Two

CODY

I rolled my head, stretching my neck from side to side. I hadn't wanted to move my furniture to rent a house for the summer in Crocus Valley, North Dakota, but the effort might've been worth it.

The office chair had a left tilt that fired up a spot in my hip that screamed and reminded me I just turned forty. The desk was too short, and my forearms were as tight as the muscles in my neck. My vision blurred, and I blinked at the screen.

"Daddy?" Ivy flounced into the room, the tulle skirt of her summer dress whispering her arrival. Ivy had never whispered a thing in her life. She was loud and brash. If my father hadn't been alive when she was born, I'd wonder about reincarnation, but Ivy displayed tact and empathy. My father had not. "When we gonna play?"

I held in my groan. I had so much goddamn work to do, and toiling away during afternoon quiet time and after both of my kids went to bed wasn't enough time to do it all. This summer was a chance to spend as much time with them as possible before they left for school. Otherwise, ten-year-old Grayson and seven-year-old Ivy would be off to live with my late wife's parents and attend the private school their mother had always wished they'd gone to in the first place. We'd been in Crocus Valley for two weeks, and all I'd shown myself and my kids was that I knew how to work.

I could use a break. I'd been staring at a screen full of numbers all morning.

I pushed away from the desk, the wheels on the old office chair squeaking. "How about now?"

Her face lit up, and she shouted, "Yay! Gray! Gray!" She ran from the room, presumably to the living room at the end of the hall, where I'd planted my son in front of the TV so I could steal a couple hours of work.

Father of the Year.

Footsteps thumped down the hall. Grayson skidded to a stop, and I blew out a hard breath. His hair stood up in all directions. The peanut butter from his breakfast PB&J was still smeared across his face. His red-and-blue Spider-Man pajamas were the cherry on top of my shit sundae. Afternoon quiet time had come and gone, and both kids were still in jammies.

I'd forgotten all about lunch. "Go get changed and clean up."

Ivy spun behind Grayson, her skirt twirling out. "Can you braid my hair? Please, Daddy?"

When she called me Daddy, it reminded me of my sister, Aggie, and how she referred to our father. There had been nothing paternal about Barnaby Knight. My three brothers and I had called him Barns because Mama had called him Barns, and to us he was a scary overlord turned dictator. Every time my kids referred to me as Daddy, I wondered how I'd feel if they called me some version of Alcott. Would they use the nickname "Cody" like my family and what few friends I had did?

"Daddy?" She did a curtsy, her tiny foot tapping the floor behind her. Losing her balance, she skittered out of view and popped back in.

The braid. Goddammit. "Honey, you know I can't braid hair." Nothing made me feel like I had Goliath fingers and zero dexterity like doing Ivy's hair. How quickly fatherhood had wilted my ego.

"Can you try?" She batted her lashes.

How the fuck did they learn that tactic so early?

Letting out a quiet sigh, I caved. "G, I'll help Ivy with her hair while you wash your face and change clothes."

"What's wrong with these?" Grayson's voice pitched higher, offended.

"They're pajamas," I said firmly. "We're going out, and we don't wear pajamas outside of the house."

"We do for pajama day at school."

The kid might become a lawyer like his mother. "Go change."

Huffing, he trudged away, his little feet pounding on the stairs, followed by Ivy's patter as she raced to her bedroom.

My phone buzzed. I glanced at the screen. A work call, and technically I was in the office. I needed to take the call.

Closing the door, I spoke as if I were in my office in the house where I'd grown up. A place that hadn't heard many jubilant kids' voices ringing off the walls.

Within minutes of discussing Knight's Oil Wells' purchase of four oil wells in Wyoming from a company that would rather divert their resources to fracking new locations, there was a knock on the door.

"Da-addyyyy. Braaaaaiiiid."

The guy on the other end paused. I briefly closed my

eyes. Some of these corporate guys could be sticklers about what they considered professional, and my daughter shouting about braids wouldn't make the cut. For the thousandth time, I considered how badly I'd fucked up by working from home. Should I load us up and go back to Montana? Put the kids in daycare and work in the office at the ranch?

"Listen, can you send me the details, and I'll talk it over with my team?" I had no fucking team. If Barns were alive, he'd growl, *Buy the damn wells. Next oil boom, we'll be raking in the money while they're left on their fracking asses.*

The last oil boom was because of fracking, but the argument had fallen on uncaring ears. Regardless, we'd done just fine, cashing in on barrel prices with our refurbished wells and minimal crew.

When the call was disconnected, Ivy was shouting for me again. I opened the door. "Ivy, what have I told you about when the door's closed? It usually means I'm on the phone."

She shrugged and pranced away, unbothered. I followed her to the bathroom off the living room. I was trashing my third busted hair tie—who *the hell* thought they should be so small?—when Grayson popped in, face cleaned, shorts and a Spider-Man shirt on, and his hair still a mess.

My gaze lingered on his shirt, and my late wife's words ran through my head. *Just because we live in the sticks doesn't mean the kids should dress like it. I grew up wearing a private school uniform, and they can at least wear something that doesn't have someone's face on it.*

The more she'd complain, I swear, the more licensed clothing my siblings got the kids.

"Don't you have a clean polo?" I asked.

He spread his hands flat on his shirt. "What's wrong with this?" His voice wavered.

I recognized the tell. He was close to losing it. Grayson had a hair-trigger temper lately, and a meltdown was impending. I'd give him the shirt if he'd spare my eardrums for now. "Comb your hair, bud."

He rolled his eyes, heaved out a mighty breath, and stomped away. Another hair band snapped. Fuck whoever invented these.

"I can't braid today," I announced, giving up. "How 'bout a ponytail?"

"Okay," she said, with the devastation of being told there were no more puppies on the face of the earth.

Crooked ponytail in place for Ivy and freshly combed hair for Grayson, we got our shoes on and went outside. The tension riding along my shoulders eased. Birds chirped all around us, hidden in the thick, green leaves of all the trees lining the boulevard and shading houses. The old farmhouse I had rented had long been crowded by other houses and a whole neighborhood over the century since it'd been built. Kids squealed from the small outside pool a few blocks away. The drone of cars was minimal.

Ivy held on to my pinky, and Grayson hopped the cracks in the sidewalk as we covered the five blocks to downtown.

We passed a long, flat, brick building that was an insurance office. Across the street was a small-engine mechanic, his garage door thrown wide open, and the steady beats of an impact drill escaping. A block beyond that was a small park with a set of swings, an old metal slide, and a picnic shelter. There was a short set of close-to-the-ground monkey bars Ivy couldn't get enough of. We'd probably end up there for at least an hour after lunch.

This meal was more like an early dinner.

Shit, I needed to get groceries, and I had a conference call that'd take half the morning tomorrow.

When we arrived at the little Hummingbird's Diner that

made the best goddamn pancakes in the history of the world, I shoved my work worries to the back of my mind.

An older couple was sitting in the corner. I nodded at them. Two older men who I didn't think ever left the diner were in the opposite corner. I picked the point farthest from them both.

The kids and I slid into an old, cracked red booth. My loafer caught on a crack in one of the black-and-white tiles, and the table wobbled. The owner of the place claimed to like the vintage look, but the cantankerous waitress said *he's a cheap bastard who thinks spending money is for fools. But what's he going to do—have it all burned with him after he's gone? 'Cause you know his family's got plans for that cash.*

The waitress reminded me of Barns.

She shuffled to our table, sticking her tongue out of the corner of her mouth as she brandished a pad and pen. I had a feeling she didn't need to write down one single detail.

"Hey, Thelma. How's the breaded cod special?" I'd grown to respect her frank opinion on the matter.

"A touch freezer burned, but Hal gives it an extra minute in the fryer so you can't taste it."

"I'll take it."

"Same as usual for you fellas?" she asked the kids.

Grayson nodded, scribbling with the crayons left on the table next to the salt and pepper shakers. The usual was the awesome pancakes, drowned in whipped cream and syrup that had never crossed paths with a maple tree. But we weren't here for the type of breakfast that would polish my Father of the Year award.

"Uh, no," I intervened. "They'll each have the flank steak with mashed potatoes and green beans."

Thelma raised a brow, and groans echoed from the kids.

"Pancakes are for special Sundays," I said. "You need heartier food."

"White or chocolate milk?" Thelma asked, like she was trying to get ahead of the complaints.

Both kids hollered chocolate.

I tapped my fingers on the tabletop. "Plain milk, please. For all of us."

Ivy let out a frustrated growl and rested her head on the table.

"Got it," Thelma said, her tone full of censure, as if she thought I should let the kids have pancakes and chocolate milk for all three meals because life was short and who cared about sugar lows.

"I got a batch of new crayons," she said to the kids, bypassing me in case I insisted on being the fun police all day. "Want them?"

My precocious daughter turned demure around Thelma. "Yes, madam."

Thelma smacked her teeth against her lips. "I ain't no one's madam." She winked at me. "Maybe once upon a time."

I wasn't sure she was joking.

Thelma left and returned to drop off the milk for all of us. I hadn't grown out of the habit, and hitting the milk made it easier to be a dad than the whiskey neat Barns had been fond of.

I rubbed my face. Why was I thinking of him so much today? He'd been gone for six months, and he'd lingered for too long before that.

The kids colored on pages that had been ripped out of old coloring books. Did I have markers and coloring books at the house?

"Daddy, did Mommy like coloring?"

Her question ignited a burning in my stomach. Meg had liked filling out documents, and she'd thrived on contract negotiations. The more she wrung out from the other party, the better she had felt about life. "Sure, she liked coloring."

"She could braid hair," Ivy said solemnly.

"That, she could." Not a single strand would dare loosen from one of Meg's braids. "I'll have to try again. Maybe watch a video."

Ivy's grin went straight to my heart. I had to do better.

After several minutes, our meal arrived. I cut Ivy's steak and ignored Grayson's groans about the mushy green beans. Before I could dig into my slightly overcooked cod, Grayson knocked his milk over.

White liquid streamed over the top of the table. I scooted out, pulling him with me, but it was too late. My shirt got smeared with milk, and Grayson's shirt and shorts were wet.

"Dad!" He began uncontrollably sobbing. His emotions were instant and hit hard, and I had little fucking clue how to deal with them. "I'm all wet!" he wailed.

"It's no problem. We'll run home—"

"I'm not done eating," Ivy argued.

"I want to go to the park!" His volume rose.

"Well, we can't—"

"Park! I wanna go to the park!" Tears streaked down his face.

This behavior was what his teacher had met with me about a month before school was out.

Third graders don't cry, she'd said, giving me an exasperated but lecturing look.

I wanted to tell her that obviously they did, and there must be a reason, and it might not have to do with the math assignment. But I'd nodded and told her we'd work on it, and I casually reminded her that it hadn't even been a year since his mom had died. So maybe fuck off a little.

I hadn't said that last part out loud.

"Buddy, hey. Buddy." I squatted at the end of the booth to make eye contact, willing him to quit screaming.

"I got the girl," Thelma said from behind me. "There's a hand dryer in the bathroom. It'll dry you both off enough to play. It's not like the Crocus Valley Garden Club will kick you out of the park because you smell like a sour cow. Half of them fit the description anyway."

I pressed my lips together. Thelma's gruff tone quieted Grayson, and Ivy blinked at her.

"You mind?" I asked. Half my struggle with going anywhere with the kids was splitting us between the bathrooms when Ivy was still too young to be set free and too old to be accidentally seeing a guy's junk.

"Wouldn't have offered if I did."

I took Grayson to the bathroom. His little body was shaking while he tried to repress sobs, but I positioned him under the hand dryer and hit the big silver button. The little machine sounded like a jet engine.

He calmed and sniffled. "Sorry."

"It happens." The kid was a klutz, though. I thought he'd grow out of his newborn pony stage with the unsteady legs and halting steps. I was riding cutting horses on my own at his age. Helping Barns tag calves. Barns would throw me on the Arabians we raised and trained, call the horse a kid horse, and sell it for more money.

Grayson had fallen off every horse he'd been on. No coordination. No balance. No interest.

Barns had been a dick about it. Meg had chided me. *He's an intellectual,* she'd say, as if acknowledging it automatically made me know how to parent.

I didn't know how to raise an intellectual. After Mama abandoned us and I got stuck looking after my siblings, I didn't experience a kid like my son. My brothers had practically been born in the mud and raised in the saddle, and while they weren't dense, they weren't sensitive like Grayson. Same with Aggie, the youngest of us all. I'd tried protecting her, and she'd only resented me and the family, leaving home and staying gone for good.

Now she was in Crocus Valley with her new husband, and I'd followed her, like we'd reversed stereotypical roles. Only I felt like she understood. She knew what it was like to grow up under Barns's rule and wanted things to be different. Hell, all of us did. With Meg gone, I was back in familiar territory but still on foreign land.

The blower stopped, and I punched the button again. I couldn't cross my arms over my chest. My shirt was full of milk. Leaning against the wall might get me dirtier than any spilled drink. Waiting for clothes to dry only gave me time to think about how much work waited for me.

I pinched the bridge of my nose. What the hell was I going to do?

Grayson's little face was tipped down while he watched the wetness slowly diminish. His blank expression was the opposite of when we walked in. He poked at the red of the fabric. "Spider-Man's dry."

"He is. Want to back up a step and let the air hit the shorts?"

"I don't care about the shorts."

"I do."

He glanced at me like he had to see if I was serious about drying the milk on his shorts. Then he did as I asked. He did a hip wiggle that would've made Elvis jealous. Then another.

"Whatcha doing, bud?"

He swirled his hips and gave another thrust. I bit the inside of my cheek. For having no balance or coordination, he liked to bust a move, but after his meltdown, he didn't need to feel like I was laughing at him.

"Moving around." He thrust his opposite hip and broke into a full-body boogie. Then he stepped back, inspecting his crotch. "All dry. Your turn."

I stood steadfastly still while I dried my shirt. Grayson whipped his hands out behind me, making web-flinging motions. Meg would hate that, but Aggie had gotten him the shirt. I should probably buy a few more plain polos that had been his mother's style so I didn't feel like I fell short of the expectations she'd left me with.

"Done." I opened the door, and Grayson sprinted out.

When I rounded the corner, I expected to see Thelma at the booth with Ivy. Thelma was nowhere to be seen, but there was a stranger sitting next to Ivy, bent over a coloring sheet of a castle.

She murmured softly to Ivy, and while I could only see the woman's back, my curiosity was turning to desperation to see her face. The curve of her shoulders was graceful, and her glossy dark brown hair tumbled down her back.

I gave myself a shake, shame filling me. I lost my wife less than a year ago.

I was *not* interested.

"Excuse me?" I said, as Grayson scooted into the hopefully dry booth.

The woman tipped her face toward me, and my stomach clenched.

Jesus. She had high cheekbones and wide-set blue eyes that combined to give her a Snow White look. Her skin practically glowed under the fluorescent lights, and those didn't do anyone justice.

"You must be Dad," she said with a smile in her voice. But for as sweet and Disney-princess innocent as she looked, there was a sharpness to her gaze that couldn't be missed. Not by me. I'd seen the shrewdness in Barns and my wife, but their critical view of the world was different than this girl's. She was sizing me up, reading me. Judging me from the button-up, pinstripe white shirt with the crusty dried milk stain to the feather-gray slacks and my chestnut-brown loafers.

"I am. And you are?" My question came out harsher than intended, but I had left my daughter with someone I . . . trusted was a strong word, but I thought Thelma would do what she said for at least five minutes.

"Tova," she said with a practiced smile. "I've already met Ivy." She took her attention off me as if it were as simple as breathing when I couldn't look away from the way her creamy skin shone like expensive satin. "And you are?" she asked my son.

"Grayson," he said, going back to his coloring.

"Grayson and Ivy. Lovely names." She scooted out of the booth, and I realized I was looming over her. I jumped back before her knee brushed my slacks.

Thelma swooped in with two fresh milks. "Gotcha new glasses. The booth is cleaned. Tova watched your girl for me." She eyed me with a hearty challenge. "She's like a daughter to me."

As if I were in the market.

If I was, Thelma's look said *no, I wasn't.*

"Thelma and my grandma were best friends." The fondness in Tova's sultry voice made me wonder what it was like to have an older family member you were close to. Barns's parents had been as cold as him, and my mama's parents had passed away when I was a kid.

"More milk is fine," I said.

Thelma snorted. "I think the words you're looking for are thank you."

Shocked, I stared at her but didn't miss the sway of Tova's ass in a pair of short shorts as she disappeared into the kitchen.

Thelma's gray brow arched higher. Busted staring at her "like a daughter." This day could be going better. "Thank you. For the help and the new glasses of milk."

She grunted and went in the same direction as Tova.

Ivy slumped over the booth.

"Sit straight, please." I sounded exactly like Meg when she'd chided Grayson about slouching. I used to tell her to give the kid a little room to be a kid.

Those discussions hadn't ended well.

Now it was up to me to fill both parenting roles. Until the kids went to live with my in-laws, like my wife had wanted.

Stuffing the dread into the pit of my stomach, I slid into the booth and attacked my cold, overcooked cod. I couldn't stop the recollection of cunning blue eyes and a smile that could light a room from intruding on my personal glowering, and maybe it was the stress, but I did nothing to stop them.

⚜

Tova

I hovered by the back door of Hummingbird's, staying far away from the dining room, when I really wanted to peer out and see if that man was as handsome as I thought.

Hadn't I learned my lesson about good-looking men in impeccably tailored clothing yet? It'd only been two days since I fled Frederick in an Uber.

By god, I had a thing for a man dressed like he was going to make a shitload of money.

The look was catnip to me. The more I sang and danced and wore outrageous costumes until I stripped down to an ensemble that could fit into an envelope, the more I liked the put-together semblance of a man who appeared as if he could command a boardroom and a bedroom.

Frederick hadn't soured my attraction nearly enough.

But Frederick had eyed me like he had secrets I'd love to know. Like he could be my dream come true.

Stern Daddy out in the seating area eyed me with annoyance, like he'd rather not have seen me today—or ever.

"That stick up his ass runs straight to his hairline, doesn't it?" I murmured as Thelma approached, smacking a pack of cigarettes against her hand. She'd quit smoking, and she refused to vape, but she'd kept a pack of cigarettes to go through the motions. She was also known to stand outside with an unlit Newport and pace and bring the cigarette to her lips without actually lighting it.

"That stick is sewn into the man's spine." She withdrew a long white cigarette and stood with the door propped open, like she was going to take a long drag and blow the smoke out the crack. "He ordered those kids green beans instead of pancakes. Wouldn't even let them have chocolate milk."

Thelma believed in grabbing life by the brass ones, but that was what had landed her in the town she'd been born in, serving those green beans and milk instead of hitting the stage.

I secretly thought she was happier here in the tiny town in the middle of the country she'd desperately wanted to get away from. The town where the closest thing she got to being scammed or conned was when the cafe owner tried to pass off half-and-half for cream.

No one messed with Thelma and the cream for her coffee.

I glanced back toward the doorway that led to the seating area. Was he still there? Little Ivy was so precious.

She'd asked me if I was Snow White and if birds cleaned my house. "He looks like he'd wither green beans with one stare."

"Is that how he looks?" Thelma drawled and took a fake drag.

I rolled my eyes and pushed away. "You know I'm not on the market."

I was hiding from the market. I had no idea if Frederick would come looking for me. I couldn't imagine why, but my mom's tragedy stayed with me and made me paranoid. Some guys couldn't stand being bested by the woman they thought they had power over. The way Mom's ex had tracked her down had haunted my grandma, and between her and Thelma, I had an escape for every relationship I'd been in. I'd never had to use the plan to the extent I did with Frederick. Usually, Thelma wired me money or hooked me up with a better landlord. One time, before she'd moved home, I caught my blind date slipping something into my drink. I pretended to spill my drink, and a half hour later, she'd picked me up.

So, yeah. A relationship wasn't in my future. I was done with men's bullshit.

I couldn't give up on money, though. The end of the month was bearing down on me, and I'd have Mom's long-term bill due. I'd pumped all of my funds into setting up my show—the dress, the face and body makeup, and advertising. Frederick had created opportunities, and I'd coasted off his lifestyle, using my money to get me to the next level and handing him any extra to "invest and grow."

He'd walled off the money garden. Jackass.

Why had I moved my checking account to the bank he worked at?

"I need a job," I said.

"You could work here."

While I was certain Mr. Uptight out there put a nice tip down for Thelma—she'd have called him shit stick or some other name by now if he didn't—I doubted the Hummingbird's patrons were heavy tippers. I wouldn't be buying a used Volvo on the gratuity left anywhere in Crocus Valley.

Besides, Thelma's retirement plan was *I'll figure it out*. I wasn't taking her tip money or her customers.

"Think I could teach dance lessons?" There was an old, empty theater next door that enchanted me. The former stage house turned movie theater oozed small-town charm and character. I fell in love the moment I saw it after I arrived. Thelma's apartment was above the drugstore on the opposite side of the theater.

She took another pretend drag. "You'd have to rent a place to hold lessons—unless those garden club bitches let you use the park. But then they'd grill you about your credentials."

I'd taken dance lessons since I was three—tap, ballet, ballroom, jazz—it didn't matter. As long as it was movement to music, I was in. Mom had seen what it'd done to help me focus and control my emotions, and she'd nurtured it. Grandma had done what she could, but there were only so many lessons she could foot the bill for while collecting social security.

"You think they'd be all judgy about burlesque?" I was used to it. Burlesque wasn't sophisticated enough for the "real" dancers, and it was too close to stripping for most. I didn't know why there was a problem with either. I didn't care to strip, but I poured years of experience and creativity into my act. I was proud of burlesque but also defensive. Maybe a little insecure.

After the way Frederick treated me—raw.

"Probably," Thelma answered, confirming my fears.

"The nearest strip club is three hours away. It's not a part of life here."

"Shouldn't matter," I grumbled, sick to death of the struggle to be taken seriously. I'd been a performer and a business owner.

If I'd been a smart business owner, I wouldn't need a job so damn badly right now.

"You and I know that." She flicked her unlit cigarette into the garbage and pushed off the doorframe. "I gotta go check their milks. That guy puts 'em down like they're forty proof."

Smiling, I tried not to run the image of "that guy" and his wide shoulders through my head. No man should look that sinful in a shirt with an off-colored milk stain hugging his impressive pecs. He wasn't a wall of muscle like a lot of the gym bros who creeped at the gyms I'd gone to in my life. Nor was he overly lanky. He was built, but like he'd earned his body through sweat equity—hard work and a meat-and-potatoes diet—instead of plastic surgeons, protein drinks, and ninety-day diet plans.

Usually, I didn't care. A person could look good with any method they wanted, but the LA girl in me was intrigued.

"I'm going to take a walk," I said. "See if anyone's looking for help."

I was about to head for the dining area when she said, "You hoping to get one more look at milk-does-a-body-good guy?"

Heat stoking in my face, I went to my toes in relevé and spun. "The back door is fine," I said sweetly, and she narrowed her eyes at me.

I breezed out the back, ignoring the pang in my chest that I wasn't going to lay greedy eyes on the uptight dad again. Milk really did do his body good. Would his ass in those slacks outshine any I'd seen yet?

Nope. Didn't matter.

Outside, I paused. Crocus Valley was like stepping back in time. The buildings were historic in a way that I didn't see in LA. Old brick of various shades, sometimes on the same buildings, which had been moderately kept up, lined Main Street. In between some buildings were newer wooden structures, also moderately maintained. Some had the undeniable style of the seventies—browns, yellows, and whites that were now also more yellow. Other buildings were from the eighties, and then a random stucco house fit into the far corner. Every decade was reflected on Main Street, and I liked the variety.

I went all the way through the alley, not scared at all to traverse a place I'd stay far away from in a bigger city. Since the space was fairly private, I added a few hitch kicks before I rounded the block to reverse my direction toward the theater.

The two-story theater with large plate glass windows flanking either side of the entrance was built with reddish-brown brick, which was the hallmark of the area. Thelma said another small town not far away was known for its brick. She'd spouted all sorts of facts on the drive to Crocus Valley from the Bismarck airport.

I owed her so damn much. I sent the manager of my mom's long-term care home a message that I had temporarily relocated and briefly explained the situation in case Frederick tried to track me or Mom down. I asked her to tell Mom I was hanging with Thelma. I'd given her the number for the burner phone.

Laughter from children playing across the street caught my attention. Turning, I found the milk-loving dad pushing his little girl on a swing. His dark hair had busted free of the severe styling and feathered over his forehead. The scowl was still in place, and he had his phone in one hand.

What was it with guys? Being a workaholic shouldn't be a badge of honor. Some, like Frederick, should've worked on bettering themselves rather than filling the well with more money than they could use in their lifetime.

All I'd need was a fraction of Frederick's wealth. I could open a dance school, give a few performances, and do things like travel to see my mom. I'd stay with Thelma. We could catch up and share fun memories of Grandma. I wouldn't only be visiting so I could nurse my wounds and figure out how to make money when all I had was a small suitcase half-filled with garments for my act. The few clothing items I'd purchased at the airport weren't job interview material.

I already owed Thelma for the Uber and the plane ticket.

"Snow White!" Ivy shouted, frantically waving from the swing as she pumped her little legs. Grayson was digging in the dirt at the base of the slide.

I waved.

"Come here!" she yelled. She turned a commanding expression at her dad. "Daddy, stop the swing." Her voice carried across the street. Powerful lungs on that one.

His frown deepened when his gaze touched on me. I was in a souvenir *North Dakota—Legendary* shirt from the airport and a pair of cutoffs quickly made from an old pair of Thelma's jeans from the nineties. They were back in style now—a win was a win, and I'd take all I could get. My only other outfits were the velour tracksuit and the extra shorts and shirt I had packed. Those were in the laundry, and I didn't have money to buy more.

I needed to find an income. I needed to secure Mom's care and figure out how to get my accounts free of Frederick.

"I'm sure she's busy," the hot dad uttered. I never got his name.

"No, she's not," Ivy insisted. "Snow White, come here!"

I could pretend I was busy, but I couldn't resist getting under the disgruntled man's skin. He wasn't Frederick, but my pride needed the boost. I sauntered across the quiet street, struggling not to put an extra sway in my hips. A silver band on the man's left hand that I hadn't noticed earlier when I was ogling his pecs glinted in the sunlight. My walk turned stiff. I wasn't looking for a relationship, nor was I looking to interfere in a marriage. I'd had enough angry wives, girlfriends, and mistresses up in my business for doing nothing but my job—which didn't include flirting or fucking with their man. Usually, I flirted with the women when I worked the crowd before my show—better tips and less jealousy that way. My performances were for the audience, not any one individual. But that didn't stop the rest of the bullshit I dealt with.

His words carried toward me as I stepped off the road and onto the grass. "Her name's Tova."

My steps stuttered. I didn't think a guy like him would be bothered to remember. Frederick had called me Fannie Grace until our third date.

"She looks like Snow White," Ivy said.

I'd take her compliment. I was dressed like the airport had lost my luggage.

"Princesses recognize each other," I said, twisting my hair over one shoulder so it wouldn't tangle in the breeze. I'd always enjoyed working with kids and their youthful exuberance and energy.

Ivy's grin melted my heart. She fluffed her skirt and tried to bow. Her hair was a few shades lighter than mine, and her ponytail was crooked. Was her mom in the picture? Not that moms couldn't be crap at doing hair. When my grandma styled my hair, I looked like I'd been run through a car wash.

"Do you know how to curtsy?" I asked. Ivy shook her head. I lifted my chin, adopted an imperial expression, and waved to the spot next to me. "Come, I'll show you."

She jumped off the swing and stopped beside me. I grabbed at my imaginary skirt. "Now, watch my feet." I put my right foot back. "Keep both feet straight. There you go. Now bend your knees."

"Isn't it like this?" She dropped to a low bow and stumbled sideways.

"Are we doing Disney bows or royal bows?"

Grayson jogged toward us. "Whatcha doing?"

"Curtyseeing," Ivy said in a singsong voice.

He positioned his feet to mimic us.

A warm wall of heat hit my side. The dad approached us, a scowl in place. I tensed, waiting to get yelled at for his son trying to curtsy.

"You have to bow, Grayson," Ivy said hotly. "You're a *boy.*"

Grayson's lips pursed a lot like his dad's. Scowls ran strong in this family. "You don't know how to bow."

"You do it like this!" She swooped into a low bow, crossing an arm over her waist.

Surprisingly, the dad didn't speak up, like he was waiting to see how his kids handled the disagreement.

Grayson did a perfunctory bow.

"That's pretty good," I said. "Do either of you know how to do a stage bow?"

The boy wrinkled his nose. "Is there a difference?"

"Guys, I gotta take this call," the dad broke in, looking once more at his phone. "I'll just be by the porta potty." His gaze swept over me, and his jaw tightened before he focused on the kids. "Stay by the swings and give me some space, okay? Should only be a few minutes."

Instead of maintaining a restroom, the town sprang for a portable bathroom during the summer months, much to Thelma's consternation. *Can't they make them look better than a powder-blue column in the middle of the park?*

"I can entertain them." I didn't know what made me offer. Something to do, probably. A way to feel useful, and I missed working with kids.

His dark gaze oscillated back to me. "You don't have to."

Was this guy allergic to help? "I promise I'm not billing you."

His eyes narrowed for a heartbeat, but all he said was "Thank you" and strode away, phone to his ear. His kids were watching me.

"Your dad's a busy guy," I said, not being nosy at all. But, you know, kids talked a lot, and my ears were open. Just in case.

"Mommy used to be a lot busier," Grayson said as he practiced another bow.

"What does she do now?"

"She died," Ivy said, her smile suddenly gone.

Oh. Sympathy welled inside. I had almost lost my mom, and it'd torn me up, but I'd been an adult. "I'm so sorry." I crouched to get on her level. Her wide brown eyes were a few shades lighter than her dad's, and the sadness went deep. "I'm really, really sorry."

She sniffled. "'S okay. She worked a lot too."

Questions piled on my tongue, but I'd already stepped in it. "A lot of adults have to work more than they want."

"She wanted to," Grayson said. He looked around, his mouth pursing. "I gotta go to the bathroom."

The only choice was the bathroom his dad was standing by

with his worried gaze on his kids. A widower. Didn't I feel like shit for labeling him all sorts of an uptight workaholic? "Can you wait for a few minutes while your dad's on the phone?"

"No."

Well, he was honest. "Okay, so maybe we can switch places with your dad." I waved to catch his attention, which wasn't hard. I didn't get the feeling the man missed much.

I pointed from Grayson to the portable outhouse and then made an arc that vaguely suggested we change places. His shoulders slumped, and the quickest defeated expression lit his eyes before it was smothered. Did I imagine it? He gave a curt nod as he spoke into the phone. Wandering toward the slides, he put more space between us, presumably so the person he was talking to wouldn't know he was at a park with kids.

"Let's go," I said, holding my hands out. "Remember to be quiet."

They clamped on without hesitation. I checked the hygiene situation of the porta potty because no way could that thing be clean sitting out in the middle of nowhere. In LA, the inside would be smeared with feces, and there'd be at least five different types of needles.

The interior was pristine and had a chemical mint smell. Huh. Not bad at all. "All set."

Ivy waited with me, practicing her curtsies.

"I never got your dad's name." I couldn't deny my nosiness, but I was helping the guy with his kids. I should know what to call him.

"Alcott."

I cocked my head. I was used to hearing all sorts of first and last names, but this one was new. "Is that your last name?"

She shook her head, her crooked ponytail flying. "Knight."

"Alcott Knight?" Classy but manly. It fit him.

"People call him Cody."

He didn't look like a Cody. When I thought of a Cody, I pictured a relaxed guy from a small town like Crocus Valley. Easygoing with a quick smile. I thought Alcott had forgotten how to smile. My gaze drifted toward him just as he pushed his hair off his forehead and swept it to the side. It stayed, like it was afraid to disappoint him.

"Only Mommy called him Alcott," Ivy said, twirling her skirt while she was standing in place.

Cody, it was.

Grayson came out, and the spring-loaded door slammed shut.

"My turn!" Ivy stormed the bathroom like a warrior princess.

It was me and Grayson. He was a subdued kid, which I didn't expect after his outburst in the diner. Was it losing his mother? How long ago did it happen?

He practiced bowing.

"Good." I dropped to a stage bow. Usually, I was topless with nothing but pasties or tassels on my nipples, but I was worried even thinking that would give stern Cody Knight a brain hemorrhage.

Grayson and I bowed and tossed our imaginary audience kisses. He giggled, and I got a glimpse of a lively kid who wanted to come out and play but had to learn to handle living without his mother. Ivy joined us when she came out.

I lost track of time, loving the fake finale we were making, when a deep "Thanks again" startled me.

I put my hand on my heart and jumped. "Ohmigod, you scared me."

The creases at the corners of his mouth deepened, but

this scowl was different. Could it be . . . humor in his gaze? "Sorry," he said.

That deep voice of his. I wanted to record it and play it back when I was alone at night. I planned to stay far away from men and relationships, but a girl still had needs.

Inappropriate much, Tova? "No worries. It's been fun. You have great kids."

The corner of his mouth almost lifted. "They are great."

Ivy beamed, then tapped her brother. "Gray, let's race." She sprinted for the slide. Grayson darted after her.

Cody didn't bat an eye. I kept thinking he'd be uptight about kids acting like kids, but this guy wasn't acting like I expected him to. Except for the scowls.

"Hey, uh, do you know where I can look for a nanny for the summer?"

It took a second to realize he'd directed the question at me. Even with only half of his attention, my belly flipped, then flopped. "I don't know. I'm not from here." His gaze sharpened, and the urge to explain myself in a way that wouldn't cause more questions was too strong. "I just left a bad relationship, and Thelma's an old family friend. I'm crashing with her until I figure out what to do."

Normally, I wouldn't spill so much of my business, but the ol' *woman running from man trouble* story was usually enough to keep people from digging too deep. They'd all heard similar stories or had their own, and they unconsciously filled in the gaps. The less often I had to evade nosy questions, the better. I wouldn't be in town long, but Thelma didn't need the gossip around her.

"You could ask Thelma, though," I offered. "She would know who's reliable and who isn't—and she'll be happy to tell you."

The side of his mouth lifted higher for a split second, then his forehead furrowed. His jaw worked like he was going to say something. Finally, he gave his head a shake. "Thank you again. For Hummingbird's and now."

"Not a problem. I'm sorry about—Ivy told me about her mom. I'm sure it's hard on them." Again, I didn't know what possessed me to keep talking. God, why had I brought up his late wife? I made a living being attuned to the crowd, but getting a read on this man beyond him being a grim workaholic was like deciphering a blank wall.

"It'll be a year in September since she died." His expression flickered. Grief. Regret. Confusion. "We're not from here either. Just trying to get away for a while." He shook himself, like he couldn't believe he'd shared that much. We had that in common. "Anyway, thank you for the suggestion. I'll talk to Thelma."

He marched to the slide. The kids looked at me like they were wondering if I'd join them. I executed a perfect curtsy. It wasn't like me to linger where I wasn't needed, but turning around and leaving Cody and the kids behind was harder than it should've been. We were nothing but strangers. He'd go back to wherever they lived, and as soon as I figured out my financial situation, I'd be gone too.

Three

CODY

I jerked awake, my heart pounding and my dick tenting the blankets in a way it hadn't done for more than a couple of decades. After being married and getting laid regularly, I hadn't thought about not getting any. If Meg wasn't in the mood, I jacked off in the shower. She'd had a lot of headaches—from stress and then from the tumor. After she got sick, and definitely after she died, I locked my libido away.

The fucker snuck out while I was sleeping. Images of creamy, heavy tits swaying over my face while she was riding me filled my head. Only when I was about to dreamgasm did the view of the face clear into sky-blue eyes and a spill of nearly black hair.

Meg's eyes had been brown. Her hair was mahogany.

I pushed a hand over my face. Dream-fucking a woman I'd just met was a dick move. I didn't care what anyone said about grief—and during Meg's funeral and after, they'd had a lot to say—it was wrong.

But for a moment, it had felt so damn right.

Ignoring my throbbing erection, I rolled out of bed and checked my phone. Messages lined the screen. Reminders about calls and appointments. One from my youngest brother, Eliot, stood out. He managed the Knight's Arabians and Cattle Company portion of the family businesses.

What the hell? No indoor riding ring?

I groaned. When I took over the books for my dad's company, I thought it'd be a fairly easy financial stream. I'd run the numbers, tell Barns and Eliot what could and couldn't be done, collect my paycheck, and concentrate on Knight's Oil Wells, the real moneymaker.

Knight's Arabians and Cattle Company turned out to be a drain on my time and energy, and the money was a damn mess. It'd taken years to untangle the chaos the first accountant had made when he'd done nothing but acquiesce to whatever Barns had demanded, funnel a little money into his own account, and leave us with back taxes and penalties.

Work was enough to reroute blood back to my brain. I tossed on a plain white polo and a pair of gray slacks before I trudged down the hallway and peeked into Grayson's bedroom and then Ivy's. They were both asleep, but it was early yet—and they were early risers.

Rubbing my eyes, I went back to the bedroom and called Eliot, bracing myself for his constant crankiness.

"Why not?" he answered. "Don't you think after being in business for fifty years, the company can afford to keep us from freezing our asses off while we train the horses?"

I took an even breath. I'd been one of those guys

freezing his ass off working horses and cattle. An indoor ring would've been the ultimate pampering.

I don't breed pussies, Barns had muttered.

"If those first fifty years had been run correctly," I answered patiently, "then yes, the company could afford to build."

"Can't we use oil money?" Frustration rang in his voice.

"It's not that easy, and oil's been down for years."

"What's it good for, then?"

We'd had this conversation already. It was as constant as quarterly taxes. "Keeping our doors open for another fifty years. Look, Eliot. The economy is shit. Barns tied up the money in the trust to pay us until we can retire, and if we want money until we retire, then we can't just build whatever we want when we want it."

"I'm not being greedy, and you know it."

"I do know it. *You* can build the indoor riding ring—Knight's Arabians and Cattle Company can't."

"I'd have to take out a loan because, like you, I only get our inheritance one year at a time and only if I'm working for this broken-down company." His frustration matched mine.

If we wanted any of the money Barns had squirreled away, we had to work for the company until we retired. In doing so, we had to clean up the mess he had made. I was living with my own issues resulting from the living trust Barns had created. Eliot was living with his.

My ass wasn't working with horses when it was twenty below zero anymore. Eliot had fought with Barns more than I had about upgrades around the ranch, improving processes, and making a more efficient company. But just because Barns was gone didn't mean we could dive in. Damage had been done for years to the bottom line.

"We can go over the accounts again," I said evenly, "but

you know how tied my hands are. Cattle prices are shit, gas still isn't cheap, interest rates have skyrocketed, the horses aren't selling like they used to, and the oil boom has nearly busted. I need more time to figure out how best to do this."

"There's gotta be grants or something."

"Look into it."

"I'm not the accountant. I'm actually breaking a sweat."

I ground my teeth together. Whenever we argued, he tossed it in my face that I wasn't working the ranch like I used to. He did the same with our other brother, Austen, who'd joined the army after high school. Wilder was exempt since he'd never quit helping while working around his job as a deputy. Maybe he should've backed off more, or he wouldn't be going through a divorce. Eliot left our sister, Aggie, alone, and she'd been the one who wanted to work just like him, only she hadn't been encouraged. Barns had taken his anger toward our mother out on her by ignoring her presence.

Eliot wasn't going to listen. He was pissed at our dad, but Barns wasn't around to be a target. I was.

Ivy sprinted into my bedroom and flung herself on the bed to burrow beneath the covers.

"I'll do some checking," I said. "I've gotta go."

"Of course you do."

"We're not opponents, Eliot. My hands are tied almost as much as yours."

"I can't run to another state and take a summer vacation."

"You also don't have kids who just lost their mother," I growled into the phone, hoping it was low enough Ivy couldn't hear in her bedding cocoon.

"Fuck, I know." His hostility was gone. "Listen, I get it. It's just . . . our hands shouldn't be so tied."

"I agree. I'll still see what I can do."

After we disconnected, I tossed my phone to the side. I had to get to the office, but I needed to situate the kids first.

I peered under the blankets and found a mass of brown hair. "Tired?"

Ivy squinted at me, her eyes bleary. "No."

She'd never admit it. "Let's grab some breakfast. I've gotta get to work."

In the kitchen, I groaned. Dishes were piled high by the sink. How could three people use so many? The house didn't have a dishwasher. I had offered to pay for one to be installed, but the landlord preferred the house's natural state. As if the dishwasher would ruin the effect of the nineties oak cabinets.

I opened the fridge. A half-cup of milk was left in the last jug. So, cereal was out as an option, but the kids refused to eat the brands I bought anyway. High-protein, whole-grain cereals weren't their thing, but I refused to buy the kind they would eat. Brownies for breakfast would be healthier.

Good old PB&J, then. I scanned the inside of the fridge. No jelly. I stuffed a hand through my hair. We were out of that too? I had already used all the sausage Eliot had sent with us when we moved, and going along those lines, the beef he'd packed into the back of my pickup was also gone.

I checked the oatmeal canister. Enough for one serving. I could bypass breakfast, but I had two kids. The yogurt was gone. No fruit except for one sad, brown banana. A reflection of the job I was doing as a single parent. That damn banana was a banner for why the kids were going to live with their grandparents.

Ivy was jumping over a seam between the flooring planks—also oak colored. "There's nothing to eat."

The kids noticed before I did. Meg's sarcastic humor

filtered through my brain. *Way to go, Alcott. Crack parenting right there.* Had our positions been changed, she would've been in the same situation, and she'd have known it. Our busy work lives were why she worried about leaving me a single dad and talked with her parents about taking the kids.

"I agree." I pushed another hand through my hair and caught my reflection in the microwave. The strands stood on end, and I looked half asleep. I couldn't go out like this. I'd look like a dad who didn't know what the fuck he was doing. "Go get dressed. I'll wake up G, and we'll go get groceries."

"But I'm hungry now."

"We need groceries first."

"What about Hummingbird's? Maybe we'll see Snow White again."

"Tova." Her soft blue eyes flashed in my head. The image from my dream wasn't dying. The curve of her bare hips was purely from my imagination, but I couldn't think about her without getting hard. "Get dressed, please."

She huffed and stomped out of the kitchen. I roused my son, told him to get dressed, then I went to clean up. I kept my polo on. The conference call wasn't online, and I didn't have to appear as if I wasn't in a home office.

Grayson appeared in the doorway of his room as I was leaving the bedroom. "Daddy, I'm hungry."

"We've gotta get some groceries first."

"Can we go to Hummingbird's?"

"Not today."

"I want to see Tova again."

She made an impression on my attention-starved kids. I had been the fun parent when Meg was alive, but now I didn't have time. A dull thud started at my temples.

"She was really nice," he insisted, as if I hadn't noticed

exactly how nice she was. As if I hadn't noticed the sensual sway of her hips, how much my fingertips burned to stroke over her skin, or thought about how her long hair would feel running over my bare chest when she—

Fuck's sake.

"Get dressed," I said, harsher than intended. I had to get that woman off my mind.

"I am dressed."

I glanced at the duck pajama pants and Teenage Mutant Ninja Turtles T-shirt. Meg had hated that shirt worse than his Spider-Man gear.

Who the hell cared?

But her litany ran through my mind. Country bumpkins. Stereotypes. Dress for success. Wasn't that what I did with my clothing? Dress shirts for in-person and video meetings, polos for audio meetings? "Since we're going to the store, go put on some nicer shorts. Maybe a plain shirt."

His nose scrunched up. "Why?"

If I told him we dressed for the job we wanted, he'd claim he would love to be a Teenage Mutant Ninja Turtle. Or he'd go put on a Spider-Man shirt. "Just while we're out, okay?"

He rolled his eyes and disappeared from the doorway.

Why couldn't we go to Hummingbird's again?

They need to learn responsibility, Alcott. I closed my eyes against the onslaught of parenting mantras I'd heard throughout my marriage. She was gone, and it was up to me to raise responsible, educated, worldly kids.

Then you should've gone somewhere for the summer other than Crocus Valley, Alcott. It's barely larger than Buffalo Gully. The small Montana town where I was born and raised had been a purgatory for Meg.

I should've taken the kids to New York. London. Rented a villa in France.

I had no one in New York, London, or France, and I liked towns the size of Crocus Valley and my hometown. My sister was here, and I wasn't sure I'd have had the guts to go anywhere else. I wasn't going to lean on her, though. I'd practically raised her, and she had her own life. Being away from the quiet and the memories and the impending change at the end of the summer was enough.

A half hour, a change of clothes for both of them, and one wonky ponytail later, we were wandering the grocery store. I was pushing the cart, and the kids were asking for every product the store sold. My phone gave random notification buzzes, but I ignored them. The morning had been stressful enough, and the clock was ticking for my meeting. We needed groceries and an early lunch, and then I'd lose myself in work.

"Can I get Oreos?" Ivy asked.

"Not today."

"Ooh, what about fruit snacks?" Grayson asked.

Meg had detested fruit snacks. "We loaded up on real fruit."

"Pop-Tarts?" he tried again.

Meg would come back and haunt me if I bought those. "Nope."

"Ugh." Ivy trailed her hand along all the forbidden items. "How about ice cream?"

"We can go to Hummingbird's for an ice cream treat later this week." I grabbed a canister of oatmeal.

Grayson eyed it dubiously. "Do we have brown sugar for the oatmeal?"

Their mom had blamed me for the brown-sugar-on-oatmeal habit. Meg had all sorts of oatmeal recipes—overnight oats, steel-cut oats, and old-fashioned oatmeal—and my eggs-and-sausage ass had a hard time making the switch. My spoonful of sugar might've been more like two, and the kids had taken notice.

"Let's grab another bag." I tried to do my best, but if I was duty-bound to carry out the oatmeal tradition for Meg, then I needed sugar.

We rounded the corner, and I got an eyeful of creamy long legs and a heart-shaped ass bending over to inspect the different brands of sugar.

My gut clenched, and that damn sex drive that had snuck out of the shadows this morning made itself known again. To be fair, I'd never seen such an amazing behind. Guilt hit me hard in the chest, and I swallowed sour bile. I had no business rating asses.

She straightened.

"Tova!" Grayson called, and when she turned, he dropped into a deep bow.

Her smile was sweeter than the sugar we were surrounded by, and she dipped into a curtsy, flaring out a pretend skirt. Her legs were a mile long, and she'd tied an old Hummingbird's shirt at her waist, showing a strip of belly.

Christ, but she looked soft in all the right places.

Ivy did both a curtsy and a bow, then rushed to crash into the stomach I'd been inappropriately admiring.

Tova laughed, the sound a tinkle of delighted chimes. She hugged my daughter back, and a knot twisted in my chest. I didn't grow up in a warm family, and while Meg strived to be the best mother she could be, she hadn't been a stereotypical warm mother.

"How are you two?" she asked, keeping her arm around Ivy's slim shoulders.

"We're getting sugar for our oatmeal," Grayson announced.

"Daddy wouldn't let us eat at Hummingbird's today," Ivy said sullenly.

Humor danced in Tova's eyes. "Oatmeal sounds just fine." She leaned down. "Sugar makes everything go down better."

Her words were innocent, but they only reignited strong memories of my dream. I needed to get away from her, but she was standing right where I needed to be. "G, grab the sugar. We gotta get to work."

Ivy stamped her little sandaled foot. "Daddy's always gotta work."

My constant well of guilt filled fuller.

Tova finally met my gaze, her own neutral. I didn't get the warm smile Ivy did. "Did you talk to Thelma about possible nannies yet?"

"I haven't had time." My answer came out curt, and I nearly winced. I didn't mean to be an ass, but her voice wound around my insides like a velvet glove.

She lifted a shoulder. "It's only been a day."

"Can you be our nanny?" Ivy asked.

An ice-cold bucket of water splashed against my face. Kids and the awkward situations they put me in. Unexpected questions to strangers and invites I had no part in approving.

Actually, this was the first time in a long time either had happened. "I'm sure Tova has something else planned for the summer."

Her smile had a strained edge to it. "Yes. I'm . . ." She laughed nervously. "You know . . . the days fill up fast."

Ivy threaded her hand through Tova's. The sight both warmed my heart and filled me with guilt that my little girl was desperate for a woman's attention.

"I would be home" came out of my mouth before I had time to think. Fuck. Was I doing this? My phone was vibrating like crazy in my pocket with notifications and missed calls. Yes. I was, and the more I thought about it, the better the idea seemed. Also the worst.

"Are you making a serious offer?" Tova's tone was curious. "You just met me."

"I haven't met anyone Thelma would recommend yet either. It's only for a couple of months. I'll be working out of the office in the house, and I can be flexible on hours." To punctuate that she was my only option, my phone buzzed again.

Like she heard it, her eyes dropped to the pocket of my polo. For a woman who was getting back on her feet, she didn't jump at the opportunity. "I don't know."

Ivy tugged on her hand. "Can you? It'll be fun."

"So fun." Grayson nodded.

My spark of regret for asking her in front of the kids was wiped out by their enthusiasm.

"I have a princess doll that looks like you." Ivy beamed.

Grayson wasn't going to be outshined. "We're not far from the park. We can go back there."

She fondly smiled at them both, but the hesitation remained.

"Pay is also negotiable," I added. Where else would I find a nanny in this town?

"I . . ." Her reluctance hacked away at my pride. What did I look like to her? An older man propositioning a young woman he'd just met, throwing money at her, when she was in an unstable portion of her life? "No pressure, Tova."

I might have to ask my sister if she could take the kids for a day so I could catch up. My soon-to-be ex-sister-in-law lived in Crocus Valley now too. She was busy starting her own vet practice, but maybe she'd be willing to help for a few hours a week. The kids missed their aunt Sutton, and they loved their aunt Aggie and her animals. The last thing I wanted to do was impose, but I also wanted to enjoy some of the next two months with my kids. "I can talk to Thelma later today for more leads."

I dipped my head and held my hand out for Ivy, who still clung to her. "Come on, guys. Let's let Tova get back to what she was doing."

Ivy and Grayson exchanged disappointed looks.

"I'd need to talk to you," she blurted out. Her gaze darted around. "About the job. In private."

"Stop by sometime today, before eleven or after two. We're the house across from the small-machine repair shop. We'll be home."

Ivy hopped in place, a big smile on her face.

Grayson said with a hiss, "Yes." Tova didn't give us a yes, but she didn't say no, and that was all my kids heard.

Her tentative smile made it seem like I might see her later and chase her right back out. I didn't know this woman. I didn't know what the hell I was doing hiring her to hang with my kids.

My other option was to move back to Buffalo Gully and tell Meg's parents they should take the kids to Helena two months sooner than expected. They had already enrolled the kids in a private school.

No. I said I'd give myself the summer with them, but I needed a hand. As much as I wished I didn't, even Meg, before she got sick, had mentioned the option of hiring a nanny to help with the kids before and after school and during the summer. Her parents had pestered her about daycare too.

After seeing the kids with Tova, I couldn't not do it. They were smiling again. Happier. When she was near them, their behavior reminded me of my siblings when we were younger. Kids being kids.

When I ran Grayson and Ivy through the store and we left to go home and unload our groceries, I was relieved I hadn't seen the last of Tova yet. And irritated. I'd forgotten the damn sugar.

Tova

I hung back by the back door of the diner. The lunch rush would start soon, but I had to stop and ask Thelma how crazy impulsive I was being.

She took a fake drag off her unlit Newport. "You want to know if taking up with the first handsome man to cross your path after Charlie-boy is a bad idea?"

I screwed up my face. She made it sound like I was jumping onto the man's lap and urging him to *take me, big boy.* "I'm not shacking up with him. I'd be working for him."

"Tova." Her tone said everything.

"He asked me to watch his kids, not lap dance for him or his business associates." It wasn't like I thought about what it'd be like to loosen a couple buttons on his shirt and soften the granite in his jaw. I *did not* think about what kind of special choreography would drive a man with iron-clad control wild at all.

No. Not at all.

"He hasn't asked you *yet.*"

She shook her head.

"Bad idea. No one knows him around here. All I know is that he has two kids and likes his milk."

"Do you know anyone trustworthy who can nanny for him?" I was strangely protective of the kids. I'd only met them a couple of times, but they'd gone from a sort of lost haze to being exuberant kids when they were around me.

My presence was enough to cheer them up, and I didn't have to put on a performance.

It'd been a long time since I felt like I didn't have to act a certain way around people depending on what they might think of me or what they wanted from me. It'd been even longer since I'd gotten to hang out with kids.

Thelma pursed her lips and flicked imaginary ashes. "The Wilson girls are teenagers. Heard the older one has a boyfriend she can't get off of. More likely to spend more time stuck on her phone when he's not around than watching the kids."

"How old is the younger sister?"

"Thirteen."

I didn't want to offer up this sister I'd never met. "Anyone else?"

She lifted a shoulder. "I think one of his neighbors is Catherine Ives. Her mom has been divorced for a few years, and Catherine is maybe twelve. Old enough to help."

A single mom lived right next to Cody? How hot was she? Why was my heart rate thumping like I'd done a half hour of barrel jumps? "I like being around Grayson and Ivy."

"Just the kids?" she asked dryly.

I rolled my eyes. "He's like talking to a brick." A handsome brick with hard pecs and wide shoulders that filled out a polo shirt in a way I'd never seen. "He's like a stern milk daddy."

But there was the moment when he unexpectedly shared information about his late wife. He could've been making it clear he was single, but I didn't get interested vibes from him. The impression I got from him was that he'd rather be farther away from me than closer.

An unusual circumstance for me. I spent too much time around straight men who had either seen me with my top off or wanted to see me with my top off. And then there was the batch of guys who wanted me to make money for them by taking my top off—and several who thought I shouldn't stop there and hated that I used pasties and tassels and thongs.

"You're going to do what you want to do." Thelma eyed me and flicked her cigarette into the trash can, where three more lay on top of kitchen scraps. It'd been a taxing morning for her. Was living with me stressing her out? "Milk Daddy," she chuffed.

"I can't have you paying Mom's bills." The only saving grace to my circumstances was that Frederick had waited to screw me over after the beginning of the month. I had until the end of June to figure out how to pay for another month of Mom's care.

Once Mom's care was nailed down, I'd turn my focus to how to deal with Frederick.

Her mouth tightened, and fine lines rimmed her lips. "I can help out, doll face." Worry flashed in her hazel eyes. "For a short time."

That was it. The issue making her pretend chain-smoke. Any more stress, and she'd light up for real and go back on a habit she'd kicked three years ago after my grandma died from emphysema.

Thelma had footed the bill to get me to Crocus Valley. She was feeding me from the diner and risking her job. I needed to work. I needed an income, and my old skills weren't going to help in a town as small as Crocus Valley.

I gave her a kiss on her wrinkled cheek. "Thank you for everything, Thelma."

"Remember, you feel unsafe at all—call me."

"Will do." The last thing I felt around Cody Knight was unsafe. He was a brooding wall of man, and pressure rode on his shoulders like a pet parrot, but his presence was comforting in a way I couldn't explain. Like he was struggling to make his way in the world and fulfill obligations as badly as I was.

But I had to talk to him first. If he bailed after he heard what I had to say, then I'd call the grocery store back about the opening they had. The pay wouldn't be half of what I needed to keep Mom where she was, but it was a start.

I slung my black tote bag, emblazoned with the logo of one of the burlesque clubs I'd danced at, over my shoulder and walked to the towering farmhouse. The old place was charming with its clapboard shutters and peaked roof, but Thelma said the landlord didn't like to put money into it. He'd rather his renters do the work themselves than hire out, and he might give them a few bucks off rent, which was nowhere near what paying a professional would cost.

I knocked on the door, and footsteps pounded on the other side.

"G, don't open the door without—"

Grayson whipped the door open, cutting his dad off. The collar of his little polo was flipped up, and his hair was mussed. Ivy was jumping up and down behind him.

Selfishly, I'd missed this. Kids were always happy to see me. I felt popular. I'd grown up an only child, getting uprooted regularly, and was eventually passed to my grandma when I was a teen. Kids gave me the friend network I didn't have when I was younger.

Cody was right behind them, his usually stony expression exasperated and his phone in his hand. He pulled to a stop behind his kids and sighed. "What have we talked about when someone's at the door?"

Grayson was unrepentant. "But we knew Tova was coming."

I smiled and tugged down Grayson's collar. "What if I

was selling vacuum cleaners? Or . . . trying to lure small children to my van with kittens?"

"You have kittens?" Ivy bounced in place again.

I laughed. "No. I'm trying to point out that you didn't know for certain it was me." I pointed to the peephole in the door. "And I know neither of you are tall enough to check."

Undaunted, Grayson shrugged. "It was you."

I met Cody's eyes, grinning. His features were smoothed back into his determined, professional mask. "Kids, go finish putting the dishes away so I can talk to Tova."

The way he said my name sent warm tendrils of shivers down my spine. His deep, pleasing voice only made me wonder how much it'd rasp in my ear in the dark.

I inhaled a shuddering breath. It'd been a while since I'd been thoroughly pleasured. Men like Frederick could be selfish in bed. I'd gotten off—if I did half the work.

Cody probably wouldn't need to do more than tell me to come, and I'd shatter.

Flustered, I dug in my tote and withdrew a bag of brown sugar. "I wasn't sure if you remembered to grab some." Cody's dark brows drew together as he stared at my present. Was he annoyed? "I gambled that since you mentioned it was for oatmeal, you were after brown sugar."

"We forgot it," Ivy announced. Grayson was still standing next to her.

Cody's expression shut down further, and he gingerly took the sugar without touching me. "Thank you." He handed the bag to Ivy. "Put this away, please." She didn't move. "Both of you—now." They scurried off, peeking over their shoulders.

The command in his voice . . . *God*. No. I did not want a domineering man.

"How much do I owe you?"

"It's fine." Thelma had given me money to grab

groceries, so technically, he owed her, but I'd reimburse her. Add it to my stack of bills.

I stepped back. He was walling himself off, and I found it alluring. I couldn't be that girl. I was old enough to know better. I was not going to be intrigued by a guy who made himself off-limits. "Can we talk on the porch?"

Before we got to negotiations, I wanted to ensure he knew who he was hiring. I'd had parents in LA get upset when they learned their kid's teacher was a burlesque dancer, as if they'd looked up anything about burlesque performance beyond the bare skin.

If he hired me, then fingers crossed he was the discreet man I assumed he was. I couldn't have the kids overhear. Crocus Valley was a small town, and I had no idea how the residents would react to my line of work. More like my former line of work. I had no idea what I'd do for a job. I didn't have money or time to build another name. Frederick would make sure Fannie Grace wasn't a desired act to book, and I was already making life more challenging for Thelma. She didn't need to bitch people out on my behalf.

He stepped out onto the covered porch. There were two dusty wicker chairs I wasn't sure would hold my weight, much less his. I drifted to the railing and stared out at the quiet street. A large willow tree swayed in the breeze in the yard of the adjacent house. Green leafy trees lined both boulevards, and tall junipers that needed trimming pushed against the railing of the deck. "I need to discuss the job."

"Yes." He stood several feet away from me, his arms crossed over his impressive chest. What would he look like without his shirt? *How the turns have tabled,* Grandma used to say. Look at me, thinking the same thoughts I held against men over the years. "Like I said, I'm flexible on salary and hours."

"I'm a dancer, Mr. Knight." Formality seemed more appropriate right now.

His brows crashed down. "Cody, please."

A deep, feminine part of me let out a dreamy sigh. "Cody it is." I almost purred the words. *Rein it in, Tova!*

A muscle in his jaw jumped, but he didn't react otherwise. "Are you trying to tell me that if you find a dancing position, you'll have to quit?"

"Sort of." I'd have to leave to make a living dancing. "I'm trying to be transparent. When I was in my early twenties, I was in different dance troupes and auditioned for bit-acting roles. Then, for the last seven years, I've been a burlesque dancer."

A furrow creased his forehead, and this close, without the distraction of his kids, I got a good look at him. His skin had a tanned, ruddy quality to it, like he'd spent a lot of time outside. He wasn't leathery, but the roughness added a manliness to him that reminded me of the Marlboro man Thelma and my grandma used to gush about.

Even I'd ride that cowboy, Thelma used to say, and Grandma would cackle, and they'd tell me I'd understand when I was old enough.

I got it now.

"How old are you?" he asked. He shook his head. "Never mind. I shouldn't have asked."

"It's no problem. I'm thirty-three." I watched for his reaction.

Relief filled Cody's face, and he coughed out a rough laugh, the sound rusty, like he didn't get to do it much. "Thirty-three," he murmured.

Memories of Frederick's reaction and why rose. "Is that an issue?"

"Not at all. I was afraid you were younger."

"Oh." Afraid? Age wasn't usually a good thing in my

field. At twenty-six, I'd been asked how I could build a dancing career when I was already at an advanced age.

"Okay, so you're a dancer."

"*Burlesque*, Cody." I waited for understanding, searching his eyes, waiting for the *Oh* moment, and then the *what kind of show will she do for me?* look. Not every club owner and venue manager was like that if they were into women, but I'd been around long enough to be ready to protect myself. "It's adult dancing, sensual, a little comedic. I think of it as theater adjacent, but, uh, burlesque is sometimes described as a striptease."

He blinked. Blinked again. His gaze intensified on mine. "Striptease," he echoed.

"I undress down to mostly topless. I mean, I wasn't covered by much, and I always had pasties—like stickers—or tassels on my nipples." The last word drifted off, and my face blazed. I refused to be ashamed of a profession I worked hard in and made enough of a living so I could provide long-term care services for my mom. So I was never embarrassed about my profession, but saying nipples around Cody hit differently. It landed lower, but also made me wonder . . . What would it have been like to perform when he was in the crowd?

"Tassels." His jaw sawed back and forth. Was he angry?

"I'm only telling you out of professional courtesy. I know how people can be and the assumptions and judgments they make. I'm proud of what I've done and how far I've come, and I'd still be successful if it hadn't been for—" I gave my head a shake. I was rambling. Because he was listening, and I didn't sense judgment from him.

"The bad relationship you left?" he asked, concerned. He crowded me, taking a step closer, and I was anything but threatened. The strongest urge to sink into his hot embrace hounded me. I kept my feet rooted. If I was working for him, embracing was the last thing we should be doing. The ideas sparking in my brain were all naughty.

But I bet he'd be good at all of them.

"I'd rather not talk about it," I said, preparing to get driven away.

"Well." He scrubbed a hand over his face. "You're good with the kids. I assume you aren't going to teach them stripteases and put any tassels anywhere?"

Shocked, I searched his gaze. All I saw was candid discernment and a desperate need for a nanny. How far did I look for problems? I'd gambled once with Frederick and lost everything. Except now I had nothing to lose and a paycheck to gain. I owed for Mom's care. I owed Thelma. And I needed to look after myself.

Only I would control my bank account this time. "Any stickers will only go on paper."

"Good luck catching Ivy before she plasters her dresser." The corner of his mouth tipped up, and I caught the most dangerous glimpse of him. My breath stalled, and my lungs seized.

The brief glimpse of casual Cody with a sense of humor and an undeniable *aw, shucks* charm got my heart racing. I struggled to take in air. I was breathing through a straw, and I wanted this man to give me life. I wanted him to lean in, capture my mouth, and make me forget I needed to breathe to stay alive.

My giggle came out strained, almost painful. "I'll do my best," I stammered. I swallowed hard and calmed my rapidly beating heart. He was back to being closed-off Cody. The wall of man I still found irresistible. "Are you sure it's not a problem? You don't even know I'm telling the truth."

"You don't know the same about me. We're both taking a risk, but I've got two kids to raise and two companies in one to run. I don't know anyone but my sister and her husband, my sister-in-law, and Thelma in town. You don't seem like you're in a much different boat."

"You have siblings here?" He was rigid, like I might expect an only child to be, but he must be the oldest.

He cocked his head like he didn't understand my question, then he nodded as if it were suddenly clear. "One of my brothers is getting divorced. My sister-in-law, Sutton, moved here because she's friends with Aggie, my sister. Wilder is still in Buffalo Gully. I have two more brothers too."

Were they all devastating to a woman's senses? I was enjoying this conversation and learning about him too much. "And Buffalo Gully is where?"

"Three hours west, in eastern Montana."

"Thelma said there's nothing but cows and oil wells there." She'd said the same about here but added coal mines and windmills.

"We also breed Arabians. So cows, horses, and oil wells." The easiness was back in his speech, and his stance had softened. This guy was uptight, but I was getting the impression he didn't want to be.

"Are two of those your two companies to run?"

His gaze went distant. "Technically, all three of them, but we lump the cattle and horses together."

"You're a cowboy?" Did that come out as breathless as it felt? This rigid man on a horse? In cowboy boots? He couldn't be real.

Not many men I met were.

He let out a puff of air. "Not really anymore. I'm a paper pusher. The oil wells our family company owns are our bread and butter." He ran his bottom lip through his teeth, doing it more in thought, but my mind took a dive into dark nights and light nips around those tassels I'd mentioned earlier.

Get a hold of yourself, Tova!

"Which brings up the topic of pay. What do you need?"

He didn't come out of the gate with a lowball number? He ran two companies. He had money. I needed money. Already, I was at a power disadvantage, and for the last two years, I'd turned negotiating contracts over to Frederick. I was still too raw to be a boss-woman negotiator. So I went for the truth. Seeing how Cody reacted would be more enlightening. "I have to be honest again, Cody, if I don't make at least five grand a month, I'll have to pick up another job."

He watched me for a beat. "Five grand?"

I nodded. I needed much more if I wanted a chance to get on my own again, but that amount would allow me to cover Mom's long-term care costs for the two months he needed a nanny while I figured out a game plan going into the fall. "I would look for evening and weekend work. I'm sure you're needing help with typical Monday-through-Friday hours. But I want you to know that I wouldn't be available outside of arranged hours."

"Six grand, and you don't have to take other work—but I might need you for weekends and evenings—and some light housekeeping."

He might need me . . .

Tingles spread through my belly and circled between my legs. Red flags waved frantically in my head. I shouldn't work for a man who made me feel like this, but I couldn't pass up the pay. I had Thelma close by just in case.

I couldn't abandon all my business acumen. Frederick had taught me an expensive lesson. "I need half upfront each month and the rest paid in weekly installments."

His gaze lightened, as if he liked to hear me negotiate. An unusual reaction, but then that had been my entire experience with the man. If it hadn't, I wouldn't be on his porch right now. "Get me your bank details, and I can arrange the weekly payments. I'll cut a check for the first half of the month so you can deposit it immediately."

I had to set up a new bank account with access granted to only me. I didn't have a car to run a bunch of errands. I hated to use Thelma's when I couldn't yet pay for gas. "Can I start tomorrow?"

Screeching resonated from inside the house, then Ivy's voice reprimanding Grayson for some dishes-related trauma drifted out.

Cody dragged in an even breath. "I'll give you a bonus to help me out today."

"Two hundred is the daily breakdown." I didn't mention I'd be working half a day today.

Grayson's yells and then loud sobs could be heard. Poor Grayson sounded like he needed a hug and a nap. I'd had several days like his as a kid. As much as I wanted to go to him, I had to watch out for myself first.

The phone in Cody's polo shirt pocket buzzed. His resolution set firmer. "I'll give you five hundred."

I narrowed my eyes. "In my experience, the other party doesn't usually go up in their offers, and you've done it twice."

"You need the money, and I need the help."

"I'm not a charity case." I was a charity case, but I didn't want to feel powerless.

"I am." He dragged a hand through his hair, loosening the hold his product had on his strands. I liked the softer look to him. "Look, Ivy is a tiny extrovert, and she needs more company than me and her brother, and Grayson's been having regular meltdowns since his mom died."

"I used to get inconsolable every time my mom relocated us." I bit the inside of my cheek. His gaze intensified, but I acted like I'd said nothing of consequence. He could be open and raw at times, and it was easy to be the same with him. No one could fake the heaviness in his gaze, and I'd lived in a city full of actors my whole life. "Go hold him. Sit quietly for a while and just let him know you're there and you know how he feels. I'll be back in an hour."

"Thank you, Tova."

I nodded and turned to go before I shoved past Cody into the house and gathered the boy in my arms. His sobs hurt my heart, but he needed his dad first. I wasn't going to replace the kid's mom, no matter how much I'd like to find out what Cody was like in bed.

Four

CODY

I rushed through finishing the dishes after lunch. I handed a plate to Grayson for him to carefully dry. Meg had been big on giving them daily chores, but we'd had a dishwasher. I relished having a few moments to do something as mundane as dishes with my kids, watching them bicker like brother and sister and prance around because they couldn't sit still. These instances reminded me of when I was a kid, before Mama abandoned me and my siblings.

She'd tell us about her hopes and dreams and make us feel like anything was possible. Which made her abandonment sting more. Nothing had been possible once she was gone. We were under Barns's rule, and without Mama as a buffer, we'd become hired help—for no pay.

I didn't want my kids to feel like I ditched them. But I also didn't want them to grow up feeling like they were never enough. I didn't want them stuck like I was.

The whole work-life-balance thing had been hard with

two full-time working parents, and Meg had often complained about how much time my job demanded when hers was similar. Her dream was to move back to Helena, or even farther west, to Seattle. But my obligation to the ranch was strong, and she'd very grudgingly acquiesced, sacrificing more of her career to live in Buffalo Gully. The two of us had been making a solid go at it. By myself? I couldn't. If Grayson and Ivy lived with my in-laws, surrounded by love and attention, they wouldn't feel like I never had time for them.

Which was the unfortunate truth.

I caught myself scrubbing a pristine plate. How long had I been washing it? My fingers ached. I wanted what was best for the kids.

Yet I wasn't sure I agreed with Meg about what that was.

I rinsed another plate and gave that one to Ivy. She was tipping from side to side, excitement vibrating from her, beside herself about Tova's impending arrival.

I was the same.

Only because I'd be able to work without distraction. Sort of. Having Tova in the house would steal my attention enough, but only because I'd have to keep an eye on her until I was reassured I could trust her with my kids.

Not because she was beautiful. My lack of focus wasn't due to the way her toned thighs flexed when she moved. And fuck's sake, I wasn't thinking about her being a burlesque dancer.

Strip. Tease.

The doorbell rang. Ivy shoved the plate on the counter and sprinted out of the kitchen, barely edging out Grayson to be the first to the front door.

"What's the rule about answering the door?" I rounded the wall separating the kitchen from the living area the entry opened into.

The front door hung wide open, and Ivy was leading Tova into the house. Tova's grin stretched her lovely face, and her eyes danced. The woman wouldn't need to remove a stitch of clothing to captivate an audience. She was alluring and sensual, and . . .

She used to remove her clothing, though. And my brain insisted on circling back to that specific topic. How much clothing? What exactly did she show? Did she undress to those damn tassels that kept flashing in my head and panties that were nothing but floss and a dream?

I cleared my throat, and she glanced at me.

"Sorry, I'm later than I meant to be." She gave me an apologetic smile. "The bank took more time than I thought." She withdrew a sheet of paper from her pocket. "They said this would get you started for the direct deposits."

"I can do that now, starting with today's pay and the first half of the month." I ran my fingers along the crisp edge of the folded document. The smell of rose petals rose up. Mama used to grow roses, but once she was gone, I didn't bother with them. Seeing them die was a small vindication for what she'd done. This was the first time since then that I smelled the flowers and didn't get resentful. "Let me show you around before I duck into the office."

Ivy hadn't let go of Tova's hand, and Grayson grabbed the other. She grinned. "I think they're ready."

I led the troop through the square living room, the floor groaning in places I'd learned to block out. In the kitchen, a hallway branched off to a half bathroom and my office. I pointed them out. "Down the other hallway is the cleaning closet and small pantry. The furnace room is the farthest back, and the door goes to the basement, but we don't use that space."

"It smells like a lake," Grayson said.

"No musty basement. Check." Tova's tinkling laughter went straight to my chest. She was a breath of cool air in the heat of summer.

I gestured up the flight of stairs that landed between the two hallways. "Upstairs are the bedrooms. The kids can show you that after we go outside." I lifted my chin toward the light filtering in through the back door by the stairs to the basement.

The kids dragged her out the squeaking screen door and into the backyard.

I stepped out just as a gusty gasp left Tova. "This is gorgeous. Look at those trees."

I hadn't thought about the backyard other than it was shaded, so I didn't have to worry about letting the kids play too long and bake in the sun. Towering weeping birch trees hugged the back fence. An old swing set with swings that creaked in the wind was on the left, and the rest was open and grassy.

Tova ran her hands over the wooden railing of the square deck, onto which the back door opened. "This must be such a nice place to sit in the evenings and watch the kids play."

It must be. "We haven't done that yet."

"Daddy works a lot," Grayson said.

Hearing that phrase was like tiny needles pricking my skin and getting left there. "The company's focused on expanding." And without the company, neither I nor my siblings would earn an income. Our supposed inheritance would go to keeping everything afloat, and I couldn't allow that. Aggie was the only Knight exempt. She'd built her life free of Barns's control, thanks to Mama.

Tova nodded, and her gaze was carefully neutral, like she was withholding judgment about a workaholic dad who hired a nanny so he could work more.

Speaking of which, I had to get to the office. "The kids just had sandwiches. They can have a snack between two and three. We'll have dinner at six." Shit. I hadn't planned that far ahead. "Would you be able to throw something in the oven?"

"You're paying me for evenings and weekends."

I was also paying her double today, but I didn't want to feel like I was taking advantage of her. She'd said she left a bad relationship, and I believed her. She likely needed a place to land for a while until she straightened out her life. The kids liked her, and she'd been open enough to ease any worries.

She was also fucking gorgeous, but that had nothing to do with my decision. I was supposed to be in mourning. I wasn't supposed to be lusting after another woman.

"I'll be in my office," I said abruptly.

Tova dragged her admiring gaze off the yard and lifted a brow toward me. "Dinner at six."

The hint of a tease in her tone should've had me on defense, not bordering on hard. Fuck, I needed space.

I gave a curt nod and marched inside. I wasn't used to hanging around women. That had to be it. I had girlfriends in high school, went to college, sowed some oats, and then met Meg. I'd supported her through law school and gotten some outside experience with a financial firm before we moved home. Other than my sister, who'd fled right before her wedding, I worked with my brothers and the guys Eliot hired to work the ranch. I was in board meetings, mostly online, sometimes in person, but there weren't a ton of women in the oil industry, and I'd been a married man.

I flexed my hand and stared at the wedding ring I hadn't yet removed. I didn't give a shit about rings, and Meg had known it, but I thought it was best for the kids to maintain some semblance of what used to be.

Squeezing my hand closed, I shut myself in my office. My kids' laughter mingled with Tova's and drifted in around the old windows. It was nice to hear them so carefree. This was good. I could get my work done and be more present when I was off the clock. Whenever that happened.

I leaned back and peeked outside. She was doing some version of a hoedown while twangy country music emanated from her phone. The move should be silly, but I let my gaze brush over her body. That shirt she tied at her waist only highlighted the flare of her hips and teased about her breasts underneath.

Pasties and tassels.

Did she wear one or both at the same time?

The question had consumed me since she'd told me. Did her breasts perk out so the tassels hung straight down? Were they like two big, creamy raindrops? Would I get a glimpse of her areolas and learn if they were a rich pink or a dusky red?

She paused and gestured for the kids to try, then she glanced around, her gaze sweeping to the window. I whipped away from where I'd been staring out, nearly tipping my old chair.

I was a goddamn pervert.

I needed this nanny thing with Tova to work out. Hopefully, she wouldn't notice how hard it was for an older man not to creep on her.

⚜

Tova

Milk Daddy worked a lot. The kids had been right about that. For the last week, he gave me minimal instructions and then retreated to his office. His list usually pertained to meetings and phone calls, with a light suggestion that I find a way for the kids to either be quiet or be noisy elsewhere.

I hated how much I looked forward to seeing his stern expression every morning. His strong features. The way his dark hair was swept off his face and styled in place with barely noticeable hair product. And the business casual dress. It was a good thing he didn't dress in a suit, or I'd melt for reasons other than the outside temperature. *No more sleek businessmen, Tova.* No more guys like Frederick who would sell their girlfriends to their biggest investors.

Only Frederick hadn't been selling me. He had wanted to give me away.

I shuddered.

"Are you cold?" Ivy asked, painstakingly coloring the castle in her coloring book that had been delivered yesterday.

"Not when that little window air conditioner is trying so hard to cool the whole house."

Heat rose, and the bedrooms were cooling off later in the day and staying warm longer in the evening. We'd abandoned playing in the bedrooms for the living room. Thelma said July could get hot and August even hotter. We might have to venture into the musty basement.

Or I could just mention how nice another AC unit would be, and it might just appear.

On my first day, I had mentioned a lack of toys. I thought Cody's jaw would crack, but he'd asked what items I meant. More than a generic green ball he must've bought at the grocery store. I'd listed footballs, soccer balls, kiddy balls and bats, jump ropes, sidewalk chalk, coloring books, paints, crayons, and just to be coy, I'd tossed in face paint and costumes to play dress-up.

Two days later, a shipment had been delivered, and I'd nearly died when the doorbell rang during one of his timed calls. He hadn't stormed out and chewed into me. He'd only popped out, gave one of those forthright nods that did it for me, and said, "Good. They've arrived."

Everything I had listed.

Why was that so hot?

Grayson pushed his coloring book away. "Can we dance now?"

The little guy had taken a huge interest in actual dance steps. The way concentration etched into his face reminded me of his dad. Ivy loved to dance, too, but she was more of a free spirit. She wasn't as interested in flexibility, coordination, or rhythm. But when Grayson got out of his head and into the beat, he displayed some promising skills, the biggest one being his interest.

"Ivy, you can bring the coloring book and crayons outside if you don't want to dance."

She nodded and gathered as much as she could. I handed some supplies to Grayson to help carry them.

My phone buzzed as we were walking toward the back door. I checked the number, and my heart sank. Mom's home. "Grayson, Ivy? I have to return a call really quick."

"I want to dance," Grayson said. The wobble was in his voice. I'd been through one tantrum, thankfully not during a sanctioned quiet time. I couldn't lose the money train this job was giving me, as the number on my phone attested.

I wrapped an arm around him. "I know you're worried, but we will dance, I promise. Can you give me five or ten minutes? I won't go anywhere, okay?"

He blinked big brown eyes at me, a few shades lighter than his dad's fathomless brown. The kid reminded me of myself at his age. Needing constant reassurance. Losing all shit when his expectations were upended. Mom hadn't dealt with it well at the time. She'd put me in dance to give me an outlet for my emotions and some semblance of structure. As an adult, I understood she had limited resources and was dealing with a lot herself. But as a kid, I would've killed for a hug and some time to process all the changes.

"I'll stand on the deck while I call, okay? We'll still be outside and ready to get started as soon as I'm done."

He nodded and drew in a shuddering breath. Poor guy. He didn't look like he was struggling. He held everything in until he blew. I bet he'd had a hard year in school. I used to be labeled a problem, and some teachers came down on me harder because of it.

My phone had gone quiet, but I called the number back. The administrator answered with a "Hi, Tova. Thanks for returning my call so quickly."

"Hey, Andra. Is everything okay?"

"With your mom, yes." Andra was a straight shooter. When Grandma and I had found this place for Mom in Springville, north of Yorba Linda, Andra had told us exactly what to expect for insurance coverage and out-of-pocket costs. In return, I made sure I was never a day late for payments. "But there was a man calling for information about her—and you."

I let my eyelids fall shut. "Frederick."

"That's not the name he gave if it was him, but I appreciate the heads-up." Andra probably had plenty of experience dealing with hostile or disgruntled family members. "He was pushy, but I told him I wasn't allowed to talk about our residents, and if he was looking for someone, he needed to go through the appropriate contacts."

All Frederick knew about Mom was that she was in the Springville facility, and I was footing much of the bill. Hindsight being twenty-twenty, I could see how he'd ratcheted up his "help" after he'd learned that fact about me. I had a large financial obligation he could exploit.

"Thank you, Andra."

"I figured you'd want to know." She paused for a breath. "In my experience, men who are that persistent don't quit easily."

"Unfortunately, that's my experience too."

"I suspected as much. Keep your head down. I've reminded my staff that some of our patients come from complicated situations, and adherence to our confidentiality policies is critical."

Relief helped tame my panic. The anger wouldn't leave. Frederick had no reason to track me down. He should've let me empty my accounts and move on. But then I might have enough to hire a lawyer.

One day.

Until then, my troubles couldn't spill over to Mom, and definitely not to her care team or other employees. I chewed on the corner of my lip as I wrapped up my conversation. All I wanted was a stable home and security for me and the people I loved. Why was that so damn hard?

When the call was done, I tucked the phone into the back pocket of my linen shorts. With my first day of pay, I had borrowed Thelma's car and went shopping in a nearby larger town that was still incredibly small, topping off the gas tank when I returned.

Grayson was in the middle of the yard, going through the brief warm-up I'd taught him. He did toe touches and jumped up like a frog. I went into the middle of the lawn to join him.

As happened yesterday and the two days before, as soon as I turned on the music, the kids from the houses next to this one piled out.

A little girl around Grayson's age draped herself over the chain-link fence. She had curly, dark pigtails and a small space between her front teeth. Kali. "Can I come over again?"

"If it's okay with your grandma." The first day I watched the kids, she'd copied the spinal twists and seated balances we did as part of our warm-up on her side of the fence. When Grayson and Ivy learned pencil turns, she was watching from the bushes on the far side of her yard. The next day, she'd begged her grandma, and I suspected her grandma was glad to let her burn off energy with someone else.

The girl tilted her head back to yell, "Grandma! Can I dance with Tova?"

Somehow, all the neighbors knew my name by the second day. Kali's grandma, Sima, reminded me of a younger Thelma. She'd come out to double-check with me that it was okay if Kali jumped in. Kali had told me she lived in Crocus Valley with her grandparents, her mom was in jail, and her dad drank himself into the ground—all her words, which I'd guess came from her grandma. I probably sounded the same when I was her age. Only my dad had preferred white powder over a family.

I didn't hear the response, but Kali hopped the fence and went to stand by Grayson. He gave her a shy smile and shifted to the side. Ivy abandoned her coloring books on the deck and lined up next to her. Grayson and Ivy had talked excitedly about having a friend over after Kali joined us last time.

Two more kids peered above the fence behind us—twins who were staying with their aunt and uncle for the summer while their parents had baby number three.

"Tova!" the boy twin, Bridger, called. His sister was Britta. "Can we come over too?"

"Ask permission first."

For the next two hours, I ran through line dance routines with five kids. The twelve-year-old from the house on the other side of the yard came out once, rolled her eyes, and stormed back inside. Catherine was in full preteen mode, but for the last two days, she'd given one longing look before disappearing inside.

I'd get her out here soon enough.

"Okay, okay," I called. "Time to cool down. Let's start with some roll-downs."

"Can we come tomorrow too?" Britta asked as she hung down in a front bend, swishing her hands over the grass.

I was in the full bend of the roll-down, my ass facing the door. These daily dance parties were becoming my lifeline. I was reminded of the days when dancing was fun and exciting and all my hopes and dreams weren't hanging on a paycheck attached to a performance. I let my head hang and closed my eyes. My hair was knotted on the top of my head, and I folded so far, the strands nearly touched the grass. "As long as you ask permission first. In fact, I should probably ask permission too." We'd been quiet enough, but I wasn't the one renting the house.

"It's fine," came a deep voice from behind me.

I rose and twisted. Cody was on the deck, a glass of water in his hand, his fingertips white, like he was fighting an invisible force to hang on to it. His dark gaze pierced mine, and that chiseled jaw was set in a harder granite expression than usual, showing nothing. Shit. Were we too loud? Then he scanned the yard, the kids, the toys on the ground, and the mass of juice boxes and granola bars and fruit snacks I had to grab a garbage bag for. Nothing in his features gave away what he was thinking.

"You sure it's okay?" I asked. "We get kind of loud." We didn't. But we could.

"I'm sure."

"Hi, Grayson and Ivy's dad!" Britta waved furiously from her latest cooldown stretch with one leg crossed over the other.

He dipped his head. "Britta. Bridger. Thanks for coming over. Kali, tell your grandparents hi."

No details missed this guy. I hadn't been sure he knew the kids joined us each day, but the noise was undeniable. He'd been working constantly since I'd started, but I assumed he tucked the kids in each night since he dismissed me before bedtime. He had them up in the morning and dressed like they were going to the office, too, before I arrived. Some days, I wondered if he had a mini-board meeting over their oatmeal with no more than one spoonful of sugar.

I had them change out of their stiff and formal clothing before we did art projects and played outside.

"Tova, a minute, please?"

My stomach fluttered at my name and sank with the rest. I should've asked him before letting all the kids come over. Was he so rigid because he was upset and hiding it from the kids? "Finish the cooldown," I said to the kids as I joined him on the deck.

He set the water on the patio table and stuffed his hands into his navy-blue slacks. I looked like a tourist standing within his vicinity with my casual shorts and the fitted pink tee that landed just above the waistband.

It wasn't a game to dress as opposite of him as I could, but the soft ballet slippers didn't help.

"Yes?" I had to tip my head back to look at him. The clear sky soared over his head, and the green leaves of the tree were stark against the blue. This starchy man did not fit in this environment with his blue-and-white-pinstriped polo shirt. I kept picturing him as a cowboy. Wouldn't he have to get dirty and stuff to raise cattle and breed horses?

The guy intrigued me. If he were a steam-pressed business guy with nothing but dollar symbols to make him attractive beyond his superficial looks, I would be immune.

But he was a dad. He had a body that screamed fresh air and hard work. To top it off, he had an edge I wanted to cut myself on. Not a bad-boy edge. Nothing screamed dangerous about him other than he was off-limits.

The man controlled my pay, though. I'd do well to remember that, and Andra's update wouldn't let me forget about Frederick.

"My sister called and invited us over for dinner," he said. "Are you comfortable taking the kids? I can give you directions."

"You aren't going?"

"I have some paperwork to catch up on, but the kids shouldn't have to miss out."

I caught a flash of regret in his eyes. He'd been buried in that office for a week. Didn't he want to see his sister? He spoke like he was fond of her.

He scrutinized me. "Is that an issue?"

His question wasn't hostile, but I didn't know him. He might smell like an intoxicating combination of cedar and sage and put off heat that didn't chase me to cooler areas like the summer sun, but I couldn't automatically trust him. Men in general didn't like to be challenged. "Well, I don't have a car."

"You can use mine."

His car was a giant pickup. I'd only buzzed around in tiny, economical sedans. The car Frederick had let me use was electric. Cody's pickup didn't look like an ego stroker either. The body had a few dings and even a rust spot beginning above the tire rim. The vehicle looked like it had done work before.

Even the vehicle was a contradiction. What was the real Cody Knight like?

Didn't matter. I didn't need to know. At all.

But I was *so* curious.

I licked my lips, and his gaze momentarily dropped to where my tongue flicked out. He grew more tense, his expression more of a mask.

"Grayson's been having at least one meltdown a day," I said. I had planned to give him a general update once a week, but sending me on a solo trip with the kids to his sister's wouldn't go unnoticed by Ivy and Grayson.

He frowned, instantly worried. "I haven't heard him."

"I've talked him through a few. One time, I just sat with him and Ivy until he calmed down. You had a meeting, so we were on the front porch." My mouth went dry. He'd been reasonable so far, especially when it came to his kids, and I wasn't just collecting a paycheck. This was my job, and I had to be honest. "You've been working a lot more than they're used to."

His jaw flexed so hard I waited to hear his teeth crack. Then he let out a long, slow breath. His gaze pierced mine, searching. "You think that's what's doing it?"

Inhaling was a struggle. This man's intensity should send me running, not wondering if it translated to being naked. *Mind out of the gutter, Tova. He's a workaholic widower!* "They miss you."

He nodded, his gaze stroking around the yard one more time. Bridger and Britta were climbing over the fence separating the yards, and Kali was twirling with Ivy. I could finally draw an easy breath with his focus off me.

"Want to come with us?"

The fresh air in my lungs froze. "Excuse me?"

"To meet my sister? You'll be around all summer, and this won't be our last time getting together with her. She might stop by once in a while." The corner of his mouth twitched, like he was in danger of smiling. "She's probably afraid to scare me off if she pops over too much. I know she'd love to have us closer permanently."

"You don't plan to move?"

"My home is in Buffalo Gully." The finality in his voice didn't make sense. He could clearly work anywhere. Would he work more or less in his hometown? Was it the memories of his wife keeping him there?

I'd leave LA in a heartbeat if it wasn't the best place to make a living. The city was very expensive, but the options were plenty, even if the market was highly competitive. Back to his question. Did I want to go? I didn't get out much in Crocus Valley, and it'd be nice to see a new place and meet other people. Yet, I wasn't looking to plant roots in town.

Ultimately, my paycheck dictated my answer. "If you need me there, I'll be there."

His expression softened again, and the furrow in his brow smoothed out. How old was he, anyway? I guessed a few years older than me, at least. Was he forty yet? "It isn't mandatory, but I know the kids would like to show you everything, and you won't have to cook tonight."

"Oh, well, sold, then."

His lips twitched. An almost smile. Good thing I hadn't witnessed the full effect of a grin. My panties would melt right off. If I was wearing any.

Five

CODY

I leaned against one of the fence posts for the pen of Aggie and Ansen's large, wooly Mangalitsa pigs. Aggie was next to me, and Ansen had Ivy on his shoulders. They walked in the pasture by the barn toward his horse, Shelby. Aggie's horse rescue had first taken in five neglected horses, but she and Ansen had both bonded with them. They accepted other rescues, nursed them back to health, trained them, but they were sold. Same with a donkey. Another donkey was in the smaller pasture with an old, retired draft horse she was also thinking of keeping.

Grayson was creeping after chickens. He missed animals. We usually went to the family ranch once a week, if not both days of the weekend, and we'd been in Crocus Valley for almost a month. No horses. No cows. No uncles.

Tova was with him, still wearing those damn short shorts. I used superhuman efforts to keep my lecherous eyes off the crease of her ass cheek and thigh. After seeing her completely folded over, full view of how nice her ass was, my temperature soared. I'd never concentrated so hard to keep blood away from my dick. Then there was her pink, slightly see-through shirt. Her bra was yellow. Did she know I could see the color of her bra? Was it the fashion these days? Would I have to steel myself to stand up for Ivy if she wanted her bra to be visible under her shirt and the school thought it was too much? I'd have to channel Meg.

"So. A nanny?" Aggie murmured when Grayson and Tova disappeared into the barn.

"I needed help."

"Mm."

"She needed help."

My sister slanted her gaze toward me. She looked more like she did when she was younger. Light reddish-brown curls surrounded her face. Less wild and more refined than when she was a kid, but not as polished as Meg had mentored her to be. Relaxed looked good on Aggie. So did being in love. "Saving stranded young women now?"

"News travels fast."

She chuckled. "Alcott Knight isn't used to being the talk of the town."

I wasn't. My siblings had roused enough drama in their day. Between Barns and his mouth, Mama leaving, Austen's antics when he'd been a kid, Eliot's decisions on the ranch, and the implosion of Aggie and Ansen's first engagement, I hadn't been centered in local gossip. Unless it was bringing Meg home to live in a big farmhouse not far from the ranch, no one paid me much mind. They had taken bets on how long Meg would stay in a Podunk town, and some days I'd been tempted to put in my wager.

"She's good with them. I wouldn't have hired her if she wasn't." The defensiveness landed wrong in my tone, and from the way a smile played over Aggie's lips, she'd heard it.

"I get it, but I hope it doesn't mean you're still shipping them off to Meg's parents."

"Jesus, Aggie. Digging in hard already?"

"With four brothers, I had to be blunt to be heard."

And we still probably hadn't listened. "There isn't a nanny like her in Buffalo Gully." I'd have inappropriately noticed. "The kids complain about daycare, and they love the one-on-one attention." Attention I couldn't give them. Meg had known it.

Ivy and Grayson were blossoming before my eyes. Opening up like a rose after a summer rain. They smiled easier, complained less, and Tova said Grayson pulled out of his meltdowns with a little talking. They'd had a few friends at daycare, some at school, but the kids in Crocus Valley gravitated toward them in a way I hadn't witnessed at home.

The reason might be due to the charismatic, welcoming-and-calming-while-being-everyone's-personal-cheerleader nanny. Tova had a way with kids, not just mine. I could see the neighbor girl Catherine and her sneer from my office, but each day when she popped outside, unable to control herself, Tova would greet her, ask her how her summer was going, and invite her to hang out too. Never pressured her. Didn't chide the girl for her attitude. Let her be while welcoming her in.

Aggie peered at where Ivy was petting Shelby's flank. My kids knew how to behave around horses, but Ansen was cautious with her. The guy had gone from someone I hadn't wanted around my sister to taking my kids for an afternoon of horseback riding. Ansen was just as engaged of an uncle as my brothers.

Aggie rested her elbow on the rail. "Don't attribute the change to just one-on-one time. It's who they're with that counts too."

"Tova's only around until we leave. She deals with Grayson's outbursts well."

She playfully swatted me on the shoulder. "I was talking about you."

"No. It's not me."

"Why?"

Not long ago, I wouldn't have bared my insecurities to my sister, but things had changed in the last year. The answer to her question came easily. "They aren't happy like this around me. I can't talk to Grayson when he's upset like she can."

"Mm." Aggie didn't sound convinced. "How do you think Curtis and Lauri would do? Would they give him a stern lecture, or negotiate the terms of how and when he would stop crying?"

I gave her a frustrated glare, but I nearly laughed. Picturing my almost-retired lawyer in-laws pulling out a pen and contract to discuss terms of a meltdown was too easy to imagine. Same with the lecture.

"I tried lecturing because that's what they'd do. It's what Meg would've done."

She didn't respond immediately, her expression was contemplative, like she was deciding whether she should. "Meg was so confident and direct, it can be hard to consider that she wasn't always right."

"How so?" I asked sharply, the obligation to be defensive of Meg and her frank personality lingering inside me.

"You're good with your kids. I don't know why you don't think you are."

"I don't think—" Her *prove it* expression halted my denial. "I fucked up with you guys, didn't I?"

Her mouth dropped. "How? We wouldn't be who we are today without you."

"You hardly talked to us for ten years—"

"I talked to you plenty."

"—Wilder's getting a divorce. Austen joined the military and left before the ink dried, and Eliot is terminally upset."

"We all have our baggage. Imagine how we'd be if you hadn't stepped in when Mama left." She put a hand on her hip, not letting me deny my way out of the conversation. "Alcott Knight, you did not let your wife convince you that you couldn't do a better job than her parents because she was so bitter about being stuck in Buffalo Gully."

"She gave up a lot to be with me."

"But she didn't give up on herself like you're doing." She put a hand on my forearm. "Cody, Meg could've been the best supportive mom in the world, but she's gone. *You* make the decisions based on the now."

My throat worked as I tried to speak.

She squeezed, rooting me in the present. "I know you're a man of your word, but in this case, it might not be best for you or the kids to keep it." Her smile was encouraging. "You give some very helpful parental lectures yourself."

Her teasing tone dislodged the rock in my throat. "I figured it was better than what Mama would do. Flutter around and commiserate about how this wasn't what she wanted out of life."

I had adopted a parenting style for my siblings, and I worried it had messed them up. Aggie's insistence made me view the past, including my last conversations with Meg, with new eyes. Meg had been strong and stoic until the end, but she'd been scared. What if her worry had spilled over, making me rethink how I would—how the kids should— live without her?

As for Aggie, her gaze flickered like she was trying to recall the instances Mama would go off about how she'd been wronged in the game of life. Aggie was too young to remember the specifics of Mama's presence. After Mama had left and before she'd died in a pointless car wreck of her own doing, she'd made it a point to save Aggie from the sort of domesticity she thought was hell. Aggie had sort of listened, minus the self-destructive lifestyle.

"I didn't realize that's what she did."

I tossed a pointed look her way, grateful to have moved on from the topic of Meg. "It was usually you throwing a tantrum."

"Was not." Her lips twitched, fighting a smile. "Eliot and Austen, maybe."

"Oh, they got on her nerves plenty." Wilder had been a rigid, do-gooding prick since he left the womb. But he'd still been a Knight brother with three other brothers. "We all gave her gray hairs."

"We'll never know. She dyed her hair every month."

I let out a soft chuckle. At Mama's funeral, she looked exactly like she did when she walked out on us. Dark brown hair curled around her face, and she had rosy cheeks, red lips, and an imperious expression even in death. It was like the mortician had known her personally.

"You should've told Tova to wear better shoes." Aggie pushed off the fence. Ansen and Ivy were heading back toward us, a flank of five horses following them.

"I wasn't married for twelve years to tell a woman what to wear." I went to the barn. The conversation with my sister continually tugged at my mind. I tucked the memory away to inspect later. I wasn't making permanent decisions after talking for a few minutes when plans were set.

Tova was crouched with a tabby kitten twining around her. Grayson held an identical kitten in his arms.

Aggie walked by my side. "We had two kittens show up when the snow melted. They must've been early spring babies."

"Can we keep them, Daddy?" Grayson asked, nuzzling one.

"We're not the animal rescue." I crossed my arms, enjoying the view way too much. Tova was squatting, her trademark smile in place. Oddly, seeing her play with my kids brought Aggie's words back to the forefront.

You *make the decisions based on the now.*

How would I do things differently? How could I?

Aggie came to a stop next to me. "When I opened this place, I had horses in mind. So far, the cat rescues outnumber horses."

"Gray!" Ivy rounded the opening of the barn, Ansen right behind her. "I got to pet Shelby!"

Her appearance and loud proclamation startled the kitten in his arms. The cat wiggled, wielding all its claws. Grayson jumped back and opened his arms so the cat could escape. The only place for the kitten to go was Tova's bare legs.

She yelped when the cat landed lightly on her legs and scrambled off her, leaving fine red lines in its wake.

"Dammit!" I barked and crossed to Tova, who was straightening and inspecting her leg, unconcerned.

"Sorry!" Grayson took my outburst on himself. Tears sprang into his eyes. "Sorry, sorry, sorry."

I put my hand on his shoulder and tempered my tone. Aggie had been right. I wasn't Mama, but I'd been there for them, and I sure as hell was better than Barns. The kid took the heap of responsibility for everything that went wrong. A trait he got from me. "It's alright, G. It's no one's fault. The kittens are getting used to people."

"It's not a problem." Tova's tone was reassuring. "I've been cut worse by a pair of heels in a kick line—and the kitten's cuter."

Blood welled up from the scratches. For such a tiny creature, it had scored all the skin of her top right thigh from the hem of her shorts to her knee.

"I didn't mean to—" He drew in a shuddering breath. A wail would come next, then he'd be embarrassed when he realized everyone was watching, and he'd feel like his visit was ruined. My son needed good memories.

"I know you feel bad," Tova said, pushing a lock of hair off his face. "And you're feeling guilty, but it happens. I've been scratched by much more ferocious kittens."

Grayson's bottom lip wavered, but he nodded.

"Hey, buddy." I gave his little shoulder a squeeze. "Would you go with Aunt Aggie to the house to get the first aid kit?"

Aggie could tell I was trying to divert his attention. He wouldn't want to be coddled in front of everyone. She held her hand out to both Grayson and Ivy. "Come on, guys. Let's do some wilderness medicine."

The request distracted Grayson enough that he latched on to Aggie. I exchanged a relieved look with Tova, and for a second, I didn't feel so damn alone.

When they were halfway to the house, Ansen went to a metal cupboard tucked into the corner. The hinges squeaked as he opened the double doors. He withdrew a small, yellow plastic box and tossed it toward me. With a smirk, he jogged after his wife and my kids, leaving me alone with Tova.

She glanced from her shredded thigh to me. "Oh look, a first aid kit," she said teasingly.

"Grayson needed a moment."

"He has such a tender heart." She swiveled her leg from side to side as she scrutinized the damage. "It's not bad anyway. Just kitten tracks. I've seen worse track marks."

She probably wasn't joking with that one. I dug into the

kit, mostly to take my attention off her toned dancer's leg. "Have a seat on the hay bale behind you."

"Won't it be scratchy?"

"Not as bad as straw."

"There's a difference?"

"These bales are alfalfa, so they're finer. Straw is from dried stalks of grain—thicker and pokier." I stopped before I went on about the different types of bales and why they were used. Aggie had mentioned my lecturing more than once.

"Pokier? Is that the technical term?"

I couldn't bring myself to look at her sweet smile as I dropped to a knee in front of her. Horrified, I realized she had a leg stretched out, and instead of lowering myself beside her, I looked like I was trying to wedge between her thighs. "Technical, yes." Be. Professional.

She drew her leg in and sat forward. "You're getting your slacks dirty."

I didn't care about pants when I got to care for her soft skin. "It's fine." I took out a couple packets of gauze and an alcohol wipe.

"Are you saying you actually get dirty once in a while?"

I opened the gauze, mildly insulted but more perplexed. "I said I grew up ranching."

She nudged me in the shoulder. "Don't act surprised that I'm surprised. I've seen you in nothing but slacks and polos, Milk Daddy."

I forgot everything I was doing. "Milk Daddy?"

She blanched. "Forget I said that."

Holding back a smile, I set the unopened alcohol wipe on the bale next to her and dabbed at her cuts with the gauze. I used my other hand to steady her leg and fuck . . . her skin was warm and softer than I had imagined. The wounds were minor, not deep, thanks to the age of the kitten, but I hated to see her leg marred. "You know I can't. Explain."

"That." She pointed an accusing finger in my direction, then circled around my face with it. "You consume inhuman amounts of milk, and you're bossy."

I was a dad. I drank milk. "How does the bossiness fit in?"

The way she swallowed and lowered her gaze to where I had wrapped my fingers around the back of her leg told me where the daddy part came in. "You're a stern man, Cody Knight."

I'd heard that before, usually from a sibling, but coming from Tova, I wasn't sure I prided myself on it. I finished dabbing and handed her the alcohol wipe, finally taking my hand off the back of her leg. Reluctantly. "I'm not mean enough to ruthlessly swipe this across your cuts."

"But I'm a wuss."

"We can wait for Aggie to come back. Or you can go to the house and use soap and water. It's probably better for your skin anyway." I'd rather she cleaned her cut, but I also liked being alone with her.

"Just do it. I don't want it to seem like a thing around Grayson."

I opened the packet, and dammit if I didn't position my hand the same way. Her muscles flexed under my touch, but she didn't move. I gently dabbed at the scratches. They were really shallow, but the stark red on her skin had made them look worse. They probably stung like a bitch, though.

"So . . . Alcott. Is that a family name?"

"Have you been dying to ask me that all week?" I arched a brow at her, and she shrugged. Holding back a smile, I said, "I was named after Louisa May Alcott."

"*Little Women*?"

I nodded and ran the wipe over the last couple of short

scratches. Mortified, I realized I was rubbing circles on the back of her thigh with my thumb and stopped. I focused on the task, afraid to see if she'd noticed. "Aggie is named after Agatha Christie. Wilder after Laura Ingalls Wilder. Austen—"

"Jane Austen. I'm sensing a theme. How many siblings do you have?"

"One more—Eliot." I waited. "His has a twist."

She puzzled over his name. "I've got nothing."

She had one thing—a hold over me. "George Eliot, the pen name for Mary Ann Evans."

"All women authors."

"Mama was big on women's empowerment, as long as it didn't include anything maternal."

"But there are five of you."

I nodded, leaning closer to make sure I cleaned her off well enough. An absurd task but a damn good reason to close the distance between us. "She felt like Barns—my dad —was baby trapping her, and when I was fifteen, she jetted. Aggie was five."

"Are you the oldest?"

I nodded.

"I can tell." When I cocked my head, she leaned forward, a smile playing over her pink lips. "Milk Daddy."

Laughter erupted out of me without warning. I sat back on my heels and propped my arm on my knee with the pink-stained wipe pinched in my fingers.

Her tinkling laughter caught my attention, but surprise was the dominant expression rippling over her face. "What?"

"You're grinning. I've only seen your stern face." She danced her fingers lightly over my cheeks, stealing my ability to breathe. Then she gasped and pulled back like she was caught lifting jewelry.

Air drew back into my lungs. I wanted her touch back on me. To distract myself, I crumpled all the garbage in my hands. "Am I that bad?"

"You've been through a lot," she said quietly. "But the kids really do love being with you." Stronger, she continued. "They talk about stuff you've done all the time."

That gave me pause. "Like what?"

"They talk about horses and working cattle. They say you catch the biggest fish."

Two years ago, I took them fishing so Meg could work on a case. Austen had been home, and we'd gone to the river. "The fish was barely a foot long."

"It was a whopper to hear them tell it."

Huh. The kids said I worked a lot, and I had narrowed our whole existence down to that, but really, it'd only been really bad since Barns had died. My talk with Aggie wanted to come out of the corner.

Later.

I rose and tossed the trash in the burn bin Aggie kept in the barn to be part of a summer bonfire later.

Tova scooted over. Was she making room for me to sit and wait for our wilderness medicine crew to arrive?

I took the seat, unable to stay far from her. When her rosewater scent reached my nose, a knot loosened inside my chest. "I didn't remember the fish. Does that make me a bad dad?"

"You're not a bad dad. Trust me—I'd know."

The glimpses she gave me into her life only made me want to know more. To talk with her for a few hours . . . or days. Weeks. Months. Hell, she'd been in my house a week, taking care of my kids, and I knew little more than her last name, where she banked, and that she left a bad relationship in California.

"You love them, but I think . . ." She licked her lips, and

I tucked my groan away. The sight of her pink tongue would have to torment me later when I figured out how shitty of a guy it made me, as a widower, to low-key lust over my nanny. "I think you could loosen up with them. I think you want to."

I stared at the straw-packed dirt between my loafers, stunned. I hadn't fucking changed clothes. When did I become this workaholic guy?

Maybe when the mother of my children suggested someone else should do the bulk of raising them.

"I've been focused on how to secure a future where they can do anything they want." I ran my thumb and forefinger over my bottom lip. I had opened up to my siblings, mostly Aggie, a lot since Barns died, but talking to Tova was easier. And I wanted to keep talking with her. I wanted her to know I wasn't uptight because I was a controlling asshole. She sounded like she'd had enough of those in her life. "When my mom died, she left all her life insurance to Aggie."

Tova cocked her head, and the artful knot of hair on top of her head bobbed. "Just her?"

"Yes. My wife knew how much it hurt me and my brothers. Her life insurance was distributed equally to our kids. They can go to whichever college they want and have enough left over for a down payment on a house."

"Nice."

I nodded. "Never thought we'd need it, but we'd had it all planned. And then we had to go through with the plan. Brain tumor."

She rested her warm hand on my knee. "I'm so sorry."

I nearly put my hand over hers. I gave myself a shake, and unfortunately, but thankfully, she removed her hand. "I didn't mean—what I'm trying to say is that even though they have a better start at life than many, I still feel pressured to provide. To make sure the family company is going strong in case my kids or any future nieces or nephews want to carry on the legacy."

"The company can't replace you." She bumped my shoulder with hers. "And you don't seem like a bad guy to hang around."

I shared a smile with her, liking how I could see the lighter flecks of blue in her eyes when I was this close. "There aren't a lot of people who can give me a solid testimony, and I wouldn't trust my brothers."

She giggled. "I was an only child. What's it like to grow up with siblings?"

I had to think about that. Voices drifted toward us, alerting me to the end of a pleasant, private conversation. "It's like living with feral animals who stitch in your hot buttons so they can push them all day."

Her laughter grew. "Sounds . . . fun?"

"My relationship with my siblings got better when I realized I was their older brother and not their dad." I didn't have time to say more. I could've sat on the bale with Tova for hours.

Ansen was next to Aggie, his long legs making his walk look like a stroll, while Aggie scurried next to the kids. Grayson was holding a white first aid kit, and Ivy had a can of some carbonated drink that wouldn't be safe to open for at least ten minutes.

"We brought you water!" Ivy announced.

I rose, ignoring how Aggie tracked my position. Ansen looked from me to his wife as if he knew she didn't miss how close we were sitting and that I didn't want either one of them to look too far into it. He caught my gaze and smirked. Fucker. He was like having a fourth brother.

But as I watched my kids dote on Tova and the way she playfully overacted her malady until my kids were giggling and arguing about who got to bandage her, reality hit. I wanted this again. I wanted to be in a relationship one day with someone who loved my kids as much as me. I wanted to stop over at my sister's place or one of my brothers' and just . . . be.

How would that happen if the kids were with Curtis and Lauri Smith? How would I meet anyone and move on from the emptiness Meg left behind?

Would I first have to admit that life wasn't like this with Meg? It wasn't light or easy. Underlying tension had been woven through our family unit.

Guilt propelled acid up the back of my throat. And now I wanted something different. How fucked up was that?

What was even more messed up? I could picture it perfectly with Tova, a girl I met barely more than a week ago. A woman whose satiny skin I'd never forget. A dancer who'd be gone from our lives in less than two months and who'd leave us wanting for more than what we did before she showed up.

Six

TOVA

Thelma squinted at me over her heavy-on-the-heavy-cream coffee. I was downing a gritty protein shake. I couldn't blend it as much as I wanted because Thelma hated noise first thing in the morning. She also hated conversation right after she woke up, and she disliked being assaulted by sunshine after she opened her eyes.

I was a morning person like Grandma had been, and it was refreshing to see mornings again after seven years of late-night performances.

I had no idea how Thelma and my grandmother stayed together for so long. They claimed they were friends and roommates, but I'd always suspected they were more. I'd also grown up with a cagey mother when it came to relationships, so I assumed they had their reasons, and I was astute enough to know things would've been different for them if their roommate status had ever publicly changed.

I couldn't have asked for a better mourning partner after

Grandma died, though. Thelma didn't sink into depression. She'd cried, said "fuck" a lot, and then got down to the business of planning the funeral and figuring out how to help Mom since Grandma couldn't take care of her. Thelma worked with me until I could bring in the money to make long-term care for Mom possible.

"He did what?" she asked.

"He tended to my wounds." I lifted my skirt and pointed at my toe. My skin tingled at the memory of his big, hot hand on my skin. Strength radiated from his grip, more than I thought it would for a guy who worked in an office all day. He looked strong, and I guess growing up the way he had was the reason, but I knew fuck all about ranching. Yet to *feel* strength? From just a touch?

If I wasn't sleeping on Thelma's couch, I would've given myself some alone time with a toy or two. Which I didn't have, thanks to my sudden departure.

Had Frederick tossed all my belongings already? I should tell Thelma the long-term facility had called and why, but I'd rather relive my time in the barn with a certain stern father and not worry her. The line was thin between pretend smoking and lighting up.

Thelma peered harder at my skin. The scratches were almost nothing, really. From the distraught way Grayson acted and how he'd insisted on bandaging me up like a mummy, one would've thought the kitten had adamantium blades sticking out of her paw like Wolverine.

A gal learned a lot during a special performance for a Comic Con after-party.

"I know they're not much. The event itself was more traumatic. Grayson's having a tough time."

Her features softened. "I would've thought Milk Daddy was a hard-ass."

"I feel like he thinks he needs to be." I took a pull of my

berry drink and chewed through the mouthful. "I wonder what his wife was like."

"Does he remember he was married around you?"

I shot her a disgruntled scowl. "Other than some thumb circles I don't think he knew he was doing, he's kept his distance. He works more because I'm around."

"He works more because he's attracted to you."

"His wife died less than a year ago."

Thelma sighed and went to the counter to refill her coffee. The galley kitchen was right off the dining area. The whole apartment was smaller than the bedroom I had shared with Frederick. "Grief is different for everyone. Some people lose their partner, realize life is short, and find love again within months. Others know they'll never get over it. Ever." If Thelma were anyone else, I'd cross to her and hug her, but she'd only get uncomfortable. Showing emotion was tough for her. Sometimes when she talked about Grandma, her pain was as fresh as the morning we lost her, and she'd retreat to the bedroom for a couple hours. "And some guys know an opportunity when they see it."

Her remark smarted more with Frederick in my history. "I'm not on the market, so it doesn't matter. He's my employer, and that's all the control he has over me."

She gestured with the coffee pot from a machine that looked identical to what the diner had to the couch where I had slept. "I can tell you're being cautious."

My newly purchased clothing was in a pile on an end table. The suitcase was open underneath, filled with the belongings I'd smuggled out but that were shoved over. It looked like I could dump the pile into the suitcase, zip it up, and run. Even my toiletry bag was packed, only taken out when I used it.

Was Thelma offended I lived like I was ready to bolt while I was here?

Habits were hard to break, and I'd leave before I caused her any trouble.

"You taught me to be smart."

"Because you grew up knowing instability." Regret darkened her expression. "Anyway, I wasn't sure about Cody Knight, but the fact that he's trying so hard to ignore you . . . gives him a few extra points."

Hmm. A begrudging acceptance from Thelma? That wasn't easy. "I've only known him a week."

She grunted. "He's a guy. Still a strike against him."

I chuckled. "I'd better head over. He's probably got the kids lined up in their formal wear."

"Betcha his wife was a stickler for looks and propriety."

"She was a lawyer." Of course a guy like Cody would go after a smart, successful woman. If we'd crossed paths in another timeline, he wouldn't have looked beyond my superfluous dancing before he wrote me off.

"Don't mean nothin'."

But it did. Was that why I had let Frederick ingrain himself so far into my life? Guys like him didn't take up with burlesque dancers. A lot of men saw dancers, actresses, and strippers as a good time—not someone for a long time.

I wanted a partner in life. I'd grown up seeing Mom's terrible relationships, but I'd also had the steady presence of Thelma and Grandma. I wanted the trust. The closeness. The ride or die.

"I've gotta get going. Love ya, Thel."

I got another grunt in return. "Love you too, doll face. Be smart out there. He didn't balk at you doing burlesque for a reason."

He had taken the news without much reaction. Thelma was suspicious. I should be, too, but I was curious about his reasoning.

I left and jogged down the stairs, landing at the bottom

and doing a passé hop. Tinkles of silverware on plates and cups hitting tabletops filled the stairwell. The cloying grease smell that stuck to the walls was growing familiar, but I'd be glad to get away from it.

Outside, clouds covered the sky, and the scent of rain filled the air. The sidewalk and street were wet. Hopefully, everything would dry by the afternoon, when we had a dance party. I lingered by the theater.

Wouldn't it be nice to bring the kids here to practice? I could put on a real performance, even join in.

But I didn't have money to rent the place or buy costumes, and all I had of my own equipment were the undergarments that had been packed in the suitcase I'd fled LA with. The garments weren't exactly appropriate for a kids' ensemble performance.

Stuffing my hands in the pockets of my rainbow maxi skirt—long enough to cover the small scratches so Grayson wouldn't stress—I walked to the old farmhouse. I'd tossed on a white tank top, but I should've packed a light cardigan. Shivering, I hugged my arms around myself.

I knocked lightly before I entered. Someone had been unlocking the door before I arrived each morning.

Ivy pranced into the room, the yards of tulle in her skirt bouncing with each step. Her hair was free. One of the first things we did each morning was braid it. When I did a crown braid earlier this week, she thought I was magic. I think Cody thought the same. "We're getting the cats!"

"Yay!" I had no details but relief that the scratch incident hadn't scared them away from cats was strong.

"We're *fostering* both cats." Cody came into the living room just as I crossed through the entry. His jaw was a chiseled marble, but he was dressed in jeans and a forest-green shirt, which only made him more imposing with his dark hair and deep brown eyes. "To get them used to kids—and loud noises."

My mouth went dry. Casual Cody assaulted my senses. He was approachable. Softer in a way a guy like Frederick never could be. While there was a grim set to his mouth, humor sparked deep in his gaze.

"Two cats?" I asked around my parched mouth. My breathing rate picked up as I raked my eyes down his body. Oh, god. He wasn't even wearing his strict loafers. On his feet were dusty, used cowboy boots.

My hormones kicked into a seductive salsa.

His attention was traveling up my skirt, drifting past my abdomen and breasts like a caress before landing on my face just as my gaze hooked on his. We'd been checking each other out at the same time.

I should be embarrassed, but the way his jeans molded to his powerful thighs sapped all thought from my brain. Meanwhile, a place farther south on my body needed to quit thinking so much. "Day off?"

"It's Saturday, for one." The corner of his mouth kicked up. "What you said yesterday got through to me. I'm due for a day off."

"Oh." I was pleased for him, but disappointment sifted through me. "You don't need me today?"

He shook his head. "Not so fast. I have two very excited kids who will be wanting to smother two very nervous kittens. And they're due for shots and deworming. Sutton said we could stop in any time this morning at her new clinic, but I need a hand."

Sutton. His sister-in-law.

Kids and kittens and vet clinics were evidence of an ideal life I'd wanted to be a part of so badly since I was a kid. Big dreams of sleepovers and dance parties and pets had faded, and I'd clung to my dance lessons, the one thing Mom had been able to keep constant. Now, I was the hired help, but excitement welled in me nonetheless. If I was going to seek shelter with an ex-smoker who snored while I scrabbled enough money together to keep my mom in good hands, then this wasn't a bad way to do it.

"One cat wrangler, at your service."

His eyes darkened, but he gestured to the door.

Outside, Catherine's mother was stepping out, juggling a tote bag, her keys, and her purse. She spotted us, eyes wide. "Oh. Good morning."

"Morning," Cody said. "Vienne, have you met Tova yet? She's working as a nanny for the summer with the kids."

Vienne was pretty with a sophisticated, indie vibe. Jealousy came perilously close to forming in my head, but Vienne's gaze was perfunctory, almost clinical behind her glasses, when she looked at Cody. His muscled shoulder was next to mine, and it'd be too awkward for me to peek at how he reacted to her.

Tova, you have no business getting jealous.

"Tova, hi. I've heard about you from Catherine."

Hopefully good things, but maybe annoyed at best since I wasn't sure how the teen reacted to my invites. "She's welcome over anytime."

Vienne floated down the stairs. Her light brown hair had blonde highlights growing out, but she'd blown it out and added soft curls. Her heeled boots paired nicely with her skintight jeans, and the slouchy, loose-knit top she wore with a mustard tank underneath was perfect for a June day. She was simple but stylish compared to my surfer-girl chic.

She crossed the wet grass between the yards, heedless of the recent rain. She stuck her hand out, her phone held in her other. A tangle of bracelets lined her wrist and matched the fall of necklaces around her neck. Classy but cool. "Welcome to town, Tova. I'm Vienne." I shook her hand. When she released me, she dropped her keys and stooped to pick them up in a jingle of jewelry. "About Catherine." She straightened and glanced at the house. "She, uh, says she prefers modern dance."

She said it, exasperated in a way I'd heard many parents in my teaching days speak about their kids' specific interests.

"I do modern stuff. We can always change it up if she joins us." I smiled. "As long as it's kid friendly."

"That probably rules her out entirely." She rolled her eyes and shoved her dark-framed glasses up her nose. "If it's not pushing the limits, she's not interested."

I'd been the same. "There are still moves we can work on. Maybe even some evenings when I'm not working?" Catherine was clearly interested, and there was nothing better than mentoring a kid who had a heart for learning. Excitement welled inside me thinking about it.

"Oh." She blinked, her turquoise eyes owlish. "I'd pay you."

My interest perked up. The more income, the merrier, but I was dedicated to the Knights. "I can't commit to a schedule."

"We could work around lessons," Cody said. I glanced at him, but his expression was unreadable. "I'd hate for Catherine to miss out because you're at our beck and call."

Touched, I didn't know what to say. He'd paid for extra time, and he wasn't going to use it? My mind dug for a suspicious reason but came up empty.

A phone started buzzing. Vienne glanced at her purse, then her gaze landed on the phone in her hand. "I've got a client waiting. Give me a schedule and a price, and I'll see how many sessions I can swing." She turned to rush toward the hybrid SUV sitting in front of her house. "Wait, you don't have my number." She waved her hands, her bracelets tinkling. "Ask Catherine. I'm sure she'll be spying on you."

"Mom!" resounded from inside the house. Vienne grimaced, and I bit back a grin. I needed to stay on Catherine's good side if I wanted to work with her.

"Give Tova my number next time you see her," Vienne called to a window and rushed off.

"Can I dance with you two?" Grayson asked. Worry swam in his eyes. Poor kid. So much had changed, and he probably feared his new passion was being taken away from him.

"We'll have our own time." I held a hand out, giving him something to anchor himself into the present with. "I was thinking we could work on a performance. Use those costumes your dad bought."

"Really?" Ivy squealed loud enough to wake anyone who wasn't already up.

"Sure." I loaded into the pickup after helping Cody buckle the kids in the back. Inside, I was wrapped in his cedar and sage scent. He didn't mention noticing me shiver, but he flicked the knob to red, and soon heat pumped out of the vents.

"Thank you," I murmured.

"No problem, California."

"California?"

"Born and raised?" he asked.

I nodded. Mom and I had moved around, but it'd been within the state's borders. The corner of his mouth ticked up while his eyes stayed on the road.

"Milk Daddy," he said quietly.

"Fair enough." In the duel of nicknames, I reigned supreme.

"I was born in Montana," Grayson said from the back.

"Where was I born, Daddy?" Ivy asked.

"Also Montana," he said.

By the time we reached Aggie's to pick up the kittens, I'd learned the name of the hospital they were born in and that their names came from some classmates of their mom's. Law school buddies Cody said his wife had lost touch with. He really didn't have many people in his life other than his family. More than me, but somehow still lonely.

At Aggie's, we piled out of the pickup. I admired her sprawling farmhouse. The inside was spacious yet simple. Perfect for a family. I would've died and gone to heaven if I'd lived in a place like this. Would've been harder on me to leave too.

Cody didn't go to the house but walked around the garage and straight to the barn. The kids sprinted ahead of him. I was in sandals again, but I rushed after him, clocking the echoes of family life I had rarely experienced, like being so familiar with someone's home you knew where they were and were free to go find them. Grandma's house used to be like that. Thelma's apartment would be, too, if it wasn't so small.

"I seem unprepared for farm life again," I murmured. The air was still cool, but I was growing used to the milder mornings.

Humor gleamed in his eyes. "A little dirt never hurt anyone."

"Says the guy covered from neck to toe."

"You're covered." He grinned. "Except for your toes."

I playfully scowled at him while pretending tingles didn't spread through my belly at the same time my sex plugged in all the neon signs that said "Open for Business."

Aggie was already kneeling with the kids. They each held one kitten. Concentration furrowed Grayson's brow as he eyed my toes. I stood by the barn entrance just in case there was a getaway kitten.

Aggie waved at me. "Nice to see you again." To her brother, she said, "I thought you, of all people, would come prepared."

He smirked. "You think the kids would wait for a shopping trip after I said we'd foster the kittens?"

She laughed. I folded my arms, watching the family interact. Aggie scratched each kitten's head. "I'll miss them, but I've got my hands full with the six-pack."

The six-pack were her barn cats, all named after sodas. A couple of them monitored us from the top of the stack of hay bales.

"Where's Uncle Ansen?" Ivy asked, rubbing her chin on the kitten's head.

Ansen entered the barn, giving me a nod as he passed. "Right here, princess." He walked to Ivy and ruffled her hair. Grayson cradled his kitten with both hands, but Ansen managed to give him a fist bump around the fur. "Sutton's waitin' for you and the new arrivals. Y'all seen her new clinic yet?"

The kids shook their heads, but they gave Aggie and Ansen a thorough rundown of how they planned to play with the kittens every day to get them used to kids.

The cats didn't appear concerned about being manhandled by children. Was sweet-looking Aggie being devious? She had to know the kids wouldn't let the cats go easily. Perhaps she and Cody had already discussed the effect on the kids.

A few minutes later, we were loaded up again with two squirming, meowing kittens and were on the way to a small steel building on the outskirts of town. No sign was up yet, and only one blue pickup was parked by the back, but Cody pulled into the square lot that didn't yet have parking stripes.

All in all, our stops weren't far from each other.

Nothing in town was more than a few miles apart at the most, but Crocus Valley didn't have a bus system. The only sidewalks were within city limits, and bike paths bordered two sides of town along the highways.

Crocus Valley would be easier to make a life in. If I stayed, I'd need a car and a place to live— No. There was no point in thinking about where I'd land after my nanny position was over. My mom and my money were in California. But so was Frederick, and he controlled my money.

The door to the clinic swung open. A woman popped her head out. This must be Sutton. She looked a little taller than me and had dirty-blonde hair tossed up in a looped ponytail.

She grinned wide when the kids rushed her, each clutching a kitten to their chests. She gave each kid a hug and nodded as they told her about how well the animals tolerated the trip.

"Go on in," she said to the kids. "The first exam room on the right." She straightened and waved at Cody as he got out. "Did you gamble they'd travel well, or you didn't think the kids would let them stay in a carrier?"

"Yes to both." Cody chuckled. "If we manage not to lose control of the cats and they don't run off before this appointment is done, I'll be surprised."

I exited the pickup and rounded the front.

"You must be Tova. Nice to meet you." Sutton didn't act surprised I had come along, but she was likely friends with Aggie and had heard about me. I'd love to know what was said. Or maybe not.

"Hi." A sudden onset of shyness struck me.

Sutton's worn jeans and plain gray sweater didn't scream money and sophistication, but she was well-educated and owned her own business. One she seemed to have started in the middle of a divorce. I hadn't even been engaged, and I'd lost everything to a man.

"Come on in when you're ready." Sutton disappeared into the clinic.

I was in public with Cody, but we were alone outside. Like in the barn, I didn't hate the situation. "You're not upset about the possibility of kittens on the run?" He hadn't gotten that upset after the kitten escaped Grayson yesterday either. I had thought he'd explode, then . . . Mellow Daddy.

"I'd be highly annoyed to have to chase kittens, but they're small yet and can't go too far too fast." He studied me. Did I seem stunned? I was looking harder for warnings than I ever had with Frederick, and I was coming up empty. Cody was uptight. Stern Daddy. But he was also relaxed at the most unexpected times. "Is something wrong?"

"One of my mom's boyfriends tried to take his belt to me for feeding his dog an hour late." An event I had never mentioned to anyone. I hardly thought of it, and when I did, it was with the air of a detached observer. All Mom knew was that he had tried to hit me, and that had been enough. We were gone by sundown.

"Shit, Tova. That's awful. And so goddamn wrong."

I shrugged. Why'd I say anything? But I liked his adamant reaction. "We left right after."

His attention was still on me. "Was that a common occurrence?"

"Yes." I licked my suddenly dry lips. The wariness from back then intruded on my present. "Why don't you care I was a burlesque dancer?"

"Was? You're not going back?"

"I don't know. I did it to earn as much money as possible. The gigs didn't always pay the best, but I wasn't restricted by hours, only by how much I could hustle."

He nodded, thoughtful. "My wife . . . Let me start with my mother. Mama touted being a feminist. And she was, but she also confused the term with selfish. Meg was a feminist for others more than herself, and I think that's what attracted me to her. She was passionate and generous."

I snorted. "I'm sure she wasn't hideous." Horrified, I pressed my fingers to my mouth, my gasp dissolving into a squeak. *Tova, shut your damn mouth!* I couldn't believe I hadn't filtered myself.

But he only grinned. "She was beautiful, yes. Her looks got me to notice her and to hit on her. But she championed women. She used to take pro bono cases for strippers. Draw up and negotiate contracts for them."

"In Montana?"

He nodded. "There are a few strip joints, but those weren't the only people who sought her out. Meg worked with entertainers and encouraged them to think of themselves as a business. She always said artists shouldn't starve, and her definition of artist was broad."

"Your wife sounds amazing."

Fondness mixed with loss in his features. "She was." He stared out the window, lost in his past.

He'd loved her, and he missed her. Did he talk about her often? Occasionally, the kids made offhand comments about their mom. *Mom didn't like when we put sugar on our oatmeal. Mom didn't like this shirt. Mom could braid really well.* But that was as far into the memories of her they delved. Around me anyway.

I didn't want to trash his whole day. "I knew I was a charity case." I tried to lighten the mood.

His attention snapped back to me, and the earlier expression was gone. "Pro bono, and no. I'm in a tough spot, and so are you. It's okay to help each other. I have the money, and you have the time."

"In my experience, whoever has the money usually has the power."

I expected him to argue with me, but he nodded. "That's been my experience too. But money won't teach my kids to dance or help Grayson handle his feelings. So you've got me there."

He complimented me more as his nanny than I'd ever been complimented as a dancer. "I bet you do a mean two-step."

A ghost of a smile played over his lips. "I was born two-stepping, California."

I'd love to find out if he was telling the truth, but it'd never happen and I shouldn't want it to. Yet I did.

Cody

Tova's earlier confession streamed through my head on repeat as I watched her joke with the kids and laugh with Sutton.

Anyone who didn't know Sutton would think she looked cheerful, like she loved her job and enjoyed her summer days. But I'd known Sutton for over ten years, since she and Wilder had started dating. I considered her family. Her expression brightened when she talked to Tova, but her eyes were rimmed with pink, like she had woken up crying. Her face was wan. The stress of the divorce, moving, and opening a new business was getting to her, but she'd never share her struggles with me.

I wished I could've talked sense into Wilder, but I was the last guy he'd listen to. He was the second oldest, and there'd been a rivalry between us that originated with him.

I could stand and dissect a relationship I knew little about, or I could ask for a little more of Sutton's time. The kids missed her, and I'd been too wrapped up in barrel prices and projections to arrange a meetup with her and the kids.

"Sutton, can I ask you a small favor in case dropping kittens and kids on you on a Saturday morning isn't enough?"

"Please," she said, squirting dewormer into the kittens' fur. "It's not as if my doors are bursting with customers yet. Just the women who got dumped by Dr. Jake." She dropped her volume for the last part.

I'd heard of the other vet in the area and his reputation. Decent guy if you were a dude or an animal. A dog himself when it came to women. "Then you should be filling up in no time."

She laughed. "One can hope. But if you want to keep the kids here for an hour while you grab cat supplies I doubt you own, then yes."

"How'd you guess?" I asked it jokingly, but she'd known how Meg was with pets. No pets had been the best kind for her. "Tova, do you want to stay or help me pick out pet supplies?" *Come with me.* The more time I had with her alone, the more I wanted. Apparently, I was shameless about it too.

I missed adult conversation that wasn't about those projections and barrel prices. That was it.

"I'd love a better chance to see the town," Tova said.

"I want to go with you, Dad," Grayson said. He'd listed several items I was supposed to buy on the way over.

"Us girls can stay here," Ivy said and plopped onto a chair with a kitten in her lap.

It'd be weird if I argued. I hadn't gotten many opportunities to talk to Tova. I should be thanking Grayson for sparing me from thinking about how that skirt draped over

Tova's hips. I didn't need to be waking up with more super-imposed images of her over or under me.

"No naming the cats until we get back," I warned Ivy.

Grayson's eyes widened as if it hadn't occurred to him missing out on naming was a possibility. "Never mind. I'll stay."

Sutton grinned. "Go ahead, Tova. Kids naming animals can be a multi-day event."

Back in the pickup, I was acutely aware that it was just me and Tova. I shouldn't have suggested just she and I go run errands. She was my nanny. I knew better, and I'd still done it. I waited for daunting regret, but nothing rose.

She crossed one leg over the other and squinted out the window. "Where do you get cat supplies in town?"

"Probably the farm and tractor place in Coal Haven." The general store in Crocus Valley would probably have what we needed, but Coal Haven was only ten minutes away and the quality would be better.

I wasn't aiming for more time alone with Tova. I *wasn't*.

"It's been an exciting weekend. I get to see Coal Haven." She straightened her long skirt over her legs. How could a garment that covered her so much still make her extremely sexy? "And I've met two more people today."

"I met Vienne at Aggie's wedding. She gave me the information for renting the house, mostly because she was complaining about the owners and how little they did with it. She's an interior designer and would love to get her hands on the place. And I'll consider Sutton family forever. I can't help my brother fucked that up."

"I don't think I've heard you swear, Milk Daddy."

"I get dirty when the occasion calls for it." Fuck's sake. Did I really let that slip out?

Thankfully, she laughed, covering my shock at what I

said. I hadn't flirted in . . . Had I even flirted with Meg after our first date?

Regardless, I shouldn't be goddamn flirting now.

She shrugged. "I've heard it all, so no worries."

"Do you perform for a tough crowd?"

She shook her head and twined her hair over one shoulder. I liked when she wore it loose like that. I pictured wrapping it around my hand and—

Gritting my teeth together, I kept an eye on the road.

"More like I perform *with* a tough crowd. Seasoned dancers learn not to put up with shit. In the early days, I played for rougher clubs, and guys in the crowd could get lewd, but . . . I learned how to take care of myself." She peered out the passenger window. "Or so I thought."

Her ex. "Turned out the trouble was closer to you?"

"I took too many chances. I should've seen him for what he was."

Anger kicked at my gut. "It's not your fault. People don't wear their labels on their forehead."

"I wish I was as smart as your wife."

Meg had been smart, but Tova seemed just as savvy. "Meg was tenacious, but don't sell yourself short. People like Meg and my in-laws only learn what they do because they study the crap people pull for a living."

"Your in-laws are lawyers too?"

"Makes for a wild Thanksgiving."

She laughed, and hell, I lived for making her smile. "My ex's parents were in the arts—the prestigious kind. Operas, art galleries, auctions. They despised me."

"Then they have no taste."

"Wait until everyone around you thinks I'm a stripper. Opinions change."

I got what she was saying, and I didn't think the people around me would care if she stripped for a living or not, but

I couldn't deny she had likely faced a metric ton of crap for her line of work. "Is that what happened with your ex? He didn't respect you because of your profession?"

Her mouth pursed. "Most definitely did not, but he was good at hiding it."

"Asshole. Did you even give him a cool nickname?"

Her mouth quirked. "No cool nickname."

"Good. He didn't deserve it." I pulled into the parking lot of the tractor supply store. I wouldn't take for granted Tova had opened up to me, but I also didn't want her to dwell on what she clearly thought were mistakes. "Time to raid the pet supplies."

We walked through the store and gathered curious looks from people who'd probably lived in Coal Haven forever. We were strangers in a small town.

"Ooh, look at this cute carrier." She brandished a pink contraption from the shelf. "It'll look like you're carrying the cats like a tote bag."

"Exactly what a man of fashion needs."

She clutched the carrier. "You know, when I met you, I thought a sense of humor was the last thing you possessed."

"What was the first thing you thought I possessed?"

"Control." She said it so quickly, I wasn't sure it was a good thing. "Do you think you'll need two carriers? Leashes, collars? Cat treats?" She wandered down the aisle. "Are you sure you're just fostering?"

The kids thought fostering meant *keep forever* in the same way they interpreted a maybe for a yes. But it couldn't be. "My in-laws are allergic to cats." When she cast a questioning gaze toward me, I realized she didn't know why that mattered. "The kids will be living with them after the summer is over." The words tasted sour.

She recoiled, shock rippling over her face. "Why?"

I pushed back the dark cloud that entered my mind

when I thought of the end of summer. "My work, and school, and daycare were rough this past year."

"Sure." Her tone echoed empty, like she didn't think I was making a good decision.

"Meg and I talked about it when she was sick." Defensiveness gnawed at my throat. Words gathered to spill over, to tell her that I didn't know what else to do. I couldn't put them through another year like the last, but I couldn't be that far away from the ranch or the wells. The kids would still be with me for holidays and the summers.

When I'd hire another nanny to watch them.

Fuck. No matter what, I lost, and so did the kids. I'd rather I lost more than they did. They'd have Curtis and Lauri, new friends, and a fresh start. I'd be stabilizing their legacy and giving them what their mother had wanted for them.

The decision was made.

We loaded up on two of everything, and the discussion was left behind. I let her pick sparkly pink collars, a flat glass dish she heard was better for their whiskers, and an automatic waterer. Next were a couple of litter boxes and a longer debate over brands and types of litter until she had me pull out my phone and look up the best options—not on the internet but on some social media app.

"Horse bedding it is," I said. "We're definitely in the wrong aisle."

She swiveled the cart. "The horse section is down farther."

I followed the sweetly swaying ass under that multicolored fabric. The muscles in her arms flexed. The morning wood I fought back every time I woke up would roar back if I didn't get my growing and inconvenient obsession with my nanny under control.

When was the last time I fought an erection in public? In a store, for fuck's sake?

My steps slowed. When was the last time I had fun shopping? Felt so light, damn near carefree? I'd like to say it hadn't been since Meg got sick, but it was before that. Long before. If ever.

I loved my wife. I missed her. I mourned her. But our marriage . . .

It'd been fine. We'd been close, compatible, and professional.

I winced. The latter was not a word to describe a marriage. Meg wasn't warm and gushy. I'd accepted that about her as long as she accepted that I didn't like to talk about feelings like my lingering resentment toward my irresponsible dead mother or how much pressure Barns had put on me.

I didn't notice Tova had turned until she backed out of the aisle. "Did I lose you in this vast metropolis?"

My lips twitched despite the heavy mental road I was traveling. "If you're worried, you can pull up GPS on your phone."

"Hmm." She tapped her chin, her gaze sweeping toward the lighter part of the store where the set of sliding doors let more daylight in. "I'll manage. Like a voyager in the mountains."

"Okay, California, Lewis and Clark your way through the store."

She laughed, the sound something I latched on to. "First, I need to make my way through the equine aisle. What is all this stuff?"

Excitement lurched in my chest. I didn't get out to the ranch as often as I wanted, and my house in Buffalo Gully was on Knight land but close to town. Growing up, I thought I'd be Eliot, running the ranch and spending my days in the elements and under the sun. But Barns had different ideas and all the money for school. I had siblings to think about, so I went to school for business and finance and parked my ass behind a desk for most of my days.

Guilt ate at my chest as I located the horse bedding. Was it "Question My Life Day"?

I was content with where I was, all things considered. I wanted to provide for my kids, do my job, and honor my wife. Nothing else fit into my plans. Definitely not Tova.

Seven

TOVA

I hauled bags of cat supplies into the house while Cody used his big, manly, nicely flexing muscles to carry in the bigger items like the horse bedding and litter boxes. We'd left the carriers in the pickup so Grayson and Ivy could practice loading and unloading the kittens.

"I can put all this away while you pick up the kids," I offered.

"Sure. Thanks."

I set the bags on the kitchen table. Whatever happened to Cody's mood in the store resulted in a major shift. Was it the discussion of his kids going to live with their grandparents? He was no longer the guy cracking jokes and showing me a level of charm I'd never witnessed.

Only now he wasn't even Stern Daddy. He brooded. His gaze was dour. When he'd popped on his mirrored sunglasses for the drive from the store to the house, he might as well have built a wall between the driver and passenger seats.

His reasons for sending the kids away were logical and seemed to be centered on Grayson and Ivy's well-being. But . . . didn't he realize how much they loved him? Couldn't he see how his absence would be like losing another parent?

It wasn't my place to say. I was just a nanny.

I'd also been that kid shipped away for her own good.

Thanks to the silence on the return trip, I'd gotten a nice view of the rolling green hills and the fields full of corn. Mom couldn't get more than five plants to grow the one time she'd attempted a garden. So many cows dotted the landscape with smaller calves at their sides. I'd burst at the seams to ask Cody about them, about ranching and what was growing in each field that wasn't corn, but I minded the wall he'd erected.

I wasn't begging for a man's attention. I had experienced enough problems after getting their notice.

"Put the litter boxes in the bathroom, and we'll close the kittens up in there to make sure they know where to do their business." And he was back out the door.

Okay, then. I might've liked his commanding side earlier, but not now.

The quiet of the house let in the chirps of the birds through the drone of the AC unit. Nothing worked harder and had less effect than that equipment.

I was the AC unit in my life.

My mood sucked, and it was because of *him*.

What was his problem anyway?

What was mine? Would I have to admit to myself that I had enjoyed talking with him? That I liked being alone with him? That I was more comfortable with him than anyone I'd ever met, and I didn't know him hardly at all?

Yeah. I'd have to confess all that. I'd also have to face my raging crush. He was hot. He was nice, like *really* nice, not *I want something* nice. And the way his ass filled out his jeans was a sin. He needed to throw away his loafers because the swagger his boots gave him was everything I didn't know I needed.

Energy hummed through my veins. While I was active with the kids all day, lessons weren't the same as concentrating on a set and entertaining a crowded club. Add in the emotions that uptight man made me feel, and I needed to do something, to do *more*.

All the items were unloaded, and the tags were off. I'd wash the cat dishes later, but I had to move. To dance. It was how I dealt with life.

I loved modern dance, but I didn't want to think about choreography. I turned on my Frederickton playlist and twisted my hair into a bun on top of my head, securing it with another lock of hair. The hold wouldn't last long without a tie, but I didn't care. With the big moves of the arms and legs and the jubilance needed to pull off the dance, the Frederickton was a perfect outlet. The fake wood plank floor was good enough to dance on. I kicked off my sandals and pushed the chairs closer to the table, giving myself a small space.

The Paul Whiteman Orchestra filled the air. I used to dance a set to this song, and it was one of my favorites, but Frederick had pushed me toward modern Frederickton music.

Fuck him.

I held up my skirt and kicked my heels out. This was supposed to be an upbeat, fun song, but rage pumped through my veins and punctuated my movements.

Fuck Frederick. To hell with the way he disregarded me.

Fuck all the men who'd stomped on me and my mom.

Especially the one who'd taken the essence of her away from me.

I threw my arms up in practiced moves, matching the steps. I didn't have to worry about undressing, pausing for effect to unhook an arm strap, or making eye contact with some random audience member. I was free.

Finally, the anger ebbed, and I was lost in the flow, pairing my feet with my arms. My skirt made it hard to put my hands on my knees and rotate my legs in and out, but I mimicked the motion without tangling myself in the material of the skirt. I rather enjoyed the challenge.

I wasn't worried about whether I forgot to put my thong on when I was unhooking my fringe skirt. I wasn't praying my pasties would stay in place while I shimmied out of my top. I was dancing just to dance again.

I was doing the heel taps with my arms held out to my sides to make it a full-body action when giggling reached my ears.

My chest heaving, I came to a stop. The kids were pressed into the entry that separated the living room from the dining room and kitchen. Cody was behind them, but he wasn't glowering anymore. His calm mask wavered, but I couldn't identify the tide of emotion he was holding back.

Until his gaze dropped to catch the rise and fall of my breasts. I was only in a white tank top, and one spaghetti strap had fallen down my shoulder.

"Do it again!" Ivy clutched one of the kittens to her chest. The kitten didn't flinch, already used to the outbursts of kids.

Cody shook himself, like he was recovering from a trance. "Sorry to interrupt."

I shouldn't have let time get away from me. He was paying me to work, not play. "It's your house."

"It's not," he said, plainly.

Tendrils of hurt curled around my throat. Was he pointing out that his presence was temporary in Crocus Valley, and so was I? A long jump logically, but my brain happily created reasons for the hurt.

"Can I dance with you?" Grayson asked.

I loved this kid's enthusiasm. "Let me change the music, and we can practice some of those swing steps you've been learning. Remember the name of my favorite song?"

"'In the Mood'!" both Grayson and Ivy yelled.

Grayson handed his kitten to Cody. "Here, Dad."

Cody juggled the fluffier of the kittens with a surprisingly gentle and ginger grip that sent the wickedest thoughts through my head about how he handled other types of pussy.

I hit the play button before I did something more old-fashioned, like fan myself. The sound of trumpets blared through the room.

I held my hands out for Grayson.

Cody stopped by the bathroom, the kitten cuddled against his chest. Lucky cat.

"Big band?" he asked.

I did slow, minimized versions of the swing steps while Grayson concentrated on his footwork. "I'm a sucker for old-time jazz and big band. I'll take a jitterbug over a twerk any day." I nodded while watching Grayson's feet. "That's right, step, step, rock step— Look at you. You nailed a triple step."

Grayson beamed. I'd started him on the single step and only demonstrated the triple step, but he just executed the move. I had the song on repeat, and we danced two more before Ivy shoved in and Grayson took a break and went to stand by his dad. Her footwork was erratic, more like we were jumping rope, and she didn't care about a single swing step. Regardless, I was having fun. Even Cody was smiling against the doorframe of the closed bathroom, holding the kittens, his arms crossed over his broad chest. Grayson stood like his small mirror image on the other side of the frame.

I danced another song with Ivy, getting silly with her. Giggling, Ivy dropped to a curtsy. "Daddy, it's your turn."

I froze, my gaze shooting to his. Alarmed, he opened his mouth like he was going to turn us both down, but then he snapped his mouth shut. "My boots might scratch the floor."

The curl of hurt was back. This floor had seen a lot in its day. Cowboy boots wouldn't nick it.

"Come on, Daddy," Grayson urged.

The stern expression was wiped out by determination. He stepped out of his boots. His socks were stark white, and he was no less imposing in stockinged feet, prowling toward me. My breath hitched.

What was going on?

He crossed to me, hooked an arm around my waist, and took my hand in his, his grip light but sure. His toe tapped with the beat, and at the top of a count, he started twirling around the floor with me.

This man could swing dance.

Laughter bubbled out of me. Forget his hot body close to mine, the way we fit perfectly together, and the ripple of strength through his limbs. He could *move*.

Frederick had been a stick in the mud at parties—the few he'd taken me to. And I'd been focused so long on making enough money that I didn't get to dance with partners. I didn't get to dance for fun.

We were limited on room, but he spun me away from the counter and the table. When he kicked a leg out with me on the right beat, I threw my head back, my laughter filling the room. The kids cheered.

Too soon, the song was finished, ready to repeat again, but he slowed until he released me.

I puffed loose strands out of my face. "You're full of surprises."

"Mama used to play around and dance with me before motherhood tapped her out." He rolled a shoulder, his eyes brighter, but his smile was almost shy. "And a teenage boy will do a lot to impress a girl."

"Swing dance did it, huh?"

"My teen crush loved doing the jitterbug at street dances but eventually dumped me for the lead in the senior play. Now they have four kids, and she teaches drama in Billings." He pushed a hand through his hair, leaving it adorably and sexily ruffled. I waited for him to straighten it. "I haven't danced like that for over twenty years."

I put my hand on my chest. "*Over* twenty years? How long ago was high school?"

The side of his mouth tipped further up. "I turned forty last year."

"Well, you still got it." In all the best ways. I meant on the dance floor, but the way his gaze heated, I bit the inside of my cheek.

"Did you dance with Mommy like that?" Ivy asked.

Grayson blinked his big eyes, and Cody grew so still, it was like the air had been sucked out of the room.

"No. Your mom didn't dance a lot."

I hated for this moment of fun to turn dreary. Their mom hadn't been gone long, and it seemed like they were stuffing away her memories, afraid of the pain. Grief was complex, but hiding from it never helped.

"But she did dance?" I pressed, looking from a solemn Cody to equally serious kids. Was I making them scratch at a fresh wound in a failed attempt to cheer them up?

Ivy nodded, and Grayson rolled his eyes to the ceiling as if it'd jog a recollection loose.

"She didn't like country music or two-stepping . . ." Cody gestured to where my phone continued to stream "In the Mood." His gaze narrowed, but not from wishing I dropped the subject. More like he was trying to explain his late wife. "She wasn't a fan of organized dance."

The kids didn't add any information, and the mood threatened to veer into somber territory. I should butt out, but I had to change it. They had to have good memories of her that didn't hurt as bad as they used to. "How old was she?"

He clenched his jaw. "She would've turned forty this December."

Forty. Seven years older than me. "Hmm." I went to my phone and scrolled through my list until a song jumped out. I recalled the playlist I put it in and selected that. "Did she dance more like this?"

As the top hit of a boy band filled the room, I swiveled my hips like I was in the club, keeping it as unsuggestive as possible in front of the kids, and waved my arms in the air.

The hint of Cody's smile was back. Success! "Close."

"Oh, yeah!" Grayson skittered to the middle of the floor. "She used to do this." He made a wave with his arms like me and moved his head around while wiggling his hips. I did the same. Ivy joined us, doing her usual jump and adding her arms.

Cody's smile grew bigger, and he stepped in, mimicking his son. Delighted I possessed the skills to help them enjoy a memory, I continued dancing. Soon, our laughter and giggles mingled with the music. We danced for at least four songs when Ivy dramatically collapsed on the floor. Cody and Grayson stopped, but they were both still smiling.

"I need water," Ivy croaked.

I shut the music off and held my hands out to help her up. "Let's get you some before you turn to dust. We need lunch too."

Cody didn't disappear and leave it to me to get water and fix sandwiches for lunch. He was at my shoulder, putting turkey on bread, while I filled three glasses of milk to go with their water. The kids piled on the stools on the other side of the island that separated the dining area from the kitchen.

"Do you like mayo?" he asked.

"Ick. No."

"Mommy didn't like mayo either," Grayson said, lifting the top of his sandwich to check for mayo. Satisfied his dad had left it off, he nodded. Whether he liked it or not, he must have needed to feel closer to his mom today.

"Did she like mustard?" I asked.

He shook his head.

"Ketchup?"

"Ew." Ivy giggled.

"Don't tell me." I snapped my fingers. "Ranch. Doesn't everyone around here love ranch?"

Cody had a half-smile in place as he pushed a plate toward me. "Yes. But not Meg."

I made a scandalized sound. "Dry?" I took a bite out of my dry turkey and Swiss cheese sandwich.

"The green stuff," Ivy said with a big grin.

"Guacamole. Mm. Good taste."

The kids were satisfied with my judgment of their mom's sandwich habits. I ate standing up, wedged in the corner. Cody didn't move to the table or to a stool. I got a front-row seat to the way the tendon in his jaw pulsed with each bite and the flex of his forearms as he brought the food to his mouth. He was so much taller than me, but there was nothing intimidating about standing this close. His earlier moodiness had needed a release, too, and his presence was comforting. Welcoming.

The way his hair was still mussed added an undeniable sexiness that rivaled his clean-cut, business-style look.

I had it bad.

The food turned to ash in my mouth. I almost regretted passing up the mayonnaise.

I was falling for a man I had no business having the hots for. Three weeks had gone by since my ex tried to prostitute me. I had no home. My job was temporary. And Cody was my boss.

That was *my* situation. This man lost his wife last year. He didn't live in Crocus Valley. He worked all the time. He was a billboard of warnings I was willing to ignore.

When I had been sitting at the vanity in Frederick's house, I berated myself for missing all the signs, and here I was dancing right past them. Frederick wasn't a good guy. Cody could very well be the best guy I'd ever met. But he couldn't be my guy.

I finished the rest of my food without tasting it. I brushed off my fingers and put my plate by the sink. The dishes could wait until tomorrow. Or Monday. "If that's all, I should get going and let you guys enjoy yourselves. As a family."

Cody watched me while he chewed. I gave him a neutral look. Did he see right through my panic? Did he know I was beyond finding him attractive? Did he realize the wicked fantasies I'd been pushing away about him were joined by domestic dreams, like what if I could have this kind of weekend every weekend? What if I had a stable home, a man who danced around the kitchen with me, and kids I adored? What if . . .

He finished his mouthful, and my gaze dropped to where his throat worked as he swallowed.

"Aw, can't you stay?" Ivy asked.

I wanted to, that was the issue. "Unless you need me to work." He was paying me to be available. I wanted to stay. The impromptu dance party was the most fun I'd had since . . .

It'd been a long time.

Cody's eyes narrowed, reading me. Could he decipher my expression, my want, my absolute terror that I would be left with a broken heart if I couldn't trust a guy I actually cared deeply about? He poured himself another glass of milk. "My inbox is quiet so far. All I have to do tomorrow is to call Eliot and find out when he's working cattle and if he wants us there."

I had no idea what working cattle meant, but if they were gone for a weekend, I could brainstorm what I needed to do when I returned to California. My mood took a dive.

"I want to go!" Grayson said.

Cody lifted a brow like it was a surprise Grayson wanted anything to do with cattle. "Aunt Sutton won't be there to play with you. She lives in Crocus Valley now."

"Will Uncle Austen be there?" Ivy asked.

"Maybe. And Wilder." Cody turned his intense gaze back to me. The spark from dancing fanned into a blaze. "We'll be fine until Monday."

"I have to go." I wanted to run, but I didn't want to leave. "I need to see if I can call my mom and . . ." Plan my future. Figure out what the hell I was going to do with hardly any money when this gig was up.

"What's your mom like?" Ivy asked, picking at the bread of her half-eaten sandwich.

My chest constricted. Such a simple, innocent question. Tears stung the backs of my eyes. "She, uh, she's quiet. Likes to watch TV and . . ." Feel safe. I swallowed hard.

"Hey, guys, wait here while I walk Tova out."

Not questioning the way he saved me from breaking down, I gave each kid a quick hug while they polished off their milk. In the entryway, I put my hand to my forehead. A dull ache settled behind my temples. "Thanks for letting me tag along this morning."

"Are you okay?"

The concern simmering in his eyes without a trace of falsity was nearly my undoing. "Yeah. Yeah, I'm fine. It's just . . ." For once, I let go. It wasn't like she was in witness protection. "My mom's in a long-term care home. She's why I asked you for so much money."

"Six grand a month isn't a lot."

I stared, dumbfounded. "It's seventy-two thousand a year."

"You're not getting benefits, and you work more than eight hours a day. Around here, seventy-two grand is a decent living, but it's not millionaire money. I imagine in California it wouldn't stretch nearly as far as it does here."

"I need most of it for my mom."

His gaze softened even more, and he swung the door shut, closing us in the makeshift coat room. "Do you need a raise?"

I needed money, but I couldn't bring myself to ask. I wasn't going to be dependent on a man again. Yet here I was. "No, it's fine. That's partly why I need to go. I need to look for jobs for after you go back to Montana." Saying the words out loud made the end date so achingly real.

His gaze darkened, and he propped a shoulder against the wall. We were standing closer than we needed to be. He'd asked me quietly if I was okay, and I had swayed toward him like I could cuddle into that big chest and forget about my worries.

"Thank you for today. For earlier." He wasn't talking about the cats.

"I know it's hard for them—to remember her and not be sad. My mom used to dance with me. She loved to dance, and she would've been a performer if . . ." I let out a long breath. Frederick had known that Mom was in long-term care, but he'd never asked why. Knowing she depended on me was all the information he needed. Cody hadn't asked either. Whether out of politeness or because he didn't give a shit, I didn't know, and I wouldn't talk more about her. "Anyway, we used to have sudden dance parties. They're some of my favorite memories, especially now that she's . . ." Unable to care for herself.

"I don't talk to them much. About her." He dropped his head to stare at the floor. "I should."

"Is it too hard for you?"

"Yes? No?" He rubbed his bottom lip between his thumb and forefinger. "Some days I don't know what to feel. Our marriage wasn't perfect, but it wasn't terrible. It should be easier to know what to do."

"Where's that written?" When he glanced up, I softened my question with a smile. "Thelma and my grandma— Well, if I didn't have Thelma to talk about everything under the sun with, I don't think I would've handled Grandma's death very well. Even when it was hard for her, Thelma would talk to me about Grandma. Eventually, we were able to do it with more laughter and less tears."

He mulled over what I said. "I never looked at it like that. I feel like if I get sappy, Meg will cross over and bitch-slap me. She wasn't one for unneeded emotion, but then, neither am I."

"It might've been part of her personality, but I'm not so sure it's a part of yours." I didn't know what possessed me to step forward and tuck a hunk of his hair to the side so it wouldn't stand on end, but I did it, running the silky strands through my fingers. "It's okay to have and express emotions. Your kids need to see it. And you're allowed to have all sorts of feelings."

I drew in a sharp breath when I realized what I was doing. I snatched my hand back, curling my fingers into my palm. He caught my wrist, his grip somehow gentle, and that thumb that had rubbed circles on my thigh stroked along my palm.

"I shouldn't feel a lot of what's inside me right now."

He wasn't the only one. "Me either."

His gaze jumped back and forth between my eyes, the energy between us crackling. I wanted to sink into the floor for what I said, but I held eye contact. Anything else would make me seem lovesick or hopeless or hopeful. None of those had their place in the moment.

Releasing my hand, he straightened. "See you Monday, Tova."

Relieved to move on from my uncomfortable admission in order to inspect what he'd said with a fine-toothed comb, I smiled. "Have a good weekend, Cody." At the door, I paused with my hand on the warm metal handle. "What did the kids name the cats?"

The electricity in the air sizzled to nothing. "They've been through five name changes so far. When we see you again, maybe they'll have settled on two."

"I look forward to it." I wasn't talking about the cats. There was nothing more I wanted to do than spend time in this house with these people. But they weren't my family. At the end of the two months, I'd be alone once more.

Eight

CODY

I let the shower sandblast me in the face while I choked my dick. That damn dream. It'd been tormenting me every morning, but after having Tova in my arms while dancing, I knew her size, how warm she was, and the way her body moved. She'd been fully clothed, nothing but her face, arms, and shoulders showing, but the dream had only grown more vivid, more detailed, and, *fuuuuck*, more real.

Christ, it was like I had felt every inch of her naked body. Her weight as she rode me, the bounce of her tits, and there'd been no tassels this morning. Nope. My brain happily painted her nipples a vibrant pink that made my mouth water.

The breathy moans. I had no fucking idea what she'd sound like, but my imagination somehow did. My balls tightened as the dream replayed in my head. Lightning laced down my spine, and blistering heat shot through my shaft. Hot jets of cum fired out of my selfish, demanding cock. I squeezed my eyes shut, both against the water and the force of my climax. I'd resisted jacking off when images of a naked Tova were in my head, but my morning wood hadn't flagged.

"Fuck," I groaned, gritting my teeth to keep something stupid from happening like Tova's name tumbling from my lips.

When I was done orgasming, I sagged against the shower wall, letting the water cascade down my body and clean up the mess. I'd have to wipe everything down after I caught my breath.

Feel better, asshole?

No. Because if I recalled any second of that vivid dream, I'd be right back where I started.

There was rapid pounding on the bathroom door. "Daddy? Everything okay?" Ivy's alarmed voice drifted in.

Shit. Getting time to stroke one out shouldn't be so hard. Maybe I should shower at night, and that'd help beat the dream back, and I wouldn't have to worry about the kids hearing. "I'm fine."

"But I heard growling."

I let my head fall back. "I was . . . singing . . ."

Her dubious "Okay . . ." was all she said. I got out and toweled off.

The rest of the morning was busy with getting the kids up, having breakfast, and finding a show they could watch when I called Eliot. The duties kept my mind off the morning and almost succeeded at keeping me from drifting back to yesterday and how nice it was to have Tova around. The joy of the dance party. I hadn't done a spin on a dance floor since . . . probably my wedding, and it certainly hadn't been swing. Work, then kids, had filled our lives.

I should've tried to get Meg to have more fun, but easygoing hadn't been her default. She was a different person, and I'd accepted the way she was, just like she accepted that Alcott Knight had a duty to Knight's Oil Wells and Knight's Arabians and Cattle Company. She'd been Meg . . . but I hadn't been Cody.

Guilt ate at my insides. What I said to Tova yesterday rose in my mind. *I shouldn't feel a lot of what's inside me right now.*

I didn't regret my marriage, but I shouldn't already be thinking about what I'd like to have. And I shouldn't want something so completely different.

"Can we go to the park today?" Ivy asked.

Grayson's worried gaze slashed with mine. "Is Tova coming over?"

"Maybe for the park—I have to call Uncle Eliot. No for Tova. It's just us." I tried to finish brightly, but Grayson's face crumpled.

"I want to see Tova. I want to dance again."

You're not alone with that, G.

I did what I'd seen her do all week. Dropping on the couch next to him, I paused the cartoon on TV, and put my arm around him. "I know. It's fun when she's around."

"I wanted to spend the day in the backyard," he whined, his big eyes filling with tears.

Ivy bobbed her head. "She's teaching us a whole dance routine."

I'd been watching like a perv peeping through a window, only I'd been on the inside looking out, spacing out of phone meetings where I didn't need to show my face. She worked patiently and diligently with Grayson and Ivy, and the neighborhood kids, demonstrating the footwork with her long, lean legs, and sometimes when she reached into the air, her shirt rode up and I caught sight of her belly.

Only a jackass would compare the view to a striptease, but fuck.

"I can't wait to see it," I told the kids. "Even professional dancers need breaks, though. She'll be back tomorrow."

"But she's only here until the end of summer." He slumped his narrow shoulders. "*We're* only here until the end of summer."

I worked my jaw back and forth. I wanted what was best for them, but I wasn't sure what that was anymore. A stable, richer home life with my in-laws seemed like the reasonable choice. Grayson would have a chance to get a better teacher in a school where he wasn't labeled a problem kid. My hometown was too small to forget his outbursts. I didn't have a nanny in Buffalo Gully, and when Tova got back on her feet, I wouldn't have a nanny if I stayed here.

But I didn't want Tova as just a nanny.

The truth hit me square in the face. I coughed against the onslaught of emotions clogging my throat.

Ivy gazed at me, sweetly innocent but also attentive. She seemed attuned to my inner turmoil, but what the hell did I know about seven-year-olds? When Grayson was seven, I had Meg. With my siblings . . . I'd been flying blind, but I was better than Barns. Just like my in-laws were better at balancing this parenting thing than me. At least one of them would be retired by then, and the kids needed the stability.

There'd probably be no dancing. More like practice debates or museum tours, all while wearing polo shirts and khakis. Just what my kids loved . . .

I didn't have time to doubt myself today, and the kids were worried about when they could see Tova again. "She'll be back tomorrow."

"Tomorrow," Grayson repeated, looking as forward to her entering our house in the morning as I was.

He'd made so much progress, yet a huge change loomed on the horizon.

I needed to talk to Curtis about getting an appointment

made with a counselor so Grayson could talk to someone. The transition might be hard on him. New town. New school. Less of me . . .

Was I making the right decision?

I restarted the cartoon. When the kids were engrossed, I went into the office, keeping the door open in case they needed me.

I dialed Eliot, but he didn't answer. He could be legitimately busy but also ignoring me since I hadn't gotten any further in figuring out how the company could pay for an indoor riding ring.

Instead, I rang Wilder.

"Yeah," he answered.

"Am I interrupting donut time?"

"Ha ha, fucker." Wilder hated the cop and donut joke, but it was also ironic that for a guy without much of a sweet tooth, he fucking loved donuts. "How much are you missing me?"

"I dream about you every night."

"As you should. What's up?"

I didn't normally call him if it wasn't for business. Wilder could act like a giant chip sat on his shoulder, but he wasn't one to talk. Sutton would back me up on that. "I'm trying to nail down dates for working cattle."

"You're coming back for that?"

"Why wouldn't I?" It'd always been a family affair, no matter how many hired guys the ranch had. Working cattle was one of the highlights of my year. I could shed the suit and watch my kids play in the dirt. Even Meg had looked the other way for ranch weekends.

"The kids. How they doin'?"

I leaned back in my creaky office chair. "They're good. I found a nanny, and she's been with us all week."

"Is that the young girl Aggie told me about?"

"She's thirty-three."

Wilder grunted. "Aggie said she was hot."

I dropped to sit normally. The chair let out a long groan. "What does that have to do with anything?"

"Just wondering if she's helping you loosen up."

"Fuck, Wilder. My wife—"

"Cody." Wilder used his cop voice. Then he sighed. "Jesus, it's none of my fucking business. But . . . we were all worried about you after Meg died, and then you want to ship off the kids—"

"I'm not shipping them off. I'm finding the best environment for them to grow up in."

"Sure."

My siblings said a lot with one fucking word. "Fuck off." For a brother who didn't talk about his feelings much, he was running his mouth a lot today.

"Got it. 'S okay though, you know."

"What's okay?" I asked, punctuating my question with massive amounts of irritation.

"To move on. Doesn't mean you loved Meg any less."

"What do you know about it? I lost my wife to a brain tumor. You lost yours because your work is your mistress."

The line went silent.

I scrubbed a hand down my face. "Goddammit, I'm sorry. I didn't mean—"

"Maybe ask yourself what you're going to lose because you won't quit working."

I drew in a sharp breath. Wilder could be tenacious, like a dog with roadkill. I could be the same. "I saw Sutton yesterday."

He went quiet again. Yeah, it was a low blow but also a relief to get the focus off my mess of a life. "How is she?" he asked gruffly.

Stressed. Sad. Lonely. I'd seen it all in the first minute of chatting with her. "Good. Her vet clinic is finished, and her doors are open. There's no sign. I'm not sure what she's calling it."

"Sutton's Animal Care. That's what Aggie said anyway."

"Simple. Concise."

"Just like her. Look, uh, Eliot wants to work cattle starting next weekend. I have it off, and Austen's coming home for leave to help with that and stick around for the Fourth."

"I'll be there Saturday."

"With the kids?" His unspoken question echoed between us. *With the nanny?*

"That's the plan," I said tightly. I had no idea about Tova. We'd probably stay a little longer than the weekend. She could get a few days off. I'd still pay her. She needed it. Would she be too proud to accept it?

She'd negotiated, and I'd sensed her need. I hadn't wanted to exploit it. Hiring her solved so many issues while creating a few I didn't know how to deal with other than stroking one out in the shower each morning.

I hated that I went to bed each night anticipating that damn dream.

⚜

Tova

I was in the park on one of the swings, my phone held so the sun didn't interfere with the screen. "Love you, Mom. I'll be back to visit as soon as possible."

My mom's drawn face filled the tablet. Her smile was higher on her left side than her right, and her wave was visible. Her goodbye was slurred. Fuck her ex ten ways 'til Sunday. I wanted to talk to her, tell her everything, and get her advice. She'd use every bit of her strength to help me get through this mess with Frederick. I couldn't worry her. She'd never admit to feeling guilty about being there for me like she wanted, but I saw it. Just like I was sure she could tell something was bothering me. Our mutual agreement to not pry would hold firm a little longer.

Andra popped her head next to Mom. She didn't have to provide care this personal, but she was there every Sunday to set up the online call with me and Mom. "Stay on for a moment, Tova." The screen flashed around Mom's simple room. "Lana, I need to speak to Tova before she hangs up. I'll be right back."

In the hallway, the image finally settled on Andra's face. Her salt-and-pepper hair was woven into even rows of braids.

My throat closed up. "Is everything okay?"

The brown skin at the corners of her eyes pinched. "Yes, but . . . a man tried to get in to visit Lana, but he wasn't allowed past the reception desk."

I let out the breath I was holding. "Good. Thank you. Your staff is amazing."

"Given her history, we band around her a little tighter." Andra's smile turned comforting, like she hoped to take the edge off the memories. "But I wanted to let you know. Again."

"Once Frederick realizes he can't get to me through Mom, he'll back off." He'd have to. He had everything of mine already. His pride wouldn't let him try again, would it?

"I can out-stubborn the best. Same time next week?"

"Thanks, Andra."

After hanging up, I swayed on the swing and stared at the thick, green grass of the park. I needed good money and a long-term job. Scrolling through job postings nearby, I was ready to give up when I spotted Vienne leaving the diner with Catherine and a guy who slouched like he wanted to be anywhere but upright. Jumping off the swing, I jogged across the street, my sandals slapping the pavement.

My scratches were healing quickly, but I'd picked a shorts jumpsuit with a longer hem to cover them in case I ran across the Knights.

I wasn't spending my time in the park in hopes I'd see them. Not at all.

My body hadn't quit burning since that last talk with Cody before I left yesterday.

Who was I kidding? I'd been in an ignited state since I'd met him, but after he swung me around the dining room and kitchen and I'd been pressed for brief seconds against his hard body, I'd been smoldering.

Catherine saw me, a spark of interest lighting her eyes before she reframed into a scowl. She tugged on her mom's hand.

I slowed. "Hey, Vienne."

The guy kept going, but Vienne stopped. Her gaze lit up. "Tova, hi."

"I forgot to stop over and ask Catherine for your number." I'd been too distracted, wishing Cody had a milk mustache I could lick off. "I wanted to check if there's an evening that works each week for the two of you." I gave Catherine a smile. "That is, if you want to work with me. It doesn't matter. Whatever moves you want—if I don't know them, we can learn them together—except for ballet. And fair warning, I suck at tap, but I was in lessons for a couple of years."

She shrugged, but the interest was back. "I like, um, just like . . . whatever. It doesn't matter."

"Freestyle it is." I grinned, loving how easily she broke.

My attempts to reach out weren't for nothing. "You can pick a song, and we'll come up with choreography."

I glanced at Vienne, but she spun and waved at the guy who was squinting at us like he didn't realize he'd ditched two whole people. "We'll be right there," she called to him, giving me a frantic smile. Did the woman always act like she was twenty minutes late for a meeting? "That's Theo. My fiancé."

Catherine rolled her eyes, and her lower lip stuck out. Was it because of the fiancé part or the Theo part?

"Nice to . . . meet him." I was glad I didn't have to experience a limp handshake with the guy. I could feel his clammy palm just by looking at him.

Vienne was so chic and energetic, and he was . . . not.

Vienne juggled her bag with her phone. She wore fewer bracelets today, no glasses, and was dressed down in white linen shorts and a loose beige shirt. "Oh, here." She thrust her phone at me. "Call yourself."

Thankfully, the burner phone's number was branded into my brain. I'd add a better phone to my long list of items I had to get for myself once I paid for Mom's care for July and settled a few debts with Thelma. I dialed it in, then hung up after a few rings.

"How about Thursdays?" Catherine asked abruptly.

Vienne's light brows rose. "Oh, um . . .works for me." She looked hopefully at me.

"Once a week until we know it's working out?" I asked.

Catherine nodded, excited, then switched quickly to subdued. "Sure."

"I'll double-check with Cody, but getting away for an hour should be fine. If he has a meeting or something, we can always reschedule."

A honk made us all jump. Vienne winced and glanced

back at Theo, her mouth pressed in a line. "We've gotta go, but if it's fine with Cody, come on over this week."

She flashed a quick smile and dragged Catherine to Theo's sport utility truck.

That guy was a douche from what I could tell. Single had to be better, but I didn't live Vienne's life, and I wasn't one to talk. I let Frederick make me think he was my knight in a crisp Tom Ford.

I wandered back to the park and perched on the swing. I stared at my phone for several minutes and finally called Cody. Calling him had nothing to do with wanting to hear his voice or missing spending the day with him and the kids. He had to clear my lessons with Catherine.

His deep "Hello" rumbled through my body. That voice.

"Hey, it's Tova."

"I know." His chuckle made me squirm. A gal's wet dream right there.

"Just in case you have a lot of women calling."

"It's been a while." His rueful response made me wonder how much of a player he'd been before he met his wife. A vision of a crowd of hot women trailing him rose in my head. Too easy to picture. I needed to keep it in mind as a warning. When he decided he was back on the market, he would be collecting as many hearts as he wanted.

"I need to check with you about dance lessons with Catherine for an hour or so on Thursday evenings. After a couple of weeks, we may want to do two evenings a week."

"I don't know, Tova." His serious tone heaped stress on my shoulders. "I don't know if I can do the types of steps Catherine wants to learn. I can't drop it low quite like you."

Laughing, I pushed my toes against the ground, so I was swaying on the swing. "You had me in the beginning, I'm not gonna lie."

"Whatever time you need, we'll make it work."

"Thank you."

"Don't mention it."

A simple "don't mention it." He never said I owed him, but more importantly, he didn't make me feel that way.

After I hung up with him, I got a message from Thelma. **Working a double. Can you water the plants?**

Sunday was plant-watering day. Glad to have something to do, I jogged up to the apartment. Cool air with a light, grease-laden scent from the diner surrounded me. I watered her philodendrons and spider ivy plants.

I put the watering can away under the kitchen sink, then leaned against the counter and looked around. I was no closer to figuring out my dilemma than when I first arrived. The clock was ticking down. Once I was released from being a nanny and received my final paycheck, I'd have a month to come up with another five grand to pay for Mom's care. Then another month. And another.

Stress undulated under my skin, and my brain hooked on to Cody's deep timbre.

Letting out a gusty breath, I pushed off the counter. Thelma's bathroom wasn't the lap of luxury, but I could still take a bath. She was working for eight more hours, and I wouldn't have to worry about hogging the bathroom.

Within minutes, I was sinking into warm, sudsy water. I set my phone on the ledge in case Thelma needed me to do more for her and slid as far into the water as I could go.

My eyelids drifted shut, and I let the pounding of water filling the tub block out the world. The problem was that once my problems were locked away, a face rose in my mind.

A square chin with a defined jawline I thought of tracing with my tongue. Dark eyes that could twinkle and obliterate my senses. A hard body that was lithe but solid and strong.

I'd felt so safe in his hold.

I shut off the water with my foot and stared at the gleam of the silver faucet. The heat from the water somehow made the vision of Cody vivid, so damn real, I could almost feel the way his big hands gripped me to spin me around his kitchen and dining room.

Tingles increased to a dull thrum. I skimmed a hand down my abdomen, the water lightly sloshing.

This was so wrong.

But who was going to find out?

I could finally get myself off and not worry about someone overhearing.

I widened my legs enough to let my hand slip between my thighs. As soon as my fingertip touched my clit, I let out a moan. A gal shouldn't go this long without getting off, but dammit, I wasn't masturbating on Thelma's couch. This tub was my safe space.

I circled my finger in a rhythm I'd had to use with too many partners ever since I learned that not all men cared whether I came or not.

Cody would care. I bet he made sure his partner's world was rocked hard before he even entered her—and then he probably decimated her. The tight control he kept reined in all day had to release. I bet sex with him was trans-formative.

Thinking about Cody was wrong.

Oh, fuck it all anyway. I let out a needy whimper.

He was so hot. Those shoulders of his. They were begging to be footrests while he buried his face in—

Another moan echoed off the walls. I was so damn close, but I didn't know the next time I'd be able to service myself. Edging could be a solo sport too.

God, I needed to come *hard*.

My phone buzzed. I opened my eyes and stilled my

hand. My hips didn't get the message and rocked against my finger.

I just really needed to get off.

Cody's name lit up the screen. I bucked harder.

He was on the other end of the phone. I just talked to him. Couldn't I fantasize about a forbidden man in peace?

More vibrating came from the phone.

I missed my toys.

I shouldn't answer. But he was calling again. What if something was wrong?

Without moving the hand touching myself, I hit "answer" with my free hand but left the phone on the ledge of the tub. "Yeah?" My voice was breathless and tinny in the bathroom.

"Tova? Everything okay?"

It'd be better if I removed my fingers from between my legs. Instead, thanks to his voice filling the bathroom, my index finger twitched. I swallowed a gasp. "No. Yeah. I'm fine. What's up?"

"Is this a bad time?"

The best timing—or the worst. I couldn't decide. "No, I can talk."

"I was surprised you called earlier, and I forgot to mention the kids and I are going to be working cattle with my brother next weekend."

An image of him with a cowboy hat shading his face and his chin dipping down while his tight body was maneuvering a horse filled my head. Damn Hollywood westerns. Damn Cody for being my personal walking wet dream.

My clit practically swelled under my touch, ready to release the restraint I had on my orgasm. My body shook. I fought back the climax. "Okay," I croaked.

"You sure everything's fine?"

"Yep." I swallowed a moan, yet I didn't move my hand.

When was masochism my thing? But this intensity? Right now? If being with him was anything like having him oblivious on the phone with my body hung off a tightrope ready to plummet into an ocean of pleasure, then I was better off living this moment up. I'd never know what it was like to be with him for real.

So, I'd indulge myself.

I teased my clit because I was feeling that naughty. "How long are you going to be gone?" Those few acting lessons I took after graduation finally paid off.

"That's what I wanted to talk to you about."

Talk to me, Alcott Cody Knight. I rocked my hips, and water sloshed, and I didn't fucking care.

There was a loaded pause on the other end. I ignored it. I was squeezing my eyes shut, biting my lower lip, and holding myself on the precipice.

So damn good.

"Want to come?"

"What?" The full-body jolt shoved me off the edge. I gritted my teeth, struggling to keep all the sound contained. A little squeak escaped, a tiny gasp, water rippled and sloshed, and I rode out what I hoped was the quickest orgasm of my life.

There was another pause. "Uh . . . The kids aren't proficient enough on the horses to help, but I'll be on a horse, so I can't chance that someone's not watching them well enough. Would you be able to come to help with them? We'd be gone for three nights."

I sagged against the cool porcelain and flipped my hands to the ledges of the tub. Water tinkled and splashed. I was exhausted.

The best orgasm to date had been from his voice.

You're in trouble, Tova.

Thinking about his offer taxed my sated brain. I should

be wary. I should pass. Risk the pay cut for four days off. But I was tired of fighting everything. So I answered now and hoped I wouldn't regret it later. "No problem." I even sounded sleepy. "I can go with you."

"All right. I'll get more details for you tomorrow."

"Okay," I murmured and stared at the phone and the seconds ticking by. For once, I didn't feel so lonely.

Another pause. "I'll let you go and finish, uh, whatever you're doing."

Oh, Stern Daddy. I already finished.

Nine

TOVA

"Tova." Thelma didn't have to say more than my name. That alone radiated all her disappointment.

"I know." I leaned against the counter by the sink in the galley kitchen. Thelma was at the table, her damp hair hanging to dry before bed.

For two days, I'd ruminated over my decision to tell Cody I'd go with him. I'd vacillated between berating myself up one side and down the other to being completely chill. The trip would be fine. *Fine.*

"You're going to the middle of nowhere with a man you've only known for a few weeks, and you'll be surrounded by his family—his people—and not know a single soul."

I nodded, my mouth dry. He'd been locked in his office all day Monday and Tuesday, only coming out to give me information for the days and times we'd be leaving. He'd thoughtfully decided to go to Buffalo Gully on Friday so I could work with Catherine on Thursday night.

I fought off more guilt. I lusted after the considerate, off-limits man.

"What the hell, Tova?" She slid out a long Newport and looked around like she was going to find a lighter and smoke for real.

"I'll have my phone with me. I can report in regularly. The kids are there. Nothing will happen around the kids." Any smart woman would have reservations about going away with a man she'd just met. A lot of my brain cells didn't work around the man, but he was a dutiful father.

She tapped the filtered portion of the cigarette against the table. "You like him."

"I do." I sighed and sat across from her. "I'd like to think he's legitimately a good man, but I'll be careful. I'll send updates on my location, and I have money if I need to make a quick getaway."

She grunted. "Good luck finding public transportation in the Wild West."

"There's an airport. Flights come in the morning and leave before noon or in the early evening. If all else fails, I'll steal his truck. But . . . I don't think I'll have to."

"You didn't think Frederick would take control of your whole life and try to traffic you either."

I slumped in the chair. "I gambled with Frederick and the house won." Panic about supporting myself and Mom had gotten to me.

She nodded, her mouth pursed. "What's going on with him?" She gave me a steady look like she knew I wasn't telling her everything I knew.

"He's tried getting in to see Mom." I wouldn't have told her, but she was worried about the Montana trip. So was I, but not for my safety. My heart was in danger more than anything else. I didn't need to get wrapped up in the Cody fantasy more than I was. Being in Crocus Valley, working as his nanny, I could be rational. I didn't need him to be real, attainable even. But since we would be returning to his home, the one he had with his wife, I might also realize just how unattainable he was.

Besides, he was shipping his kids off, and the idea still broke my heart.

"What are you going to do about him?" she asked.

It took a second before I realized she was talking about Frederick. "Nothing." He'd take one look at Mom and see that she couldn't tell him anything. Mom was mostly nonverbal. She could communicate with one-word answers, but they were slurred thanks to the stroke and lack of care afterward. "I'm more afraid his attempts to get to her will make the staff think having Mom around is a danger to the other residents and kick her out."

"Can they do that?"

"I don't know. Frederick isn't an idiot." Saying it out loud was freeing. He was a clever man, and I'd lost in the battle of wits. I'd had to worry about survival, and he didn't.

I had even more worries now, but being with Cody didn't resonate as a gamble. I had rapidly developed an affection for him I hadn't had for anyone.

Thelma shook her head. "Maybe we should get Frederick a message," she said. "Tell him if he tries to enter that place one more time, you'll file a restraining order, and he can explain publicly why the son of Mr. High and Mighty Opera House chased off his girlfriend."

The bad publicity threat would work the best, but he could also spin it so I was the bad guy. The crazy ex-girlfriend. If he hadn't yet, he'd have me blacklisted from the entire entertainment industry. I'd return to California for Mom and figure out the job aspect later. If Frederick destroyed my reputation, I could find work in Las Vegas and be half a day's drive away.

"I don't have the power to risk it. He'd twist it to make me look awful." I couldn't afford another game of wits with him. "It's best I lie low, and being on a ranch in the middle of nowhere would help."

"Hmph." She puffed her unlit cigarette. "I don't like it."

"I'll be fine. Cody isn't Frederick."

"But at least we know what Frederick is."

I opened my mouth to tell her that I knew what Cody was. He was a devoted dad who was afraid he'd mess up, so he was pushing his kids away. The man was restrained, but it wasn't because he couldn't control himself. He wanted to do right by everyone in his life, but by closing off his feelings, he didn't realize it was those emotions he needed in order to make the right decision—for himself and everyone else.

But I was the nanny, and I'd have to remember my place if I wanted to get back from this trip with my heart intact.

Cody

Buffalo Gully was less than three hours from Crocus Valley, so the Montana weather was no different. The partly cloudy sky and light wind were stark reminders that I worked in an office after growing up toiling outside every day of my youth. I used to tell myself I was lucky—I could choose my line of work when Barns could've flexed his control and put me in charge of the ranch like Eliot was.

Standing in front of my house outside of Buffalo Gully,

I wasn't sure how lucky I was. The desk and chair had chains on them I couldn't escape.

Wouldn't it be nice to have some cattle of my own? A way for the kids to experience ranching without the life consuming them?

No. Those days were done.

Wilder leaned against his white patrol SUV with his arms crossed, inspecting me. I'd grown used to seeing him in his uniform of khaki pants with a brown, almost black, shirt and a brown, almost black, felt hat. He'd been parked by a popular speed trap like he'd been waiting for us and followed me in once I hit Buffalo Gully city limits. Tova's wide gaze had plastered on me until I explained he was one of my annoying younger brothers. She got a quick introduction to Wilder before the kids dragged her into the house.

His presence was the only thing that helped take my mind off the phone call from Sunday. Had she been taking a bath? Doing dishes? Did a person make those noises when washing a plate?

I'd heard a breathy moan. A little gasp. And they weren't from fucking dishes.

Fuuuck. I jacked off in the shower morning and night, and if Tova hadn't been home with the kids, I'd have been stroking one out at noon too.

Ever-present desire, more acute since the car ride in a cab surrounded by her rosewater scent, fisted itself hard around my insides. I tightened my abs and willed the feeling to vanish already. I couldn't take much more of this torture, and now being home, where I had lived with my disgruntled wife, wasn't helping the flurry of emotions inside my chest.

I met Wilder's steady gaze. "Something on your mind?" I'd been a dick on our last call, and the feeling he was going to return the favor was strong.

"That's your fucking nanny?" Wilder asked.

I didn't appreciate the disbelief in his voice. It wasn't awe at her beauty or how her tank top was the exact shade of blue as her eyes. He didn't leer at her legs, which could make a guy drive off the road, or the way her ass filled out her tiny jean shorts. He frankly did not buy that I hired her to watch the kids and no more.

"Yes," I said tightly. "I know you're single now but behave."

His expression darkened. "The divorce isn't finalized. I can thank Barns for that," he muttered.

Our father had tied up our inheritance with the Knight businesses, and the process added more time and legal fees to his divorce. Still, I was pleased to hear he wasn't out hunting for a Sutton replacement and that he wasn't eyeballing Tova with more than rampant curiosity.

"Sutton's feeding our cats while we're gone." And playing with them. Guilt was a band around my heart when I thought of giving them back to Aggie to find a home when the kids went to live with their grandparents. Each morning, Cheetoh was curled around Ivy's legs in her bed, and I found Grayson hugging Lilac before he'd get dressed or eat breakfast.

Wilder eyed me, his expression carefully blank, but his question was loud and clear. Why was I telling him?

"Just wanted to let you know she's in our lives. I don't think she'll ever not be my sister."

He gave a curt nod. "I understand," he said gruffly. "Glad she's in your kids' lives."

"Me too."

"It'll be harder when they're in Helena."

I slanted a hard gaze at him, and he shrugged unfazed. I rolled my eyes. "Grayson's gotten a lot better." Thanks to Tova. "I don't want him to go back to school where everyone assumes he'll have problems."

"You don't have to explain it to me."

"Don't I?" I had to explain it to everyone I came across. Aggie often gave me a guarded look, and she'd been the one to urge me to take some time and get away with Grayson and Ivy before they left. I knew she was hoping I would change my mind.

There was Tova's carefully blank reaction. And now Wilder.

Would Austen and Eliot have opinions?

Of course they fucking would. They were Knights.

Wilder's radio squelched. He turned away and spoke into the handset clipped by his collar. When he spun back, he lifted his chin. "See you in the morning. I've gotta go deal with a stolen pickup."

"Is crime getting that bad?"

He grimaced. "Goddamn oil fields. Guys think they can make money in the middle of nowhere while breaking laws. But no, this time it's Guy McCormick. He's got dementia, refuses to be put into a home, and then argues with his wife. This is the third time this week his pickup hasn't been stolen. Delilah sold it three years ago."

Guy and Delilah McCormick had lived in the same house by the elementary school since well before I was born. I didn't envy Wilder for dealing with a couple we grew up getting lemonade and cookies from. "See you in the morning. Bright and early."

He hopped in his sheriff's department SUV and took off. I faced the house that was supposed to feel like coming home, and instead, I was full of trepidation. Looming in front of me was an imposing, two-story farmhouse with a wraparound porch and an equally expansive deck on the back that faced the valley on Knight land but was as close to town as possible. Despite the bushy trees and sparse brush on the property, the house was fairly isolated. The closest neighbor was over half a mile away, heralding the outskirts of town.

When I thought of this place since Meg's death, it was with cool detachment. A structure to hang my hat in and store all my kids' belongings. I'd rather work in the office at the ranch than in the house, and we were too isolated for the kids to have neighborhood kids who could hop a fence or ride a bike over. I wasn't sure how to feel about being here. What kind of mind-fuck would it be to walk into a home I shared with my wife and lust after the nanny?

I came to Buffalo Gully with a plan. Tova could hang with the kids while I got a few groceries for the four days and three nights we'd be here. When we weren't sleeping, we'd be at the ranch.

Solid plan, Cody.

I went to the front door. The porch didn't creak like the one in town, and Wilder had stopped by to crank the AC. I could finally get a decent night's sleep. As if rising heat and an old air-conditioning unit were why I wasn't sleeping well.

Walking through the house, I didn't look around. I knew what I'd see and where everything was. This house was no longer a home. We had slept here. We had eaten here. We'd all spent a ton of time at the hospital in Billings and then hospice.

For a heartbeat, I envied the kids for leaving at the end of the summer. They could go to a home without all the heavy memories. Without the mantle of "what-ifs" and "should've beens."

I followed the voices to Grayson's bedroom. Tova was holding the long neck of an old Epiphone guitar.

She lifted her gaze to mine, her eyes filled with question and awe. "He said this is your old guitar. Does that mean you play?"

"Would you believe I learned to impress a girl?"

She laughed. "I'm sensing a theme."

I craved her smile and drank her in like a man who hadn't had a drop of water all week. I'd barely had a drop of her, deliberately abstaining from all things Tova since that torturous phone call.

Yet I wasn't putting up a fight in my house.

"He was teaching me to play," Grayson said matter-of-factly, "but the noise hurt Mommy's head."

Tova flinched but recovered quickly. She gave Grayson an understanding smile. "That was thoughtful of you to store it so nicely in your closet so she could feel better."

"Can I learn to play?" Ivy asked.

Grayson had been close to Ivy's age when I'd started working with him. We'd only managed a few hours here and there, but that was all he'd needed. What the kid lacked in athleticism, he made up for with musical talent. Just like the dancing. He had coordination when paired with a tune. Perhaps the noise helped him concentrate.

"It's my guitar." Grayson angrily reached for the instrument. Tova released her hold like she was afraid to damage it. "He said I could keep it in my room."

"Grayson," I said, sensing a meltdown. No one would blame him. We were back in an environment that was so damn familiar yet just as foreign as another rented house. "Remember how excited you were to learn? Ivy is, too, and I'd love to teach both of you someday, but it's not happening this weekend because we're here to help Uncle Eliot."

"Can you show Tova how you can play?" he asked, handing me the guitar.

The familiar weight in my hand summoned memories. Of missing home while I was in college. Delight in the concentration of learning to play. Next came understanding. I would finally quiet the to-do list in my head when I played. Nothing seemed as urgent or as critical while I picked out a melody. Was that what my son needed? A temporary escape from all the expectations? The freedom to just be?

I glanced around the small, square bedroom. His twin bed was in one corner, his dresser in another. If I sat on the bed, they'd pile around, and Tova would either have to stand or sit on the bed with me.

Not happening.

"Let's go to the living room." I could take the upholstered window seat, and Tova and the kids could sit on the couch and chairs.

I was like the Pied Piper leading everyone out of the room. I dutifully plastered my gaze on the floor to walk through the hallway full of artfully arranged photographs. I didn't usually avoid looking at the family photos Meg had hung around the house before, but with a woman I couldn't quit thinking about fucking? It seemed wrong.

When Ivy announced, "That's my mom," I briefly squeezed my eyes shut.

"This picture is so cute," Tova gushed. "Tell me about it."

I didn't have to turn to know which one she was talking about. Meg hired a friend to do a photo shoot one summer. The girls wore ivory-colored dresses, while Grayson and I wore polo tops in a similar shade. The day had been hot, and Meg had been extra uptight that day. Family pictures always did that for her.

"I don't remember," Ivy said.

Should I be grateful? The day hadn't been miserable, but photo shoots hadn't been a fun family activity.

Grayson peered at the photo. "Mom got mad at Dad for telling jokes."

Tova sent a questioning glance my way like she couldn't

believe I'd tell jokes while working to look like a perfect family.

"I meant to lighten the mood," I explained. "Meg was trying not to be frustrated with her friend and keep her cool with the kids, but we were all tired and hadn't eaten supper yet."

"Getting the right photo can be stressful." Tova put a hand on Grayson's shoulder. "And you have kids in almost white clothes on green grass? I bet your mom was worried."

Tova had nailed the day, and Meg, in one take.

"That was the only picture that turned out." What Tova said clarified my understanding of the day. Like the kids, I remembered the curt words hissed back and forth between us while we struggled to emulate a happy, carefree, and spontaneous family. None of the words described us. "The photographer, bless her innocent soul, brought bubbles, thinking she was in for a carefree summer shoot."

"It wasn't carefree," Grayson said in his best Eeyore voice.

"Until the bubbles!" Ivy said jubilantly, her smile triumphant. "I remember now."

"That picture was when the photographer turned on a bubble machine she'd kept hidden." I finally looked at the photo. Meg's mouth was open, surprised as hell, a direct contrast to her crisp dress and tightly wound hair. The kids were delighted, and my grin was full of stark relief, giddy at watching Grayson and Ivy try to race to the bubbles instead of bickering with each other. The image was full of movement, lightness, and charm. The photographer had captured a feeling we couldn't otherwise achieve without the impromptu bubbles.

This picture was a perfect representation of what we'd been like. An uptight family, interspersed with moments of lightness.

Would they get more of the uptight or more of the light with my in-laws?

My hand tensed on the guitar, a dawning realization pushing at my brain.

"The bubbles were fun." Grayson's concession lifted the mood, and I shut off my mind.

"I'm glad they worked." Tova propped her hands on her hips and studied the photo. "The bubbles helped the photographer capture the real you." She gave me an almost shy glance. "All of you."

Tova wasn't afraid to talk about Meg. But then she likely wasn't having naughty dreams about me and therefore wasn't feeling like a lecher out of place in this house.

I gripped the guitar and sat on the bench. A cool blast of air rode up my back from the vent between the bench and the window. Sweet, cool air that helped me focus.

Tova took a seat on the couch, a kid on each side of her. She folded a long leg under her and wiggled to get cozy. Hugging the kids, she murmured to each one about how excited she was to hear me play.

A lump formed in my throat. Whenever I brought the guitar out before, I'd hear *Oh, that thing again?* We couldn't blame the brain tumor on Meg's sensitivity to sound. She'd been selectively sensitive.

I hadn't realized the kids had noticed so much. Tova must think we had been an awful, rigid family.

We had been quite a few times. Some days, it felt like all the time.

I tried to swallow the emotion clogging my chest, but the guilt was too thick, almost tangible. Because I wanted this. I wanted a woman to be impressed with what I could do. I wanted my kids to be excited about something I enjoyed. I might've learned guitar in college to get noticed by a girl in the dorms across from mine, but I truly loved doing something so different from what I was raised to do.

Tova lifted her gaze to mine, and her smile faltered.

What did my expression look like? I schooled my features to hopefully come off as passive when inside a storm raged. I wanted so much more than what I'd had, and I was shitty for it.

I cleared my throat and tested the strings. I messed with the tuning until I was satisfied. "Okay, see if you can guess this song." I strummed out a few chords of Dolly Parton's "Jolene" and watched Tova's thrilled smile spread across her face.

I would be a shitty guy for a little bit longer.

Ten

TOVA

I lay in the guest bedroom, covers thrown back, sprawled across the bed. Goose bumps dotted my skin, but I didn't care. After being restricted to a scratchy couch, I wanted to utilize each inch of the queen bed.

The house was cute. The inside reminded me of Frederick's place, oddly enough. The two-story country home didn't resemble the mansion in anything more than its vibe. Someone like Vienne designed this home. They decorated it. The insides were tasteful, almost subdued. Organizing bins filled the kids' closets and the kitchen was ordered with near military precision. Nothing that described what the family was like could be deciphered from the décor.

How stifling.

I wasn't a slob, but if I had a home that was all mine, I'd want to relax in it. I would sprawl like I was doing now. I would have throw pillows that I actually put my head on when I lay on the couch to watch TV. I'd have a cup by the fridge—all the time. Just for water. Just in case.

I could fully unpack my suitcase for once in my life.

I'd pull the trunk out of storage that Thelma was keeping for me. The blankets Grandma crocheted would be on the back of the couch. I didn't care if they didn't match a damn thing. I'd find the pictures she cross-stitched and the kitchen towels. I had an entire bundle of embroidered dish towels Grandma had saved from her mom. She told me to use them. "If they don't end up ripped and stained, they're pointless," she'd said.

I giggled when I thought of using them in Frederick's immaculate kitchen. His personal chef would've gotten a kick out of the one with the words "This towel isn't the only thing that's dirty" sewn onto it. Frederick would've hemorrhaged and kicked me out.

I should've used them.

Straightening the blankets, I tried to burrow into the pristine sheets and go to sleep.

No luck.

I flung them off again and let the cool air sweep over me.

A guitar twang made me sit up. Was Cody awake?

The moods that man had been through since we arrived made my head spin and my heart ache. How hard was it to be back here? Happy memories didn't bounce off these walls. The only two rooms that looked like they were lived in were the two offices across the hall from the guest room. The bedrooms were upstairs.

A longer melody played this time. Slower. Sadder. It stopped.

I shouldn't be nosy, but I stood anyway. I wasn't wearing a bra under the souvenir shirt I'd bought at the airport, but the garment was baggy and it was dark. Padding through the house, I followed the sound to the back deck.

Twice as large as the one in Crocus Valley, it had the same unlived-in feel as the rest of the house.

The glass sliding door was open. The music was louder, a melancholy tune that was also sweet. I couldn't come up with the name, but I knew I'd heard it before.

I crept to the screen door and peered out. Flies buzzed around the yard light, and the tang of citronella hung in the air. I barely noticed any of that. Cody reclined in a chair, the guitar at an angle that didn't look comfortable to play. His feet were kicked up and bare, and he had no shirt on.

No shirt.

Shadows cloaked him, but I suddenly had a cat's night vision. His long, slender feet that were usually hidden in loafers, and occasionally, if I was a lucky gal, cowboy boots were crossed at the ankles. Was every part of him sexy?

I couldn't see his chest, but I was desperate to. I pushed open the screen door before I decided if it was a good idea or not.

He stopped playing and cocked his head back. "You might want to come all the way out. You're lettin' bugs in."

I stepped out and closed the door behind me.

He strummed a few notes. "Sorry if I woke you."

"I couldn't sleep." I pulled out an Adirondack chair next to him and curled into it, hugging my arms around myself. The air wasn't cool, but it wasn't warm either. "Besides, you're not the loudest thing out here." The croak of what must have been a hundred frogs filled the air. Maybe some crickets. The noise was like the country nights soundtrack for movies.

"Must be different for you."

"Sort of, but not how you think."

His long, talented fingers softly strummed a few strings. He was so damn relaxed, but his chest and stomach still rippled with strength. I could watch him all night.

"Where I lived before was so big no noise could get inside if the hired help didn't allow it." His quiet, easy contemplation must've been why I kept talking. "I lived with my ex in a mansion, believe it or not. Beverly Hills." I cocked a brow like I knew the idea of me roaming a huge estate like the lady of the house was ridiculous.

"Moving on up," was all he said.

"No, I moved backward." I leaned my head against the wooden back of the chair. "I thought . . . I thought I knew better."

"The prince turned out to be the frog?"

"Yes." Why was it so easy to talk to this man?

I didn't know him that well, and I should be wary. But I also wanted to tell someone my story. To share what had happened without waxing on about what I should've done and how I needed to protect myself in the future.

"I thought he genuinely found me at one of my shows. I didn't realize he was on the hunt. I was used to men like . . ." I nibbled my lower lip. No one knew the full story of my life but Thelma, and while it was tragically common, it was still mine. Some days, my past was all I felt like I had. "My mom had poor taste and low standards. I grew up determined to be different. I ditched a guy as soon as he seemed controlling or irresponsible with money, or if he had a temper that could turn into more. I was smart. Street smart. Then I wasn't."

He didn't respond but lightly flicked his fingers over the strings like he knew the ambient noise made it more comfortable for me to speak rather than face silence.

"He was rich. Charming. He seemed to treat the people he hired decently." If decently meant he didn't see them. I mistook a lack of outward cruelty for kindness. "And he pretended to be supportive of me, of my hopes and dreams. I didn't realize I was a mark. I thought there was a chance, and I was cautious, but he lured me further into his web."

"He fell into the controlling category."

I let out a long sigh. A light breeze ruffled my hair, and I inhaled a long stretch of clean, fresh air. No exhaust fumes. No human stench. No fake fragrances. This place was real and so different from what I was used to. Just like Cody. "I had to make a new category for him. I'm used to two-bit losers. Small-time scammers and perverts. Frederick is a predator." I hugged myself tighter, and it wasn't because I was chilly. "He booked one of the clubs I had a steady gig in and wanted me to perform for his biggest clients—and then fuck them."

The notes turned into a screech. He flattened his hand over the strings and stared at me. "Tell me that fucker is in a gutter with his balls crushed."

Rage played over his face, but I remained relaxed. Cody was my safety net. A buffer between me and a cruel world that didn't care about girls who just wanted a place to call theirs.

"I wish. Thelma saved my ass. Again." He cocked a brow, but I left it at that. My story was easier to tell than my mom's. "I had switched my bank and investment accounts to his company and my management to him. I figured I didn't have much money anyway. It all goes to Mom. But I was saving some, and thanks to his investing, I was earning more, but I'm locked out."

"You can't get to it." A hard twang resonated into the night. "That fucker. Does he know where you are?"

"No. He's . . ." I licked my dry lips. "He's, uh, looking for me. I think."

"What about your mom?"

"She doesn't know where I am." And she couldn't tell Frederick. "I gave my contact information to the home. I don't know why he doesn't just go find another target but then he invested two years in me."

"To traffic you."

I nodded. Heat burned the backs of my eyes. I hadn't cried once about Frederick. A sign I hadn't cared enough. Yet I had a feeling when it was time to part ways with the Knights, tears would stream down my face.

"He's a bastard. Anything you need, tell me. My brothers and I might just be dumb hicks from the country, but we've got resources."

He used the perfect mix of righteous protection and humor. I smiled. "Oh? You've had to use them?"

"We ran off Aggie's husband."

"A different one?"

"Nope. Ansen."

Grateful for the change in subject and his blanket support, I smiled. "That sounds juicy."

"Barns—my dad—paid him to marry her ten years ago. I thought something was up, but I couldn't get to the books until everyone was so busy before the wedding. I confronted Ansen, Aggie told him to fuck off, and me and my brothers made sure he did."

"Ten years ago? How are they together again?"

"She'd never confess to me, but Wilder said she and Sutton got drunk one night, and next thing we knew, Aggie had hired Ansen and swore there was nothing between them."

"And now they're married," I mused. "So romantic."

He grunted and plucked a string.

"If you're not her brother," I added.

"He's a good guy. He probably was then, too. Barns was one of those controlling men you'd want to stay away from." A troubled frown played over his mouth. Cody sounded determined not to follow in his footsteps.

"Frederick definitely isn't a good guy."

"He's a pussy."

I liked the rough side to Cody. "He has the money to be a bully."

"That may be true, but it doesn't mean he's not a coward. A good man will do what's right no matter what, no matter how hard it is, and no matter how much money they have."

"And you, Cody?" I was close to whispering, desperate to hear the truth. "Are you a good man?"

"I'd like to think so."

He didn't sound so confident. I kept pushing. "What's the hardest thing you've done, no matter what, where money didn't make a difference?"

He strummed a few strings. The sounds were lower, deeper. Sadder. I didn't think he was going to answer me, maybe he didn't have anything, but he ran his thumb down the strings and said, "Stay married."

Cody

What the hell did I just say?

Tova's lush lips parted. She must think I was lowering myself to her ex's level. I had no other explanation. The words had popped out, like they'd been caged in a dark, terrifying corner of my mind and escaped at the worst possible time.

"You weren't happy?" she asked softly.

The strings anchored me to this world. I wasn't lost in the past. The guitar marked a time before Meg. The last time I felt like myself. "I wasn't unhappy."

She was quiet for a beat. "I understand that more than I thought I would."

I glanced at her, surprised, but I was met with an understanding stare. "You do?"

"I wasn't in love with Frederick. But I thought we had a mutual relationship, and I was okay that it wasn't built on love." Her smile dipped. "I know it's not the same as you and your wife, but I get it."

"I loved my wife." I plucked the G string. I should've been doing guitar therapy since the funeral. The sound soothed my nerves, made my world seem like it was spinning in the right direction. "I respected her more." I hadn't thought a lot about my relationship with Meg as much as I had in the last few weeks. It just was. Like when Mama left, and I was it for my siblings. It just was. The kids needed a stable home, and my in-laws fit the description better than me. It just was. I was thinking about it all now. "I knew I was a lucky bastard that a woman like her was interested in me. That she moved here, away from the city, and still managed to kick ass at a job made five times more difficult because she was stuck with me."

"I think you're selling yourself short."

"You didn't know Meg. She was amazing." I strummed over all the strings again. "But she was also Meg. Prickly. Moody. Ambitious in a way where she'd never be satisfied in Buffalo Gully. She wasn't warm, and she kept her emotions tightly wound until I wondered how deeply she actually felt." I plucked the strings harder. I forced myself to be gentle. The last thing I wanted was for the kids to hear me. "Even when the tumor was diagnosed, she was practical. Almost businesslike. I thought maybe it was a defense mechanism. What the fuck did I know about finding out I was dying? But . . . I'm not sure. She was ruthlessly efficient and almost harder on me

—and the kids," I finished with a sigh of resigned admission.

"I didn't know her, but it sounds like a defense mechanism."

"I don't know," I murmured. "We were married for twelve years, and at first it was fine. Then Grayson came and life got busier, and she seemed to thrive on the stress, but she wasn't a doting mom. I was surprised when she got pregnant with Ivy. She said it was so they'd have each other to play with. Like cats."

"Not every mom acts like she walked off a sitcom." Tova didn't sound horrified. I hadn't known what to think when Meg had compared our kids to pets.

"She loved them, don't get me wrong. In her own way. I guess . . ." Was I really going to say it? The sentiment that had kept me awake. The astonishing realization that had taken years to figure out came to me minutes after seeing Tova in the house with my kids. "It's not the way I wanted to love."

"Oh, Cody." She unwrapped her arms from herself and scooted to the edge of the chair, propping her elbows on her knees. "You remained the devoted father and husband out of loyalty?"

"She was my wife. I wasn't going to leave like my mama did." Another jolting twang. Frustrated, I put the guitar on the smooth, metal outdoor table. "Sorry, I didn't mean to dredge up my childhood trauma."

"We could do that weird competition thing people do with scars and try to one-up each other."

"I loved her." The words had to be said. I wasn't convincing myself. I was reassuring myself.

"I know. I can tell." She reached toward me, and I couldn't move. When she closed her warm, small hand around mine, I was a statue, as if I was afraid to scare off the beautiful, wild creature who had entered my life. "It's okay to have complicated feelings about people who are gone—or are even still with us."

She didn't have to tell me who she was talking about. Her mom.

"I'm really glad you're here," I said gruffly and covered her hand with mine.

"Me too."

We were side by side, but we were each crowded on the edge of our seats, leaning against the armrest.

"Tova." I stared at our shadowed hands. Those emotions I kept a tight hold on were unfurling. I had questions. Confessions. I felt things.

"Yeah?" she asked, breathless.

"When we danced the other day . . . I almost kissed you."

"I almost let you."

My breath wheezed out. The slight confirmation that she might feel anything close to what I did chiseled at the flimsy wall I'd built between us. I'd fought my attraction for weeks, and it was only growing stronger. "When I called you last weekend, were you . . ."

"Yes."

A final answer. A triumphant answer. I knew it. I craved more of what I heard. "I wanted to be in there. I wanted to be the reason you made that little squeak."

"You were." She drew her lower lip in between her teeth. There was fear and uncertainty in her eyes. Her admission could have driven a giant wedge between us, but instead it obliterated my mental guards.

"Christ, Tova. I want you so damn bad." I slid out of the chair and dropped to my knees in front of her, my hands on her legs. Her bare fucking legs, with skin so soft it shouldn't be possible. Her soft gasp was swallowed by the night, but she didn't tense. If anything, she edged closer to me. "Do you know how much I've dreamed of getting that little moan out of you?" I stroked my hands up, the thin fabric of her shorts the only thing between us. "Do you know how often I get off with the image of you in my head?"

That should send her running.

It didn't. She pushed her hands through my hair and tipped my head back. The porch light backlit her. I saw the beauty who sold out performances. I'd pay my entire life's savings to watch her dance.

"I thought I could keep myself in check, but god, Cody. You're just so—" Her mouth crashed onto mine, and any restraint I had left was gone. Eradicated.

The flavor of mint and coconut ChapStick filled my mouth. Two tastes that were now my favorite. I dragged her to me, her ass nearly falling off the seat.

She whimpered and widened her legs to make more room for me. I deepened the kiss, stroking inside her hot mouth with my tongue. She met me stroke for stroke. The woman kissed with abandon, just like she danced. And like when she danced, she made me want to free myself from rigid expectations. I wanted to be that guy again. The one who learned new skills for a girl. The guy who enjoyed a relationship instead of trying to keep up, afraid that getting left behind meant failure.

I ran my hands over her lush hips and under her baggy shirt. I groaned. Her skin was warm and velvety. "How do you feel so soft?" I licked across her lower lip.

"Moisturizer," she gasped. "Keeps the body makeup from caking."

"I'd love to see you perform." I kissed along her jawline and laved a path down her neck. She tipped her head back with a low moan. Score one for me. "The way you move is like a special gift just for me."

She tightened her hands in my hair. "Cody." Need filled her voice, bordering on pain, and well, I couldn't have that.

I pulled up her shirt and leaned her back. She arched just as the hem passed her breasts. I groaned again. "No bra?"

How had I not noticed?

I hadn't been fucking looking, or I knew I'd be toast. Thanks to the dim light, I couldn't make out much, but her nipples were a rich pink and pebbled so tightly they were begging for relief. Just like my goddamn dream. I dipped my head and drew one into my mouth. Her breathing was ragged, and she hugged my head to her, a silent plea.

How was this my reality right now?

"I don't usually wear underwear to bed either."

"Jesus." I licked across her nipple and looked up at her. "Show me."

Her chest rose and fell, her full, round breasts right in front of my face. Perfect. All of her was perfection, and if lightning struck me from the dark sky, I'd die a happy man.

She flicked her tongue out to run along her bottom lip. I hooked a hand around the back of her neck and caught her mouth again. That tongue was mine.

She made the sexiest mewl and squirmed against me. She only broke away to say, "See for yourself."

Fuck, yes.

She was sitting, and I was impatient. I put my hands on her thighs, touching her as thoroughly as I wanted to the day she got scratched, and brushed upward, going higher and sweeping under the hem of her shorts. They were loose and easy to tug to the side.

I wished the sun was high overhead so I could get a full view of her glistening pussy. What I did see amplified the desire pumping through my veins and pounding in my dick. My damn mouth watered.

"You're bare, Tova." I didn't care either way. She could

be as natural as possible, and I'd still be on my knees, ready to sate myself on her. But I liked the unobstructed sight of how fucking wet she was.

"You haven't seen the G-string I wear to perform. It doesn't cover much."

I lifted my gaze to hers. "Do you still have it?"

She nodded. Her hands had left my hair when I was sneaking a peek, and she gripped the armrests. "Not with me, though."

"And the tassels?" The question came out guttural. I was obsessed with the idea of her tassels.

She nodded again. Part of her shirt had fallen over one breast, but her other nipple held the rest at bay. Like my own personal peep show.

My little striptease.

I grunted and pushed her legs wider. The shorts stretched to hide the perfect view from me, but I shoved them to one side.

"I need to taste you."

Her needy "yes" changed me. I no longer thought, analyzed, or planned. I took.

I descended, my punishing grip keeping the aggravating material out of my way. I couldn't bother with the time to take them off. Licking through her, her salty sweetness coated my tongue. My lust ratcheted impossibly higher. "Goddamn, you taste like heaven."

I tongued her clit, and she bucked into me. "Cody," she hissed. "Just like that."

"Tell me how you play with yourself." I circled her swollen clit one more time. "When you're thinking about me."

She rolled her hips again, demanding more. I let her have it.

A mix of a whimper and a moan left her. "It doesn't take

much." I hummed against her and was rewarded with a flood of heat. She was close already. "Your voice is enough to get me off by itself." Another hum. "God, *yes.*"

Need clawed at my chest. I only paused long enough to say, "Keep going."

She anchored her feet on the edge of the chair, giving me as much access as possible. "I think about how well you danced, and I think you must be dynamite in bed."

My chuckle vibrated into her, and she shivered. "I like to think so."

"Quit talking." Her fingers were twisting in my hair again.

"Yes, ma'am." This time, I set a pace and threaded a finger into her. So fucking wet. I had no more blood left in my brain. My entire supply throbbed in my erection.

She groaned. "When you say 'ma'am,' I can't hold back." Her breath stilted over a gasp. I thrust my finger once and that was enough. "Cody. Oh my god, Cody. Yes. Yes!"

She came hard. Heat flooded from her, and I kept lapping at her little nub. Her body shuddered against my face, and I planned to keep going, to get another orgasm from her, to hear my name spill from her lips because part of me was inside her. I watched her as I devoured her.

A light flicked on above us from the house.

"Fuck." I scrambled back until I was a few feet away from her and caught her stunned blink. She hurried to drag her shirt into place. Craning her neck, she glanced up, worry, shock, and dammit, disappointment etched into her flushed features.

I'd fucked up as soon as I touched her.

‡

Tova

. . .

I was too afraid to move. I couldn't get busted on my third week of being a nanny with the face of the dad in my crotch.

Ugh. I knew better.

The stark terror blazing across Cody's face told me everything. He regretted all of this. He didn't want to be attracted to me. He wasn't ready to rebound. And we were in the house he'd shared with his dead wife.

Another light flipped on. A faint "Daddy?" could be heard.

Cody pushed back and up. "Shit. *Shit.* Wait here."

He rushed inside, and I was left with a throbbing core and a bruised ego.

I rubbed my hands against my face and sat up. My shirt and shorts were still crooked. His command resurfaced. *Wait here.*

I couldn't do that. Did I want to sit outside and find out if I was going to be fired or not?

Before I went to bed, I texted Thelma and told her all was well. Would I have to call in an SOS? I didn't picture Cody pushing me out of the house and slamming the door behind me, but I also didn't know him that well.

Or worse, would he ask me to stick around and be his striptease piece of ass?

Would I say yes?

I had made a monumental mistake with Frederick, and it affected my ability to care for my mom. This seemed so much worse. A two-month gig, and I'd fucked it up for a hot dad playing guitar without a shirt.

I got up and crept into the house. I would crawl into bed, and maybe he'd see that I was gone and decide to pretend he didn't lick me to an amazing orgasm. I couldn't even get myself off that fast or hard.

Could I pretend what we did never happened?

I risked using the main-level bathroom. I could hear his low rumble upstairs while he consoled a crying Ivy.

I was responsible for her being scared that her dad had ditched her in the middle of the night. My track record was getting better and better. The sink had recently been used. Of course, he'd had to clean me off of him before consoling his distraught kid.

I chewed on my guilt while I washed my hands and splashed my face. A quick glance in the mirror, and I skated my gaze away. My face was flushed, my eyes bright. I might be filled with remorse and regret, but my body was humming and hoping for more.

I hated to think Cody was feeling the same, only his remorse was likely more acute. I made mistakes when it came to men, but I wasn't used to being the mistake.

Opening the door, I was met with a tall, grim, still shirt-less man blocking my way.

I gasped and slapped a hand over my mouth just as the inhale was turning into a yelp.

My brain calmed, immediately registering the broad expanse of his chest and how he was towering over me, and I liked it. The wide shoulders capped with muscle. The abs begging for my fingers to run over them. The hard pecs with the scattering of chest hair. Cody wasn't manscaped, and I didn't know that was my thing until now.

"We should talk about—"

"I know." But I didn't want to hear it. "It was a mistake, and I probably shouldn't work for you, but I'm stuck for at least the weekend—"

He planted a finger on my lips. "Nothing about me feels like what we did was a mistake." He stroked his hand along my jaw, and I stared at him, perplexed. This wasn't the confrontation—or shunning—I expected. "Yes, my brain is trying to tell me that it was wrong, but I think it's because . . ." His gaze stroked around the bathroom like he was taking in the whole house. He shook his head. "How do you feel about it? Are you okay?"

He was checking on me? I nodded, unsure what to say. Did I tell him I was silently panicking but wanted to climb him like a stage ladder? Reveal that I was willing to drop to my knees and return the favor? Or better yet, remind him that the guest bedroom was right behind him, and how handy was that?

"I'm okay." I *so* wasn't okay. His tongue had altered me. No one should be able to elicit that much pleasure with a body part. He didn't have to be controlling. I'd hand over my life to get more of what he could do with his mouth.

"Are you sure?" He pulled his hand away, his expression resolute. Did he think his touch was influencing what I said?

Was it?

I thought hard. He deserved an honest answer. "I'm afraid I messed up. I'm a little ashamed that I've been your nanny for three weeks and things have already gotten sexual with you. I worked hard to be taken seriously in my line of work. The nature of it made it more difficult, and here I am, wanting to jump into bed with you."

His gaze softened, and humor lit his eyes. Then it faded. "If we weren't in this house, in Buffalo Gully, where people would talk, things would be different. I'm a recent widower with a hot nanny."

My heart stuttered.

"I don't think I'm ready for the speculation," he admitted softly. "Just like you, I don't want to be a stereotype, someone people assume is a lonely dad who's lusting after the younger nanny."

"Seven years is hardly scandalous."

His smile was quick. "I've been feeling older." He shook

his head. "I want this to be a decision between us. You and me. No one else, past or present. I'm dealing with my feelings about being a widower and moving on, but I want you. I like you. I like your outlook on life, your kind nature, the way you naturally understand my kids. You're an amazing person, and I'm not at all ashamed to be attracted to you. But our circumstances make it seem sleazy. Make me feel like a creep, and if anyone found out, that'd only make it worse. And I can't forget that you're stranded in Crocus Valley, and we both plan to ditch the town soon. Makes the whole decision almost moot."

I processed what he said. His stark confession was calming when I thought I'd be left disappointed. He was going through a lot internally, and I understood what it was like to be labeled and struggle against it. He had kids to think about, and we were like two planets in the universe. Our paths crossed once in a lifetime.

I didn't know a thing about astrology other than I was a Taurus and naturally stubborn.

What did I want?

This snack of a man in front of me. The rest went much deeper than what we'd be allowed in the remaining time we had together. My gaze dropped to his left hand, where his silver wedding ring was covered in shadows.

He noticed and flexed his hand. He studied his ring for a moment. "I kept wearing this for the kids. They've been through so many changes, but . . . When I help at the ranch, I usually take it off." A ghost of a smile passed over his mouth. "Meg picked the ring she wanted because she knew I had zero fucks to give about my own wedding ring."

"It's nice." The ring was solid, like I assumed their marriage had been. A solid marriage wasn't necessarily a passionate one.

"She had good taste." He drew his brows together. "But

I still think of it as more hers than mine." He tugged the ring off, and I let out a soft gasp. Silver flashed in the light as he held it up. Just as quickly, he closed the jewelry in his fist. "Meg wanted her ring to go to Ivy, and I put it in her jewelry box. I'll add mine, and it'll go to G. I'm not living in the past, Tova," he said softly. "But I'm trying to figure out my present, and the one clarity I have is how much I want you."

The warmth flowing through me wasn't only from my earlier orgasm. Removing his ring wasn't performative. I'd lived with and around people who wanted me to think they were someone else so they could take advantage of me. Cody was different. He was conflicted, but only because he wanted to do the right thing for himself, his kids, and me.

Cody Knight was a good man.

"I want you too," I finally said. "I also like you." I loved what he did to my body. "We can table this until we get back to Crocus Valley, and then anything between us there can stay there, and we'll both go in knowing it's temporary."

His jaw didn't clench until the word "temporary" came out. My gut wrenched at the same time.

He stroked his gaze over me. "You really are amazing," he murmured.

Almost shy, I smiled. He leaned in close, his forehead tipping toward mine. Power radiated off him, tension flowing through his body. I met his eyes, the bathroom light highlighting the amber flecks in his deep brown irises. "Good night, Tova," he said and peeled himself away.

"Good night," I whispered to an empty doorway.

These were going to be the three longest days of my life. My next message to Thelma would say I'm fine, but I'd be lying. It should read **My raging case of lady blue balls is going to strangle me, but when I get back, I might get the ride of my life. Can't wait. XOXO.**

Eleven

CODY

Dust hung in the air, and the sun dropped lower in the sky. It was late, the day had been long, but half the cattle had been run through. My body ached from a much-needed day of moving around in nature. I smelled like horse sweat and nervous livestock.

When I returned from the tack room after putting my saddle away, I found my brothers leaning against the wooden pens built into the garage for bottle calves.

I took off the old cowboy hat I'd had for years and ran a hand through my hair, warm and damp from working in the sun all day. "Say it now, fuckers, before we get into the house."

Tova was hanging with the kids in the main house where I'd grown up, though it looked little like it did when I was a kid.

Eliot lived there now. He'd remodeled the kitchen and the living room and was redoing his old bedroom. I didn't ask him why he didn't take Barns's old bedroom. None of us would want to spend a single night there before it was gutted and redone.

Eliot folded his arms. They all looked the same as me. Dusty. Sweaty. Tired but exhilarated. Wilder was out of his uniform for once and looked like the brother I grew up with. Austen did as well because he kept all his ranch clothing at the house and stayed with Eliot when he was in town.

"Just what do you think we're going to say?" Austen asked, a shit-eating grin on his face. "I wanted to ask how your kids are thriving under such a hot nanny. Or is it you who wants to *thrive* under her?"

I narrowed my eyes at him, but I didn't hide my flinch well enough.

Wilder's brows went up, and Eliot made a choking sound. Austen chortled.

"Was that why you warned me away?" Wilder asked. "You and her?" He snorted. "'Just the nanny.'"

Eliot turned an alarmed gaze toward Wilder. "Are you looking to get some?"

"No," Wilder scoffed. "This isn't about me."

"Good." Eliot kept his glare on him. "You don't need to hurt Sutton more than you have."

Austen's grin stretched wide, ready to antagonize any vulnerable brother. "What if Sutton's found plenty of guys who want to keep her company? Hey, Cody, what'd Aggie say about that other vet in Crocus Valley?" The bastard was a fire starter, but he'd taken the attention off of me and Tova.

A red swath worked its way up Wilder's neck. "Shut it. She's not fucking around." His searching look landed on me.

"Don't think so," I said, throwing him a life preserver.

"But all the women he's scorned are getting her business off the ground."

Wilder grunted and folded his arms like Eliot. He appeared to be a solid post in a windstorm, but the winds raged inside of him. I lost hope he'd get his head out of his ass and stop the divorce before the papers were signed.

"Back to the nanny," Eliot said.

"Tova."

He smirked at my not-so-subtle hint to quit calling her the nanny. "Right. *Tova*. Something happened?"

"None of your business."

"That's where you're wrong," Austen said, getting uncharacteristically serious. "Today, I got to see my brother Cody again. You weren't 'Mr. Stick in the Ass' working the corrals. I think—I could've been hallucinating—you even smiled."

"Fuck off." I wasn't cranky until now. The atmosphere between me and Tova this morning wasn't as awkward as I'd feared. The air had sizzled between us, a quiet current only the two of us knew about. I wasn't going to let my brothers make it weird.

"Speaking of fucking . . ." Austen arched a dark brow.

"No," I snapped. I would've, though. I'd been so close, and Tova hadn't seemed ready to stop at some oral.

Some oral. Understatement of the year.

I had the best sleep last night that I'd had in months. Even my persistent erection had been placated by Tova's orgasm.

"You got protection?" Austen asked.

Eliot glanced from him to me.

Confused, I gave him a *what are you talking about?* look.

"Condoms," he said. "Rubbers. Raincoats. Love glove."

"No glove, no love," Eliot added.

Oh.

Oh, *shit*. My world slowed on its axis. Wilder's expression mirrored what I felt. Protection? When was the last time I bought condoms? Goddamn, it'd been years. Where would I even— No fucking way was I getting condoms anywhere in the county. Talk about gossip spreading like wildfire. The widower bought rubbers and had a hot nanny. What was two plus two?

I saw the same questions play through my brother's features. He hadn't thought about getting laid since Sutton left him, either, and from the sick tint to his features, he didn't like thinking about sleeping with anyone else.

Get it together and win her back, idiot.

But my advice didn't help me. Fucking condoms.

Eliot elbowed Austen. "I think we need to teach our big bro about the birds and the bees."

"Fuck right off." My face was hot. Goddammit, I didn't blush.

Austen studied me, that stupid grin glimmering under the surface. "You keep talking about fucking—"

I growled and stomped toward the entrance of the barn. The laughter of kids could be heard, and I shot a warning glare over my shoulder. No more talk of fucking or Tova. She was playing in the backyard with the kids, and while the barn was a good hundred yards away, I couldn't have her knowing how nosy my brothers were. I didn't want her to regret joining us.

"Cody," Eliot said, stopping me short. "It's nice to have you back."

"I'll be home in a little over six weeks."

"That's not what I meant." Eliot glanced around but didn't move closer to me. "It's what Austen said. You haven't been the same since you came home with Meg."

I stalked toward him, shame branding my steps. "What are you saying?"

Wilder and Austen inched closer to Eliot, but that didn't stop the bastard from running his mouth. "I'm saying I know you loved her, but you changed for her."

"She gave up a lot to be with me."

"You gave up a lot to be with her," he shot back.

Austen moved between us. I wasn't going to hit my brother—any of them. Probably.

"We know she moved here against her will, and she wasn't happy," Austen said quietly. "But the decision was hers as much as yours. You don't need to punish yourself for the rest of your life over it."

I wasn't.

Was I?

I gave them all a sweeping glare before I marched out of the barn. Was I more annoyed that my brothers touched on a major source of guilt? I had gotten married and couldn't make my wife happy. I'd been willing to change only so much for her happiness.

Or was I upset over the sensitive topic they probably didn't realize they touched on? I was acting like my old self, but in a couple of months, I wouldn't have my kids because I couldn't make them happy. And Tova was moving somewhere she could have a life, and that wasn't Buffalo Gully. I was coming home at the beginning of August. Alone.

⚜

Tova

The guys had gone late yesterday working cattle. Tonight was almost as late, but they planned to have a cookout to commemorate being done.

I found the whole ranch life fascinating. Green

surrounded us, but the landscape wasn't a manicured sprawl. I didn't know what the native or invasive plants were in Montana, but the lawn surrounding the house wasn't plain old grass. Dandelions dotted the yard and lined the ditch, along with what Ivy called wild morning glories. Grayson called it bind weed. Either way, we braided a few flower crowns out of the stuff.

I enjoyed the glimpse into Cody's life before Crocus Valley and into the rest of his family.

The polos and slacks Grayson had on in Crocus Valley were only a portion of his wardrobe. His closet in Buffalo Gully was packed. I asked if he attended private school, and the *duh, no, it's Buffalo Gully* look the ten-year-old had given me was impressive.

Ivy didn't own a single piece of denim, yet the guys wore it like a second skin.

The brothers all resembled each other. A family of panty-incinerators. But they were individual in the way they stood and their default expressions. The brother from the army had a permanently wicked gleam in his eye. Austen. He had an ease about him the others didn't possess. The opposite of Cody. Wilder was the deputy, and where Cody was the serious sibling, Wilder encompassed everything brooding. He was a little more relaxed than when he was in uniform yesterday. Eliot was the rancher, and he walked like he carried the weight of all the horses and cows on his shoulders.

All the brothers possessed this little twinkle in their eye that they only brought out for certain and rare reasons. I bet they'd been a menace to the single women of Buffalo Gully growing up.

And now.

None of the brothers amped up my heart rate like Cody. Cody in his business casual. Cody in cowboy boots. Cody with a cowboy hat shading half his face, except for that knowing gaze that now said he knew what I tasted like. All of it. Devastating. Then Cody on a horse sent my ovaries through puberty a second time when I witnessed the tight but flexible set of his body on a horse.

I fanned myself with a hand even though the heat wasn't awful today.

"Do you like steak?" Grayson asked for the third time. He was worried I wouldn't like the food. He'd been concerned I wouldn't like the house or getting dirty when we toured the property. He thought I might feel overwhelmed by all the horses and cattle. The cacophony of mooing when they were working cattle and the random clangs of the gates they lined the cattle in were unusual noises and sometimes startling.

None of it stressed me out. I was used to the clatter and smells of the city, so this was all new, but in some ways, it was similar. Instead of a throng of people and sidewalks, there were livestock and corrals. Instead of skyscrapers and businesses, there were barns and shops and sheds.

The only stage I could perform on was if I twirled through the pastures like in *The Sound of Music*.

Those were hard concepts to get through to a kid whose mom hated this life. "I like steak, and since I'm not cooking, even better," I assured Grayson.

"You hate cooking?" Ivy asked, scandalized. I'd been making lunches and suppers since my first day working.

"No, but I like a break from doing something every day, even if I enjoy it." Except for dancing. The kids made sure we got our stretches and practice in while we were playing outside. They were delighted to learn a flying squirrel was a dance move.

The guys swaggered up the winding dirt road from the barn to the house. A flank of four cowboys.

I went from city girl to having a major thing for cowboys.

For one cowboy.

Excited nerves rippled through my belly. That casual swagger. The rolling gait and the way his cowboy hat shaded his face. He was hell on my senses. I could cross to him right now and drag him . . . somewhere. What was sex in a barn like?

Eliot clapped his hands together. A puff of dust came off his gloves. He took them off and slapped them against his thigh. "Ready for some grub?"

"Grayson told me a lot about your grilling skills." I smiled at Grayson, who adamantly nodded.

Ivy perched on the deck stairs next to me. "He calls himself the Grill King."

"I had a crown," Eliot said. "But I lost it."

"A king never loses his crown," she said solemnly.

I nudged her and grinned. "We'll have to make him one."

She brightened. "We can make it out of dandelions!" She darted across the yard, stopping to pick flowers as she went. Grayson stood like he was going to follow her.

Cody smiled at Ivy's exuberance. He swung his dark stare to me. Electricity sizzled between us. Could the others feel it? Was it obvious I had a thing for this guy?

Yes.

I noticed Eliot elbow Austen, who glanced between us like he was in on a secret and giddy about it. Wilder was the only one who was subdued. A sense of loss emanated from him. I didn't know his and Sutton's story, but it was clear he wasn't happy about it coming to an end.

"Tova's teaching me how to dance," Grayson announced as loudly as if he were standing in a pulpit.

Cody nodded. "Grayson's taken to it like a horse to a dirt bath."

I smiled at the pride in his voice.

"No shit?" Eliot said, oblivious to Cody's censuring scowl. "Maybe some two-stepping will help you stay in the saddle." His tone was gently teasing, and Grayson nodded excitedly.

I didn't need to come to his defense, but I was too used to citing the benefits of dance to guys like Frederick. "Dancing is excellent for the core, and while I've never ridden a horse, I assume it requires a lot of core strength."

Wilder's eyes flared. "You gonna correct that, Cody?"

My stomach clenched. Crap. Was he pissed he had a dancing nephew? Guys could be so—

"She's been here for days, and you haven't taken her riding?" he finished.

I didn't catch the unintended innuendo until Austen snickered. Eliot cleared his throat and looked down, his lips twitching.

I nearly choked on my next breath. What had Cody told them about us? I couldn't picture him talking about something so intimate. Was I not playing it as chill as I thought? How obvious was it I wanted to plaster myself to this man?

"Uh, no." Humor and curiosity mingled in Cody's dark gaze. "I didn't realize I had such a grave error to correct."

"Can we go riding too, Dad?" Grayson asked.

"Tomorrow," Eliot said, walking toward the grill. Austen followed him. "We'll eat and drink tonight." He pointed at his nephew. "Milk for you, little man. And in the morning, we can ride."

"If some of us can wait that long," Austen muttered under his breath, earning a hard scowl from Cody.

Heat crept up my face, but I couldn't hold back my smile. "Really? You don't mind?"

"No," Cody said. "You can't stay on a Montana ranch and not ride a horse."

"I'll ride with Grayson," Wilder said. "Eliot or Austen can take Ivy, so you can handle Tova."

That one I caught and nearly snickered myself if it wouldn't be a signal that I wanted Cody to handle me.

Austen's body shook with suppressed laughter. He was the clown of the bunch, but I didn't miss the way mirth sparkled in Wilder's eyes. He'd phrased his words on purpose.

The guys liked teasing Cody, and Cody needed it. I was starting to like them. What was it like to have siblings simultaneously looking out for you while also frustrating you to no end?

"Ivy!" Grayson darted toward his sister. "We get to go riding tomorrow!"

He took the playful energy with him, and the men's speculation landed on me.

"So . . ." Austen said, more serious than I'd seen him all weekend. He folded his arms, seemingly content to let Eliot get the grill ready. "What kind of dancing do you do?"

"Uh . . . well." This was tricky. I was still a cautious city girl, even though I was in the middle of nowhere. Cody knew my former career, but I was still alone with four men, three of them I'd only met days ago. "I've worked in clubs and . . ."

"A stripper?" Austen asked, but his question wasn't lecherous. More matter-of-fact.

"Not exactly." *Please don't let this be a mistake.* Thelma would be there if I needed her, but I didn't want to send an SOS text. I owed her so much already. "Burlesque."

"Like the movie?" Wilder asked. "Sutton watched it all the time."

"Technically, that's more cabaret."

"I dated a stripper once," Austen said. When he caught Cody glaring at him, he shrugged. "What? She owns the joint now. Smart lady."

"Which is why she's not with you," Eliot added.

Austen had the same glare as his brother, but then he relaxed. "Nah, she wanted freedom from all men and never planned to get married."

"Good decision." Wilder's tone wasn't a commentary on his brother but was aimed at the institution of marriage. His brothers sent him worried glances.

"So, burlesque?" Austen seemed like he was directing the attention away from his brother, and I adored the sweet gesture. "Boas and shit?"

"I use fans in one of my acts. I like to have the flapper look. That way the humor fits in better since it isn't thought of as a serious time period, being after World War I and before the depression." I relaxed as I spoke. Only genuine interest and mild curiosity were in their expressions.

"Cool," he said, and they all nodded.

Cody was watching me with a hint of a smile. "She even got me to swing dance."

I beamed like a porch light hung inside my chest.

Eliot whistled. "Ask Jenna Mae Rogers how well that worked out."

"The theater girl?" I asked, enjoying that I was now part of the ribbing.

Austen howled with laughter. "Dude, you admitted to that? Wait until you tell her you learned guitar, and that girl didn't date you either."

The guys snickered, but the acute memory of the guitar from last night rose in my head.

Flames engulfed my face, and the heat only grew when Cody's burning gaze landed on me. "I've shown her how well I play."

Austen laughed and clapped. Eliot did a lot of headshaking, like he was the old man of the group. But Wilder had that brow lifted. The man said little with his mouth and a lot with his expressions. He knew exactly what Cody showed me, but he wasn't making it public.

I respected these guys. They respected me.

Eliot smacked Cody on the back. "I'm hungry. Time for food. But hey, leave the kids here tonight."

"Eliot—"

"They can sleep in Aggie's old room." Eliot talked over Cody. "I have Austen sleeping over to help watch them."

Cody's panicked gaze landed on me.

I froze, unable to process what a sleepover meant. Cody and I alone in a house he didn't want to touch me in. A house that filled him with conflict about his past life and his present and how there was no future between us.

"I'm here to work." I glanced between them. A wall of Knight men, three of them trying to get me alone with their brother. "I—I wouldn't have anything to do."

"I don't get much uncle time," Eliot replied smoothly. "They are my only niece and nephew until Aggie and Ansen get busy."

"And I think they are getting bus-ayyy," Austen added. The rest of them shuddered.

"Jesus, Austen. None of us needed to hear that." Wilder grunted, shooting him a glare. "I can come over tonight too. They like getting rides in the patrol car."

"So that's it." Eliot clapped his gloves together. "We'll have a sleepover, and you can get a tour of the mighty Buffalo Gully."

As if he sensed how uncomfortable Cody and I were, thinking we were getting thrown together when we weren't ready, Wilder pointed to the sky. "It's supposed to be clear out tonight. You'll have to check out the stars after dark."

All the guys murmured appreciatively.

I latched on to an activity that required clothing—I assumed—and couldn't be done from Cody's bed. "I've never done stargazing, unless you count Hollywood actors."

"I can take you to the south pasture," Cody said, acting as casual as me. "There's almost no light out there."

"It's like clubbing," Austen said, "but with cattle and no music."

"I look forward to it," I said. But I was looking forward to being alone with Cody more.

Twelve

CODY

I crumpled the small brown paper bag I found on the driver's seat and stuffed it in a cupholder. I was going to kill my brothers. I would make them pay somehow.

Tova swung her legs in and glanced at the destroyed bag.

"My brother left his shit in my truck," I said with no further explanation. The brother in question was likely Austen, the dickweed. My teeth were going to crunch if I clenched my jaw any harder.

"You guys seem close."

"Yeah, we kind of are." I didn't realize until I said it that I treasured the fact that we were still close. My relationship with them was one of the few things I could thank Barns for. "Nowadays, Aggie doesn't make working cattle an event like we do, but she always got pushed out of a lot of the family work. None of us felt like we had time to watch her, but she's as much of a cowboy as the rest of us."

When I called myself a cowboy, her eyes dipped down to

my chest and the dusty shirt I was still wearing, then to where my cowboy boots disappeared under the dash. I'd shower when I returned to the house. This trip was about showing her something she hadn't gotten to see before.

Sparks kindled under my skin. I was going to be a Fourth of July sparkler with an erection if she looked at me like that again. I started the pickup and punched the truck into gear. The sun was almost all the way down, and the sky above us was darkening to a midnight blue.

"Aggie has her new horse rescue anyway," I said to distract both of us from wondering how we were going to split into our separate rooms without it being weird when we arrived at the house. "So, she couldn't come down, and we were all together for her wedding earlier this month." I sped down the road, leaving a cloud of dust in my wake.

"I didn't realize she and Ansen were newlyweds, but it's cool you all still talk and meet up. Like a built-in friend group." There was a wistful quality to what she said. "I think Mom would've had more kids if she . . ." She stared out the windshield at the flurry of bugs zooming through the headlights. "If she found a decent guy to settle down with. My dad definitely wasn't one."

She shifted in her seat, and I thought she'd leave it at that. She'd opened up about her dickwad of an ex, but she was quiet on the subject of her parents.

"He was an addict," she finally said. "Might still be, I don't know. He didn't want a family and ditched Mom as soon as she found out she was pregnant."

"I'm sorry."

I caught her shrug out of the corner of my eye.

"She never remarried?"

"She never married, period." Her sigh was barely audible. "But she wanted to be in love so bad. Thought she needed a guy to be happy, but she found all the wrong men."

"That sucks."

"It does, and I always wished for siblings. It's been fun watching you with your brothers. Maybe Grayson and Ivy will be close like that when they get older." She peered out the passenger window. "Oh, wow. I can already see the stars, and it's not completely dark."

"By the time we reach the south pasture, the sun will be all the way down, and you'll get a better view of the Milky Way."

The soft caress of her attention landed on me. "Like . . . the whole thing?"

"As much as will fit into the sky." I had cursed my brothers for putting me in this position, alone with Tova, when we weren't ready, but I was grateful I could show her this. Give her more memories that didn't involve a workaholic dad who couldn't quit thinking about her.

"Cookouts and stargazing," she murmured.

"Not exactly what you do in the city?"

She chuckled. "Cookouts, maybe. Although I've never been to one, and the only stars I see are when I'm going home after a show in the middle of the night. Movie stars who are usually drunk or high and pretend to not want to be noticed."

"You'll find a few of those stars in Montana too. They like to buy land here." The silence between us was easy, but a focused tension rode through the air. Did she feel it too? Just in case, I didn't want her to think the sleepover meant I expected to start where we left off. That night caught us both by surprise, and after our talk, I didn't want to backtrack on any progress we'd made. I didn't have her for long. "About tonight, please don't think the sleepover means we have to do anything we're not comfortable with."

"I know," she said quietly. "I appreciate it, and I know what situation this puts you in."

The house. The big empty house that no longer felt like a home but had too many memories to ignore.

I stopped at the gate and hopped out. The pickup's headlights lit several feet past the gate. Once the gate was open and I drove in, I got back out to close it. Once I was back behind the wheel, Tova fully turned her body to stare out the passenger window.

"It's so dark," she said, her voice full of awe. "It's like it goes on forever."

I parked at the top of a rolling hill. I knew my family land by heart, and at the bottom was a stock pond. Killing the engine, I said, "I have a blanket in the back. Let me spread it out in the bed. With all the lights off, maybe we won't get eaten alive by mosquitos."

She laughed. "I guess there's always something waiting to draw blood in the dark no matter where you are."

"It's the size that matters." I died inside at my joke, but she kept laughing as she got out.

I dug the blanket out from a compartment in the back seat where I stuffed some winter supplies. Giving it a good couple of snaps in the air, I walked to the back of the pickup.

"I'm afraid to wander too far from the vehicle," she murmured.

I could make her out well enough. The sky soared over us, full of tiny pinpricks of light, and the dull glow from town shone brighter without bigger towns around to stifle it.

I dropped the tailgate, rolled the bed cover back, and spread out the blanket. "Go ahead. Have a seat and enjoy."

She climbed up, and I averted my gaze. It didn't matter that I couldn't see definition; my mind happily filled in the blanks. Toned legs up to the ass I wanted handfuls of. A round bottom temptingly close to my face as she crawled in to stretch out on the blanket.

She was wiggling to get comfortable. I could hear it, and that was enough for me to keep my back to her.

"Okay," she said, slightly out of breath and *fuck*. "There's room for you."

"I'm good standing."

She didn't reply. Did I hurt her feelings? I was between her legs the other night, and now I acted like I might sprint into the pasture.

"Wow, it's so pretty," she said after a few moments.

I craned my head back. The Milky Way spread above us, the stars packing together like they were following a line that cut a swath through the middle of the sky.

"Wow," she said again.

"I haven't stopped to look at it for years." Contemplating the star-filled sky, I crossed my arms. "I used to see this all the time. Took it for granted, I guess."

"It's like city lights. I remember thinking I'd never tire of seeing LA lit up at night, but then it became just part of what I saw every day. I've never seen this, though. So many stars." The blanket rustled as she sat up and pointed. "Look —a plane."

"If we sit here long enough, you'll see a lot of planes. It's like a highway miles above us."

She didn't lie back down but crossed her legs, her feet hanging off the end.

"Comfortable?" I asked.

"No." She chuckled. "I feel like I've been lied to my whole life. The movies make it look romantic to lie in the back of a pickup to watch the stars."

"But really, you have the ridges of the pickup bed digging into your back and butt."

"Exactly," she said, laughing, cutting off with a gasp. "A falling star."

"There are some peak times for meteor showers. I haven't thought about checking those out in years."

"Let me guess—you used to come out here and watch meteor showers to impress a girl."

It was my turn to laugh. "Maybe once or twice."

"Hm, I'm sure you weren't watching the stars the whole time."

"How do you think I know the bed of the pickup isn't comfortable?"

She gave me a playful shove. "When I first met you, I never would've thought you were that guy."

"Milk Daddy doesn't try to impress girls?"

"No, they're too busy falling at your feet."

"That hasn't happened in a long time, California."

"Well, you impress me."

This girl. She wasn't being flirty, and that made her words snuggle around my heart even more. I turned around to face her. My eyes were adjusting better, and it was like the light of a thousand stars grew brighter just so I could see her better. "How did I do that?"

"By being you. Is that too sappy?"

Grinning, I put my hands on her knees. Her muscles briefly tensed under my skin, but she didn't move her leg. I couldn't keep from touching her. My restraint only lasted so long, and we were out here all alone. "Yes, but I like hearing it."

"First, it was how you brushed off what I did for a living."

My mood darkened. "You shouldn't be shamed for it."

"Well, I have been. But when that big order of toys showed up, I might've been a little impressed again."

"You said you could use them." I should've known what my kids needed.

She scooted closer. "See, that's the thing. I'm used to having to justify what I think or want." Before I could ask who made her feel like shit besides that motherfucker Frederick, she continued, "And then there was the dancing. Quite impressive, Stern Daddy. And the guitar. Then when you were shirtless."

While I loved hearing what had mesmerized her, I couldn't take credit for my appearance. Sure, I took care of myself, but Barns hadn't been an ogre. Genetics got me a lot further than my sporadic workout routine. "None of that's important."

"Am I supposed to say the way you sit behind that desk for hours and make soooo much money is hot, Mr. Knight?"

She was using a sexpot voice on purpose, and goddammit, it was working. The sound was curling around my dick and inviting all the blood in my body to join. "Yes," I said roughly. "I make a shit ton of money to keep our doors open and fix what my father ran improperly."

"I admire your work ethic, but I'm not impressed by big, bossy businessmen who think they rule the world with a word. Just like I'm not impressed by men who get their way with their fists. I'm infatuated with the guy who'll learn a dance for a girl. Who'll take up an instrument just to get noticed. The man who takes his nanny out to look at the galaxy instead of going right home to get into her pants."

"I told you that you didn't have to—"

She put her finger on my lips. "I know. But your brothers gave us a night to be alone, and you're not taking advantage of it. You've been worked up and tense, probably wondering how weird it'll be when we get back to the house."

"I have." She had a sixth sense about what I was going through inside. Her understanding filled that empty hole in my chest. "I don't want to go back on what we talked about."

"Me either. You seem like a really good man, Cody."

"I want you, Tova." The confession came out ragged. I wasn't a good man. I was just a flawed person who wanted to do the right thing. "I've wanted you since I met you, and I wasn't ready."

She huffed out a soft laugh. "Neither was I." She flattened her hands on my chest. "I fled to Crocus Valley to lick my wounds while I was down, but you've done nothing but build me up."

Anger at how she lost everything rippled under my skin, but I didn't want her asshole ex infringing on our time together. I tipped her chin up. She was at the edge of the tailgate. I couldn't remember if she scooted that close or if I dragged her. My hands were gripping her thighs, but not hard enough to tug her toward me. Maybe. "We can get your money back. Thanks to Meg, I have connections. Her parents—"

"Are you going to tell them that the strip-teasing nanny you want to have a fling with got into a bad situation with a guy?"

My jaw locked up. I didn't like hearing her downplay her accomplishments, but my pulse jumped at the thought of telling my in-laws about Tova. She shouldn't be a secret, but I wasn't ready to share her or open my desires up to scrutiny. "We can . . . It's not . . ."

"It's okay." She stroked her hands up my chest to my face. "You aren't ready to tell your in-laws you're moving on, even if it's not serious, and I'm not ready to air my dirty laundry to people I don't know and who are much smarter than me. Having your wife's parents in our business seems a little too much, too soon."

"This is between us." There was a lot more between us than raging hormones, but I wasn't ready to evaluate the matter. "But I will help you if you want me to. I could make a few calls."

"We'll see. It's only been a few weeks."

Her noncommittal brush-off wasn't what I wanted to hear, but I also understood she didn't want to be indebted to me. We were each on our own journey, and our paths would only converge for another month and a half.

Suddenly, the time frame was miniscule. Just like this evening would be over and we'd be in the pickup and going back to the house, the weeks would fly by, and then Tova would be going her way and I'd be coming back here. Alone.

I cupped her cheek, rubbing my thumb along her jawline. "I know I said we should wait, but I haven't showered, and you—"

"Like having you dirty and all to myself." She pulled my head down, and my lips crashed on hers.

Again, she said exactly what I wanted to hear. With a groan, I pulled her closer to me. She wrapped her legs around me, and that erection I was trying to hold back was present and demanding. The sound of our breathing got lost in the symphony of the bugs and the crickets. I was attuned to her. Her needy little whimpers when I licked into her mouth and found her tongue were my guideposts.

She broke the kiss long enough to whisper, "What exactly are we going to do?"

"Everything, Tova. I want everything." Raw admission. I couldn't hide how much I wanted her in this moment. I'd be going back to pretending to be a guy who worked all day while a nanny cared for his kids instead of being a desire-filled man who often thought of burying himself between the legs of this woman.

"I don't have . . . And you don't have . . ."

Her hot breath wafted across my cheek. My face was close enough to hers I could tell she bit her lower lip. "We can do a lot without protection."

Protection. A low chuckle rumbled out. I held her to me and lifted her off the bed of the truck.

She yelped and clung to me as I walked to the passenger side. "Cody!"

"Just so happens one of my jackass brothers left a pack of condoms in the pickup."

She went still in my arms. "The bag?"

I nodded and opened the door. I got us loaded inside carefully without hitting her head on the doorframe. She straddled me, and I pulled the lever to lay the seat back.

"I'm on top," she said, intrigued.

I breathed in her soft, rosewater scent. "You set the pace, California. I don't want us to do anything you're not ready for."

"What about you?"

"If you knew the dreams I've been having since I first saw you, you'd know I'm ready for exactly this."

"This?"

I nodded and tugged her shirt over her head. "This." The inside of the pickup was darker than it was outside, and I mourned the loss of light, but I also needed the shadows. They softened the moment between us, made it more intimate. Less real, and maybe it made me a jackass, but I needed to *not* be reminded why having sex with my nanny was a bad idea.

She unhooked the latch of the bra between her breasts and let it slide off her shoulders.

"Fuck." I palmed each of them, touching the creamy

mounds like I'd never seen anything so magnificent when I had just two nights ago.

She moaned into my touch, arching her back while I rolled her tight nipples between my thumbs and fingers. "Cody. Your hands are rough." She placed hers over mine. "I love it."

"Some big, bossy businessmen work with their hands."

"Yes." She was riding me, and I didn't think she knew it. My dick was getting ground between us, and if I let her keep going, I could probably come in two minutes.

But I wasn't letting her get me off first. "Are you wet for me, Tova?"

"I'd rather you find out for yourself." She leaned over me, and between the two of us, we wrestled her shorts off her. She was completely naked on top of me. I didn't need a spotlight to tell me she was fucking perfect, pink and rosy in all the places my filthy mind imagined.

I slid a finger through her slit. "You're fucking soaked."

She rolled her hips against my hand. Wet and so damn hot, I should be worried about burning myself, but I was willing to stroll into the middle of a fire pit if that was what it took to get my hands on her.

As if she realized how unbalanced the clothing situation was, she worked at my waistband. I sucked my abs in, suddenly frozen.

The other night, I'd kept my pants firmly in place. My jeans were like a safety net. As long as they were in place, I wasn't going to unintentionally impale Tova, as ridiculous as it sounded. This was intentional.

She popped open the clasp and met my eyes as her fingers brushed my hard-on.

I hissed and drew my hands back. A vise tightened around my chest, and I couldn't breathe.

She freed my cock and leisurely pumped up and down, slowly, like she knew I needed a minute.

This was new, yet so achingly familiar.

"Are you okay?" she murmured.

I pulsed in her hands. My erection said it was fucking fantastic, but my brain was skidding in the mud of my thoughts. "I'm fine," I rasped.

"If we're going too fast, just say so."

"No." What I thought was panic before had nothing on the fear of her removing her touch.

I forced myself to move, spreading my fingers on her thighs and brushing up to the rounded flare of her hips. I dipped my thumbs into the crease between her leg and pelvis and moved inward. Then I was back in her wet heat, stroking the finger of one hand over her clit while kneading her ass with the other.

She rocked again and pumped with my strokes. Pleasure radiated up and down my spine, growing stronger with each lap. We were in sync, and the rapid patter of my heart steadied into a solid thrum.

As much as I hated ditching her ass, I had to bring her head down for a kiss. She kept her fingers circled around my cock as she kissed me. I threaded a finger into her, playing her body like I was producing the most beautiful melody in the world—and I was.

She let a moan escape, her lips parting against mine. I invaded her mouth and plundered her with my tongue to the rhythm of my finger.

A needy mewl came from her. I had to hear more. Tonight was just us. We didn't need to hold back.

"You can be fucking loud here, kitten."

"Kitten?" she whined, getting too lost in her impending climax to question my impromptu nickname further.

"Let it out."

"Cody!" She was so damn wet I didn't want to quit, but the way she was fisting my cock and how she bucked the closer to her climax she got, I was going to come much quicker than I wanted.

Her explosion wasn't just a sign of how well we fit together. There was more between us. Respect. Laughter. Life.

I nibbled down her jaw and lined her graceful neck with kisses. She tipped her head to the side, a loud moan leaving her.

"Let it go, baby. Let me hear you."

"Cody." She pumped her hips against my hand. Her grip tightened on me, and I gritted my teeth. "Cody, Cody, Cody," she chanted.

"Let go, kitten."

She exploded, slicking my hand with her release, her hips swiveling and grinding into me. "Yes! Oh. My. God. Yes!"

I was on the edge. As much as I wanted to revel in her release, to coax more from her, I had to get my dick out of her grasp, or I was going to blow. I clamped on to her wrist, unwilling to end early.

I'd learned more since my younger days how to impress girls, and it wasn't ejaculating in her hand before I got to feel what heaven was inside of her.

"You gotta let me go, baby." The strain in my voice was clear. "I'm gonna lose control."

She unpeeled each finger away. I removed my hand from between her legs and rested it lightly against her hips, needing a second to get myself back from the ledge. Heavy breathing from each of us filled the cab.

She lazily met my gaze and grabbed the paper bag. "Ready?"

I was almost past ready. "Put it on me."

She took out the small box. Three condoms.

Fucking condoms.

A neon sign for how my life had changed. I had a woman I'd only known a few weeks perched on top of me, gloriously naked with a fresh orgasm glow, and she was opening a condom packet. I was no longer Alcott Knight, a married father of two. I was Cody Knight, a single dad who had the hots for his nanny.

Watching her roll the damn thing onto my straining cock was like an out-of-body experience. This wasn't happening to me. I wasn't doing this.

Only teenagers fucked in a pickup in the middle of the night. I'd been that teenager.

Now, I was forty damn years old. I had two kids. A future I was navigating like I'd been blindfolded and tossed into a dark maze. And I was about to have sex with a woman I didn't know a lot about but felt like I *knew*.

Her deft fingers finished rolling the condom on. She gave me another hesitant look. "Do you want this?"

"Don't fucking stop, kitten." Everything outside of my cock might be confused, a little cloudy, but I wanted this.

I needed it.

She situated herself at the tip, a steadying hand on my chest and one on the window. Then she carefully sank down.

Each inch she covered me robbed me of more air. I hadn't had sex in well over a year, and this was intense. Staggering. Like I had zero control and wanted to randomly thrust until all the delirious pressure was gone.

But I didn't. She deserved better than a man who couldn't keep his shit together.

An eternity, but really only a second later, she was seated on me. I was inside her, and she was in my arms.

"Are you sure you're okay?"

I gazed into the shadows covering her face and gathered

her closer to me. I might be spinning into an abyss or willingly flinging myself in if it meant I was inside her, but yes. I was fine. "Let me show you."

I rolled my hips up, and she went liquid in my arms. "Cody. So good," she moaned.

The confines of the pickup made it hard to move, but we didn't need much space. My world was orienting itself, centering on her. I was crazy about this girl.

And now that I had her, I wasn't going to waste our time together. "I'm going to make you come again."

I could make out her sexy grin in the dark. "Are you doing it to impress me?"

"No—that would be showing you we can finish the rest of the pack of condoms before we go back to the house."

Her throaty laughs went straight to my dick. I slid my hand between us and found her still-swollen clit.

"Oh, god, Cody," she groaned.

A swell of energy shot down my spine, tightening my balls. "Tova." I clenched my teeth and buried my face in her neck, continuing to drive into her, meeting her downward motion with a tight thrust that hit the right spot.

"Cody." She started chanting my name again. She was close, and I teetered on the edge.

I lightly nipped the skin at the base of her throat, and she jerked, heat blooming between us as the climax hit.

Fucking finally. I let go. My release shot out and I held her, like the top was going to blow off the pickup and carry us away. Desire filled my senses, and all I knew was the ecstasy flooding my body and the warm woman in my arms who was the cause of it.

She collapsed on top of me, and I sagged into the seat. Only our heavy breathing filled the air once again.

"Are you good at everything you do?" She traced a circle

on my chest. I couldn't wait to be with her when we could stretch out and be entirely undressed.

"It takes practice. Like I said, there are two more condoms."

Tova

We were on the front porch. My legs were rubbery like I'd been doing a kick line all afternoon, but the rest of me was as relaxed as if I'd spent a week at an all-inclusive spa.

The frogs were as loud as the other night, and the sky was just as dark as when we'd left the pasture. Cody unlocked the front door of his house, but he didn't open it. The porch light danced across his finger-combed hair. It'd been my fingers doing the dragging through those soft strands.

"To say I enjoyed tonight is an understatement." He hesitated.

I put my hand on his strong forearm. My skin tingled from head to toe, and lingering aftershocks zinged through my core, reminding me that it agreed with his statement one thousand percent and would like to know when we could do it again. But once we left the pasture, we were back to our agreement to wait. "I understand, Cody. We're going inside and going to sleep in separate beds, and it's not going to change how I feel about what we're doing."

He brushed a tangled lock of my hair behind my ear. "You're pretty special, you know that?"

He made me feel special in a way I'd never experienced. I'd never had the sense of being treasured by someone like him. Possessed, yes, and I had ignored the prickles of unease from those exes. But not revered. Cody acted like he was in awe of me. We were standing on the porch of a home he'd lived in with his wife and kids, and his feelings weren't as sorted and neat as he wanted them, but he was taking the time to make sure I was okay, that I understood it wasn't me who was the issue.

He cupped the back of my neck and brought his head down. The kiss started tender and grew demanding. Only the frogs and the crickets witnessed the electricity flowing between us, growing until we generated our own lightning storm.

After all the orgasms we'd just had, how could I be aching and ready for another? From a kiss?

Slowly, he pulled away and tipped his forehead to mine. Our breaths mingled in the night air. "Good night, Tova."

"Good night, Cody."

He pushed the door open and ushered me inside first. I gave him a smile over my shoulder and shivered at the dark, heated look in his eyes. One foot in front of the other, I went to the guest room, the burn of his gaze on my back the entire time.

I'd wondered before what it would be like to wake up to this man. I still wanted to know, but I was comforted going to sleep knowing exactly where I was with him. Tomorrow, we'd go back to single dad and nanny, and if we never broke out of those roles again, at least I had tonight.

Thirteen

TOVA

"You did it with him." Thelma waved her hand up and down my body. I wasn't dressed any differently than normal in jean shorts and a loose shirt I could move around in for a day of dance lessons. "You're glowing, doll face." Her lips flattened.

She worked later this morning, and I was having my chunky smoothie before heading out.

"It's not like that." I took another pull on my straw.

She tapped her unopened pack of cigarettes on the table and locked me into a silent face-off about my trip.

I returned home with Cody and the kids last night. Instead of diving right into a secret sleepover, we decided to give it a day and figure out what to do. Crocus Valley wasn't as invested in Cody's personal business as Buffalo Gully, but neither of us wanted the neighbors to speculate on my hours. I couldn't exactly sleep over and never be seen coming or going.

I wanted to come a lot.

I *had* come. A lot. My body hadn't quit humming, and it'd been all I could do not to climb into bed with him the morning after we woke up in a child-free house to find out if he was as virile before noon.

I didn't know if he'd brave getting more condoms in town, and I wasn't going to ask. The weekend had been surreal, a quasi-vacation unlike any I'd ever had, and if it turned out to be a one-time occurrence, I wouldn't have my hopes up.

How was Cody going to adjust to returning to his routine? To having time to think about how something between us was more trouble than he wanted?

What if he didn't want to risk gossip trickling down to Grayson and Ivy? We had too many neighbor kids over to get caught sneaking a kiss. Thankfully, because I needed to quit thinking about when was the next time I could get close to Cody's cock.

He was magnificent with it.

"You're blushing." Thelma sighed. "He got you with the magic dick."

I choked on a mouthful of gritty smoothie. "Thelma." Cody had earned my blush, though. "He's the most generous guy I've been with." She rolled her eyes, and I shook my head. "Really, it wasn't serious, and he brought me home in one piece. He even put me on a horse and taught me how to ride." My nerves were only just calming down. Give me a full auditorium over a creature four times my size with its own mind. Seeing Cody ride a horse had been so worth it, though. "Not once did he offer to share me with his brothers."

She didn't laugh at my lame attempt at a joke. I was partially serious. Cody had constantly asked me throughout the weekend if I was doing okay or wanted to leave early. He hovered close to me during the cookout, like he wanted to make sure his brothers weren't crowding me. As for his brothers, I'd never felt more like one of the bros. They didn't leer at me or make sexual comments, and I never caught one staring. If I did, they were watching Cody interact with me with mixed reactions of curiosity, relief, and an overall sense of watchfulness. They'd been worried about him after his wife died.

What was it like to have a big, supportive family?

"So you two are just like . . . fucking around?"

Anyone else would make it sound like a bad thing, but Thelma was cautiously optimistic. "Yeah, I guess. Maybe. As long as we can keep it from the kids. We don't want them to think something's going on. He's still planning to ship them off to his in-laws." I heard my own judgment. I worried for Grayson. I didn't know their grandparents, and I'd only heard about Meg, but Grayson possessed a sensitivity she hadn't. Could they nurture a kid different from their daughter? Ivy would be fine. She was probably a little replica of her mother, but she'd still miss valuable time with her dad and also with her aunts and uncles.

"And you don't agree?"

"I think the kids should stay with him, but maybe not in Buffalo Gully. He's putting his job ahead of them, using his wife as an excuse, and saying that he's a single dad with a full-time job."

"Do you resent your mom dropping you off with us?"

I swirled my straw in my glass. The leap between the kids' circumstances and mine when I was younger wasn't far. Was I bitter about Mom dumping me? Yes, but I only had happy memories of living with Grandma and Thelma. Sure, we'd had our own struggles, many of them centered around Mom, but I'd had a good life with her and Thelma.

"I'm more resentful about Mom not trusting herself enough to live on her own and support us."

"She had a fear we couldn't cure."

"She had daddy issues."

"Yeah, well." Thelma smacked her lips, contemplated her pack of cigarettes, and carefully set them far away on the table. "She took her own daddy's leaving hard."

Grandpa left for another woman and started a new family, forgetting his old one. My dad chose a substance, and it was easier not to take personally.

Easier, but not easy. And ultimately, like Mom, I had fallen for a real bad boy who wore a coat of polish like camouflage. Only I wasn't going back to California to be with him. I would return to fight Frederick.

I ached at the thought of leaving Crocus Valley, but really, without Cody, what was there for me? Thelma would worry more if she was around to see me struggle.

Figured I'd finally meet a nice guy at a time when we couldn't stay to see if we worked. Cody was someone who treated me right and who I didn't feel the need to protect myself against. Was I delusional? Or was it only because we were temporary?

I hated the idea we were ending, but I'd take all the orgasms I could get. "I'd better get going." I gave my glass a quick wash and set it on the drying rack by the sink. Then I gave Thelma a peck on the cheek and was out the door.

The humidity in the air clung to me, and the clouds concealing the sky were dark and heavy. A fresh smell of impending rain hung in the air. I was almost to the house when Kali darted out her front door.

"It's going to rain!" Her panic rang through the quiet street.

"Looks like it."

"How are we going to practice for our performance?"

Her grandma came out of the house, barefoot and wearing a quilted robe, her thinning gray hair pulled back into a ponytail. "Kali, don't bother Tova about the dancing."

Kali's eyes glittered, and she rose to her tiptoes. "But we already missed Friday and yesterday."

I hated letting her down. Grayson had made sure to work on the steps. He was invested in the idea of a backyard performance before the end of summer, but since Ivy wasn't as into it, I didn't think Kali and the other kids had their hearts set on it like Grayson. I should have known better, but it'd been years since I'd taught children. "How about I talk to Cody? Maybe we can practice inside, but we'd have to be really quiet."

Could five kids dancing be quiet enough?

"That'd be great!" Kali gave me a huge grin, turned it on her grandma, and ran back inside.

Sima met my gaze, her mouth in a rueful twist. "Let me know if it doesn't work out. I'll break it to her."

"Thank you. Too bad we can't use the old theater."

"Why can't you?"

"I'm sure there is insurance and rent and—"

She waved her hand like she could erase my concerns. "Let me talk to my husband. Maybe he can work something out with Dave and Shelly."

Dave and Shelly were the theater owners, but the place had been closed for months, according to Thelma. Regardless, I didn't have rent money. "I appreciate it, but it's okay. We'd need bathrooms and water fountains." The kids wanted to hydrate every seven minutes.

"The plumbing works. Bill just fixed a leak there last month. I'll get back to you." She shuffled inside. I stared at the screen door for a few extra moments and then crossed to Cody's house.

My excitement rose higher with each step. A performance. In a theater! I didn't care if we did it in the backyard and the lawn wasn't mowed or it was drizzling. I wanted to witness the accomplishment on the kids' faces. Their achievements and pride were my own special drug.

I went to knock, but Grayson's wails reached my ears. Instead, I tried the door. It swung open. Ivy was burrowed into the corner of the couch with an iPad propped in front of her face. I could see through the living room into the dining room and kitchen area. A puddle gleamed on the floor, and Grayson's cries were coming from that direction.

I smiled at Ivy. "Good morning."

She poked at her pad. "Morning." She was in purple leggings and a Disney princess T-shirt today, the one her uncle Austen had given her. No dress, and her hair was loose. She wasn't back to looking like she was dressing for the office at the start of the day. Had Cody decided on casual, or had it been a rough morning?

From the way Ivy was checked out of whatever was happening, I voted on tumultuous morning.

I crept into the kitchen. The deep murmur of Cody's voice was like a siren's song, drawing me closer. When I turned the corner, I found Cody in gray slacks and a light green dress shirt, crouched next to Grayson's chair. The boy had his head down, sobs wracking his body. He wasn't in a polo and khaki shorts.

Cody glanced at me. His gaze momentarily heated and swept down my body, making my shirt and shorts feel like one of my burlesque outfits.

Two seconds later, he was back to businesslike. "He spilled on his Spider-Man shirt."

Right. No polo shirt meant he got to wear what he liked, and he loved that shirt. I gingerly stepped over the white splatter. A large pool continued to drip off the table. I sat in a chair on the other side of the table. "It's so upsetting when I feel great and I'm wearing my favorite things and then I spill on them."

Grayson's cries quieted.

Success. Sometimes, just having someone understand was half the battle. "And then I'm worried I won't get the same mood lift even after I wash everything."

His head moved against his arm with his nod.

Cody gave me a grateful smile, then his jaw tightened. "His grandpa called, asking if he was getting excited for August."

The big move. Sympathy welled inside me, directed at the distraught kid.

The meltdown wasn't about the clothes or the milk. A clock was ticking down to more change in his life. He couldn't verbalize it, but I felt what he was feeling. When I noticed Mom adjusting her routine, I'd board an emotional roller coaster, and it didn't take much. Sometimes, she packed a bag for me like it was a fun activity and our little secret, then put it in the closet to look like we hadn't touched it. Or we'd take a drive, but it wasn't to the ocean or a park. She was really looking at open rentals. She never said she was preparing to leave a guy, but I knew the signs.

Grayson knew this new world he felt safe in was coming to an end, and my heart went out to him. I couldn't help with his dad's decision to send them to their grandparents, but I could help with the spilled milk.

"Can we go find another shirt?" I asked Grayson. "I can throw that one in the wash."

"It's going to rain today," he moaned.

"I know. Kali was worried we might have to skip dance lessons too." I wasn't going to ask Cody in front of Grayson if we could practice inside. If the answer was no, there'd be another breakdown.

"We can't dance today?" Ivy called from the living room.

I didn't control the weather, but the sense I let all the kids down beat in my veins. I should've thought of alternate plans in case of bad weather.

"We'll see," Cody said. He rubbed the spot between his brows. "I have a call this afternoon. An important one."

So no indoor practice. I shouldn't have said anything to Kali. She was going to be devastated. I doubted the owners of the theater would let a stranger and a bunch of kids take over.

Frustration that I had to keep making do and falling short swept through me like the Santa Ana winds. One day, I'd have control of my life. One day, I could make decisions about what I did and where.

Today was not that day.

Cody scrubbed his face and checked his watch. "I've got a meeting in a few minutes. You good, bud?"

Grayson nodded and pulled at his wet shirt. "Yeah. But what if it rains?"

I glanced at the back door. Where light usually shone through, the clouds in the window were a dull gray. "Maybe we should get some practice in this morning. Kali might be able to join us, and I'll call Britta and Bridger's aunt to see if they can come out early."

Just as I said that, loud raindrops splattered the windows. Damn. I traded worried gazes with Cody.

"We might have to figure out a rainy-day plan."

Grayson drew in a shuddering breath. "What about our performance?"

Poor guy. All his feelings were getting poured into today's missed practice. I'd met professional dancers who didn't stress as much about a few canceled sessions. "We can pull it off."

Ivy appeared at the opening between the living room and dining room. She held her iPad screen out. "It's supposed to rain all week."

Shit sticks.

Grayson's breathing quickened. He was near sobbing again. He could sense the impending change, and enduring a shift in the schedule today, or all week, wasn't helping.

Cody ducked his head to catch my eye. "What about using the house?"

My rising hope crashed when I recalled his upcoming meeting. "You're in meetings all day?"

"I should be done by four. Can you sneak in a late practice?"

I nodded before any other obstacles invaded our practice. "I'll let them know. But I'll also tell them to be flexible, just in case."

"Thanks, Dad." Grayson launched himself off the chair and plastered his milk-soaked chest against his dad's pants.

I tensed, muscle memory waiting for the inevitable shouting like my mom's boyfriends used to do when I inconvenienced them. Cody only exchanged an amused look with me and patted Grayson on the back. "No problem, bud. We'll work things out when we can."

Ivy jumped up and down. "Yay! We're having company! We haven't had company before." She darted back into the living room to—I didn't know, but she was excited to entertain.

Cody's grimace was quick. "No, we haven't had much for company over the years." He checked the time again and mouthed a swear word. "I've gotta get to the office." He raked a hot gaze down my body, then caught my eye. My belly did yet another flip, as if I hadn't seen him almost every day since I'd been in town. "Do what you need to do. I'll make sure I'm done by four."

"Thank you."

He gingerly stepped around the milk splatter. "Sorry I didn't have time to clean this up."

"No problem. Grayson can be my scrubber while I throw a load of laundry in."

When he passed me, he lightly touched my arm, fingertips to bare skin. Desire that should've been thoroughly sated flooded my blood vessels. I didn't know when we'd get to do more than a discreet tap, but it didn't feel like soon enough.

*

Cody

I was in my third meeting of the day, and I needed to get this wrapped up by four, but I wasn't in a position to hurry proceedings. The guy on the other end required my full attention. Weston Duke was the CEO of King Oil, and once he learned I was working from Crocus Valley, the conversation went from King Oil contracting a portion of our wells to Weston peppering me with questions.

Are you from the area? How long have you been there? Ever get to Coal Haven? Do you know the Barrons?

The last question derailed everything. The phone buzzed against my ear with texts I hadn't read yet. Ordinarily, I'd love to chat—my new brother-in-law was the nephew of Weston's old boss. Weston used to be vice president of the refinery outside of Coal Haven. His five kids had been born and raised in Coal Haven until he got the job at King Oil.

The old King Oil owner had retired as CEO to spend more time with his family. I didn't think Weston's ethos matched the desire. The man traveled nearly constantly, and he answered some of my emails as late as three in the morning.

I checked my watch, grateful Weston didn't insist on video calls, and couldn't see my restless squirming. If I hadn't taken WD-40 to the chair, it would've squeaked through the whole meeting.

"I'd like a tour of what you have." He said it so abruptly after waxing on about Coal Haven, I didn't realize I had spaced out while checking my watch for the eightieth time.

"Mr. Duke?"

"Weston, please."

We weren't exactly equals in the industry. Knight's Oil Wells made a lot of money, depending on the economy, but guys like Weston owned guys like me. I had to stay sharp to get my employees and my family the best deal.

We were doing fine. But we'd do even better if we contracted with a company like King Oil. We'd stay more consistent during the ups and downs associated with a larger, Montana-based firm. King Oil was known for doing good business, but they also preferred to be as local as possible.

As for entertaining a visit from the CEO, that was a little more inconvenient. I didn't want to leave the kids for what time I had left with them to go on a business trip, but I also hated to drag them and Tova out of town when I saw how important their dance practice was to the other kids involved.

Grayson's adjustment to traveling was witnessed with the milk incident this morning and Ivy's excitement at having friends over, something Meg had avoided if at all possible, often telling me *If I wanted to take care of more kids, I would've had more kids. Feel free to be the one to take leave and entertain, Alcott.*

That settled it. I would trek to Buffalo Gully on my own and ask Aggie for an auntie overnighter. "I can be back in Buffalo Gully whenever you need."

"I can fly into Coal Haven. You have some wells right over the border, correct?"

"Yes, Mr.—Weston."

"Great. We can make it a day trip. I don't want to take you away from your kids."

Relief was a cool pack on my forehead. "Thank you. I appreciate it."

"I remember what it was like. My kids are all adults, but when they were younger, my old boss used to be very conscientious about family time. I'll fly in at nine, we can be done with the well visits by two and get back to Coal Haven by four. That'll give me time to stop in at the refinery while anyone I know is still at work." His old stomping grounds. "Does next Tuesday work?"

I didn't bother to check my schedule. As considerate as he was being, I'd make it work. "I can pick you up, or will you arrange a car?"

"No fancy car service for me, Alcott."

Right as we disconnected, the doorbell rang. Just in time. Tova said she'd keep the door open to make sure no one rang the bell, but doorbells were irresistible for kids.

I checked my notifications. Three missed calls and five emails. The texts were from Aggie. I was in the middle of reading them when I heard Ivy announce, "Welcome."

I stilled and listened, loving the glimpse into their day. A small perk of a home office. I worked a lot, but I wouldn't get these experiences if I had an office elsewhere.

"We have tea and juice for after our practice." She

sounded regal, like her mother. Instead of sadness, I found myself smiling.

They were all quiet, and I guessed Tova was talking. Moments later, there was a knock on the door.

"Yes?"

Tova poked her head in. She'd gathered her hair into a floppy bun on top of her head. This morning, she'd had it loose to caress her shoulders, and I acutely remembered how soft the strands had been against my bare chest.

I wanted to fuck her again.

I needed to sink inside of her and hear those little moans leaving her because of me.

We'd gone through three condoms like I was back in college. I thought I'd be stiff and sore, like I had run a 10K after taking a few years off, but all I could do as I lay alone in bed the morning after was remind myself that I had no more condoms and I sure as fuck wasn't buying them within a hundred-mile radius of Buffalo Gully.

"Sorry about the doorbell." Worry played over her delicate features.

"My call had just finished."

She sagged against the frame. "Oh, thank goodness."

Her concern bothered me. At first, her efforts didn't go unnoticed or unappreciated, but it was more. And now that I knew her history, I wasn't sure. "Tova, even if a kid went screaming through the house, I won't lose my shit. I promise. It happens—as long as it doesn't happen all the time. A random doorbell is life."

"Thank you. It's odd how old habits are popping up. Must be the house and having new people in my life." Her smile was soft. "And I'm not used to such a chill guy."

"I'm anything but chill."

"You're uptight about the right things."

The men in her life had been shit. "Don't worry about

it. Even if I do get upset, I can just let it fester for a while before I cool off. Okay?"

"Okay." Her nod made her decision to trust me visible. "I also wanted to make sure you were off the phone before I blared music and stomping filled the air." Laughter filtered down the hallway, and my reality tilted. I was in a different world than the one I grew up in. My brothers fought. Aggie talked loudly in order to be heard. But laughter? Not as much after Mama left.

And before Meg died? The house was quiet. It was a place for us to catch our breath, recuperate from the office, and raise some kids. But we had kept to ourselves, and our social lives revolved around our respective jobs.

"Stomp away," I assured her. I brandished my phone. "Also, my sister is wondering if you'd like to go out with her, Sutton, and Vienne to play darts."

"Darts?"

I nodded, unsure what LA had for dive bars with dart machines. "It's very low-key, and they play at a bar in town."

"Oh." Her luminous eyes blinked as she deliberated. "I've never played."

"If you can throw a small object, you can play." A smile tugged at my lips. "My sister's asking you out."

She returned my grin. "In that case, I could try darts. Why me?"

"Aggie is new to town too. Sutton as well. They might want to make some friends." My smile widened. "Also, fair warning, my brothers have big mouths when it comes to all of our business."

She glanced down the hall and stepped in farther. "She wants to find out what's going on between us?"

"That's not Aggie's style, but I'm sure she's heard all about the weekend and the sleepover. She won't pester you over it. If she asked you out, then it's because she wants to get to know you."

She thought for a moment, chewing her lush bottom lip as she worked over her final answer. "I'll go. Thank you, Cody."

"And thank you for this morning. Grayson was . . . vulnerable. You're amazing with him."

"Kids can sense when things are going to change, and sometimes the small schedule shifts are just too damn much."

"Tova!" Britta called—or was it Kali? "Can we start?"

Tova grinned and ducked out, closing my door quietly.

I knew the meltdown hadn't been from the milk. The timing after Curtis's call was impeccable. Before I had decided to send them away, I had talked to the kids about living with their grandparents, and if they'd had big objections, I wouldn't have made the plans. They had seemed disappointed, a little scared, but then their mom had just passed, and I'd told them living with their grandparents was ultimately her idea.

They were kids, dumbass. What would they say? *Why, actually, I think the adjustment to life in a bigger town, a brand-new school, living with people who we're used to spoiling us but would now set strict bedtime and screen-time limits might be as shocking as getting detention because a teacher doesn't understand the presentation of grief in children.*

I blew out a breath and rubbed my eyes. Was I doing the right thing? Before we moved to Crocus Valley, I wasn't sure.

That wasn't true, was it? I was in Crocus Valley because my sister had sensed my quiet resignation, and she'd pushed me to take some time. To think more about it.

And I'd done it. Had I been hoping to change my mind?

To find a compelling reason to cause my in-laws even more upheaval after losing a kid?

But I would be losing mine for much of the year.

I stared at my scribbles from the call with Weston Duke. If I could land this contract, the company would be more stable. I could turn some duties over to the King Oil team. I'd have more time on my hands.

There was still Knight's Arabians and Cattle Company and that damn trust.

I dialed Eliot before I had much time to ponder the thought that came to mind.

He answered with a "Yeah?"

My brother always sounded cranky. "I love you too, bro."

"Shut it. You only call when you're giving me bad news."

"I do not."

"Do too."

My last call to him had been to shitcan the idea of the indoor riding ring. Before that, I told him I was leaving for the summer. More financial woes after I got full access to the books Barns had poorly kept. Going back, there was the call that Aggie was taking up with who we thought was her shitty ex. At the time, we didn't know Ansen was actually a decent guy. Then there was the call that Meg had passed. "Fair. I do."

He grunted. "What now?"

"About the trust . . ."

"We talked to Lorenzo. Barns was pretty clear. It's all in that damn trust. You, me, Austen, and Wilder are tied to this place if we want the money."

Eliot had known nothing else, hadn't expressed wanting to do anything else. A comment Aggie made months ago filtered through my mind. *Eliot said he took over because none of us were going to.*

We'd all assumed it was what he wanted. We'd gladly backed out, except for Aggie, who'd never been allowed in, and left it all for him.

Was that why he was a permanent grump?

"One thing my wife always used to say was that nothing was ever definite in law. 'It depends' was her motto." Loss tugged at my heartstrings, but there was more fondness than normal. Meg had been a beast of a lawyer, and I'd been proud of her. She'd love that she was helping me cut a few ties to the ranch because of her.

"I don't mean to be a dick, I really don't, but Meg's not here to fight the contract with us."

I didn't take offense. He'd delivered his point gently, which was a lot for Eliot. "If Meg were here, she would've poked holes all over that contract. My point is—there are holes. Do you want to find them?"

"What do you mean?"

"I'm working on a deal with King Oil."

"Yeah, you mentioned it, but I'm not celebrating until the ink's dried. Even then, it doesn't really affect me. You're not like Barns, robbing from the left hand to give to the right."

I appreciated Eliot's confidence in me. Barns had floated the ranch with oil money. He'd overlooked cost-saving, efficient practices because the oil prices had been in our favor. When cattle was good, those got us through the rough oil years. And the horses? Those were a drain no one wanted to talk about. A business that should've been nothing more than a supplemental revenue stream. Instead, Barns had made the Arabians his empire. Only he hadn't kept up with the times, and it had cost us. The horse breeding business was sponging off the other companies.

Now that Eliot was managing the horse and cattle side and I was in charge of the oil part, we were working to rectify that issue. Which meant Eliot had to figure out how to make the cattle profitable again and decide if the horses were worth keeping.

"I don't know if what we'd find would help you. The rest of us have other jobs, and being forced to work the ranch isn't helping our family lives."

"As if that would've made a difference for Wilder." The decree motivated Sutton to ask for a divorce. "Austen doesn't give a shit."

He didn't. Barns was giving him a smaller portion of the money for his time in service. Still, Austen would lose a lot if he didn't work for the family company. "There has to be a way to give us some freedom."

"To get you your inheritance without working your ass off for the next thirty years at a second job?"

"Basically. We might figure out something that helps you."

Another grunt. I couldn't tell if he wanted us to find anything or if he didn't care. "I'm sure we can at least hire a bookkeeper or another accountant to work under you and play around with the hours and titles to satisfy the trust. As long as you show them the ropes. I don't have fucking time."

Hiring someone while I move into a supervisory role might actually work. The weight was already sliding off my shoulders. "You sure about that?"

"Do whatever you gotta do. I don't have a family to lose . . ."

"You might someday."

A third grunt. "Right. There are single women flocking to Buffalo Gully daily who'd love to marry a man who spends more time with heifers than her."

"Isn't there that new dating show for farmers—"

"You can fuck right off."

I chuckled. I didn't want Eliot to be lonely if he wanted a partner. But I was still a brother who enjoyed getting under his skin. "Let me put in a call with Lorenzo. See what comes up. Worst case, we're stuck doing what we're doing until retirement."

And we'd all be fucking lonely bachelors who had to put an oil and cattle company first. Tova would have long moved on, and hopefully, my kids would still talk to me when they were adults.

Fourteen

TOVA

I was in a small-town bar as noisy as any city club with a fraction of the people. I held a red Solo cup, but instead of containing alcohol, mine held darts.

"Okay, so this game is like a countdown to zero," Aggie yelled over the noise. The wood bar, wood walls, and wooden ceiling acted as an echo chamber that also provided good amplification for the cranked jukebox. Forget the theater. I should ask the bar if the kids could perform here. The acoustics were outstanding.

"We're not competing, are we?" I asked.

Vienne wasn't flitting around for once. Her game face was on. Her expression looked like she took out her opponents with darts to the head.

"Not really," Aggie said, twirling a dart around her fingers. "This is just practice for league. You and me against Vienne and Sutton."

Sutton was grabbing drinks for us at the bar. She was

leaning on the bar top, one knee cocked, her boot on the footrest, and at least two men were checking out her denim-clad ass. Her hair was in a tight braid from work. Mine was in its typical haphazard top bun, but I wasn't wearing jeans. I stayed in the white tank top and long skirt I'd had on when swing dancing with Cody. My nerves were keeping me warm against the AC pumping through the place.

How long had it been since I'd gone out with gal pals?

How long had it been since I'd had gal pals?

A few feet away, Vienne tipped her neck from side to side and narrowed her eyes on the target board.

"Is she going to kick my ass for real?" I asked Aggie.

"No. That dart board is going to be Theo's face for the next two hours. I'm not sure what he did, but she growled about him when she first arrived." We shared a look of mutual disrespect for Theo before she turned to Vienne. "Why don't I go first, then you, then Tova can try it out. By then, Sutton will be back."

Vienne nodded. Her jaw was on perma-clench tonight. She'd left all her bracelets on her left wrist, but her right was free for throwing. I watched her stance, the way she aimed, and her throw. Aggie threw similarly. It wasn't a hard game, but there was skill.

A drop of adrenaline pumped through my veins. I liked the challenge. It was my turn. I put my sandaled toes on the line of grungy white tape on the floor and flung my dart.

"Nice," Aggie said, gathering her hair back into a fluffy ponytail. She tied it off. "What were you aiming for?"

"Uh . . . the bullseye?" I'd hit a black triangle that lined up with the number twelve.

She nodded. "Yeah, not bad. You can try aiming at different places. Not all games are about the bullseye. I'll bog you down with the rules after you get a feel for throwing."

Sutton stopped at the table we were surrounding.

"Sorry, Aggie. All they had was plain sparkling water, no flavored."

"No problem." Aggie cracked the tab and took a swig. "Mm. Tasteless. But at least I won't need to call for a ride if I drink too much. Ansen's out with his dad and brother tonight."

"As long as it's not Fireball," Sutton said.

Aggie snorted, holding her fingers to her mouth to keep her drink in. She swallowed and looked at me. "The last time I had Fireball, I ended up with my ex as an employee. That was Ansen. Did Cody tell you the story?"

"Some of it," I said, passing my darts back and forth between my hands. I'd never been this nervous on stage, but none of the crowd had been my friends.

These ladies weren't my friends either. But . . . they could be?

As we made our way through the game, I heard about Aggie and Ansen's story. Vienne grinned—she'd heard it all before—and Sutton interjected with details since she'd been a participant.

Vienne stepped to the line, her face a mask of concentration. She took aim. Her dart hit, and her score dropped to zero. "Yes!"

We clapped, earning a few glances from the other patrons. A guy close to our age at the video slots leered at us, but our group was gathering looks from most of the guys in the bar.

Sutton put down her cup of darts. "Should we play again in a few? Maybe 501?"

"As long as we don't cut girls' night short, I don't care," Aggie said.

Vienne nodded, and I found myself bobbing along with her. I was part of their group. Girls' night. I hadn't really gotten to experience this when the night wasn't centered around work.

When I was younger, Mom and I moved around too much. When I lived with Grandma, I was too absorbed in learning to dance well enough to make a living and care for Mom. As an adult, I had friendly acquaintances, but I met everyone at dance tryouts or gigs. The undercurrent of competition never went away.

"So, how's the job?" Aggie asked as she slid onto her stool and straightened the yellow summer dress that made her freckles stand out. The cowboy boots were the perfect choice to go with the dress. If she'd worn sandals, she wouldn't have been able to launch herself out of her pickup like she did when she swung by Cody's to get me.

"Good. The kids and I are working on a routine to perform before they go back to Buffalo Gully—before they go to their grandparents. A few neighborhood kids are participating too." The more I thought about Grayson's milk incident earlier this week, the more I wondered if Ivy wasn't burying her emotions in the iPad and not only avoiding the drama.

Aggie wrinkled her nose. We were on the same wavelength about that. "I keep hoping he'll change his mind. I know I'm being selfish, but I like having them in town. I've seen them more this year than I have the rest of their lives. Is this performance open to family?"

"I'd love to see it." Sutton nodded, then stilled as if she wondered if she'd be included as family. "I guess it's up to Cody how many people he wants at the house with all the other kids' families."

"Grayson and Ivy would be thrilled to have you both," I reassured them. "Sima called yesterday. She talked to the theater owners, and they weren't willing to rent the theater for practice, but they said we could at least have the performance there. I think Sima and Bill might've paid for the night." Sima had never said, but Thelma swore the theater owners weren't that generous.

I know Sima would've done it for Kali, but the number of people I owed continued to rack up. I didn't know how I'd pay them back and get my assets from Frederick and take care of Mom, and the thing was . . . no one acted like I owed them. Thelma brushed me off when I mentioned a payment plan. Sima wouldn't admit to renting the theater for a night. And Cody's family had provided food for the cookout and never highlighted my lack of contribution.

"Can't wait. The theater is going to make it so special for the kids," Aggie said. "How was the trip to Buffalo Gully?"

"It was—I mean— You know . . ." I swallowed hard, wishing my hard seltzer was a straight shot of bourbon, something that would sear my throat and make me forget I'd had sex with this woman's brother. What could I say? *Buffalo Gully was great, but my favorite was the fuckfest I had with your brother in his pickup in one of your family's pastures.* Somehow, I didn't think that'd go over well.

Sutton's mouth pinched like she was biting her cheek. Aggie's brows were raised.

Vienne squinted at me. "You and Cody, huh?"

"N-no . . ." I didn't owe these women the truth, but my brain refused to acknowledge that fact. I wanted them to like me. I wanted to hang out with them in a way that had nothing to do with acts and performances or sharing resources for our shows.

I wanted real friends. But I wouldn't be in town long enough to keep them.

Aggie's grin spread wide. "You and Cody."

Sutton's eyes flared. "Seriously?" She smiled and put her hand on her chest, but relief refused to find me. "Oh, thank

God. I mean, after Meg's death, he got so . . ." She snapped her fingers like she was trying to think of a word.

"Rigid," Aggie filled in. "Uptight. Moody. Withdrawn."

Sutton pointed at her like she had won a game show. "You're the winner. He was all that before, especially when she got sick, but this was, like, worse."

Now relief crashed over me. They took the information in stride. They weren't even surprised. Weren't they suspicious of my motives? I didn't have to prove myself to them, and that just wasn't how my life had worked. "You guys don't mind? With his past, and since we're both in town temporarily, we don't want to bring attention to ourselves."

"He's not my brother or my brother-in-law," Vienne said, "but I know it sucks to have your personal life the center of attention."

"He is my brother," Aggie said, "and since you've entered the picture, I've actually seen him smile and do family stuff with the kids."

I circled the cool can in my grip. "He's been working a lot again." He wasn't as uptight, but he was back in the office like he had been before the trip.

"Of course he has. It's his default. He thinks he has to save the world, and he forgets that people would rather have him around than have the family money."

"Wilder has a similar trait," Sutton muttered.

"Wilder needs to learn how to spend time with anything other than his cruiser and his sidearm," Aggie said sympathetically.

"And his boss." Sutton nodded, her lips pursed. I tried to picture her and Wilder as a couple. I wished I was around to see it, but the idea that they were divorcing when they each seemed like they'd rather not was already sad. It'd be harder if I saw how much they meant to each other.

"Look, I'm the baby of the family," Aggie said, "so I

didn't get to witness a carefree side to Cody, but I felt like it was always there. And when he opened up to me, of all people, after Meg died, I knew I was right. To know he's actually allowing some of that out around you gives me hope."

"Well, don't hang all your hopes on me." I might not have had to prove myself to them, but I didn't want to be an impending disappointment. "It was just a fling, and I honestly don't know if it'll be repeated. We don't want the kids to see something and get the wrong impression."

Vienne leaned forward, her bracelets tinkling on the tabletop. "What I'm hearing is that the kids are cock-blocking you."

"Not at all. I mean, yes, naturally, but it's fine. They come first."

"What I'm hearing is that no one's coming," Sutton said with a snicker. She fist-bumped Vienne.

"No." I chuckled. "Eliot took the kids one of the nights we were there. That's the only reason we . . . ." I could *not* finish. I wasn't used to discussing my sex life, and I did it with Cody's family—and a neighbor. Should I have kept my mouth shut?

I was doing the same as them. Trusting them at face value. But I'd spent a lot of time around fake people, and I didn't get that sense from any of them, and I liked that they acted the same with me.

Aggie tapped her chin. "Let me talk to Ansen. We've been wanting to take the kids for a trail ride. I'll let you know what night."

"You don't have to." Was it weird to have a sister's help arranging a booty call? I wasn't a prude city girl, but this was just odd.

"I know," Aggie said. "I owe Cody for a lot. This is the least I can do."

Vienne snorted. "By helping him have sex?"

"I didn't grow up around rutting studs to be shy about it." A wicked gleam flashed through her hazel eyes. "Cody stays out of my business if he's in hers."

Sutton was taking a drink and choked on a laugh.

I started laughing too. I liked these women. A faint cloud of sadness passed over my good mood. I'd be leaving them when I went back to LA. Sure, I could stay, figure something out. But Mom was in California, so I had to go. I couldn't afford to move her, and I wouldn't abandon her like she'd done to me.

Vienne ran her bracelets as far up her arm as they'd go and then resettled them back at her wrist. "Say, Tova. I wanted to ask about your lessons with Catherine."

She was hesitant enough that I tensed. Was tonight too good to be true? "You found out I used to do burlesque?"

She shook her head. "Come again?"

Shit. I hadn't talked to her like I had with Cody. I had been too excited. "I should've told you first. I worked as a burlesque dancer for many years."

"Cool," both Sutton and Aggie said.

Vienne twisted some of her bracelets. "And you're worried I'd be upset?"

I nodded. "People have different reactions."

"Oh. God, Catherine would think that was so cool." She shook her head. "No, my dad always repeats that old saying about opinions."

"What old saying?" I sifted through my brain and came up short.

Aggie raised her hand. "Opinions are like assholes, every-one's got one." I snorted a laugh, but she kept going. "Only my daddy used to say 'if I wanted to hear what an asshole thought, I put my ear under a horse's tail.'"

Sutton chortled. "I heard him once say that to one of the neighbors."

"No worries. I've seen you work with the younger kids, and you're good with them." She traced a finger on the tabletop, tentative. "Actually, Catherine's been talking about how you and the neighborhood kids are doing the performance—"

"Oh, I won't be dancing."

"Why not?" Genuine confusion filled her eyes.

I glanced from her to Aggie to Sutton. They stared back expectantly, waiting for a valid reason why I wasn't dancing with the kids. It was almost like they wanted to see me perform. "I don't think it'd be received well." No understanding lightened their gazes. "Because of what I used to do? People don't understand it."

"The burlesque thing?" Vienne asked, perplexed.

"Even if I do a completely separate dance, some might worry, and I don't want to upset anyone. I'll keep it just about the kids."

Aggie pressed her elbows against the table. "Do you have a recording of your routine? I bet it was amazing."

Sutton sighed wistfully. "I can barely two-step. I had to rely on Wilder to basically drag me around the dance floor. I'd love to be able to dance."

That was an easy fix. "I can teach you. As long as I'm here. What do you want to learn?"

She smiled. "The street dance basics—swing, two-step, Texas two-step, maybe a couple of line dances so I don't need a partner."

"Got it. Let me know when you're free." I turned to Aggie. "Did you know your brother can swing dance?"

She got a faraway look in her eye. "Maybe? He's ten years older than me, so it wasn't like I was at the bars with him."

Vienne began tapping the table again. "I'd like to pole dance."

Delighted, I grinned. I hadn't expected the harried mom to ask about pole dancing, but it was like finding out your new friends liked pineapple on pizza as much as you. "I can teach that too."

Her eyes lit up. "You can?"

"It's an excellent exercise. You can get a tension pole for your house. I don't know what you'll get in before I have to leave, but you can learn some on your own too." Could I pack a lifetime of friendship into a month?

She gave me a knowing look. "But will I without you there to hold me accountable?"

I chuckled. "Yeah, that's sometimes the hardest part."

"I'd love to learn too." Sutton's cheeks flushed red. "I need a different exercise than wrestling kittens."

"Too bad you aren't staying in town." Aggie flicked the tab on top of her can, her expression sly. "You'd have a full class just for pole dancing."

"Word is already out that you give kids dance lessons," Vienne said.

"I really do miss teaching kids." I smiled at Vienne. "Working with Catherine is a treat. Older kids who are brand new can still do more than the littles. They learn the steps quicker and advance faster. I know I've only worked with Catherine twice, but she's doing so well."

Vienne snapped her fingers. "That's what I wanted to talk to you about." She fiddled with her bracelets. "She won't come out and say it, but I think she'd like to do a piece in the end-of-season performance."

The joy that blew through me was as cool and fizzy as the seltzer I was drinking. "Watching kids go from wall-flower to performing in front of an audience is one of my favorite things. I'd love to see her do it! I'll figure out how to bring it up so she doesn't know you talked to me."

She released her hold on her jewelry, a relieved smile crossing her face. "Thank you." She let out a gusty sigh. "I wish you were staying. I finally have friends, and now that I'm single—"

I thought I missed something, but surprise etched through both Aggie's and Sutton's faces.

"You are?" Aggie schooled her excited expression to concerned. "Are you okay?"

Vienne gave her a reassuring *I saw that, and it's okay* look. "I'm fine. I didn't want to be a downer, so I didn't say anything. I broke up with him last night. It's like losing a pouty teenager. I have Catherine for that, only she's more ambitious and less condescending. I'm done with man children." She slumped, her lips in a troubled line. "It's just . . . It was nice to have someone to do things with. A partner, even if he was a shitty one. Why aren't there any decent guys around? I mean, Aggie brought two of them to town, and they got snatched up right away." She held up her hands. "Not that I want your men. I'm just sayin'—some days it feels like Dr. Jake is my only choice, and he's a bad decision I'm not willing to make."

"Please don't," Sutton said. She flexed her hand, her gaze on the tan line left behind on her bare ring finger. "Some days I'm tempted to put my ring back on and see if he'll quit finding subtle ways to ask me out."

Aggie smirked. "I'd say tell him you're still married, but I don't think that stops him."

Sutton shook her head. "It doesn't, or I wouldn't have half the clients I do. Scorned husbands won't let him touch their animals."

"Is it selfish that I'm glad it's getting you enough business to stay in Crocus Valley with me?" Aggie asked.

"Not as long as you keep putting up with me on my mopey days." Sutton's expression shuttered, but the grief of ending her marriage couldn't be hidden. "I have two shoulders for you to cry on, Vienne, but I'm not going to lie—I'm glad you let Theo go. He wasn't good for you."

Vienne took a swig out of her can. "He sucked in bed too. I'm putting it out there—I want an ambitious guy who's not afraid to work hard for a living—unless he's already rich. I'll take that too. I want him to dote on me, like my kid, and is it too much to ask that she likes him too? I want him to be considerate. And hot. And so damn good in bed I can't think straight the next morning."

Aggie lifted her beer. "Amen."

Sutton and I did the same, and we clinked cans.

I didn't have kids, but Cody checked all the boxes. His kids adored him. I adored them. The life I wanted was right here. A home. Friends. Thelma. A man with flaws, but none of them dangerous to me unless you counted breaking my heart. But he was leaving, and my mom was across the country. As much as I wanted to stay with Thelma, I had nothing here. There were no guarantees I could open a dance academy and have enough students to pay bills. I had too many expenses before I reached the point of being able to rent.

All that added up to me having to leave too. If I was used to one thing, it was starting over. Just once, I wished I didn't have to.

Fifteen

CODY

Aggie called yesterday. She asked to take the kids today so they could go to Ansen's brother's place in Coal Haven tonight. In the morning, she'd take them horseback riding before the heat set in. When I talked to the kids, they were thrilled.

Hell, I'd been fucking beside myself with excitement. I was like a teenage virgin whose prom date said she'd suck his dick after the prom grand march. I went all last week hardly touching Tova. She worked over the weekend so I could make arrangements and gather data for Weston Duke's visit, which meant I'd been stuck in the office. Again.

And I was back in the office. Tova helped the kids pack, and I broke away from my computer during lunch to chug some milk and give them hugs before they left. I wanted to be there when Aggie picked them up, but I had another meeting when my sister said she would swing by.

A half hour ago, I heard them running to the door and

flinging themselves at their aunt and uncle. Then laughter between Aggie and Tova carried to the office. I ground my teeth together, hating I was missing the sight of happy kids and how well my sister got along with my nanny.

I'd be free tomorrow when she dropped them off, dammit. I'd make sure of it.

And Tova was so much more than my nanny, but my nanny was all she'd been since we used the last condom in the pickup that night. I was back to vivid dreams and stroking off in the shower.

I hadn't even had a chance to sneak a kiss.

I scrubbed my face and listened to my accounts manager drone on about the various lease renewals we had for the wells on land not owned by Knight's Oil Wells. She was great at her job, but she also still worked like she was getting paid by the hour. I didn't subscribe to the idea a salary meant getting as much time as I could out of my employees. If we could do this meeting in an hour, she wouldn't need to drag it out for two.

When she paused after the last data point, I tried to jump in, but my virtual assistant swung right into reviewing the itinerary for Mr. Duke's visit. "Did you want to tour any of the wells not on Knight property?"

"No, we'll be contracting for Knight-owned minerals first." Paperwork was easier to manage when Knight held the mineral rights, owned the wells, and was one of the parties signing the contracts. I seized the opening. The drive to get the job done and move on had been strong since returning from the ranch. I'd missed my kids leaving, and the bitterness wasn't fading. "Thank you for getting all that arranged. We'll touch base again this time next week to make sure all the final preparations are in place for his site visit."

When everyone had disconnected, I leaned forward in my chair, propped my elbows on the edge of the desk, and dropped my head between my arms. The backs of my shoulders were tight. Overall, I was tenser than normal.

It could be the long hours in the shitty chair. The time behind the desk. The angle of leaning to peer out the window at Tova with her long legs going through the moves with the kids. My favorite was when they were just messing around and she danced around, her laughter mingling with everyone else's.

The sound was becoming necessary for life.

A notification dinged on my computer. A reminder my workday wasn't over yet.

Fuuuck.

I had just opened an email with a reiteration of today's meeting from my accounts manager when there was a light knock on the door.

"Come in." I ditched the email because the only person at the door could be Tova, and she was more important than my inbox.

She peeked in, her dark hair not in a top bun like normal but pulled back with corkscrew curls framing her face. She looked even younger, but in an old black-and-white-photo way.

"Hey, is your meeting done?" she asked softly.

"The meeting is. Now to answer a million follow-up emails." I ran through calculations like I was Einstein, but there was no way I could step away from the office for the afternoon. Would Tova stay? I didn't want her waiting on me.

Would Tova be offended if I fell on her like a starving beast, then went right back to my inbox? No, she deserved better. "Are you heading out? Maybe we could do something for dinner?"

We hadn't talked about us when we discussed the kids going with Aggie. The kids had been around, and she'd been carefully and professionally neutral. I had struggled to be the same.

"I wanted a few minutes of your time," she purred.

My dick stood at attention just as she casually swung the door open. My back hit the chair, and all the air whooshed out of my lungs. I was riveted.

She wore long, sapphire-blue gloves, and peacock feathers poked out from behind her head on one side. She was gorgeous, as always. But what she was wearing had me in a chokehold I didn't want to be released from.

She had black velvet heels on her feet, and her long, creamy legs were bare. I stroked my gaze up her legs until I hit the juncture between her thighs, where only a scrap of fabric matching her gloves covered her. Thin straps that were nearly useless circled around each hip, and I'd die a happy man knowing if they disappeared between her ass cheeks.

I could linger there forever, but then I would miss another view of the curves of her belly, the way her waist nipped in on each side, accentuated by how she was standing, and the lacy bra that covered way too damn much for being so skimpy.

Fringe hung off the cups of the bra to tease the skin of her belly.

"Goddamn."

She pivoted to the side, sticking her ass out. "Do you like what you see, Mr. Knight?"

I groaned, both at her formal use of my name and at the confirmation that there was nothing more to her panties than string that trailed through globes I could sink my teeth into. "I've been dreaming of devouring every inch of you, Miss Evanson."

Looking pleased, she spun to the other side, the move

smooth and practiced. "Your sister told me to remind you that you're working too much."

"I might need a few more reminders if that's how you're giving them."

"I also wanted to thank you for replacing the air conditioner."

After being in my house with central air, then returning to the flagging AC in the old farmhouse, I bought a new window unit and one for the upstairs and submitted the receipts to the landlord. I didn't care what he fucking did with them. I wasn't boiling at night anymore. "You should've said something earlier. I would've done it sooner."

She sauntered toward me, one heel carefully placed in front of the other. A saucy, sensual walk. Blood evacuated my brain, and I was nothing but a lust-ridden male ready for her to release my leash by saying *go*.

"I left the dress that goes with this behind in California," she said, stopping just two feet in front of me. Her rosewater scent closed around me. Heaven was near enough to touch, but I didn't want to ruin the show.

And that was what this was. A private little show. Just for me. As if she dug into my brain and saw how badly I wanted to see her perform. Like she knew I was already her number one fan.

I was obsessed with her.

She tipped forward and propped her hands on the armrests of the chair. "So, you're ahead of the game. I'm already in my underwear."

"You're fucking gorgeous." I trailed my finger along the edges of the trim hanging from her bra. "But I also can't wait to see you naked."

A sexy pout plumped her lips up. My brain barely registered that she wasn't wearing thick stage makeup. Nothing but lip gloss and maybe a light touch of mascara, yet she was a fucking knockout.

"Don't you know, Mr. Knight?" That breathy voice she used was going to make me come in my slacks. "We don't get naked."

"I'm willing to wait until after the show."

Her smile was saucy as she tugged her bra straps down. Then she wiggled her shoulders as she reached behind her. My pulse jumped. Was she taking her bra off? I couldn't tell if she was wearing pasties or tassels, and I needed to know right fucking now.

Just as her bra loosened and would've slipped down, she turned and peeked at me over her shoulder as she slipped the damn thing off all the way.

"Kitten, you're fucking killing me."

"Speaking of kittens . . ." She tightened the chokehold she had on me with a slow sway of her hips. Side to side. Side to side. "I have to shut the door, or they'll come in and interrupt."

She ditched the act and marched toward the door, butt cheeks jiggling, so damn tempting. After closing it, she wiggled her hips again and shot me a flirty look while holding her bra in front of her chest.

"That's how I want to see you close every door in this house."

"A gal sometimes has to improvise." She sauntered toward me, her bra frustratingly covering all the important parts.

I clenched the fingers of each hand. She was so close. I could touch her. But then that'd be the end of it. She was giving me a glimpse into her life. A special feature only for Mr. Knight. I wasn't fucking it up.

She slowly turned around, and when her back was to

me, she held the bra out to one side. Then dropped it. My heart nearly stopped.

Pasties or tassels?

She turned her head to peer over her other shoulder. The sway she did with her hips turned rhythmic. Enraptured, I kept my gaze on her fleshy cheeks. I could lean forward and nibble them.

But I didn't. I was an avid audience.

"Mr. Knight." She adopted the sultry purr of a 1920s sex kitten. "Is that a pistol in your pants, or are you happy to see me?"

Despite the desire raging through my veins, I chuckled. "I'm very happy to see you."

She linked her hands behind her neck and turned her face into an arm. "I heard there was one thing you really wanted to know."

"Yeah?" The word came out guttural.

She spun, and there they were. Fucking tassels, swinging gently, a few strands tangled.

"I knew it." I didn't sound human. I sounded exactly like that guttural, ready-to-rut beast. "Christ."

"This is the point where I strut around the stage and get a few more laughs while men and women stare at my tits." She leaned on the arms of the chair again, tits and tassels in my face, right where I preferred them. "But I really want the performance to be over so you'll touch me."

That was all I needed to hear. I snaked a hand around the back of her head and dragged her onto my lap. The old chair squeaked, but I didn't care. I claimed her mouth. She tightened her fingers in my shirt and moaned into me.

She pulled back. "I want you to know, I'm not asking you to quit working for the day. But I thought you deserved a break."

I didn't care how many questions were waiting in my

inbox. I nipped at her lips. "I can't seem to give a fuck about work when you're around."

"Yes, you do. But you're really horny."

"God, yes," I groaned, diving back into her mouth.

Our tongues danced together before the demand for more pounded at my temples. If I released my dick, the day was over. And ultimately, I'd feel like shit that I left the office for sex and barely popped out to wave my kids off for the night when they left with Aggie. Tova knew me better than I did.

I swiveled the chair and closed my laptop. I set her on the edge of my desk. "Tonight, you're mine. But I'm going to leave you with a little reminder."

Her blue eyes shone, even bluer thanks to the sapphire on the rest of her body. "Promise?"

I loosened my tie and leaned forward, spreading her knees apart. "Keep the shoes and gloves on, kitten."

She blinked and looked at her hands. "I forgot them. Mr. Knight, you made me forget an entire sequence of my show."

"Damn right I did." I lowered my head between her thighs and shoved the tiny fleck of soaked fabric to the side. "Tova, you're wet for me again."

"Yes," she whined and propped her hands behind her, knees falling farther apart, the backs of her heels resting on my shoulders.

I licked through her slit and tightened my hold on her hips. She was sweet and salty and so damn addicting, I didn't think I could force myself to come up for air.

I lost myself in her. *Too long* kept echoing through my mind. Too long between the night in the pickup until now. Too long before I could have her again.

The sense that something had to break to get what I wanted scrolled through my head. Something had to give so I could be the dad I wanted to be. The man I wanted to be.

"Cody." Her back was bowed, her tits straining for the ceiling, the individual threads of the tassels draped over the slopes of her breasts. I could see her like this every day—tassels or not.

What was it like to wake up next to her?

"Stay with me tonight." My mouth hovered over her swollen clit. It glistened, begging for me to finish her off.

"What?" She undulated her hips again, seeking release.

"Stay with me tonight. In my bed."

She nodded. "Yes, now keep going."

Fuck yes. I flicked my tongue out. "Just like that?"

"Cody, you're killing me."

I smiled at her use of my saying. "I'm sorry, kitten. Was it this you wanted more of?" I gave her another quick lick.

Frustrated, she clamped a hand in my hair and tugged my head closer.

Chuckling, I let the reverberations ripple through her skin. I unclenched a hand from her ass cheek and slid a finger inside her. Hot and wet, my fucking favorite.

"Come for me, kitten."

A long groan left her right before she went taut. "Cody!"

"Louder," I growled.

"Cody, Cody, Cody." She shook against my face, her walls clenching around my finger. My erection hounded me. *Tonight.*

I kept going until she pushed on my head. Then I pulled away, licking my lips. She was spread wide open in front of me.

Perfect. I'd be erect for a month. Minimum.

Yet a concern niggled at the back of my mind. We'd had sex in the pickup the only other time we'd been alone together. She should know that getting inside of her wasn't the only thing on my mind. She was the entire package, and I wanted to be with her. "How 'bout I take you dancing tonight?"

She puffed a loose strand of hair out of her face. "Cody Knight, there's not a damn thing I'll say no to when your face is in between my legs."

"Aw, kitten—I'm going to tuck that fact away for the future."

Tova

An obnoxious alarm went off, and I cracked an eye open. A strong arm was banded around my middle. I stretched as much as the solid wall behind me allowed. The annoying beep was unexpected, but I got to wake up next to Cody in a real bed. I'd take an early alarm to experience the heat of a guy who'd done nothing but make me feel safe and give me so many screaming orgasms while doing it.

Cody finally moved and tapped the alarm off on his phone, then wrapped his solid arm back around me.

"It's early," I groaned as the sleepy haze wore off. It'd been a while since I'd been so stiff. I was used to my burlesque routine. I wasn't used to swing dancing and two-stepping for hours and then coming back to have another few hours of sex.

Cody was insatiable. I loved every minute of it and the industrial-sized box of condoms he'd bought.

"Sorry, I forgot to change it since I don't have to get the kids ready and feed them breakfast." Cody nibbled along my ear.

Just like that, heat kindled between my legs. I squirmed and was prodded in the behind by an impressive erection.

"'S okay." I didn't want to sleep the morning away. I didn't know if I'd get many mornings like this.

We were running out of time.

The thought was a cold splash of water dousing my desire.

"What's wrong?"

How could he tell? He couldn't see my expression. Was his dick a mood ring? I went cold and set off an alarm. "I'm getting in my head, that's all."

The muscles in his arm flexed. "Want to talk about it?"

I wanted to talk about all of it, which was the problem. I had already told him about Frederick. I wanted to spill my guts about Mom just to have one more person in my life to help with the burden, and god, didn't thinking about her like she was a problem make me feel like a total dick? More than anything, I wanted to vomit my fears about leaving Crocus Valley and have him tell me it was fine, somehow there was a future beyond the end of July that included both of us. That he would stay in this old farmhouse that wasn't his and didn't hold the memories he'd locked out when I met him. I wanted him to tell me there was a place I could rent and teach dance classes and I wouldn't get called a hussy in online reviews for doing burlesque and I would find a job that would pay me enough to afford rent. All in Crocus Valley.

It was a lot.

A lot for me to deal with, and a lot to dump on him.

The pressure built in my chest. I didn't have anyone to talk to about my worries. I couldn't dump them on Thelma. Aggie, Sutton, and Vienne were barely more than acquaintances, no matter how much I could see us all hanging out as friends. And I was still living out of a suitcase and sleeping on a couch.

I had to release the valve. Just a little. Or a lot. "I hate myself for letting Frederick know how much I need to take care of my mom."

He went quiet. Several moments went by. "Are you scared to tell me about her?"

"Yes," I whispered and sniffled. A single tear rolled out and slid the short distance onto the pillow. "She was afraid to be on her own, but she had the worst taste in men. The bar was on the floor. Her last boyfriend was abusive."

"The dog food guy?"

"Dog Food Guy was two before her last boyfriend." I clung to his arm around me like it was a life preserver. "I thought she was finally leaving, but she brought me to my grandma's in Yorba Linda to stay with her and Thelma. I thought it was temporary, but then we got the call. Mom was in the hospital. The old excuse that she fell down the stairs was obviously a lie." The back of my neck flushed hot, and the strength of my tears pressing against the backs of my eyes was almost as strong as when I'd been younger.

"He put her there?"

Another hot tear eked out. "Yes. She left me with Grandma until graduation, and she stayed with that guy. He kept abusing her. She wouldn't admit it, but we knew. Grandma tried to help. I tried to talk Mom into moving in with me when I was twenty, but she stayed. She landed in the hospital again. Head trauma."

"Fuck."

"We tried to get her to leave, but she went back." His hold on my body was my anchor. I had to finish the story. I had to let someone in, and dammit, I trusted Cody. "While she was rehabbing, she had a stroke. He didn't take her to the hospital right away. Thought she was messing around."

"Aw, Tova. I'm so damn sorry." He buried his nose in my neck. I continued to grip him. The story was spilling out. Cody had no financial control over me. He wasn't Frederick. I was safe with him.

Tense energy leaked out of me.

I did feel safe with Cody. My heart might be hanging out on a clothesline, but I was safe with him. He might hurt me, but only because he wouldn't change his life for me, and I couldn't hold that against him. He was doing what he thought was right for his kids. I didn't agree, but when it came to us, I trusted him.

The rest of the story gathered on my tongue to be told. "Grandma, Thelma, and I took care of her as much as possible. Between her injury and the stroke, she lost a lot of verbal communication and fine motor skills. She can walk with help, but her right side is weak. She needed a lot of therapy, and she still needs routine treatment, but she can't take care of herself. Then Grandma died. Funding and disability and who covers what and how much—it's a nightmare. A confusing mess that somehow still leaves thousands owed per month. Grandma did what she could, and I picked up extra work. It was easier when I wasn't alone." I drew in a ragged breath. When I returned to California, I'd be alone again.

"Then you lost your grandma, and Thelma moved?"

I nodded. "After Grandma died, the cost of living in California was too high for Thelma, but I think the memories of Grandma were too hard for her anyway."

"And Frederick got to you when you were the most stressed, like an absolute fucking predator."

How could Cody be so intuitive, so understanding? "I met him after a show, and I was so fucking tired. I taught classes from ten a.m. to six p.m., and I booked performances as early as eight at night. Then I'd perform, sometimes at three or four different venues a night, or I'd have a show at eight and then another at two in the morning. I booked as many as I could. When Frederick interrupted the rat race, I saw a chance to breathe for a moment." I was weak.

"It's still not your fault."

"I lost everything, and because I took the risk, I might've cost Mom her care."

"*You* didn't. And you're not going to let her down."

"Know anywhere I can get a job for seven or eight grand a month with no degree and only dance experience?" My joking tone fell flat. I let out a breath. Spilling my history had been cathartic. "I'm not looking for you to solve my problems, Cody. It's just nice to talk about it. I know Thelma will help me, but I hate to put that on her. What she makes in tips a day can barely buy her a nice dinner."

"You have a big heart, Tova Grace."

I liked hearing that version of my name. Any name Cody said was music to my ears, but then he wouldn't choose one to manipulate me with. "You know what my stage name used to be?"

"Hm?"

"Fannie Grace."

His chuckle vibrated against my back. "I was definitely riveted by a fanny." He pressed another kiss behind my ear.

"I'm sad about us," I blurted out and squeezed my eyes shut again.

He stilled, then nuzzled my hair, his hot breath wafting down my neck, creating delicious shivers. "I am too. The rest of the month is going to fly by."

"Three weeks."

"Three weeks," he said softly. "Do you . . ." His chest moved against my back with his breathing. "Do you see yourself staying?"

"No."

"Never?"

I was afraid to look at him. This conversation would've been impossible if I got lost in the warm depths of his brown eyes. "I would have to move Mom closer, and Frederick convinced me to sell my car and use his car service. He claimed it was safer, and he could invest the money I made from the sale and grow it." Which he'd done. And he'd kept it.

"But it only made you more dependent on him." He was incensed for me.

I'd met the perfect man, and I'd have to leave the perfect man. He wasn't willing to move out of Buffalo Gully. LA was firmly out of the question. "There's no way for me to make a living here. I doubt the refinery or coal mine needs a dance instructor."

"Is that what you're going to do for work?"

"Yeah? I mean, I love performing, but what I'd really love is to perform for me. To do a number I created because I wanted to. Because I wanted to share my artistic expression. Before, I had to sell my act to a crowd. I had to perform for them, but I'd like to learn what my own style is again after all this time." I let out a wistful sigh.

"Why don't you?"

"What do you mean?"

"At the end-of-season performance. The kids can perform. Then Catherine. Then you."

The girls had thought I'd perform, too, and Cody made it sound so easy. I'd been so excited when I told him that Catherine was thrilled to learn a routine for the end-of-season dance. I couldn't stomp over her performance. "That would be showing off."

"The kids would be delighted."

"Yeah, but they're biased."

"Their family would also like to see their kids' teacher

dance. Otherwise, they might wonder if you really had skills."

"Do I need to get my tassels?"

"Yes, but not for them. Seriously, ask the kids and see what they say."

Ask the kids. So simple. But also reasonable. The performance was growing into more than a backyard shindig. "You drive a hard bargain, Mr. Knight." I used the same purr from last night.

"I drive a lot of hard things."

He pressed his erection between us, and I bit my lower lip, loving the solid way he held me and the promise of the ecstasy that cock could bring. He took my heavy conversation and held it close, lightening my load. Affection swelled, but it wasn't accompanied by the giddiness of a new relationship or even a temporary fling with amazing sex.

Longing crowded around the edges of my mind. When I arrived in Crocus Valley, I knew what I'd lost. Money, pride, and the ability to properly care for my mom. Leaving Crocus Valley, I'd be walking away from the future I had wanted for myself. The one I envisioned I was working toward before the shitty landlords and crappy venues and the predatory ex.

I had a glimpse of a family who accepted me for me. Not how much money I could make them. The kids even liked Thelma, and there hadn't been many people outside of my own kin who liked prickly, defensive Thelma.

Everything I'd ever wanted was in Crocus Valley. A cozy home. Friends. A man who made me swoon and who treated me like I was special for no other reason than he couldn't help himself. A man who acted as if my dreams and fantasies were important. But I couldn't leave my mom like she'd left me.

"We have some time before I have to make a call," he

said roughly, and I realized I was grinding my ass against him. "I want to take you just like this and then fuck you again in the shower."

My body clenched and went molten. "My face is going to have the orgasm flush when your sister drops the kids off."

"Damn right." He twisted to grab something behind him, probably a condom. The crinkle of the wrapper confirmed my assumption, and then he was sheathed and sliding into me. Pleasure ignited. I could stay like this forever.

The groan he let out made it sound like we hadn't fucked in years when it'd been hours. I fisted my hands in the sheets as he slowly stroked in and out, letting the pleasure build and wipe away all the regrets.

I wasn't going to meet another man like Cody. Not in California, not anywhere in the world. So I'd hold these next few weeks close to my heart and use these experiences to get through all the hard times coming my way.

Sixteen

CODY

My arms crossed, I leaned against my pickup in the parking lot outside of the small Coal Haven airport. The wind ruffled my hair, cooling the way the sun beat down on me and soaked into the material of my suit. Good thing I didn't choose black. The light gray kept me from boiling alive while waiting for Weston Duke.

The hot prickle of sweat on the back of my neck could be from talking to my father-in-law on the phone.

"Are the kids getting excited?"

"They're nervous about the change." I'd leave it at that. Grayson grew more morose when the end of summer was mentioned. Ivy fretted over the cats and whether their new owners would be as good to them as us.

No amount of reassurance helped. For any of us. I'd miss those little furry missiles playing and scampering and making my kids laugh.

Curtis chuckled. "Lauri and I are trying to decide which one of us is going to retire."

"Neither of you wants to?" They had professed how much time they'd have to dedicate to the kids when they'd helped me the first few months after Meg passed. A spark of something I couldn't identify lit in my chest. If I wasn't waiting for Mr. Duke with a million things on my mind, I might think it was hope that my in-laws would back out, and I'd have no choice but to figure out how to be a full-time single dad who had a damn good excuse not to work so much.

"Well . . ." I heard the way he sucked in air through clenched teeth like he usually did. "You know, we've discussed different options. Both of us part-time. She's not —she doesn't— And I, well . . . Retiring is complicated."

How complicated could it be? They'd had successful, lucrative careers for decades. They weren't worried about health insurance or savings accounts, and they owned their house. Was I not the only one having second thoughts? "Are you sure—"

"Oh, yes, don't worry about that," he said hurriedly. "Helena will be better for the kids than Buffalo Gully."

I agreed, but my stomach was twisting and churning. The Helena plans were growing closer, and doubts and what-ifs invaded my thoughts more each day. I hated the idea of not seeing my kids for weeks at a time. Sure, I'd travel to visit them, and they'd come home—only Buffalo Gully wouldn't be their home.

Crocus Valley fit my idea of a home more than anywhere else. My sister and brother-in-law hung out with the kids. They had their aunt Sutton. They had friends, thanks to Tova and the recital.

Curtis was speaking, and I'd missed half of what he said. "—we can be there on the last Thursday of the month, leave on Friday, and have the weekend to move. I know the King Oil contract is important, and you're going to be busy."

Panic spread through my veins. "Friday won't work."

"You're coming here early?"

Fuck no. I pinched the bridge of my nose. Decisions had been made. Plans were in progress. "No, but the last Friday of the month is their performance."

"Oh?" He sounded interested.

"You remember I mentioned Tova?" She wasn't my dirty secret, but the mind-fuck of telling my father-in-law about the woman I was sleeping with wasn't avoidable. "They've been working for weeks on an end-of-season performance. It's Friday night at the old theater in town."

"Like a dance recital? Grayson talked about learning steps, but I didn't know they were having a program."

"They're working hard on it, and they're pretty excited."

"We can change our departure date to Saturday. That's no problem. Lauri and I would love to see their performance."

I bit my tongue. I didn't want the kids to leave Saturday. The only hard date I had was July 31, which landed in the middle of the week. My rental agreement was up then, and we'd have to move. But I'd unintentionally kept the date they'd land in Helena foggy.

Or had it been intentional?

"They'd love to have you." I counted down in my mind.

Two weeks.

Two goddamn weeks, and I was back to being alone. I wouldn't have my kids, and I wouldn't have the woman I wanted to spend my life getting to know.

I was in bad shape.

"You have an extra room we can stay in?"

Motherfucker. I wandered around the pickup, a hand on my hip, glaring at any unfortunate vehicle in my sight.

"Yes," I gritted out, trying to sound inviting and failing. "We'd love to have you stay with us." I'd have to behave myself. I couldn't let them see I was into Tova. Their reaction would be another problem to deal with, and I had enough.

"All right," Curtis said, matter-of-factly as ever. "Well, we'll see you then."

Two more weeks.

Goddammit.

I stuffed my phone back in my suit coat pocket and swiped at the beaded sweat on my neck. A mosquito buzzed around my face, and I caught it in my fist and flicked it away.

I had to get it together. The conflict inside me about the changes coming up wasn't my visitor's problem, and since he could solve some issues for me, I needed to make sure his tour was enjoyable and that he was impressed with Knight's Oil Wells.

My time ran out. Weston strode out of the airport, looking exactly like his picture on the King Oil website. I expected an entourage, but no one followed him. He carried nothing but a black computer bag slung over his shoulder. I'd never met the guy in person, but despite being dressed similarly to me only in a darker shade of gray, I could almost picture him swaggering across a fighting ring.

As he approached, the ridge on his nose became more apparent. The characteristic had to be what gave him a thuggish first impression. I didn't know his age, but he was older than me, though by how much was hard to say. He had a little more gray at the temples than I did. His swagger was both casual and powerful, but the smile he aimed my way showed me the real reason why he dominated the boardroom.

"Alcott Knight, we finally meet." He swung a hand out for a punishing handshake. My grip was firm enough not to get crushed. I didn't have anything to prove. If Barns were still alive, he'd probably stand here for five minutes in a silent war over who had a stronger grip.

"Glad you could make it, Mr. Duke."

"I was serious when I said Weston was fine."

"In that case, call me Cody." I didn't care what he called me, but the familiarity might help persuade him to work with our company.

He cocked his head. "From Alcott to Cody, huh?"

"My mama named me and my brothers and sister after classic female authors. I got Louisa May Alcott, but my hometown isn't a place for formality."

He chuckled, the crinkles in the corners of his eyes fanning out. He loaded himself into the passenger seat, setting his bag at his feet. "Thanks for the ride. Mind if we head to the refinery first? I don't want to miss anyone if we get back too late." He grinned. "Can't waste the whole day working."

"No problem." I mentally tossed the itinerary out of my head and turned out of the lot and onto the highway that'd take us out of town.

We passed through Coal Haven, and he pointed out the turn to get to where he used to live with his family. A few nostalgic comments from him followed about the changes, and then we were on the way out of town.

The refinery was only a few miles from Coal Haven, between Lake Sakakawea and the railroad.

"What brought you here for the summer?" he asked.

"Family." Ordinarily I didn't say much about my personal life to people I'd just met. I preferred to bypass the questioning looks and the loaded *How are you doing?* with work contacts who hadn't known about my wife. But for some reason, Weston's laid-back air inspired me to be the same. "My wife passed away almost a year ago."

"I'm sorry to hear." He didn't sound surprised. A guy like him would make sure he was informed.

I nodded, not feeling the usual tug of despair, wondering how the hell I was going to adequately raise two kids and keep two businesses financially afloat. "My sister moved to Crocus Valley. And I thought it'd be a nice getaway while I'm still close to everything. My kids are, uh, moving schools, and we might be apart for a while."

He went quiet for a few moments, his fingers tapping on his knee. "I have to admire Barnaby. He set up Knight's Oil Wells for remote work. A lot of guys would've ditched the ranch for the money and a corner office."

Not my father. "The money was a way to remain on the ranch, and it's better to stay close. My youngest brother manages the horses and cattle, but I'm the financial guy. My other brothers are still involved too." We had to be, but Lorenzo would check on the extent to which we were tied to the companies.

"All that can be remote unless you like getting your hands dirty."

God, yes. I wanted to spend more time in the sun and less time under an LED light. With that damn trust, it wasn't possible. "Barns's dying wish was to have us stay with the family companies. He tied us to it." I had no problem admitting my situation to Weston. He gave off a down-to-earth vibe that made me think he'd understand and realize working with me and Knight's Oil Wells wasn't working with my father.

His gaze burned into me, but I kept my focus on the road, willing the speed limit to suddenly bump up another twenty miles an hour so I didn't have to get into the subject further. I didn't want to lose his confidence in me or the company.

"It's not a coincidence King Oil reached out to you now, Cody."

I glanced over. His expression was considering, like he wasn't sure he should keep talking. He didn't have to worry. I knew why. "My father was a hard man to deal with."

He dipped his head. A confirmation. "That he was. He had a good head for business, but if you don't mind me saying—he was also shit at it."

My laughter was like a pressure release valve. I could probably spill all the trust issues Barns left me and my brothers with, and Weston would understand completely. My father hadn't delved far into the oil world, but his reputation went further. "Agreed."

"I've been impressed with you, though, and if I could poach you, I would."

I was on King Oil's radar as more than the owner of some wells? The only confirmation I got that I was good at my job was the low turnover rate and the fact that our doors stayed open during some challenging economic times. Hearing a guy like Weston low-key offer me a job was a compliment. "I'm honored, but I can't move to Billings."

"You can move anywhere, Cody. It's whether you want to or not." He dug out his phone and glanced at it, then shoved it back in his pocket. "That can wait. Anyway, I'm surprised it's the move that's an obstacle and not the fact that you wouldn't be at the top anymore." Since I was CEO of both of my family companies and Weston Duke would continue to be the head of King Oil. "Billings would have more schools to consider for your kids. More activities. More recreation."

My teeth were locked together. His offer sounded perfect and was absolutely the last thing I wanted. Grayson and Ivy would be raised by teachers and daycare while I was stuck in an office. At least I'd been in a home office. Besides, it didn't matter. "I need to be close to Buffalo Gully."

He made a noncommittal grunt. I doubted any job offers would come my way. "It's home?"

No almost flew off my tongue. It was where I lived, but it'd ceased feeling like home a long time ago. The house in Buffalo Gully was as much of an obligation as my job. The only times I treasured in my hometown were when I was working cattle with my brothers, and the last time I was there had only been the best in memory because my father was gone.

And because of Tova.

"Yes." My answer rang empty. "It's home."

"My wife didn't want to move to Billings. She claimed Coal Haven was where we should be. I told her that home was where she and the kids were." I nodded, but he shot me a rueful look. "I'm not sure she ever agreed with me."

"Yet you left anyway." I didn't mean to sound censuring. I was mostly curious. His wife sounded like my conscience telling me that change didn't need to happen, that if you were content somewhere, it was okay to stay.

I hadn't been content in a long time.

But he spoke as if his wife had moved with him. Where was Tova going? We were barely in the dating phase of a relationship, and I couldn't move my kids to California.

"We moved," he said. "My youngest is going to college in the fall. Things worked out."

"Good." Was it, though? For a guy who was open about his thoughts and details, he was suddenly succinct.

As if he noticed that he wasn't willing to expound on whether the move was a good thing, he shrugged. "You make a decision, and then you make it work."

I'd made a decision. Did I want to make it work? "New decisions can always be made."

"And then you make those work. The real circle of life."

There were situations where I didn't have a choice. My mama had left, and Barns wouldn't step up to the parenting plate. It was me or no one. Meg got sick and passed away. I tried to keep our life the way we had it, and it hadn't worked. So I'd made a different decision, one I thought would finally make her happy since I'd failed when she was alive.

Aggie's gentle but firm words ran through my head. I was here now, not Meg. I had to make decisions about what was best for us. Including me. It was time to make up my mind again.

I was falling for Tova, but I was prepared to leave her behind. The question was becoming, was I prepared to stay and watch her go?

Was I brave enough to ask her to stay for me?

Tova

It was Sunday, and while I planned to spend the day with Cody and the kids, I was in the park to talk to my mom. I'd told her I was staying with Thelma for a few months, that things with me and Frederick didn't work out. She didn't pry if she suspected there was a lot more to the story. Today, I wasn't on a swing since that'd be in the full sun. Instead, I took a seat at a picnic table under the shade of a giant tree after making sure there was no bird poop.

"After this, I'm going to meet Cody and the kids at the pool. It's a perfect day for swimming." Cody wasn't working as much since I used my burlesque skills to remind him he was keeping himself deskbound too much.

In actuality, I didn't think he needed prodding. He seemed to want to spend more time with the kids. And with me.

Mom's left eye crinkled at the corner. A hint of her former smile.

As I was talking, telling her about my day, a pressure built in my chest, a hot weight that grew heavier with each memory of the week I recounted. "I wish you could meet them, Mom. They're awesome kids. Grayson is such a good dancer. I love his passion. I hope when he goes to Helena, his grandparents will listen to Cody and enroll him in lessons. But he's even talking about trying football. He was so excited when I told him that a lot of athletes take ballet lessons."

Mom dipped her head. The tablet she was talking on was propped so she had to look down, but I could see her face clearly enough. We'd started off using the keyboard for her communication, but she'd grown tired, and she was content to let me talk.

"Ivy's a riot. She's a princess, and she's a warrior. She knows what she wants, and she doesn't follow the crowd. I feel like she must be a miniature of her mom. Grayson's sensitive, and I suspect he gets that from Cody. Cody is just so . . ." Charming. Sincere. Thoughtful. "Well, I'll tell you all about him when I see you again."

I'd probably talk her ear off for months about Cody. He bought food I liked. He helped prepare lunches and cook dinners. Some evenings, he would grill using the little charcoal grill that came with the house.

Shouts caught my attention. Grayson and Ivy were sprinting across the road with Cody hot on their heels in jeans and a loose gray Knight's Arabians and Cattle Company shirt plastered against his wide chest.

"Guys, look both ways!" he called, frustrated. The street

was quiet, and there were only two cars parked outside of the diner.

"We did!" Grayson waved wildly, and Ivy was prancing next to him.

I almost cut Mom off and hurriedly hung up, but I tightened my grip. I'd wanted her to meet them, but I wasn't prepared for them to meet her. They didn't know about her medical struggles or that she was in long-term care. My breathing shortened, and a trickle of sweat started at my hairline.

I talked about Mom to Cody, and opening up had been huge for me.

I drew in a slow breath. They were kids. They were good kids. They wouldn't use Mom to get to me, and I was acting paranoid. I didn't want to be that person, just like I was tired of compartmentalizing people in my life.

"Mom, uh, we have company." I gave Cody a tentative smile, and he mouthed sorry. I lifted a shoulder. When the kids met her, they'd be one step further into my life. The Knights' fingerprints would be all over my life.

I didn't mind. As the kids crossed the last few yards between us, my excitement rose. Anxiety aside, I loved my mom. I loved Grayson and Ivy, and Mom would adore them. She used to love hearing stories about the kids I taught.

I gave Cody a reassuring smile, and his expression warmed.

"Are you talking to someone?" Grayson scooted next to me on the bench, heedless of bird droppings. This park had a lot of them. He leaned in to peer into the phone. Ivy crowded on the other side, standing behind my shoulder.

"Guys, this is my mom. Lana Evanson."

"Hi, Lana Evanson," the kids said in unison.

Mom nodded, and the left side of her mouth tipped up.

The right hitched up a little. Her little wave was visible on screen.

"Mom had a stroke, and she's working on her speech and movement, so she might not say much. She can type, but we've already been talking a lot. But trust me, she's listening."

The kids nodded and waved, not caring one bit. They had a rapt audience with Mom.

"Are you still in California?" Grayson asked. When Mom nodded, he continued, "Did Tova show you the park?"

"Have you met my daddy?" Ivy asked over her brother.

My gaze shot up to Cody. He'd stuffed his hands in the pockets of his jeans, his expression equal parts amused and uncomfortable. Morning scruff was still on his cheeks. What would his stubble feel like between my legs? Heat swamped me on this already hot day. Now wasn't the time for those thoughts.

"No, she hasn't met your dad yet," I told Ivy.

Mom's eyes were dancing, and damn, it was good to see. I'd never introduced Frederick to her, and he'd never been interested in meeting her, just knowing about her. When I introduced a man to Mom, I wanted to make sure she knew he was someone special. I didn't want her to worry I was with a guy who didn't treat me right, and while Frederick had treated me well in a lot of ways, deep down, I must've known his actions and motivations were superficial. I'd instinctively known he wasn't Mr. Right but Mr. Right Now.

Cody was Mr. Right, but he could only be a Mr. Right Now. He would be a guy worth crying on Mom's shoulder that I lost him. But I wouldn't. I was strong, and I was going to make my life right. Men like Frederick could not be allowed to walk over girls like me. I wasn't going to pass him off to victimize some other woman. I would do what Mom never could and make Frederick pay.

Somehow.

Cody was the guy who gave me the confidence to stand up to Frederick. I'd be happy for Mom to meet him.

He stepped behind us and leaned in close. His cedar and sage scent wrapped around me, so damn familiar and tempting. I didn't get nearly enough of him. "You'll have to give Tova some room if I'm going to meet Ms. Evanson," he said to the kids.

"Lana." I smiled, relieved that if he had reservations about the sudden family meet and greet, he didn't show it. "She hates going by Ms."

I angled my phone over until his chiseled jaw filled the screen.

He waved. "Hello, Lana."

Did Mom notice how devastating his smile was? How close his face was to mine? Could she see that he was nothing like the guys she had in her life? I'd have plenty of time to fill her in when Cody and the kids moved. The date was circled on my mental calendar.

I brought the phone back, and the kids squished my head trying to get into the frame.

"That looks like a hospital room behind you," Ivy said.

"My mom spent a lot of time in the hospital too," Grayson added.

I chewed the inside of my cheek, unsure how the kids would handle Mom's situation. "It's like a nursing home."

Grayson nodded. "Mom was in one of those for a while."

"She didn't like us to be in there with her," Ivy said simply. "Do you let Tova in yours?"

The topic was heavy, but her question was so innocent I giggled. I had thought they'd be serious, but they stated facts, almost sounding excited they were subject matter experts about Mom's room. "Yes, she lets me visit her. I go as often as I can."

"Good." Ivy crossed in front of me and perched on my lap between me and the edge of the picnic table. "Hey, Missus Evanson—Lana, who's your favorite princess?"

I was trying to think of what Mom would say when she pressed her lips together. A slow "Belle" came out.

I was about to translate when Ivy sat back, pleased, almost knocking her head into my chin. "She's in my top five. With Elsa. And Merida. She shoots bows. Hey, you know my uncle has a bow and arrow? Eliot. Uncle Wilder probably does too."

"Uncle Austen uses guns," Grayson added.

I couldn't envision easygoing Austen packing. I glanced at Cody. "He's military police," he clarified.

"Our new uncle doesn't have a bow," Ivy said. "I've been to his house."

I didn't have to worry about speaking for Mom if they asked questions that would tax her verbal skills. Mom wouldn't be able to get a word in anyway. The kids told her about the dance performance, their summer, and the two kittens, Lilac and Cheetoh.

Mom's shoulders shook with her laughter. The kids' visit delighted her, and I didn't realize how much I was smiling until my cheeks ached.

I squeezed them to me, so damn glad I got to know the Knight family. Even more grateful I got to spend the summer with them. My heart would break when they left and I left. I was used to being a temporary memory, but I wished I could have something permanent like this for myself.

Seventeen

TOVA

Thelma rocked in a chair on the porch, watching the kids. A golden can of decaffeinated Diet Coke hung from her hand instead of an unlit cigarette. She had one leg draped over the other, but it was the relaxed hang to her shoulders I loved to see. She was enjoying herself.

First the call with my mom. Now Thelma was joining the cookout with Aggie and Ansen, Vienne and Catherine, and Sutton.

"This is new." Aggie waggled her finger at Cody talking to Ansen by the grill. Thelma and I were sitting at the plexi-glass-topped table on the porch with the other women.

"He didn't have cookouts before?" The evening was his idea. He'd been lost in his head more since he'd met with the guy from the big oil company. He'd said it went well, but I'd been deep in my lust since seeing him completely suited up. Then he'd put on his mirrored sunglasses and dropped a devastating grin that melted my panties right off.

But his suit had nothing on the jeans molding to his ass and draping down his long, powerful legs. He had his cowboy boots on, a plain black T-shirt, and those damn sunglasses that tempted me to scale his body until his mouth was at my—

"If he did," Aggie said, pulling me out of a desire-driven hot flash, "I didn't hear about them, and I doubt anyone was invited."

"*I* can even tell he's more relaxed than when he first moved in." Vienne had left her jangles at home, wearing four different necklaces instead. She fiddled with a metal charm in the shape of a paintbrush.

I had one leg crossed over the other. Aggie nudged my shoe with the toe of her worn cowboy boot. "Whatever you're doing, keep doing it."

"We've been trying as often as possible." I took a drink of my hard seltzer to keep from grinning. Since the night she'd had the kids, Cody and I connected at least once a day. Usually after the kids went to bed. I'd stay, and instead of falling on each other like sex-starved teens, we talked. I told him about my day or if I had talked to my mom. He asked at least twice a week if Frederick had interfered with Mom or the long-term care center. So far, he hadn't made a third attempt.

Vienne sighed wistfully. "I miss good sex," she said under her breath.

Sutton nodded and slid her gaze toward Aggie before dropping it to the porch floor. Like me, she couldn't exactly talk about how phenomenal her experience with a Knight was with Aggie. I didn't have siblings, but I was certain I wouldn't want to hear about their sex lives.

"At least it's made the breakup easier." Vienne watched Catherine practice her steps. The girl had been over last night, helping get costumes ready. Catherine could sew like a pro. I could've used one of her in the wings of my performances for wardrobe malfunctions. "The lack of any bedroom skills isn't anything I miss, although I do miss waking up to a warm body in bed. Even if he did snore and complain my feet were too cold. But Catherine's been so much happier. Like a weight has lifted off her shoulders, and I don't think it's just because she's excited about next Friday."

"It's going to be so fun," Aggie murmured. She rested a hand on her belly, and Sutton's eyes narrowed. I caught Sutton's gaze and lifted my brows. Aggie noticed the exchange and playfully glared at Sutton. "Damn—is there nothing I can get past you?"

Sutton held up her hands like she was proclaiming her innocence. "It's my job to determine what's pregnant and what's not."

Aggie laughed. "I'm not a cow."

"Good thing, or I'd be sticking my arm in your rectum."

Vienne coughed into her drink. She wiped her mouth as she swallowed and set the can down. "I haven't lived on a ranch for so long, I almost forgot the humor."

During one of our nights out playing darts last week, she told me she grew up outside of Crocus Valley. She had left for college, got married, and moved back when Catherine's dad left.

They were laughing, and I smiled, glad to be part of the joke. I didn't have any experience with cows or with vets or with friends, but I liked this. I liked this world.

I wished I didn't have to leave.

But being with Cody for the last few weeks, knowing him for not much longer, had only stoked my need to fight Frederick. To go back to California and make sure he didn't get away with what he did. It wasn't fair. I was a victim, and he shouldn't get richer from it. He tricked me, and there had to be a way to get my money back.

I'd return to California, work three jobs if I had to, but I'd pay for Mom's care and hire a lawyer. I might not have a chance to go up against Frederick this year. Maybe not next year—how much would legal fees be?—but I'd do it, dammit. He wasn't getting away with screwing me over and trying to use me.

I came to Crocus Valley to hide and lick my wounds, but I was returning to fight. All because one guy with a magic dick treated me well. Like I was worth something.

"Did you tell Cody yet?" Sutton asked.

"Cody," Aggie called. She flashed a shit-eating grin toward her husband. "I'm pregnant."

Ansen actually blushed, but his grin was wide and exhilarated.

Cody stared at her for a second, then a big smile spread across his face. "No kidding?" He held his hand out for his brother-in-law. Ansen smacked his palm against Cody's outstretched one. "Congratulations, guys. Really. That's exciting." His grin didn't fade, and he looked back and forth between his sister and Ansen.

I swallowed a sudden swell of emotion full of need and . . . envy. I was happy for them. Thrilled. What they had was special, and it was hard not to give up my plans to try for the same thing.

"It's early yet." Aggie shrugged, but she was beaming. "I couldn't hold it in."

"No matter what, I'm there for you. Really." He glanced at Ansen. "Both of you."

"I thought maybe you'd recite the cost of having a kid so soon after marriage. It's an expensive life decision," Aggie joked.

I could picture the Cody I first met lecturing Aggie on the bottom line.

He chuckled. "Don't worry. The numbers are running through my head."

Instead of milk, Cody had a longneck hanging from his fingers while he ran the grill. I watched his forearms flex and the easy way he took a pull from the bottle. The girls chattered about due dates while I fought off "what-ifs."

What if I could have this? What if I was the one announcing my pregnancy? What if . . .

"Food's ready," Cody announced. Ansen helped him get the burgers and hot dogs on the table.

Needing to keep my hands busy and divert my thoughts, I stood. "I'll go inside and get the rest of the food."

Sutton came into the house with me to grab the potato salad Thelma made and the veggie and fruit tray.

Sutton hitched the bowl under an arm and balanced a fruit tray in her hands. "I can't believe they're leaving next week. I'm going to miss them."

I clutched the plate of cut-up celery, carrots, and kohlrabi. Three bags of buns hung in my other hand. "It's going to be different. Then I'll be gone soon after." I clung to my determination, otherwise, I'd cry.

"I know." Sadness rang in her voice, but she smiled. "I'm glad I got to know you. Does it sound bad that it's been ages since I've made a new friend? You and Vienne."

"It doesn't sound bad. I'm the same."

"I guess it's easy to feel like you're the only one. I imagined you having a huge friend group."

"I was too busy working." Would I change when I returned? I wouldn't be able to if I was going to make the money I needed for Mom and lawyers.

Aggie and Vienne piled in.

"I'm going for your buns." Aggie took the packages from me.

"I worked hard on them," I joked. I focused back on Sutton, and once more, the words *why not* ran through my head. Why not be honest and forthcoming? "I was pretty isolated in California. I worked a lot, but then . . ." I'd never told them why I was here, and I hadn't planned to, but for some reason I wanted to spill all the details. "I met a guy, and I ignored some warning signs because it was nice to have someone help me." I gnawed on my lower lip. These girls wouldn't fall for the same bullshit I did. Then I recalled what Cody told me about why Aggie and Ansen broke up. She'd been younger, but suddenly I assumed they'd understand instead of thinking the worst. "He's in finance, and he took control of my money, and I thought since we were engaged, it was probably fine. I always had an out. I guess I just expected to have time to plan to leave like my mom usually did with her shitty boyfriends. Only I didn't. He bought out one of the venues I performed at for the night, and he expected me to personally perform favors for his clients."

"That bastard," Vienne hissed.

Aggie shook her head, her eyes spitting fire. "We need a horse, a rope, and a big hole."

"I'll castrate him," Sutton offered. "I'm quite good at it."

Aggie nodded. "She is."

Their instant support washed over me, leaving a cozy warmth I had never experienced before. Rather, I'd never experienced outside of Cody before. "I wouldn't want you to do a good job castrating him. Do your worst."

"I'm so glad you got away from him," Vienne said, giving me a quick hug that was so motherly, I fought back tears. Instead, I concentrated on the cool metal of her necklaces brushing my skin. "What a cocksucker."

I sniffled, playing it off as a righteous sniff. "He thought I was the cocksucker."

"We all are, for the right guy." She scoffed. "Only not many men understand that it's our choice."

Aggie propped her free hand on her hip. "Has he left you alone since you ditched his scummy ass?"

"He's tried to find me, but my mom's long-term care center wouldn't give him access." I hadn't told them about my mom either, but I would love to tell them about her. Only there was no time.

They only nodded, and a chorus of "good" rang out.

Vienne yanked the veggies from my hands like it was Frederick's head and she was going to smash it. "You tell us. If he tracks you down here, he'll have to face a whole crowd ready to nail those shriveled rotten balls of his."

The thought cheered me. The scenario would never happen, but I could revel in the fantasy.

We piled out, and the guys were sitting on either side of Thelma, listening to her tell them about what Crocus Valley used to be like when she was a kid.

"That theater was one I used to perform at when I was in school," she said proudly. She'd told me that at least three other times. She'd never verbalize it, but she was excited to see another generation take the stage.

Finally, something I could do for her.

Cody assessed me, a slight question in his eyes. He'd noticed how long it'd taken us to grab less than one item each. I smiled to let him know everything was fine.

Everything *was* fine. And then it wouldn't be, but a night like this would get me through a lot.

⚓

Cody

Everyone had left an hour ago. I put the kids to bed, but they'd asked for Tova to tuck them in and read books. Now it was after nine, and we were waiting for them to fall asleep so we could do very adult things.

Oddly, but not surprisingly, the sex hadn't become my favorite part. Being inside Tova would always be one of my favorite activities, pure heaven, but just sitting with her, chatting about the day and sharing stories of the kids, ranked at the top.

My feelings were more than just like. Went beyond enjoying her company, but I wasn't ready to look that hard at what I really felt beyond lust and deep affection.

I was sprawled out in a chair on the back porch next to Tova. I had my legs kicked up on the railing and was quietly strumming my guitar as a way to defray my nerves. She had her feet on the railing too, near mine, and I could barely concentrate on stringing a few tunes together with the bare swath of her legs so close.

The little wispy top she wore covered more skin than I wanted it to right now.

"Can I take you for a drive?" I'd done things to impress girls before, but I wasn't sure how my surprise tonight would land. She might be thrilled until I told her about what was on my mind.

I'd given myself time since the day I spent with Weston Duke. The clarity I experienced wasn't impulsive, but I wanted to be sure. Damn sure. My decision would ripple out and affect others.

Confusion plumped her lips, and I pictured nipping at her sweet flesh. Later.

I hoped we'd get a later.

"You want to get the kids up?" she asked.

"I asked Vienne earlier if she or Catherine could come over for an hour or so before sundown."

"You think we're going to need the whole hour?" Her teasing smile almost persuaded me to prove that yes, I could use an entire hour. She knew it because I'd already established that fact.

I grinned to lessen the butterflies piling into my stomach. "Two minutes or two hours, it's the lady's call, but no. I have something to show you."

"I've heard that line before."

I laughed and dropped my boots onto the porch. "Mind texting Vienne to see if Catherine can come over?"

Only a few minutes later, we left Catherine behind in the living room. She wore a big grin and was so damn proud to be babysitting.

I drove through town, my stomach clenching and my nerves threatening to spill everything before we got to our destination. I pulled onto the highway that would take us to my sister's. Getting closer.

How would Tova react? What would she say?

"You have to show me something at Aggie's place?" she asked.

"Nope, but we'll be close to her house."

She didn't respond. The only sound in the cab was the smack of bugs hitting the windshield.

I put myself on autopilot. My mind was a mass of questions, the various outcomes of tonight playing through like erratic dancers in too small of a room.

She scratched at her knee. Was she nervous? Did she trust me? I wasn't sure what she thought I was doing, but I also hadn't been a traumatized kid turned almost-exploited adult.

"Are you excited to be an uncle?" Her question carried a hint of longing, as if seeing my family expand only made hers feel smaller.

"I hadn't thought about becoming an uncle, especially not recently. I had my kids, and Wilder and Sutton never mentioned their plans. Meg had hated people hounding us about when we were having kids, so I learned to never ask. Eliot and Austen seemed to make sure they were never fathers, so I just wrote off being an uncle as not going to happen. Now, I can't wait." I aimed my grin toward her. "I'm going to buy her kids every obnoxiously loud toy possible."

Her light laughter was a welcome change from her pensive silence.

I could spend a lifetime getting that sound out of her.

Would she let me try?

I snuck another glance at her, but she was gazing at the sun hovering above the horizon with a stunning display of purples, pinks, and oranges cutting through the wispy clouds in the sky.

"Beautiful sunset," I murmured.

"Yeah," she said softly. "Mom and I used to drive to the beach and watch the sunsets."

"Thanks for letting me meet her."

She hadn't talked about the call beyond telling me her mom enjoyed chatting with the kids. I'd loved watching her relax and enjoy the conversation after we'd intruded.

I took my boot off the gas. The area I wanted was nearing. Today was the first day I'd spent my time in jeans and boots without working at the ranch.

I stopped off the road on the grassy approach with faded, tire-worn tracks. No fence blocked entry into the field, but posts were placed on either side of the approach, and metal fencing stretched out in each direction from them. This pasture had been used for haying for the last few years. Beyond us were forty acres, with cows in the distance to our right. That pasture was fenced off and part of the property. The peaks of Aggie's house and shop were visible across from us.

My palms were growing sweaty against the steering wheel. "You know why I'm excited?"

She shook her head, her lower lip sucked in between her teeth.

"Because I'm building here." I swept a hand toward the windshield, my heart pounding. I hadn't been this nervous —ever—asking a girl out. But I also wasn't asking her on a date.

Shock flared in her eyes. "What?"

"I'm buying this land. I'm building a house. The kids are staying, we're keeping the cats, and tomorrow, I'll tell them and my in-laws." I blew out a hard breath. I said my plans out loud.

As soon as I dropped Weston off at the airport, my mind was made up. I'd called Lorenzo, and he verified what I had hoped. There were, indeed, loopholes.

Perhaps I should've talked to the kids first, but I knew their answer. I'd been seeing their anxiety for months, and I'd wanted to cement my plans before discussing the change with them. My communication with the land broker— Ansen's brother—had been over email, and I'd asked for discretion until I could tell everyone myself.

Tova was first on my list. Then the kids. And my in-laws. I'd put no more thought into telling Curtis and Lauri than knowing I had to do it. They could be a force when they disagreed with someone, and they might argue against the kids staying.

It was an argument I'd win, but I wasn't looking forward to it.

"That's great." She grabbed my hand, her eyes swimming with emotions I couldn't identify. "I'm really glad you decided to move. I think Crocus Valley will be good for the kids."

This was it. My pulse hammered between my ears. I wasn't making a deal, I was trying to build a future with the woman I was falling hard for. "That's what I wanted to talk to you about. Would you consider staying with us? Being with me?"

The strength of her grip faltered until her hand went limp. "Cody Knight, are you asking me to go steady?" Her gaze wavered despite the teasing purr she'd used when she gave me the private dance.

"Yes," came out of my mouth when I wished it was her I was hearing it from.

She opened her mouth, then snapped it shut and directed her gaze out the windshield. "This place is heaven, but it isn't mine. Crocus Valley isn't my home. I don't have anything, Cody."

"You'd have us." Fuck, that sounded lame. I'd give her whatever she needed, but wasn't that the problem? Giving her everything made her feel controlled. Helpless.

She shook her head and blinked back a rush of tears. "And what? You'd pay me to be your nanny while we dated?" She swiped at her eyes. "Don't you see what that'd make me? It's just like Frederick, only I'd be willing."

My defensiveness rose. "Are you saying I'm like him?"

"No." She jerked, removing her hand from mine. "But you want me to stay, and you're going to offer to let me live with you and the kids. You're going to insist on continuing to pay me, then I'll officially be the nanny you're fucking." A sad, frustrated sound left her, and I wasn't sure if it was aimed at me or herself. "I want more than that. I need more than that. It's one thing to fall for you when I fought it, but after next week, it'd be an arrangement. I love your kids, Cody, but I can't. I have to be able to take care of myself. I have family too."

When she said it like that, I sounded like a fucking douche and not a guy who was desperate to keep being around her. "Then don't work for me. But stay in Crocus Valley. Let's see where this goes. You have people here who'll help you figure things out."

Anguish filled her eyes. "I thought you understood that I can't. Twenty dollars in tips a day at the diner isn't going to pay for Mom's care. It isn't going to fly me to California to visit her. I can't just leave her there."

"You can see if she'd want to move up here. Healthcare has to be cheaper here than in California. I'll help—" I clenched my teeth together.

She was furiously shaking her head. "I can't hand my fate over to another man."

"I don't want to be just another man. I care about you, Tova. I don't want to use you. I want to be with you. I want us to have a chance."

She threw her hands up. "Don't you see? If it doesn't go anywhere, you're fine. You have a house. You're going to have a ton of land with a cute little—" Her gaze slid toward the dips and valleys where the cows were disappearing. "Gah, is that a creek? You're going to have your family. My friends aren't even *my* friends. They're your sister. Your sister-in-law. Your neighbor. Things go south between us, then where am I?"

"I know you're used to dealing with assholes like your ex, but we're good people."

"Everyone thinks they're good until they don't get what they want." She pressed her fingers to her forehead. "I know you're a good man, Cody. But staying would mean letting

Frederick have everything he took from me. It'd be like . . ." She blew out a hard breath and turned her pleading gaze to me. "It'd be like giving up, like Mom did each time she left a bad relationship for something she thought was better."

"Tova."

When I imagined this talk, I had no idea it'd go to shit like this. I thought she was feeling what I felt. The tumble into an abyss I would end up flinging myself into later. Because she was worth it. She was worth risking impending heartbreak, but what if we worked? What if we went all the way and made a family? And what if it was good? What if we were what the other needed, and she'd have so much more than whatever she'd left behind with her ex?

She slumped in her seat.

I desperately searched for ways to rescue the conversation, but I could only stick to the fact that she didn't want to try. Her past was too ingrained in her. The trauma she'd been through as a kid and what she'd witnessed, paired with what happened to her as an adult, wouldn't let her move on. "So that's it? When this week is over, we're just done?"

She swallowed hard. Fear bloomed in her gaze and was smothered quickly. "Yes, I think it'll be easier that way."

Nothing about this was easy. "You're leaving right away?" My question was like a straw mat to hang on to for a life raft. I'd take every second with her.

"I have to fight Frederick so I can take care of Mom."

I was glad she wasn't planning to let Frederick walk into the sunset, but I also doubted she'd ask for help—from anyone. "By yourself?"

She nodded, lifting her chin. A picture of pride. Of destructive independence.

I let out a sigh. "At least keep my number if you need help. I know a lot of lawyers, thanks to Meg."

She blinked at me, her eyes shimmering. Blinked again.

I held her gaze. "I mean it. Call me if you need anything. No strings."

Her perplexed stare changed to resigned acceptance. "There are always strings, Cody. Can you take me back now?"

Eighteen

TOVA

Heavy, stifling, forlorn silence filled the drive back to town. I shrank into my seat, but not once did the universe answer my silent plea to make me disappear. I wanted to hop out of the moving vehicle and sprint to the airport.

Unless I caught a ride in a crop duster or had a private jet, I wasn't flying out of Crocus Valley.

Plans furiously formed and came apart in my brain. A small damn puzzle of options.

How could Cody expect me to stay and enter into a relationship that was just like the one I fled from? I had less now than I did with Frederick.

My traitorous brain tried to insist Cody was nothing like Frederick.

As if I didn't fucking know that!

I wasn't in love with Frederick. This was scarier.

Cody pulled to a stop in front of the rental house, his

287

brows drawn together and his stare on the sleek maroon car parked on the curb that hadn't been there before we left.

Maybe Kali's grandparents had visitors. I got out and stopped when I saw the older couple sitting on the porch. Cody rounded the back of the pickup and slowed when he caught sight of them.

The man looked like he walked off a golf course and straight onto the porch. He had dark sunglasses pushed into his gray hair. The woman was dressed similarly, with a light sweater slung around her shoulders as if she got cold easily and all the time. Her hair was the perfect shade of silver, and I doubted it was from a bottle. She gave off a regal air, and her demeanor screamed intelligence.

"Curtis. Lauri," Cody greeted.

My gasp sounded before I could stop it. Meg's parents. The grandparents who didn't know Cody was staying in Crocus Valley. The in-laws who didn't know their widower son-in-law had been fucking the nanny all summer.

Half the summer.

"Alcott. We decided to come early and spend the week with you to help with the transition." The man, Curtis, rose from the porch swing. His curious gaze kept swiveling back toward me.

"We thought it'd be easier on the kids if they had a few extra days with us." The father-in-law's gaze continued to jump to me and return to Cody. When he slipped his attention to Cody's empty left hand, my muscles twitched to sprint to Thelma's apartment. "Sorry, we should've called. Is that room still open?"

"It is," Cody said, his tone ringing empty.

Lauri's sharp gaze pinned me. "You must be the nanny. Tova, is it?"

I nodded, afraid to speak.

This couple was intimidating. This couple was like the parents who complained that a burlesque dancer shouldn't be teaching their kids the grapevine. This couple was probably more like Frederick's family, the Baldwins of the Baldwin Opera House. Educated. Cultured. Wealthy. Everything I wasn't.

"The young girl who won't let us in said you and Tova went for a drive?" Sharp curiosity in Lauri's voice hid a deeper emotion I didn't want to see unleashed.

She would hate me if she knew. I was sleeping with her daughter's husband, and she'd been gone for less than a year. My stomach churned.

"Catherine wouldn't let you in?" Cody asked, confused, and walked toward the porch.

Curtis's chuckle was surprisingly relaxed. "Hard to be mad at a pit bull protecting your grandkids. She's quite firm for a kid. Was clear we had to wait until you got back and confirmed our identity. Good choice for a sitter." Again, his gaze swirled toward me as if to ask, *Are you?*

I wasn't, and this was a good time to leave. "I'll head back—give you all time to settle."

Cody's jaw worked. We looked at each other, a quiet conversation moving between us.

We need to talk, from him.

You know now's not the time. Don't tell them about us.

It's not their business. But this isn't over between us.

You know it has to be.

With my final unspoken thought, he said, "See you tomorrow." It almost sounded like a question.

"Oh, that won't be necessary," Lauri said cheerfully. "We're here."

My heart dropped like a stone in a water-filled pothole —a short, hard distance. "I—I have—the kids—" How did I argue with them? I couldn't be done with Grayson and Ivy. I had a whole week left with them.

You should've thought about that before basically dumping their dad. I was so upset with myself, I almost internally addressed myself as Tova, my dear.

When would I learn? I had no power. When I wasn't useful, I was handed off.

Cody gauged my reaction. "Tova's working with them on their dance routine. They'll be sad if she doesn't show all week." To me, he dropped his voice and asked, "Come by after lunch at least?"

Again, I heard what he didn't say. *I won't tell them about us. Since there is no us anymore.*

I squared my shoulders. His in-laws admired Catherine for looking after the kids. I cared about them, too, and had nothing to be ashamed of. "Nice to meet you both. I'll see you tomorrow."

With one final glance at Cody and the sad but accepting expression on his face, I rushed toward Thelma's apartment.

Inside, I slid my suitcase out from under the end table. I didn't know what else to do. I'd broken up with Cody before we got a chance to really be an item. His in-laws were in town, and they'd know. A sharp couple like that who could spout more knowledge in five minutes than I'd learned in my life would know what I was doing with Cody. The performance was on Friday. I needed to be here for the kids, but at the same time, I couldn't stay.

The urgency to go pounded at my temples, clouding out logic.

It was after ten, but Thelma shuffled out, wearing nothing but a gauzy white nightgown that fell to her knees. Skinny white shins full of blue, spidery veins stuck out beneath the hem.

"Sorry," I muttered, trying to be quiet.

She eyed my suitcase. I dumped my pile of folded clothing off the end table and into my luggage. She crossed her bony arms. "He turned out to be a shit stick?"

I hiccupped. I wasn't crying, but tremors wracked my body like I was holding back sobs. I growled and sat back on my heels. The only cock and balls I'd draw on a mirror for Cody would be an ode to his magnificent set. "No." I pushed my palm against my forehead. "He's still a decent guy. Doing the right thing."

Like staying for his kids. Asking me to basically go steady. Taking a giant fucking risk.

Would it be much of a risk, though?

I had Mom. Frederick had my money. My fight and my purpose were in California.

So why did it feel like I should fight for my happiness and stay here? Why did it feel like Cody Knight and his kids were my purpose?

"Going somewhere?" Her question was carefully light.

"Yep."

"Because of the decent guy who does the right thing?"

She wasn't going to quit asking. Sighing, I rolled to sit on my butt, and crossed my legs. "He asked me to stay."

"So, you're leaving?"

Frustrated that she wasn't already pulling up flight information, I pushed my hair out of my face. "You know what it's like. He has all the money. All the resources. He said he'd help move Mom here."

"That's awful," she said sarcastically.

"Thelma."

She cocked her head, waiting. When I didn't continue to argue, she huffed. "Tova, are you running because you're not safe or because you're scared?"

"If I'm scared, that means I'm not safe." The flurry in my mind settled. My statement should be right, but logic started poking through. What, exactly, was I scared of?

She circled around me and dropped onto the couch that'd been my bed most of the nights I'd been here. "If you think he's a threat, I'll have you packed up and on a flight in seconds. Why don't I think that's the case?"

"You don't trust him." I did. A giant red flag. You could only trust someone until you couldn't.

"I trust him as much as I trust anyone. But . . . I think he could be one of the good ones."

"Could be." I shook my head and folded a pair of shorts. "Until he's not."

"California's not the answer."

"What about Mom?" Thelma was supposed to be on my side. She was my ride or die. Why was she idling?

"She'll want to be where you are."

"But Frederick—"

"You can't afford a lawyer. Neither can I. And if you go back and take him on, his legal team is going to eat you up and spit you out, and then what?" She pressed her thin lips together and shook her head. "Move your mom up here where we can take care of her."

"But the jobs—and the way he'll just get away with what he did—and—"

"For God's sake, Tova."

I recoiled. Thelma came off as perpetually cranky, but I rarely heard her lose her temper.

"You've held on to the thought of leaving like it was a rope and you were hanging out a helicopter. There was no other option but to leave." She rubbed at her temple. "I blame your mother. God help me, I've kept it to myself all these years, but I can't watch you make the same mistakes."

"What mistakes?"

"Leaving when you're only upset. Leaving when you're uncomfortable. Don't get me wrong, I love your mother, but I don't think Lana should've settled. And a few of the men she picked were doozies. But she left a lot of relationships out of fear—and it wasn't for personal safety. She was afraid to trust that a decent man wouldn't leave her like your father did. Like her father left her. She was scared she couldn't take care of you on her own if she got her heart broken. I thought you were strong, but I've only seen a similar pattern."

"I'm not like Mom," I said hotly. Immediate guilt welled inside my stomach. "I've been careful about the men I associate with."

"Have you? Or have you self-fulfilled a prophecy? Is your need to make Frederick pay because he has so much of your money, the fight would be financially worth it? Or because you're using it as an excuse and tying the reason to your mom in order to justify not staying?" She stabbed her finger in the direction of Cody's house. "You're like the kid I remember when you're with him. You're not afraid to make friends. You're doing what you love even while you're doing what you have to. It's been less than two months, and yet you're not the same girl I picked up from the airport."

What she said sank into me one sentence at a time. "I never planned to stay."

She threw up her hands. "You don't ever plan to stay. You work out a getaway plan with me for each date. I swear, when you told me what you were doing with that slick bastard Frederick, I thought you were looking for a reason to be a victim."

I gasped, scandalized. I opened my mouth to demand not to be blamed, but she stuck her palm out.

"No, Tova. I'm not saying it's your fault, but you knew

better. You even said it. It was like you had to prove that you're alone in the world and people are out to get you."

My teeth clicked when I shut my gaping mouth. Hot tears pricked my eyes. "So, what? I stay? And live happily ever after while teaching a few kids dance every week and living off my rich, handsome husband?" That should have sounded worse than it did.

"No. I'm saying you should do what really makes you happy and maybe accept some help. You don't want to feel obligated toward Milk Daddy, then let me help. We'll get Lana settled, and you'll open that dance studio."

"With what money?"

"With the money you make," she said, exasperated. "You've been in business too long to play clueless. Quit it."

I winced. Thelma never spoke to me like that. My brain slowed and switched the lens I looked at life with. I thought about when I first met Cody, how uptight he was. Then the first time we danced. Seeing how much he loved and worked hard for his family. And finally, the pride and excitement and even fear on his face when he showed me his future home.

He was brave enough to change.

But he had the resources.

I met Thelma's hard but caring gaze. Her mouth was set in a flat line, sick of my shit.

Maybe I was a little sick of my shit too.

He had the resources, and I could, too, if I got over myself. Trusting Cody had been easier when I thought we were temporary, when I had the safety net of an end date. Then he turned my assumptions upside down and made a decision that yanked away my net. He'd asked me to stay. I'd have to trust I was more than a rebound. I'd have to be confident I was more than a woman he had access to. Beyond Cody, I'd have to have faith in myself.

And I was halfway out the door.

Tears tracked down my face. "I don't know what to do."

"Ah, honey. None of us do. But you've gotta let someone in. Trust yourself to know when it's the right person."

I did know. That was why I was trying so hard to leave.

Nineteen

CODY

I woke before everyone, which was easy enough when I couldn't quit replaying last night's conversation. I'd gotten a restless, frustrated night of sleep. Could I have done more? Said something different? In the end, I made the offer, and she rejected me. She came to Crocus Valley with her own life and her own goals, and ultimately, I wanted to support her. She wouldn't let me, but that was her choice too.

The start of the morning was the same as the others, but I was different, and the rest of the day would differ too. When Meg was sick, she had preferred the world kept turning and took the drama with it. The day she died was another workday as far as she was concerned. She'd been out of it long before that, but I kept up the show for her. Wore my work clothes like I was going to the office instead of her deathbed. Pretended everything was normal. Never let the act drop.

The problem was that I kept it up for way too long after.

Time to remedy that.

I had breakfast sandwiches made and milk poured by the time Grayson stumbled down the stairs. He yawned and rubbed his eyes, still in his red Spider-Man pajama shorts and shirt. Ivy bounced down with him, also in her purple princess nightgown.

"Yummy!" she said, sliding behind her food.

Grayson gave me a quick hug before he did the same. The days when I made them dress before breakfast were over.

"Hey, guys. We need to talk about some things." I took my seat, but I'd already eaten. "Your grandparents showed up last night."

"Yay!" Ivy grinned.

Grayson smiled, then turned serious. "Wait. They weren't supposed to be here until Thursday. Are we leaving early?" His voice pitched up, and panic filled his eyes.

I shook my head. "No. Definitely not."

He heaved out a breath. "Okay. Good."

"But that's what I'd like to talk to you both about." My in-laws were still sleeping, tired from the long drive and the time change. "What if instead of you two living in Helena with them, we moved to Crocus Valley?" While they both stared at me, dumbfounded, I continued, "I'm buying that land for sale across from Aggie and Ansen's place. We can build a house, have animals. What do you think?"

Ivy narrowed her eyes. "So we can keep Lilac and Cheetoh?"

"I think we should get a dog too," I said.

Ivy grinned. She took a bite from her egg sandwich. Sitting primly, with her mouth full, she said, "Let's do it."

Tense, I checked Grayson and found his expression blank. "What do you think, bud?"

He got up and rounded the table. Throwing his little

arms around me, he buried his face in my shoulder. "Thanks, Dad."

Fuck's sake. I'd been putting this kid through hell with the plans I thought would benefit him when I was just too much of a coward to think I could do it on my own. "I'm sorry I ever thought of sending you away." I turned so I could embrace him. "I thought it'd be best for you and Ivy, but it's not. We found what's best for us."

Ivy slid out of her chair and came toward us. We held on to the group hug for several moments before the stairs creaked. My chest burned hot. I'd made the right choice.

Lauri's sandaled feet hit the bottom of the stairs, and her surprised gaze lit on us. She had a toiletry bag under her arm. Cheetoh skidded on the floor in front of her, chasing Lilac. "Oh." Her mouth turned down. "Cats."

"We're building a new house, Grandma!" Ivy ran to Lauri and threw her arms around her.

Lauri lifted a brow in my direction as she patted Ivy's shoulders.

Shit. Here we go.

Curtis appeared, and Lauri shifted out of the way as she said, "New house?"

"We're staying in Crocus Valley," Grayson announced proudly, going to hug his grandparents.

After the hugs, Curtis ran his hand around the waistband of his cargo shorts in short bursts of tugging. "Staying?"

This was where the morning started to differ from other days. I'd be doing what I felt was right versus what I thought I should do. "Yes. I need to talk to you two about something, but I wanted to make sure I told the kids first."

Grayson and Ivy went back to the table.

Lauri shifted her bag to her other arm. "Curtis, find me

some coffee. I don't think I can hear this conversation without caffeine."

A tense half an hour later, both of my in-laws had used the bathroom, and Curtis had found large to-go cups of black coffee at the gas station on the outskirts of town.

We were in the backyard now, letting the kids play. Grayson and Ivy knew what they needed to. They didn't need to face their grandparents' reactions to the decision.

"You decided to buy land and build a new house?" Curtis shook his head. "Isn't your work still an issue?"

"Yes. The trust's lawyer is defining exactly what working for the company means as far as the trust is concerned. If I go back and work cattle twice a year, which I would anyway, and audit the records of a bookkeeper Eliot hires, then I'm still technically an employee of Knight's Arabians and Cattle Company."

"Wouldn't you be considered a contractor?"

"I don't have to be." I could look at the books once a week. Once a month. I didn't fucking care. I needed one of my jobs taken off my plate.

Curtis nodded. "I thought Barnaby would've made sure to cover all the bases. Wasn't he specific?"

"He paid Lorenzo to cover the bases," I said, leaving out my suspicions. "The trust only insists we work for the ranch."

"The same Lorenzo who knew he'd be working closely with all of you and who knew it'd be best to stay in your good graces," Lauri filled in.

I shrugged. I never claimed to know legal bullshit, but I knew enough to get myself out of this mess. What worked for me could work for my brothers. And yeah, we'd play awfully nice with Lorenzo if he was looking out for future generations along with his largest account.

I'd like to think my father kept the parameters open to

interpretation, to give us some sort of breathing room, but he never had before.

"So, that's it? No grandkids?" Lauri had one leg crossed over the other, and her foot bobbed with a pensive energy. Was she sad, like me, and afraid to let down Meg?

"You're always welcome for however long you want to stay. You always have been." They rarely utilized it until after Meg passed. Unlike me, my in-laws thrived in their careers.

"The drive takes a solid day," Curtis said gruffly. "Sunup to sundown—when the roads are good enough."

Meaning much of the winter was iffy. I nodded and stomped down the guilt. They were grandparents. They had to know this was best for the kids. But when and how often they visited was up to them.

"But we do have a lot of vacation we should start using." Lauri rotated the lid of her cup. "Does this decision have anything to do with your pretty young nanny?"

Her tone was carefully neutral, but I wished she'd show what she was thinking. I didn't want to fear moving on. Did they think it was too soon for me to meet someone? Would they ever approve? Would their reaction impact their relationship with the kids?

"She's, uh, not as young as you think." Tova's age shouldn't matter, but I didn't know how unstable the ground I treaded on was. "And no. Tova's leaving for California after the performance."

I dropped my gaze to the floor. The conversation about keeping the kids had been a nice reprieve from thinking about my discussion with her last night.

"But there is something between you two?" Curtis asked, his jaw tense.

I drew in a slow breath. As much as I'd avoided thinking about my in-laws finding out about my non-relationship, I'd also played through different scenarios until I came to a conclusion. "Please know it's with my sincerest respect that I say it's none of your business."

Lauri's inhale was sharp. A red flush crept up Curtis's face.

I couldn't leave it at that. "No matter what, I want you to know that what Meg and I had was real. If she was . . ." My voice broke. I missed my wife, but I wasn't the same guy she'd been married to. I was a different version of Alcott Knight. "If she was still here, we wouldn't be talking about this. She and I would still be arguing about when to move away from Buffalo Gully, and I swear I wouldn't put it past her to die in order to prove she was right and I was wrong."

The comment might've been in poor taste, but no one had known Meg like the three of us. She'd have made the same joke. A fond smile graced Curtis's face. Lauri ducked her head.

"And for a long time," I continued, my voice rough, "I didn't think the kids and I would get out of the status of us being us but without her. The thing is, without her, we're not the same. I'm not. The kids aren't. And we have to continue our lives, learning what makes us happy now."

Lauri blinked but a single tear escaped down her cheek. Curtis cleared his throat, but his eyes were squeezed shut, and he was pinching the bridge of his nose.

I clenched my jaw. I said what I had to say. About Meg. About Tova. About the move.

The back door creaked open. Tova peered out, her eyes wide, as she took in Lauri and Curtis fighting their grief. "Oh my god. I'm sorry."

"No," I said, practically jumping up. Dressed in the multicolored long skirt that showed off her hips and a tight white crop top that revealed a strip of bare abdomen, she was a vision. "We were just talking. About everything."

Clarity dawned in her gaze, and I lifted a shoulder, a

silent communication that they'd figured it out, or I wouldn't have outed us.

"I didn't realize it's so late." I couldn't think of what else to say to diffuse the discomfort in the air. "Did we miss lunch?"

"No, I'm early." She was still in the doorway, too afraid to come out farther. I wanted to reassure her it was fine but I was scared anything I did would send her scurrying away.

"Tova!" Grayson streaked out of the sandbox and sprinted to Tova.

She stepped out, letting the screen door shut behind her.

"Good morning!" He dove into her embrace, and it was the first time I was jealous of my kid.

Ivy was a second behind. "I never thought you'd make it," she said dramatically.

Tova laughed. "An eternity has come and gone since we read *The Little Engine That Could* before bed last night."

Ivy hung her head back. "It's been forever."

"We have a lot of practice to do," Grayson said, ever the fifty-year-old in a ten-year-old's body.

"Well, I wanted to steal your dad for a minute." She held up a set of keys. "I got the keys to the theater, and I want to inspect it before we meet to rehearse on the stage Thursday." She lifted her uncertain blue gaze to mine. "I don't want to go alone, and I—I thought we could talk."

I was soaking her in, but her words sent a flame of hope bursting over my damn head. I didn't know what she had to say, but it had to be better than the *No, I'm leaving* I got last night.

"You two mind hanging out with the kids while we check out the theater?" I asked Lauri.

She tore her stricken expression off the kids and Tova. "Yes," she said hoarsely. "That's fine."

I met Curtis's gaze to make sure it was fine with both of

them, and he nodded, dropping his gaze and clearing his throat again.

This had to be tough for them. Watching me and the kids move on. I only hoped they'd continue to be a part of the kids' lives.

And I'd be left wishing Tova would've been a part of all our lives.

Tova

I had my arms wrapped around myself as I walked next to Cody. He looked good. Sexy, as usual, and again in jeans, boots, and a black shirt that should carry a warning sign. *Caution: You're Wet.* I yearned to plant a kiss on those pensive lips.

A car passed us, the lady behind the wheel waving. Everyone waved here. She probably knew who I was. Knew Cody's name. Maybe she was even coming to the performance. From what Thelma said, chatter was spreading through town. The community was delighted to see kids in the theater again.

Proof that my purpose had been misdirected.

Last night, I thought of a little adjustment I wanted to make to the performance. A surprise I hoped the kids could keep secret.

Cody wasn't talking. Was he waiting for me?

I could go first. I owed it to him. "I thought I was going to interrupt you working."

"I took the day off."

"Really?" I asked before remembering I rejected him

yesterday and planned to beg forgiveness today. "The entire day?"

He chuckled. "Yes." His smile vanished. "I had to talk to the kids about moving to town and then break the news to Curtis and Lauri. Their arrival precipitated events."

"How did the kids take it?"

"So damn happy I'm plagued with eternal guilt."

I chuckled. He was hard on himself, but that was likely what had molded him into such a good person. "And your in-laws?"

His dry laugh was foreboding. "Shocked. We were discussing the move and Meg when you showed up."

"Oh my god." I stopped and faced him. "This isn't an emergency. Do you need to go back?"

"No. I said what I had to say." He ran his thumb and forefinger over his lower lip. "Curtis figured us out."

I would've panicked, but Cody's calmness blew a cool breeze over my nerves. "What did you tell him?"

"I nicely said it was none of his business."

"Oh." Touched, I just stared at him. The man who was so concerned about what people he cared about thought about him had stood his ground.

"Shall we?" He gestured to the door of the theater.

"Right." He didn't know I was coming to ask him if he meant it. Was he willing to date a poor-as-hell dance teacher who wasn't sure if she had students? I juggled the keys, found the one for the deadbolt, and opened the door.

The glass square on the wooden door was frosted with dark paint. I tried a light switch, and a dim bulb in a round fixture on the ceiling cast a sickly glow over the interior. A musty smell enveloped us as soon as we walked in.

"Well," I said.

"So," he said and started laughing.

I giggled. "It's not . . . *bad*."

"It's not good, Tova." Smiling, he tapped on the wall and walked through the lobby. His steps echoed on the wooden floor, but the squeaks were at a minimum. "It's sturdy enough."

An old concession counter was against the far wall, facing the door. A ticket window with no plexiglass was to our left. The bathrooms flanked us, one on each side, and a hallway disappeared on either end of the concessions counter.

"Definitely has promise," he said, and I wanted to sag. I saw potential but also a lot of work. He felt the same, and my stomach unknotted.

"You think so?"

"You said Kali's grandpa took care of the plumbing, the electricity works, and I don't see new stains from water damage on the ceiling."

"The owner said a new roof was put on ten years ago."

"There ya go." He disappeared down a dark hallway to our left. A light flipped on, no brighter than the entry.

"It needs a makeover," I said, following him. "But I like the character."

So much wood. Like an old theater with history. I was enchanted. I'd treasure the one night—two with the rehearsal—I got here.

I faced the raised stage. Two sections of red padded chairs spread out between me and the stage. The wood could use a finish and some stain, but the heavy red velvet curtains hung proudly on either side. On the ceiling, there was missing paint and exposed wood beams where the old movie screen had once been anchored.

"He said the curtain doesn't move anymore. There are two changing rooms backstage, and the wings are small, but they do the job." I followed Cody to the edge of the stage. The lights weren't any better in here, but it was perfect for a performance. "And a large storage room at the very back."

"It'll do the trick." He pressed his hands onto the edge of the stage and leaned over to look around. "It's not bad once your eyes adjust."

"I might have to find a couple of standing lamps to keep on stage so the audience can see clearer. I'll look a little more, but I don't see any obvious hazards."

He turned and propped his ass against the edge. He folded his arms. "You wanted to talk?"

I licked my lips again, a nervous move. Usually, he tracked my tongue, but his gaze was steadfastly on mine. "Yes. Um . . ." I pushed a hand through my loose hair. My hair tie was around my wrist. I'd had to get out of the apartment before I talked myself out of facing Cody.

"Tova, it's okay. I'm not going to hurt you, whatever you decide."

He continued to say the right things when he didn't have to try to catch me. In his mind, I was already gone, yet he was reassuring me. I paced in front of him. "But you can hurt me so much more than others because it's not my pride or my money involved this time. It's my heart." I stopped to look at him. A muscle twitched in his forearm, but he didn't speak. God, this was hard. "And Thelma called me stupid."

"She did what?"

"Not verbatim." I switched my pacing direction. "She called me a coward. Not exactly, but that's the gist of it."

"Why?" He snaked a hand out and gently cupped my elbow, pulling me toward him. With his hot skin on mine, I was helpless but to follow.

"Because I run like Mom did. I don't trust. So when something good happens to me, I don't believe it. I don't have faith that I'll be able to take care of myself no matter what happens. It's why I gave up teaching dance. I thought

I'd never be able to support myself with it. It's why I was ready to leave. I assumed I can't do it here, but I'm not even trying." My heart was beating like I was in the middle of a marathon. "The truth is, I don't want to leave. I want Mom up here with me. I want to be with you. I love your kids. But —but I'm scared."

His gaze warmed, showing me nothing but support. "I'm fucking terrified too, Tova."

"You are?"

He nodded and drew me closer. "Is my decision the right one? Am I spending too much money on land and a home when I already have a house? Will my in-laws cut themselves out of the kids' lives and blame me?" He tipped my face up, his calloused fingers a welcome sensation under my chin. "Mostly, I'm scared I fell in love with you too quickly, that everything I've done to impress girls in my life was really because you were in my future, and that I'll always be unhappy because you're not with me."

He was just as scared as me? The huge ball of anxiety in my gut unraveled. He didn't have anything to lose—materialistically. Like me, he was afraid for his heart, yet he hadn't shied away from telling me. "You think you're in love with me?"

"I also feel like a dick for saying I've never felt like this before, but there you have it. I'm in a different place in my life, and what you make me feel is like nothing before."

My heart was a dancer in the middle of the stage, collapsed in on herself. Then she slowly rose until her body was long and her arms were stretched to the sky. Toes pointed, ready to move in any direction needed. After being closed up so long, the unfurling felt good, felt right. Like I had nothing to lose and everything to gain.

Cody had so much to lose. He was leaving behind one life to start another with me, and there were no promises.

But we'd be together. "Can we be scared with each other? Can we date while I figure out how to open a dance academy and teach pole dancing lessons for Sutton and Vienne?"

His smile was like seeing my heart unfold. Slow at first and then stretching wide. "Let's be scared with each other—and naked."

A giggle left me. I was light and free and so damn happy I could float up to the new roof. I wrapped my arms around his neck. "That's my Stern Daddy."

"I'm not as stern these days. My nanny made sure of it." He dropped his head. "And I like having a whole lot more than milk on my tongue. I'm also interested in hearing more about your pole dancing."

With that, he plundered my mouth. I tipped my head back to welcome him in, and the relief that what was between us wasn't over was stark and warm and glorious.

Cody spun me, setting my ass on the edge of the stage. I immediately wrapped my legs around his waist.

"You know how much I love this skirt?" he growled.

I had bought it for the length, but I kept wearing it for the hungry look in his eyes. "I like it because I don't have to wear underwear with it," I murmured against his lips.

He jerked his head back and searched my face for the truth. I lifted a brow.

"Fuck," he groaned. He captured my mouth again for another long, lingering kiss. "I'd take you right now if it didn't seem wrong to fuck in someone else's building."

I planted a kiss on his jaw. "I think Sima paid for the day, so it feels extra wrong to get naughty on her dime."

"The next time I have you, kitten, it's going to be when we don't have to hide what we're doing." He was rubbing circles on my ass with his thumbs, and like the first time he'd done it in the barn, I didn't think he realized what he was doing. He was an expressive, passionate man.

"I like the sound of that." I cupped his face. "I fell in love with you really fast and hard, too."

"Good." He didn't bother hiding the smugness in his expression. His dark eyes turned serious. "I hope you're sure. Because I want you there when we tell the kids about us."

"I'll be there." I wasn't running anywhere anymore.

Twenty

TOVA

The rush backstage was heady and addicting. The kids' energy was riding so high, I had to prepare for a possible crash. I used a calm, proficient tone when talking to them, ensuring they had no glimpse into the turmoil inside of me.

I faced a small throng of nervous kids. Ivy hung on to my hand. She'd been clingier since Cody and I told them about us. We'd had a long talk with them when Curtis and Lauri went golfing for an afternoon. Grayson had given me a lingering hug, told me he was glad I wasn't leaving, and then he'd been all about the performance.

Ivy had asked if I would live with them. No. Not yet. As much as I wanted to get off Thelma's couch, I wasn't ready —and neither were they—for me sleeping in Cody's bed all night. Physically, I was so on board. But Cody and I weren't just Cody and me. We had the kids to think about, and a slower transition would be better for them.

So the two of us were officially dating. Boyfriend and

girlfriend. Next week, I had a meeting with the theater owners to discuss renting the space for lessons.

I was doing the Frederickton on "Cloud Nine."

"Eyes on me, dancers." I pointed to my face. I wore my performance costume underneath the long skirt Cody liked. My ensemble was a cheap black bodysuit that covered everything to keep the focus on the art and not my anatomy. My gauzy shirt was pink and purple and orange. I bought it as soon as I saw it. The colors reminded me of the sunset the night Cody asked me to stay.

I had another skirt to change into before it was my turn. A ribbon skirt that would shift and twirl around my legs. My contemporary dance routine was a simple freestyle. I'd flow to the music. Nothing but freedom. Like what I felt.

Grayson shushed Kali as she chattered with Bridger. Britta was fanning herself, as nervous as if we were performing in Carnegie Hall. Ivy was shifting from side to side, watching her princess skirt move with her. Catherine, who'd turned into a mother hen during our week of afternoon rehearsals, finished the job of flagging down their attention.

Once they all quieted and were looking at me, I smiled, a nice, serene expression that didn't belie the turmoil inside me. "Okay. Five minutes, and then I'll go out and introduce us. When I turn to the side and gesture to the wing you're waiting in, Catherine's mom will start the music. As soon as you hear the first note, you walk out in a line following Grayson."

A series of nods topped the shifting, nervous bodies. I knew how they felt.

A hot hand landed on my shoulder, and the cedar and sage aftershave that I craved surrounded me. "Anything you need me to do?" Cody murmured in my ear.

I shook my head but turned my back to the kids. "Is everyone here? Your in-laws came, right?"

The atmosphere between me and Curtis and Lauri had been polite. More like tolerance on their end. When I showed up each afternoon after giving them the morning with the kids, they were nice enough, but their gazes were assessing, their lips set in a line.

They didn't hate me. But they weren't enthusiastic about me. They were giving me a shot, and that was all Cody or I could ask for.

I think I'd really like them otherwise. If there'd been no Meg and we'd met outside of the Codysphere, I would've liked their frank attitudes and sardonic sense of humor.

They were dealing with Cody's differing parenting style, which was at odds with how their daughter had done it. No more polos. No more oatmeal. No more strict routine. But Cody still had a routine, I was included, and the Smiths were adjusting.

"Curtis and Lauri are here. They wouldn't miss it." I couldn't read his expression when he turned, so we were shoulder to shoulder, our backs to the kids. Quietly, he said, "More than everyone is here."

My shock threatened to immobilize me. "More than everyone?"

He nodded solemnly. "The seats are almost full. Anyone in Crocus Valley who doesn't have a job they have to be at is here."

My nerves threatened to spill out of the cage I'd locked them into. "I'm going to puke."

"Good puke or bad puke?"

"Stage fright," I said in a ragged whisper. "I haven't had it this bad since I was a kid. I'm not even getting paid for this performance."

His eyes filled with understanding. I wasn't getting paid,

and the show was an advertisement for my future dance academy on its own, but it was so much more than that. This performance showed how much I cared—about dancing and teaching dance. How much I adored the kids. How much I wanted to be accepted in this little town that held my future in its hands.

The kids could perform and move on. I was the outsider. I was the one who wanted to be accepted. If I wasn't, it wouldn't make sense to ask Mom to move. I'd have to find somewhere else to start over.

"You'll do fine," Cody said, disrupting my mental spiral. "More than fine, like you always do. They'll love the show, and they'll love you."

I hadn't won his in-laws over, but they didn't live in town. Crocus Valley wasn't LA. I couldn't just move on to the next venue. I had to make the venue a success and then have the town's support.

"Tova." He wrapped an arm around my shoulders and said into my hair, "There's nothing to worry about. It's all fallen into place. All you have to do is dance and enjoy yourself."

He was right. I pursed my lips and let out a long breath. "Okay. You're right. I'm making this too much about me."

"I didn't say that." He rubbed my back, and I soaked up the strength in his touch. "It should be about you. But you're looking after the kids, and it's my job to look after you."

Not long ago, I would've bristled against the way he said it. But he took care of me. He didn't control me.

I squeezed his hand. "I'm good, thank you. Go sit and enjoy the show."

A minute after he left, Vienne popped her head into the backstage room and gave me the thumbs-up. Her wide grin rippled over me, tying off frayed nerves. Between her and Cody, I was ready.

I passed the thumbs-up to the kids. "Everyone good with the changes?" All of them had been on board with my surprise. My nerves flared bright like all the stage lights were on me. I hoped Cody liked what we were doing.

Time was up. I walked out onto the stage. I wasn't blinded by the glare like on a lot of stages I'd been on. The theater needed new stage lights, but like the rest of the building, they were good enough.

The only drawback was that I saw all the guests.

Cody was next to his in-laws in the middle. Ansen sat next to him. Then Aggie and Sutton next to her. Aggie grinned and waved from the front row. Thelma had one leg crossed over the other, and her default cynical expression was gone. Her expression was bright with anticipation, just like when I was a kid, and she and Grandma would be in the front row of my recitals.

Eliot and Wilder were behind Cody. Eliot had his phone out to record for Austen, who couldn't take leave, and he said he'd send a link to me for Mom. Cody's idea.

God, I loved that man.

The rest of the chairs were filled with both strange and familiar faces. Hal, the cook from the diner. The owner had approved closing the diner until the show was done, and then he was offering an ice cream cone special. The couple who owned the theater were in attendance. Cashiers and stockers from the grocery store filled the seats. Attendants at the gas station. People I hadn't seen out of their cars but who would wave as they drove by when I walked between Thelma's place and Cody's house or sat in the park.

I rubbed my hands together. "Welcome." The word came out tenuous. Shaky. My cheeks heated.

I was a performer. I showed my tits to crowds every

night for how many years? I could do this. "I'm glad you could make it. The kids are very excited to show off their skills, and they have worked so hard. I'm impressed with each and every one. At the end of each dance, every performer would like to have a moment to speak." I clapped my hands together. "Now, without further ado, it's my honor to present 'Summer Dreams.'"

I turned to the side and flung my arm out to welcome them on stage.

Vienne was in the wings. She hit a button on her phone, and music streamed from the Bluetooth speakers we positioned on either side of the curtain. I backed off the stage once Grayson moved. My smile was going to swallow my face. My nerves were gone. Only happiness was in its place.

This.

This was what I was supposed to be doing with my life. And the man I wanted to do it with was in the audience.

If I could give another performance, my mom would be in the audience.

Life couldn't be better.

Cody

I hadn't heard about the kids giving a speech, but after the first dance, the weak spotlight hit Grayson as he stepped forward. "I'd like to dedicate this dance to my mom. She liked to work hard, and I think she'd be really proud of how hard I worked."

Goddamn. Emotion slammed into my chest, stopping my breath. Grayson was right. Meg would be so fucking proud of her little dancers. And Tova had given him the stage to acknowledge it.

I snuck a glance at Curtis and Lauri. Their eyes were shining, as I was sure mine were.

After the second dance, it was Ivy's turn. She executed a perfect curtsy. "I'd like to dedicate this performance to my mom because she used to braid my hair the best. And I'd like to dedicate it to my dad for trying so hard to braid like Mommy."

I chuckled, which helped me keep the swell of pride and appreciation and grief at bay. Tova peered out, her mouth puckered like she was nervously chewing on the inside of her cheek. I caught her eye and dipped my head. She was fucking perfect, and I'd have to spend my life showing her.

The rest of the kids' numbers went by with equally sweet dedications. Each kid received a giant round of applause.

Grayson looked confident and happy in a way I'd never seen, not when he was playing with his toys or when he was at the ranch. Ivy's boisterous energy had found a natural outlet, and my kids were the stars of the show. The parents and families of the other kids probably thought the same about their kids, but I didn't care. Mine were stars.

This summer had been good for them. It'd been good for me. For all of us. We'd found our place, and I found someone I wanted to spend my life with.

Tova felt like coming home. To a home I hadn't ever experienced. Meg and I had been compatible and loyal, but we didn't fit together. We'd had to change ourselves—our ideals—to have a life with each other.

Tova and I could be ourselves with each other.

"I'm so excited to see Catherine," Aggie whispered next to me.

My sister was barely pregnant, but whenever I saw her, I

was so damn grateful to be a part of her life. That my kids and I would be right on the other side of the road and across a pasture from her. Our kids would grow up knowing each other.

Catherine tiptoed out as new music started. Vienne slipped from behind the curtain to sit in a free chair next to Sutton. The girl would be babysitting my kids when I took Tova on date nights. More signs this community was perfect.

Tova would be in a dart league with Vienne, my sister, and Sutton. And after tonight, she'd have so many damn signups for her dance academy she'd wonder why she ever worried it wouldn't work.

Christ, I was so looking forward to my life with her.

When Catherine was done, she dedicated her performance to her mom. Vienne snuck behind the curtain, dabbing at her eyes, and another melody played. An instrumental tune that made me think of summer, birds singing, and sunshine.

I'd get to see the woman of my dreams doing what she loved.

Tova twirled out, her skirt swirling around her long legs. Between her shirt and the fabric of her skirt, she was like a ribbon caught in a graceful wind, moving to the beat and evoking emotion from the audience. Happiness. Contentedness. Relaxation.

The song continued, and I was riveted. Her hair was down. It was like she was covering as much of herself as she could to let the dance shine through. Like she had to prove to herself one last time that she wasn't what her shitty ex had pigeonholed her into. She was an artist. Her work was to be enjoyed, not used.

I knew the show would be over soon, but I told myself I'd get to see more of this.

As the song wound down, a heavy, slow clap started at the back. Tova slowed her spin, her gaze following the direction of the clap. Because she was looking, we all did.

"Bravo," said a man I'd never seen before. He was wearing a black suit with a light-colored shirt. I couldn't make out the color in the dark, but everything about him screamed money from head to toe. "Bravo," he said again and ceased his hard clap.

Anger kindled inside me at what I expected was meant to be an insulting interruption. I glanced back at Tova. She stopped, her foot that had been lifted behind her hitting the stage with a dull thud. Her mouth was hanging open, fear in her eyes.

I rose, upset that she was bothered, but the man barely noticed me. His gaze was on her.

"When do you take off your clothes?" he asked, loud enough there was no mistaking what he said.

Her mouth snapped shut, and her eyes gleamed with unshed tears. "Frederick. How did you find me?"

⚜

Tova

Oh, god. Ohgodohgodohgod. What was happening?

"How did I find the woman who flaked on her performance, leaving me on the hook for thousands and ultimately costing me millions?" He tipped his head, arrogant as always, and let a piece of paper flutter to the floor. One of the announcements Vienne hung around town. "Tova, my dear. You aren't exactly a mastermind. And your mom's ex was very free with his information." He spread his hands out. The button of his suit coat strained as the flaps spread apart. He'd found me, and he'd worn a suit while doing it. An extra rub to prove he was better than me. "Are you aware you're letting a cheap stripper teach the children of your community?"

"I was not cheap," I insisted, as if the defense would help. As soon as the words had left his mouth, I was back to being that insecure girl who was afraid that, deep down, she couldn't make anything out of herself.

Kids' faces were peering out from behind the backstage curtains. I waved them back, but they didn't move. Shivers racked my body, like I was about to sob or scream or sprint out of the building.

Cody was already standing, but he stepped out from the seats. "You need to leave."

Frederick's face contorted with his sneer. He eyed Cody, judging his jeans and the polo shirt he usually wore for his non-video meeting days. When his gaze landed on the cowboy boots, the smugness in his expression bloomed. "Did she get to you with the promise of sex? You do realize making men think they could have sex with her was how she used to make a living."

"It doesn't matter how she used to make a living. You're an insulting jackass, and you need to go." Cody's tone was hard, sending delicious shivers through me.

Frederick laughed. He goddamn laughed.

I fisted my hands. "I danced burlesque, but Cody's right. It shouldn't matter how I made a living. You're insulting, disrespectful, and you tried to pimp me out." I lowered my voice and internally apologized to the parents and grandparents who'd be asked what a pimp was tonight.

The gasps in the audience were an acute reminder that we weren't alone. Half the town was witnessing my humiliation.

I'd have to leave. I'd never be welcome here. It didn't

matter how good I was with kids, no one would want me working with them after the way Frederick made me sound.

He ruined my chance. He was robbing me of my future once again.

"Tova, Tova, Tova." He tsked. "You were the one using me for my name and my money."

This time, I wasn't going to run. The damage was done, and if the kids and everyone here were going to see me get torn down, I would show them I wasn't a willing participant. "I might've done burlesque, which for some reason you think should be beneath contempt, but I didn't manipulate someone into turning over their financial information. Nor did I steal all their money after they refused to be given out to their highest investors like a free travel bag when someone opens an account." I clapped my hands to my chest and feigned innocence. "Oh, you want to invest a hundred million with me? How about my girlfriend for an hour?"

"I stole nothing," Frederick said calmly. "In fact, you owe me for what you did."

I clenched my fists at my sides. "I did nothing but protect myself. You're not welcome here, and you need to leave."

"Before you go," Cody said, folding his arms and standing in front of me, the only physical barrier between me and Frederick. "Give the lady back her money."

"I'm not going to listen to a trollop's man candy," Frederick sneered.

"You can listen to the man candy's lawyer, then," Cody replied calmly. "I'm sure a guy such as yourself doesn't want the details of such a lawsuit spread to the press."

Today was the first time I witnessed Frederick turn pale. The first time uncertainty was in his eyes.

Cody didn't move. "That's right. You walked into this

town expecting to find a bunch of local yokels who don't know the terms fraud and libel. You thought you'd take advantage of someone with fewer resources than you, and we'd all just be so damn impressed."

Frederick narrowed his eyes.

"But guess what, asshole? I was raised by a man who used his money to get his way. I've dealt with your type my entire life, and now I have the resources to make sure Tova doesn't have to."

Frederick's jaw clenched. "She was nothing but a stripper."

"And she's going to teach me how to pole dance," Vienne piped up.

"She can teach pole dancing?" someone called from the seats, her tone full of nothing but excited interest. "I want to learn."

I nodded, not knowing who spoke. This wasn't the time to sign on clients, but I'd hate to pass up on a future student because of my shitty ex.

Frederick glanced around. The energy from the crowd was supportive. Glares were directed his way. It was like I could walk off this stage and be caught in a cloud of understanding.

"Well." Lauri rose. Her phone was in her hand.

Oh, no. This was it. I was in the coffin, and I thought since the lid was open, I could climb out and scramble for my dreams. Lauri's grim expression would be the final nail. "I've seen all I needed to see."

She flashed her screen. I thought I caught a glimpse of Frederick, one of the many pictures of him in various financial magazines. Had she researched him that quickly? I was impressed. "I'm Ms. Evanson's attorney. And you will be hearing from me."

I couldn't register what she said. Her claim didn't make

sense. I was nothing but an apt viewer like the rest of the crowd, intent on Frederick's reaction.

Frederick snapped his spine back in place. His gaze stroked down her body, eying her sensible walking sandals, her navy-blue linen shorts, and the solid white tee covered with a loose-knit navy-blue shawl. It was probably her silver hair pulled back in a simple ponytail that wiped out any credibility in his mind.

He laughed. "My lawyers will have a field day with you."

"Please, Mr. Baldwin."

He stiffened at her use of his last name when he hadn't introduced himself and couldn't see her phone.

"I've been chewing through men like you before lunch for thirty years. It'll be my pleasure to do it again."

He rocked back on his heels. "My lawyers—"

"Can call. You need to leave." Cody gestured toward one of the hallways in the back of the room and advanced on Frederick.

"That man is mean," one of the kids whispered off to my right, where they peeked out from behind the curtain.

"He's a loser," Catherine said with full authority.

Frederick stumbled back a step. His gaze flew to mine, and everything that happened slammed into place. A completed puzzle. Lauri offered to represent me. She hated Frederick just from the few minutes he'd been here, and she supported me. By helping me, she accepted me and Cody, however hard it was for her. I'd figure out how to pay her fees.

Vienne had offered solidarity in front of everyone. So did another person I doubt I'd ever talked to. The kids had my back. I was the one with power and resources because of the generosity of people who cared about me.

I smiled.

Red flushed Frederick's face. He rushed Cody and shoved him.

Cody flung Frederick's arms off of him. Eliot, Wilder, and Ansen jumped up and swarmed behind Cody in seconds. Curtis even rose and dusted off his shirt.

Cody didn't explode against Frederick. He casually glanced at Curtis. "Think that's good enough?"

"A lawyer's answer is always, it depends." Curtis tipped his head from side to side, his lips pursed. "But it'll look like self-defense to me."

Cody glanced over his shoulder, sent me a wink, then faced Frederick. Cody's punch was lightning-quick. Frederick's head snapped back, and he reeled, almost falling. Then Cody grabbed Frederick by the lapels and dragged him out of the theater.

"What did you— You broke my nose!" Frederick squirmed and struggled, but he was useless against Cody's strength. "Get your hands off me!"

Cody's brothers followed them out.

I gazed at the crowd. They were looking from me to the exit.

I exchanged a look with Thelma. What did I do now? She nodded her encouragement. To what?

Whatever I thought was right. I never felt the need to explain myself, and there wasn't much need to—or time. But Frederick had aired my laundry and acted like it was the dirtiest. I had a chance to explain myself. To tell them how much this town and the Knights meant to me.

"I'm just a girl who loves to dance. The only thing I love more is teaching others so they can find their own delight in it. That's all I want to do here. Dance, teach, and hang out with my most favorite people in the world."

"Damn straight." Thelma held her hands above her head and clapped.

The audience joined in. Aggie put two fingers to her mouth and wolf-whistled. I was dying to know what was going on with Cody, but there were people who worked hard for today and needed their time to shine.

I waved the kids out. "Time to take a bow."

Hesitantly, they took center stage, and I joined in with the applause to support these kids. The rest could wait. I wasn't going anywhere.

Epilogue

TOVA

Applause rang through the theater like it had almost exactly a year ago. I stood behind all the kids, taking my bows with them. The second annual summer show was over.

The timing was perfect. We'd moved into our brand-new house. The theater would close for a couple of months this fall to finish some remodeling.

My theater. The one with the marquee Cody had built and put my name on.

Thanks to my pit bull lawyer, Lauri, I got all my money back. She hadn't been satisfied with Frederick returning my assets. She'd gone after damages—for trying to traffic me, for stalking, and for the theater stunt. Thanks to the high-profile last name Frederick was so proud of, he settled without a fight. The threat of family shame and public humiliation had been enough.

Cody leaned over and murmured something to Mom. She had a spot in front for her wheelchair. Accessible seating was one of the first changes I made to the theater after I bought it with the settlement money.

I'd tried to pay Lauri, but she'd refused. *My pleasure,* she'd said, and she meant it. If Meg had been anything like her, Ivy was going to grow into a fearsome woman, and I couldn't wait to see it.

Mom's eyes twinkled, and she clapped her left hand against her thigh. We'd asked her to move to North Dakota almost immediately after I decided to stay. She hated to leave the center that had become her home, but she wanted to be closer to me. Cody said she could stay with us after the house was built, but Mom insisted she'd be more comfortable in her own space with her care team close by.

She was in a nursing home in Bismarck. I could visit her a lot easier than when we'd both been in California. The kids decorated her room with artwork, and she hadn't missed a single recital. She'd been next to me with Thelma at my intimate outdoor wedding to Cody last October. Cody's siblings had been there, along with Sutton, Vienne, Catherine, and the kids from the summer recital. Everyone important in my life and Cody's had attended.

Catherine helped me herd the kids off stage.

"You guys did so good," I said to them all. "I can't be any prouder than I am right now."

Ivy threw her arms around me, her face squishing against my belly. "Thank you."

Strong arms embraced me from behind. I closed my eyes and leaned into Cody's touch.

"The audience is excited to meet the performers, Miss T."

I grinned. My students called me Miss T. My pole dancing class insisted on calling me Fannie Grace.

Grayson and Ivy had wanted to know what to call me

after Cody and I married. They stuck with Tova, and that was just fine. Cody and I supported memories of their mom and encouraged celebrating Meg as much as possible. Her pictures with the kids hung with our family pictures in the new house.

I caught Lauri blinking tears away every time she walked by. She'd confessed that she'd been terrified I would wipe out memories of her daughter. I admitted that I was terrified she'd never accept me. Now I called her and Curtis my in-laws, and they referred to me as a daughter-in-law, too, since Cody was like a son to them.

As the kids filed out to meet their families, I tucked myself into Cody's side to follow.

He caressed his hand over my stomach. "You were amazing. I'll never get tired of watching you."

"I wasn't sure how people would handle watching a pregnant lady dance."

He dropped a kiss into my hair. "Everyone's going to want to be pregnant and dancing."

"Maybe not Aggie so soon." Aggie had a little girl they named after Ansen's mom, Aurora. But they claimed there were too many A names, so they called her Ro.

"I wouldn't be surprised if that's what she's going to tell us at the cookout tonight."

I laughed and put my hand on top of his. I couldn't wait to have this baby, but I was loving being a mom to the two most amazing kids I'd ever met.

Grayson was not only my most dedicated student but also Crocus Valley's newest football and baseball player. He danced for the passion and played sports for the friendships. Ivy had a gaggle of friends and wasn't interested in anything more organized than the annual summer recital, and only because she didn't want to be left out.

A little over a year ago, it was just me. In a few months,

I'd have three kids and a whole town coming to my performances. Half the theater was filled with family.

Out in the lobby, people were gushing over the kids and handing out flowers. Many came to thank me for the show. It was becoming a highlight of the season.

Eliot was holding his little niece, Ro, tucked into his shoulder, and chatting with Thelma, my mom, Aggie, and Ansen. Wilder had said he had to work and couldn't make it. Vienne and Sutton were talking off to the side, and Vienne had an arm draped around Catherine. Sutton and Wilder's divorce had gone through almost a year ago, but Sutton hadn't acted like she wanted to date. Austen wasn't able to come. He used his leave when Eliot needed help working cattle.

Everyone who had come to town would be at our place for a meal, and then there was a big street dance tonight with a live band. I was thrilled to take Cody out for a spin before my center of gravity was too lopsided to swing dance.

Thelma pushed Mom's wheelchair toward the door. I twined my hand around Cody's.

"You two going straight to the house?" I asked.

Thelma turned and flipped the little purse she carried her comfort cigarettes in. "You gave me a key to the place. I plan to use it."

"We want you to," Cody said, taking over Mom's wheelchair to load it in the van we purchased to transport Mom in. While he loaded and talked with Mom, Thelma turned to me.

"I'm proud of you, doll face. I'm proud of those kids." She pointed to the theater towering over us and then to my stomach. "And I'll be proud of that little doll face." She squinted at me. "You got a bag packed?"

"Nope." My luggage was empty, and I only filled it when Cody and I went to Buffalo Gully to help with the cattle and horses and when Cody had to train the new accountant.

"That's my girl." She leaned in. "I've still got your back, though. You know that, right?"

"Always."

She nodded like there was no doubt, and there wasn't. "You picked a good one. Cody's a lucky man."

Thelma got behind the driver's seat, and Cody came to stand next to me to watch them drive away.

I poked him in the side with an elbow. "She said you're a lucky man."

"She's right. I'm the luckiest Milk Daddy around."

———

Thanks for reading!

What happens when Sutton starts sneaking around with her best friend's brother...who's also her ex-husband? Will Sutton and Wilder be able to hide their exes-with-benefits relationship from his family or will they decide to make a real go at a reconnection in An Unfinished Memory?

To get a glimpse of Cody and Tova's wedding, get a bonus epilogue when you sign up for my newsletter at mariejohn stonwriter.com.

About the Author

Marie Johnston writes paranormal and contemporary romance and has collected several awards in both genres. Before she was a writer, she was a microbiologist. Depending on the situation, she can be oddly unconcerned about germs or weirdly phobic. She's also a licensed medical technician and has worked as a public health microbiologist and as a lab tech in hospital and clinic labs. Marie's been a volunteer EMT, a college instructor, a security guard, a phlebotomist, a hotel clerk, and a coffee pourer in a bingo hall. All fodder for a writer!! She has four kids, cats, and a half blind Corgie.

mariejohnstonwriter.com

Follow me:

Also by Marie Johnston

Return to Coal Haven

Violet Promises

Daisy Whispers

Poppy Kisses

Crocus Valley

A Reckless Memory

A Temporary Memory

An Unfinished Memory

A Fearless Memory

An Endless Memory

Coal Haven

Make Me Whole

Make Me Shiver

Make Me Blush

Make Me Dream

Make Me Exhale

King's Creek

King's Crown

King's Ransom

King's Treasure

King's Country

King's Queen

9 781951 067656